# Songs

### Of the

# Satyrs

Edited By
## Aaron J. French

JournalStone
San Francisco

JOURNALSTONE
YOUR LINK TO ARTISTIC TALENT

Copyright © 2015 by Aaron J. French

All rights reserved. No part of this book may be used or reproduced by any means, graphic, electronic, or mechanical, including photocopying, recording, taping or by any information storage retrieval system without the written permission of the publisher except in the case of brief quotations embodied in critical articles and reviews.

This is a work of fiction. All of the characters, names, incidents, organizations, and dialogue in this novel are either the products of the author's imagination or are used fictitiously.

JournalStone books may be ordered through booksellers or by contacting:

JournalStone

www.journalstone.com

The views expressed in this work are solely those of the authors and do not necessarily reflect the views of the publisher, and the publisher hereby disclaims any responsibility for them.

ISBN:        978-1-942712-24-4        (sc)
ISBN:        978-1-942712-25-1        (ebook)

JournalStone 2nd Edition:    February 27, 2015

Printed in the United States of America

Cover Art & Design:    Gary McCluskey
Edited by:        Aaron J. French

# ACKNOWLEDGMENTS

I want to thank and dedicate this book to Jonathan Rex and Randy Reynolds for all those endless hours of inspiration. The idea for this book germinated with you two; it's been a long road, but it has finally become real! I would also like to thank Stacey at Angelic Knight Press, Gene O'Neill, Dave Farland, Rhys Hughes, Steve Rasnic Tem, John Everson, Lisa Morton (for the prospectus), and Jessica at Wicked East Press for allowing me to get this project off the ground. And finally, I want to give a personal thank you to Jodi for all her hard work and help with the fantastic editing assistance and copyediting skills. This book wouldn't be as good as it is without you, and I got to learn a lot, so thank you. To anyone I may have forgotten—dig in your hooves!   -
*Aaron J. French   -   February 2014*

**SONNET 129**

> The expense of spirit in a waste of shame
> Is lust in action; and till action, lust
> Is perjured, murderous, bloody, full of blame,
> Savage, extreme, rude, cruel, not to trust,
> Enjoy'd no sooner but despised straight,
> Past reason hunted, and no sooner had
> Past reason hated, as a swallow'd bait
> On purpose laid to make the taker mad;
> Mad in pursuit and in possession so;
> Had, having, and in quest to have, extreme;
> A bliss in proof, and proved, a very woe;
> Before, a joy proposed; behind, a dream.
> All this the world well knows; yet none knows well
> To shun the heaven that leads men to this hell.

~Shakespeare

# Songs of the Satyrs

# TABLE OF CONTENTS

# INTRODUCTION

## JUDGMENT

When I am debating whether to purchase an anthology, I give little weight to the theme or shared universe or cover illustration of the book. First, I scan the list of contributors. This weighs heavily in my decision to buy the book or not. Do I trust and respect the various writers who have contributed their time and effort here? Occasionally, there may be one writer in the list of contributors that I admire so much that I will purchase everything with his/her byline. That happens very rarely anymore, because I'm picky and that list of must-have writers is very short; and those writers I really like mostly write longer stuff—novellas and novels. But there is another more important factor weighing in on this buy-or-not decision. It is the name(s) of the editor or editors who have brought this anthology together. Now, I realize many readers often pay scant attention to the editors of anything, unless it is Ellen Datlow, Gardner Dozois, or a name of that stature. But I think when buying an anthology the editor(s) should be of primary significance.

Often, the best editors are just *that*: they are only editors (e.g. Ellen Datlow). Occasionally a writer I admire will also edit something for some reason (Gardner Dozois). But being a good writer doesn't necessarily qualify someone to be a good editor. Because being a good editor requires a number of characteristics. Damon Knight was a good writer, but perhaps a better editor. He said that when an editor placed his name on his book he was selling *good judgment*. Good judgment being the primary characteristic of a great editor. Not automatically buying stuff from your friends or from *big* names in the field. I know T.E.D. Klein once bounced a Stephen King story for the *Twilight Zone Magazine*. Damon bounced a number of stories by well-known writers for his ORBIT series, including one by Harlan Ellison—a story that won major awards. Damon said that even had he advance knowledge regarding the reader/critical reception of a story, he wouldn't change a thing. He didn't bounce Robert Silverberg's Nebula-winning short story, "Passengers," but he required Silverberg to revise it *five* times. So included with that judgment characteristic is *integrity*. A really good editor realizes he does himself/the big-name writer no good by publishing something of inferior quality.

No question that Aaron J. French is a fine young writer. Elsewhere I've mentioned that one way to judge the health of a genre is to chart the number of emerging good young writers. Right now we have good young writers popping up everywhere in dark fiction. Aaron is one of these writers, on the crest of a breaking new wave.

But the question here is about Aaron J. French's qualities as an editor. I have been in one anthology he edited, and have read another. I've just completed reading *Songs of the Satyrs*. I don't know if Aaron automatically buys stuff from his friends, but I suspect he doesn't. My sampling of Aaron J. French's editorial efforts indicates to me that he is indeed a very fine editor. He puts together good books, including the one you hold in your hands.

So write down Aaron J. French and place his name with other reminders—on your fridge? Then read everything he writes and buy the anthologies he's edited because the guy exercises good *judgment*.

Gene O'Neill
December 2012
Napa Valley, California

# TRAGÔIDIA

## John Langan

Dying—he was in sufficient pain to suppose—James Bourne lay in the back of Pascal's ridiculous half van, his Kangaroo, being driven along the road east from Aigues-Mortes. He had not been to the local hospital often enough to be certain, but he had a strong suspicion Pascal was not headed in its direction. At a guess, they were racing for Provence, for the Camargue proper. That was all right: he could die there as well as anywhere.

***

The worst part was his teeth. As much as anyone could, Bourne had become accustomed to the pain in his shoulders, his hips, his knees. He had taught himself how to move in ways that did not add to his discomfort, and when such discomfort was inevitable, how to move quickly and calmly. He had accepted the shriveling of his desire, and of his cock. To be frank, now that the chemo was done, and his gut no longer felt as if it had been scraped raw, he could tolerate the disintegration of his bones in much better spirits.

His teeth, though: none of the doctors had been able to account for the ache that spread from them through his gums into his face. It prevented him from reading for any length of time. Such pain was not part of the general list of symptoms for metastatic osteosarcoma, so they had blamed it on the chemo—until he finished the treatment and his teeth showed no improvement. For the doctors, it was one more reason for the "atypical" with which they prefixed his diagnosis. Already, he had had the sense that he was moving from a patient to a paper, an interesting case to be presented at their next professional conference. They increased the dosage of his pain medication, and the most honest among them estimated that, at the rate the disease was progressing, his teeth wouldn't be a concern for much longer.

For a short time, the stronger pills had helped to quiet his teeth, had allowed him to concentrate sufficiently to complete his arrangements for traveling to Provence, to finish his final re-reading of Keats's poems. By the time the flight attendant rolled him off the plane in Marseilles, however, two of the pills were barely adequate to the task. (He had tried three, but they had plunged him into a thick blackness through which the pain had stalked him like a hungry beast.) After he had arrived at the *auberge*, Pascal had brought him pitchers of sangria, and these, combined with the medication, had allowed him to savor a plate of Pascal's *daube*, served with the creamy rice particular to the region. "It's a miracle," he'd proclaimed through a mouthful of beef. Pascal had grinned broadly.

It wasn't, of course. The time for miracles, if ever it had been at hand, was long past. A few days after his arrival, the mix of wine and medicine began to lose its efficacy. He experimented with increasing the amount of sangria he drank, but it had little effect, and anyway, it was a shame to treat the wine as a means to an end, and not an end in and of itself. A brief period of grace had been his: he would try to be satisfied with that.

\*\*\*

There were five of them. One grabbed his chair from behind and dumped him onto the alley's cobblestones. The rest set to work with their feet. They were holding long sticks, which they used next. Bourne struggled to shield his head with his arms. The sticks struck his body with dull thuds. He could feel his bones not breaking, but pulping. His attackers were men, far older than the late adolescents he would have assumed would mug an old, crippled professor. One of them was wearing an expensive-looking leather jacket. He wanted to tell them to take his wallet, it was in the knapsack draped across the back of his chair, they were welcome to its meager contents. But one of the sticks had connected with his jaw, and his mouth was numb.

He imagined Pascal had run for the police. He would not have blamed him if he had run away at the sight of five men armed with sticks.

The world withdrew. He wondered if it would return. Perhaps it would be better for everything to end like this, unexpectedly, quickly.

When the world came back, it brought Pascal's worried face hovering over his. A group of men surrounded him. He did not think they were the same men who had beaten him. At Pascal's command, they knelt beside him, took hold of his arms and legs, and hoisted him off the ground. An avalanche of pain swept over him. By the time it had passed, he was sprawled in the back of Pascal's Kangaroo, and they were driving east.

\*\*\*

A week after Bourne checked-in to the *auberge*, while he was sitting outside his room by the pool, soaking in the heat of the midday sun, Pascal appeared with a narrow glass bottle half as long again as his forearm and a pair of plain glasses. Hissing when his fingers touched the hot metal, he grabbed one of the chairs scattered on the concrete apron surrounding the pool and dragged it next to Bourne's wheelchair. He unstoppered the tall bottle, and poured not insignificant portions of its clear contents into the glasses. Bourne accepted the glass he was offered, and returned Pascal's silent toast.

The *eau-de-vie* hit him like a blow from a big man. He was sure his expression betrayed him, but Pascal pretended not to notice. Instead, he leaned in close and said, "It's bad, this sickness."

"The worst."

"That's why you come back here?" The sweep of his hand took in the *auberge*, the Camargue, Provence.

"Yes."

"For the Marys?"

"The town?" Bourne said. "Or the church?"

"The church."

"Why? Have there been reports of miracles performed there?"

Pascal shrugged.

"No," Bourne said, "I was never that good a Christian. I used to tell my students I found the Greek gods more to my liking. I fancied I could feel them here, next to the Mediterranean where they had flourished for so long. But now . . . 'Great Pan is dead,' eh?"

"What does that mean?" Pascal said.

"Nothing. It's a line from Plutarch, his piece on the failure of oracles. A sailor whose name escapes me heard a voice from shore instructing him to announce the death of Pan to his destination. I think it was his destination. He did so, and there was great lamentation. Report of the incident reached the Roman emperor's ears, and he took it seriously enough to establish a commission to investigate it."

"Bullshit," Pascal said. His cheeks were flushed.

"I—"

"You know who Pan was? Everything." Another sweep of the hand. "He was one of the old gods—as old as Zeus, maybe older. You think something like that dies?"

"I never knew you were a pagan."

"Eh." Pascal looked down. "My father had many books about these things. He told me about them."

"He was a scholar?"

"Something like that. He is dead many years."

Another sip of the liquor brought more words to Bourne's tongue. "I was going to write a paper about Pan—about his presence in the literature of the last couple of centuries. English literature, I mean. That's why I read Plutarch, for background. I was going to start with Keats, *Endymion*. There's a hymn to Pan in it. Keats calls him, 'Dread opener of the mysterious doors / Leading to universal knowledge.' It's the culmination of a series of descriptions of his role in the natural world. I thought I might talk about Forster, too: he has a piece called 'The Story of a Panic,' about a group of English tourists who go out for a walk in the Italian countryside and are overcome by a feeling of inexplicable terror. It's clear they've had a brush with the god. Oh, and Lawrence—he refers to Pan in a short novel called *St. Mawr*. A failed artist described him as 'the God that is hidden in everything;' he's 'what you see when you see in full.' "

"Yes," Pascal said. "Exactly."

"Something else I'll never get around to. I remember thinking I needed to look into Swinburne, to see if I could use him as a bridge between Keats and the Moderns. Ah, well." He finished the last of his drink. "We have discussed it, so it will not vanish from the world, entirely."

"Nothing does," Pascal said. He refilled their glasses.

\*\*\*

When Pascal turned right off the main road, Bourne thought that it was into a driveway, that he had eschewed the hospital in favor of a familiar clinic or doctor. But they continued driving, deeper into the marshland bordering the road. He had the impression that they were traveling a considerable distance; though it was hard to be sure, because they were moving more slowly, and the road they were following bent from left to right and back again, and every time the wheels jolted in and out of a pothole, a white rush of pain filled him.

The road they were on ended in a small clearing. Pascal parked the Kangaroo at the entrance to it. Before he had finished stepping out of the car, its rear doors swung out. The men who had attacked Bourne were standing there. He was too surprised to speak. They grabbed his useless legs and hauled him forward, catching his arms and lifting him out of the car. Led by Pascal, they carried him to the other side of the clearing, where a gap in the wall of marsh reeds admitted them to a footpath. His ruined bones ground together. Pain as immense as the sunlight washing the sky surrounded him.

Mosquitoes whined about his head. Reeds clattered to either side. The men bore him to the foot of a spring the dimensions of a bathtub. Grunting, they turned around, so that he was facing the direction they had brought him, and lowered Bourne to the ground. His head tilted back, and he could look over the water at the stone from which its source poured. Gray, grainy, the rock had been carved into a face whose features had been weathered to the limit of recognition. What might have been horns, or might have been hair, curled above a wide face whose blank eyes seemed to stare into his above the water that poured from its open mouth.

A hand slid under his head, raised it to Pascal crouched beside him. He was holding a dented tin cup which he raised to Bourne's lips. The springwater was cold, a benediction. He felt as if he could almost speak.

The hand was yanked away, and his head flopped backwards. Pascal pressed a knife to his throat, and cut it.

*\*\*\**

A couple of days after he'd first arrived at the *auberge*, once the worst of the jet lag had passed, Bourne rolled himself down the handicapped ramp at the front door to the dirt lot where the guests parked their cars. The lot was empty. He pushed across it to the thick lawn that reached to the marsh. The chair jounced as he wheeled it over the grass to one of the short trees stationed around the space. Once he was under its branches, he halted. His chest was heaving. His arms and shoulders were searing. Sweat weighted his shirt. He sat gazing at the island of green, where Pascal would hold cookouts if the mosquitoes weren't too bad. Sometimes, he hung lanterns from the trees. Bourne looked at the tall reeds that marked the lawn's perimeter. How long ago was it he had ventured into them, felt the ground slant steeply down to the water?

A chorus of insects was buzzing its metallic song. In the distance, a white bird lifted into the air. He did not know the name of the insects, or of the bird.

\*\*\*

Dying was not as hard as he had feared. There was a burning across his throat, and something leaping out of it that must be his blood venting into the air. His body shuddered, too injured already to do any more. Far overhead, the sky was pale blue, depthless as pottery. Closer, water chuckled as the pool was replenished. Then everything went away.

\*\*\*

Bourne heard water, and realized that he had never stopped hearing it. He was in water, floating, but when he attempted to stand, his feet found the bottom easily. He rose into darkness—into the night. A crescent moon hung low in the sky. *Artemis's bow,* he thought. He stepped out of the pool and found his legs strong, the thick hair on them saturated. The joints seemed different, as did his feet, which felt hard, almost numb, but he adjusted to the change without difficulty. His arms, his chest—his cock—were large, bursting with life. Something weighted the sides of his head, but his neck was thick enough to bear it.

In front of him, Pascal and his five accomplices were prostrate on the ground, uttering words in a language he shouldn't have been able to understand but did. They were welcoming him, imploring his blessing. They were the reason for the shape he had assumed; their belief held him to it. It would be simple enough to shuck it, to assume the form of a horse, or bird, or tree, or reed—of anything, of all. *Pan.*

For the moment, this form would do. He caught Pascal by the neck and lifted him one-handed, bringing him face to face with what he'd summoned. Pascal's eyes bulged. The acid stink of urine filled the air. He supposed he owed him a debt of gratitude. He lowered but did not release Pascal. He opened his mouth. It was full of enormous teeth. They bit through Pascal's skull with ease. It crunched like a crisp, fresh apple.

The rest of the men were shaking. Their fear clouded the air. He inhaled it, then brought their god to them.

— *for Fiona*

# Casting Lots

## Jodi Renée Lester

"Oh, Chris, you must come. Mom and *Dud* are having their meeting tonight. They're reading the Big Book and I'll be confined to my bedroom. It's soooo dull. I mean, really."

Chris had the picture-perfect image of Maria as she carried on, stretched out on the couch, cord twisted around her finger, putting on airs. Twelve-year-old debutante, with a princess phone to her ear.

As if she had to convince him.

". . . and we'll steal snacks. I can already smell something yummy in the oven. Baked goods . . ."

Chris tied his sneakers, grabbed his jacket, and left the house. Though it was shorter through the woods by distance, the trees would only slow him down. He kept to the street, walking along the flat and winding road that skirted the woods until he reached the other side.

Outside Maria's house, outside her window, a streetlamp flickered on, a yellow glow asserting itself in the slowly fading light. No cars on the street yet. He may not have to meet any guests.

Chris climbed the flagstone steps and pressed the button that had long ago lost its luster. Muffled chimes sounded inside and grew louder as Maria's mom opened the door.

"Chris. What a wonderful surprise. Now you come in here." She ushered him into the house, turning on the light in the foyer.

"Thanks, Mrs. W. Maria didn't say I was coming? I'm sorry . . ."

"Never. That's quite all right." She clamped her hands on his shoulders and steered him toward the back of the house. "I think she's in her room." Her broad smile looked painful.

Chris politely loosed himself from her clutches and headed down the hall. As he came to her doorway, Maria looked up at him and smiled from her bed. Propped up on a pillow was a walking cast where only hours earlier she had worn a shoe.

"What happened to you?" He joined her on the bed, staring at the fresh white plaster. "Is it broken?"

"No. Only a sprain. Good thing Dud's an orthopod, otherwise I would've spent the entire afternoon in an emergency room."

"So?"

"I fell out of a tree. You know the one I like. I was sitting on the big branch up there and here came your brother lumbering along. I was all prepared to scare him when I lost my footing and fell. Poor Richie, not only did I scare him, I practically landed on him. He didn't tell you?"

She grabbed his hand and put it to her head. "Anyway, I've got a knob now, too. See?" She laughed and kicked out her injured foot, then handed him a felt-tip pen. "You can be the first to sign my trophy."

"Thanks."

"You smell that? Mom should be in soon with a plate for us. She's been fussing all about me. She thinks missing a practice or two will ruin my skating career." She rolled her eyes.

"How long do you have to wear that thing?"

"Not long. Not long at all."

Mr. W. breezed into the room with a tray. "Chris, you mind the time. It's getting late." He tilted his head toward the window.

"I will, Mr. W."

"Looks like there's one of each for each." Maria's dad set the tray on a footstool. Two milks and an assortment of freshly baked cookies, bars, and cakes.

"Thanks, Dud."

He left the room nodding wearily as if the nickname took a little bit out of him each time she said it.

Maria giggled and Chris joined her. He knew she only called him that to get his goat.

"Sign." She thrust the pen at Chris.

He put the pen to his lip, visibly working out what to say. Finally, he shrugged and, on the bottom of the cast, wrote:

*Dear Maria, your first cast. One heck of a milestone. Maybe* Dud *can make one for me, too. One of each for each. Ha-ha.*

He added two dots and a grin and signed it, *"Yours, Chris."*

"What does it say? I can't read it from here." She stretched and leaned until she could see it, then smiled and raised her big white boot, giving his shoulder a hard push. As her foot fell back to the pillow her eyes widened, noting the green ink smear left on his shirt by the sole of the cast. She grabbed the tray. "Let's eat these things."

He looked out the window. A long, dark car pulled up to the curb. Steam swirled in the headlights just before they blinked out. The windows were shaded and it looked as if no one was in there.

"Is it time yet?" Maria asked.

"It's getting close." He would wait until people stopped arriving. He took her hand and held it in both of his. "I really am sorry about your foot, you know."

"Don't be. I'm just glad I didn't land on Richie. We'd both still be lying there, turkey vultures picking our bones clean."

They each grabbed a cookie and looked to the window. Night was moving in.

***

"Oh, Chris. You weren't watching." Mrs. W. swept right in.

"It's okay. I'm leaving right now."

"Oh no you're not. You go call your father. Tell him I'll send you home first thing in the morning. I won't have you running through the woods on my watch. You don't want to get caught there at night."

"It's okay, I'll run real fast!" Chris protested. He jumped up and headed for the door. "I'll take the road, I swear."

Mrs. W. followed him out toward the foyer, then gripped the top of his head and turned it like a lid on a one-gallon jar.

"Phone," she said, using his head to maneuver him in the direction of the kitchen. "And make it fast. I have a meeting to get started."

"Yes, ma'am."

He took slow heavy steps. Hopefully Richie would answer. He crossed his fingers. On the fourth ring, he heard it pick up and turned his back to the doorway for privacy.

There was a long pause, a sound of fumbling as the person at the other end took time to get the handset from cradle to ear.

*Richie.* Chris sighed relief. He looked down at the countertop to conceal his conversation. "Richie," he whispered as loudly as he could without being heard.

"Where are you?"

"Is Dad home?"

"Not yet. Where are you?"

"I'm at Maria's. Mrs. W. is making me stay here."

"You're a dead man."

"C'mon, Richie, cover for me. I'll be home first thing in the morning."

"What do you want me to tell him?"

"Nothing unless you have to. In that case, I don't care, just make it good."

"You're playing with fiiire," Richie taunted.

"Shut up," Chris said.

"Okay. But you owe me one."

"Richie, wait. Why didn't you tell me—"

The phone clicked.

With more levity in his voice than he would ever use with his father, Chris added into the dead receiver, "Okay, Dad. See you tomorrow."

Mrs. W. was waiting outside the kitchen door. She ushered him back to Maria's bedroom.

"No funny business, you two. You're not getting any younger." She smiled and backed out of the room. She closed the door and they heard it latch. Maria's cheeks blossomed rosy red.

***

He should have been asleep. He did drift off for a bit, but it was shallow sleep.

How long had he been lying there? An hour? Three? He didn't want to know. His bedspread and blanket had already been shoved to the foot of the bed. His body wrestled, fighting wakefulness with energetic legs. He felt like he could run a mile or two while his upper half trailed behind.

Chris drew back his sheet, felt a chill as the cool air touched his feet. His ankles extended a little too far out of his loaner pajamas. He'd made her promise not to tell anyone, even if they were only long johns.

He felt the weight of his eyelids, wondering whether he would sink deeper into true sleep. Or should he open his eyes and start all over?

Another position maybe.

He rolled over on his side, rested his cheek on the back of one hand. He felt unsettled. Sleep was the only way it would disappear.

The streetlamp outside set the curtain aglow.

His heart raced. He heard the faint sound of voices—a lullaby or prayer. A rite of passage.

He listened to Maria rustle and moan and then emit a giggle that sounded more like a bleat. Her arm flopped over the edge of the bed, fingertips just inches from his nose. He gently poked the palm of her hand. Her arm retracted.

Chris propped himself up on an elbow, watched as she pulled her arm in. She nuzzled her hand briefly then wiped her cheek with the back of it. One quick sleepy motion, and then her thumb was in her mouth and she rolled over, turning her back to him. She twitched slightly and was sound asleep again.

*Some debutante.*

Chris giggled, pressing his face into the pillow. No way would he sleep now.

Once Maria's breathing was steady again, he crept across the room, putting his ear to the door and grasping the brass knob. He gently turned it. The door wouldn't budge.

He tried the other direction and pulled. No give. Then he remembered, at night, they kept it latched on the other side.

She had told him how they had found her one night, standing on the pool steps. Sleepwalking.

"It was the *shallow* end," Maria had told him, annoyed at having to be locked up like a caged animal.

"Creeeepy," Chris had said, shaking his head slowly, looking at her in amazement.

"You're creepy!" Maria had pushed him away from her, and he had fallen exaggeratedly over on the couch.

He turned away from the door and surveyed the room, then stopped at the window on the way to Maria's desk. He could barely make out the mailbox in front of the house. Fine points of light radiated from its corners, casting little rainbow halos. Faint outlines of cars lined the street. A figure moved past, a dark blur.

Chris's heart picked up its pace.

On the bulletin board over her desk, a bunch of pictures were tacked up, photographs and drawings, including one Chris had done for her—a black stallion running wild. He scrunched his nose at it, a moment of embarrassment and an urge to take it down.

Maria's library card was wedged in the corner between the cork and the wood. He pulled it out, bent it back and forth testing its strength, and returned to the door. He had to work it a bit, but was finally able to wedge the card between the door and the frame, slipping it up and down a couple of times until he felt the latch. He turned the knob, pushed the latch up, and was free.

At once he was assaulted by the heady smell of incense, thickening as he proceeded down the hall.

The voices were coming from much deeper in the house, beyond the family room, beyond the kitchen. The living room, where he rarely went.

The house was dark, but he thought he was familiar enough with it to get some water without being discovered. He waited in the hallway for his eyes to adjust.

He moved toward the voices, toward the source of the smoky scent.

The voices started to thin out, falling off little by little, until there was silence.

He plotted his course.

He now heard music, barely audible, with intermittent, sparse conversation that he could not make out. He looked in that direction, toward the other side of the family room where a short hallway would lead him to the dining room. Beyond that was the living room.

From where he stood, he could see nothing. The arched entrance to the hallway was completely black. Thick smoky tendrils, slowly swirling, beckoned him into the corridor.

He went deeper into the darkness, crossing from room to room, shadow to shadow, ducking behind furniture as he got closer. Farther into the dining room, he saw shades of gold illuminating shadows. Chris crouched down. Flickers of light swayed on the walls, shrinking, expanding, breathing to the rhythm of the music.

He crawled toward the living room. Just beyond the entryway was a table cornered between a large sofa and an easy chair. He held his breath and crawled in beneath it.

From where he sat, it looked like every surface had a burning candle or two or more on it.

Over the edge of the sofa, a well-manicured hand limply held a goblet above him, casting a huge bouncing shadow on the wall and ceiling as amber liquid swirled within it.

There was some whispering, then a giggle.

Across the room two pairs of legs dangled over the edge of a Papasan chair.

Through the beveled edges of the glass tabletop, a distorted pair of legs in brown tights and boots hung over the arm of the easy chair.

A thick stream of smoke rose from the center of the room—the incense, now mixed with the smell of cigarettes and grass and melting wax.

There were small sounds, hushed voices, even one he'd heard before but couldn't place. A woman laughed with delight.

A single chime sounded and the whispers faded to stifled breaths. Shadows dashed across the room, arms in silhouette reached for seats, bodies shifted, getting comfortable, getting ready. The brown legs pulled out of sight and in their place a hand dropped down in front of his face, inches away, wielding the biggest pearl he'd ever seen, *a jawbreaker,* surrounded by a ring of clustered diamonds.

All he heard now was faint music and a single voice. Mr. W.?

"It's been a while since we've all come together like this. I know we're all excited. I know I am."

A murmur rippled through the room.

"To keep things moving smoothly, I will send you out in pairs. Head straight out to the cabana where you can change and don the clothes of our ancestors. Everything you need should be there, but keep your boots on so we can move swiftly. The sooner we arrive, the sooner we can begin. We will congregate on the deck before heading down. Grab a lantern on the way out, one of each for each. It gets pretty dark.

"Remember, once around the room you will all open your eyes and then, on my cue, you can go. Shirley? We'll start with you."

"Uh-huh. Okay. Right," a woman replied almost in a whisper.

The man had everyone's attention as he began speaking. His voice was hypnotic and droned on, talking about a flame, ". . . keep your eyes on the flame, the dance of the flame, the center of the flame, the heat of the flame, the calm of the flame, the center of the flame, the power of the flame.

"When I count ten, nine, eight, seven, six, five, four, three, two, one, when I count down from ten you will be asleep. Asleep but aware. Aware of my voice. You are in the heart of the flame now, the heat of the flame, the sound of my voice. Ten, nine, eight, lids heavy, seven, six, five, lids flickering as the flame flickers, four, three, lids shut, and two, falling to one, asleep. You are now asleep.

"You can hear my voice. All you can hear is my voice. Shirley, can you hear me?"

"Yes."

"Are you asleep?"

"Yes. Asleep."

The room was filled with heavy breathing, a room full of deep sleep.

Chris let his eyes fall shut. The last thing he remembered was the rest of the room, one-by-one, confirming their sleep state.

***

Chris awoke. The room was dark. He was still underneath the table, curled in a ball, cold in the chill of the abandoned room.

His knees cracked as he crawled out from beneath the table. He peeked over the couch. The sliding glass door to the pool was ajar. He shimmied through the opening and, seeing no one, stole across cold cement.

Water reflected distorted rings of light onto the shadowed wall of the cabana. Once past the deep end he stepped down onto the deck, rough planks of redwood beneath his bare feet. It was darker here. His belly tightened as he reached out for the rail. He walked blindly, hands feeling their way along. A splinter pierced his finger. He pulled it out, sucking the bead of blood. He looked through the tall trees. Golden light shimmered far off in the distance. He descended into the woods.

As he entered the thick forest, cicadas fought against crickets for voice. It was no mere hum; it was loud and electric, disorienting.

Chris carefully stepped through damp bark and twigs toward the heart of the woods. Low-lying ferns brushed gently against his ankles. He knew to avoid veering to the right where the shrubbery was rougher and likely to tear up his feet. The treetops reached toward the sky as the tip of a paintbrush would toward an empty canvas. Down the tall and naked trunks Chris saw snakes where only yesterday thick ropey vines had coiled and drooped.

He picked up his pace, eager to flee the damp and dense forest, toward a small clearing which he knew was nearby. With each breath, he tasted moisture in the air that on this night nearly gagged him. He spat, trying to rid his tongue of the vile flavor.

Upon reaching the open space, he shivered, wiped his brow of sweat. He paused to get his bearings and catch his breath. There was a sudden break in the sound of the crickets and cicadas, which resumed unevenly, overlapping, and Chris had the sensation of the ground shifting.

He continued forward, with only a vague memory of the rich firelight awaiting him beyond.

He moved through a patch of younger growth, weaving his way through the forest with the innate agility of a young deer. Just as his momentum reached its peak he was stopped short, caught in cobwebs. Fighting them, he became twisted up and panic nearly suffocated him before he realized the cobwebs were no such thing but merely cloth draped over a branch.

He unwound himself and looked about. Clothing—shirts, trousers, and frocks—similarly hung over the surrounding branches. The fleeting sense of peculiarity was instantly overcome by the drive to continue on.

The trees were no longer familiar to him. They stood black against the midnight sky, like false trees on a stage setting. And although still tall and slender, they had flattened out, no longer organic, appearing as if their branches were covered with burlap.

A gold fleck shone from one of them and then another. He approached cautiously, afraid of another trap. As he neared these strange trees, they regained their depth and structure and he realized the branches were strewn with black hats. He touched one to be sure and ran his hand along the wide brim, fingers feeling the brass buckle that adorned it.

There were bonnets, too. No mistaking it. His stomach clenched. But as quickly as the feeling had come over him it passed, and though he slowed his steps even more, he could not stop.

Once again the atmosphere changed ever so subtly. The cicadas and crickets re-synchronized, but now the sound was louder, the vibration in his head almost deafening.

He had no idea where he was. But surely this was his forest. He knew it well.

And following this unseen force, he walked on and immediately kicked something, nearly tripping over it. It did not roll but slid ahead carving a path in the dirt. He crouched down and carefully felt before his feet, recovering the object.

It was a boot. A man's boot, flat and sturdy, with metal rods extending out the top, and as the moon slid from the clouds, he saw a graveyard of similar footwear, discarded carelessly, crude leg braces glinting in the gentle light.

"There you are," came a whisper from behind him, and Chris whirled around to face it.

Maria had crept up and now giggled at the start she had given him.

"Shhhh," Chris quieted her. She wore a white cotton shift, one foot still bound, though now covered with earth, the other bare. "Maria, what . . . ?"

Then the moon passed behind the clouds again and she put her hand in his and let him lead her. And through the cacophony of the cicadas and crickets, he was certain she was urging him, hissing:

"Faster, faster!"

And though she was limping, he could not stop, for now he saw a flicker of light, golden orange sparks, and shadows of living things.

Chris ducked behind some bushes and Maria ducked with him.

They edged closer, together, until he saw a dark body laying on a spread of leaves and grass. It was a large animal. As he got closer, he recognized hooves and horns. Chris followed its gaze and his attention was drawn to a group of figures moving about a ring of fire. Some might say they were dancing, but it was an awful, awkward dance.

The world went quiet. Maria took his lead. A flute picked up where the insects left off. It was a familiar tune, and as they got closer, he saw there were no goats, for the figures had the arms of humans that swung as they frolicked in the dangerous light. And they had horns and wicked faces and passed a leather sack around and sucked from it eagerly. Maria tugged at his hand and led him into the circle of fire, pushing him into the fray.

Chris landed on his side and bumped his head. The music stopped. Maria's bound foot held him down and the soft blond hair of the young girl's leg glistened in the firelight.

Everything around them was silent and still now except for the crackling flames. Chris struggled to lift his head. There stood Mr. and Mrs. W. in the center of the blazing ring. They looked on with expectant pride.

Maria bent down, hands on her hips, and thrust her gleaming, grinning face into Chris's, forcing his head back to the ground. She pressed her boot more firmly into his chest, as if using him for balance. She then began tearing away at the cast with a blade, discarding the plaster piece by piece into the fire.

Tiny beads of sweat sparkled across her brow as she worked at it and when only one piece remained, she threw up her arms victoriously, one hand still wielding the blade, the other the final square of plaster from the sole of her cast—the one that bore Chris's inscription.

Maria looked to her father. His strong chest gleamed as the firelight flickered across it, his large powerful arms raised to the sky.

"Look, Daddy. He came," Maria said, beaming up at him.

"You did good, child."

Maria pitched the final piece of plaster into the flames. The crowd that had been watching silently in anticipation cheered. The flutes started up again and so did the merriment, and the living things danced, slowly closing in on Chris.

Chris looked up at Maria, confused, betrayed, and then down at his chest where her foot was digging into him. Where the cast had been there now was a cloven hoof. He looked back up at her and she smiled at him.

It was the smile of her mother.

# Founding Fathers

## K. H. Vaughan

The clearing in the woods was set well back from the park entrance and was littered with the detritus of years of parties. A couple dozen kids sat on logs or the remnants of a couch that had been dragged out there years ago, its upholstery stained and reeking. Others stood around the keg.

Jess wouldn't normally have come to this sort of thing, but it was Costa's party, and Denny was Costa's friend. Costa was already on probation for an alcohol violation. The R.A. in his dorm was a real hard-ass, so Costa had dragged this keg out into the woods at Founder's Park down the hill from campus. Stale beer in the dark surrounded by empties, trash, and used condoms. This shit was for high schoolers.

Some girl shrieked as a frat boy waved her sports bra around in the air, hooting. He threw it up into the tree branches. Everyone laughed while she slapped at his shoulder.

"This is so stupid," Jess said. "Let's get out of here."

"Aw, it's not that bad," Denny replied.

"Really?"

Denny looked around. A freshman girl was puking in the bushes while her friend held her hair out of her face. But she'd gotten there too late. The friend now held the vomit-soaked strands gingerly as she muttered support and encouragement, trying to keep from getting puke splatter on her sneakers and jeans.

"Yeah, you're right," he said. "This is pretty bad. Lemme top off our cups and we'll go."

They cut through the woods on the far side of the park, leaving the noise of the partygoers behind them. Deeper in it grew quieter, despite the expanse of the city around them.

"Whoa, what is that?" Denny said.

"What is what? Come on, I need to pee."

Denny let go of her hand and picked his way through the brush toward a dark obelisk situated beneath some branches. Getting closer, Jess could see it was a statue tucked away in the trees. A leering creature formed in marble—half man, half goat—crouching on a pedestal. It was ancient and stained. Green moss hung from its weathered horns.

"Denny, I want to go home," she said.

"Yeah, yeah. Just hold on a second." He hunched down by the base of the pedestal and began brushing at the filth and grime. "Can't see," he grunted.

She sighed loudly at him, then found her keys and shined a small pen light on the area he had unearthed.

"Sixteen seventy-four." He whistled, touching the engraving on the base. "Weird. It's classical style but they didn't do much of that in the Colonial period, especially with this kind of subject matter."

"That's my history major," she said.

"Yeah. Something strange . . ."

He looked around as if confused and then suddenly reached for her, kissing her urgently. Within moments he was peeling away her Albemarle University sweatshirt and bra, exposing her full breasts to the moonlight. She was flushed and breathing heavily.

"We don't have any condoms," she said.

"I know. But I want you now."

Her mind raced. Had she missed a pill? She decided she didn't care. She gasped as he entered her, and somewhere deep in the recesses of her mind she imagined the sound of drums and flutes.

They stayed in bed at his place all weekend, ordering pizza and leaving only to get wine. Monday morning she realized that she had missed her nine-thirty class and hadn't written two papers that were due. Denny pulled her back to bed, and she surrendered willingly.

\*\*\*

Jess pulled herself away for a couple of days to get caught up on school. She liked Denny, but this was insane. Constant fucking. Inventive positions that seemed dreamlike and strange in the sober light of day.

She'd never been prudish but now found herself spontaneously blushing and horny while sitting in lecture. She almost came once just daydreaming about their experiment with the reverse cowgirl. She excused herself from seminar to run to the bathroom, finishing herself before racing across campus to Denny's room.

Denny hadn't changed or bathed. His room held the deep musky smell of sweat and sex. His computer screen was plastered with windows open to porn sites, the monitor framed with empty liquor bottles and tissues like an X-rated shrine to penetration.

He grunted and pulled her inside. After the first hour, she realized his hands were stained with dirt and moss.

"Denny, have you been out at the park again?"

"Yeah," he said. "It's just got me curious. That monument is out of place period-wise. It's something the Founding Fathers would have to have built, but they were strict Presbyterians. They didn't embrace statuary anyhow, and that thing is practically pagan idolatry."

His honors thesis was on the influence of religion in politics during the late seventeenth century, so he would know. She really didn't care much at the moment though, not when he was so close in the room. She stroked his face—which was well into five days' worth of beard—and kissed his salty flesh.

"Why don't you explore something more current?" she breathed into his ear.

***

She couldn't get a hold of Denny later that evening. He wasn't answering his phone. She considered trying to find him, but where to look?

She took a long shower in the common bathroom at her dorm, enjoying the spray of steaming water on her flesh. Her nipples tingled as she massaged and soaped herself, and before she realized it she was masturbating with the hand shower, shuddering and moaning. Two girls from her floor giggled as she left the stall, and she blushed, fleeing to her room.

No sign of Denny yet. Thinking about the moss stains on his hands, she threw on some clothes and drove down to the park. He wasn't there, but someone—certainly Denny—had been cleaning the statue.

She'd not gotten a good look at it before, and with the filth and growth removed, she could see its bestial goatlike features and squat muscular body more clearly. Those eyes with their horizontal slits had gazed at her when they had made love that night at the party. She felt lightheaded and reached out to steady herself, her hand coming to rest on the muscular marble haunch.

Art and history were not her subjects, but she could tell that the style of the sculpture was wrong for the period, as Denny had insisted. It was grotesquely real and primitive in its lines and detail. Denny had dug out the accumulated dirt and leaves around the base of the pedestal beneath the cloven hooves. The base was wider than she had imagined.

She drove back up the hill, planning to go back to Denny's room, but something made her turn off and go back another block. She passed Club Passion a second time. Neon lights and nude women in silhouette. The sign said it was amateur night with a cash prize. Ridiculous. She had never considered stripping before.

She drove around the block three more times before parking. Up on stage she writhed and moaned: excited, horny. The crowd of men watched her with undisguised atavism. The music was throbbing, urging her on, some DJ mix of trance with a primitive flute echoing through the background.

In the changing room, the other girls glared at her and whispered, "Bitch has done this before."

She won five hundred dollars and the owner offered her a gig weekend nights.

***

"I've just been in a weird place," she told Samantha afterward, as they drank wine in her friend's room. "I mean it's been a little over a week now and it's like I can't think about anything but sex. And Denny has turned into some kind of animal. If he's not on me, he's surfing the Internet for porn."

She didn't mention the strip club, gyrating and bending over in front of complete strangers. She wasn't sure she wanted to talk about that yet.

"You should relax as long as you're enjoying yourself. I can't get attention from anything that doesn't run on batteries right now. Sometimes couples just get like that. When my dad started dating his new girlfriend last summer they were at it constantly."

"Eww!"

"You're telling me? I caught them on the couch. Oh God, he was behind her and his big white gut was rippling around and all I could think about was video I had seen of elephant seals going at it."

"God, that's gross. Thanks for that image. Really."

"I know," Samantha said. "No one wants to hear about their parents having sex."

"Well—I don't mean that I feel bad about it. It's just . . . different. I almost feel weird that I *don't* feel weird about it. Because it isn't like either of us."

"As long as you aren't doing anything dangerous."

They talked for several hours, drinking merlot and smoking a couple of joints. Samantha was taking a course on human sexuality and they went through the chapter on hypersexual behavior and laughed. She was pretty sure they didn't have any kind of neurodegenerative disease, and they weren't doing drugs—or at least nothing that would send them on a sexual bender.

She flipped through the textbook, checking off positions they had tried in her mind. She realized she was feeling drunk and woozy. It was hot in Samantha's room. She could hear drums and flutes.

"What is that music?" she murmured.

"Oh God, Sasha down the hall has been on a Depeche Mode kick lately."

Samantha was braless beneath her T-shirt, and Jess could trace her nipples along the light cotton fabric. Samantha caught her eyes and Jess shifted on the bed. They kissed, giggling. They had kissed once before playing spin the bottle at a party, but it hadn't done anything for either of them then.

This time she grew hot and wet immediately and they locked tongues, stripping off their clothes and burying themselves in the exotic sameness of each other.

\*\*\*

She found Denny in his room the next afternoon. He smelled of sweat and perfume and other women, and without a word he peeled away her panties and bent her over the couch, his thrusting like a pounding drumbeat. His sweat dripped on her neck and back. The last thing she remembered clearly was the sound of drums as she began going in and out of lucidity.

In fact there were drums all around, and naked slaves holding burning brands, their dark skin glistening with sweat and oil in the torchlight. The flames glittered on the polished wood and marble of the hall. Or was it a church? She could remember walking in the cold echoing space once when she was a girl on a grade-school field trip. The beautiful lacquered millwork and brocade tapestries along the walls. She squinted at small, engraved plates that labeled each artifact of colonial history in the dry and sterile space, while their docent, prim and proper, cautioned them not to touch anything.

Now in the past, what looked to be a future governor's mansion, filled with heat. August men dressed like English lords in embroidered silk and tight wigs encircled women in various states of dress: fine velvet gowns and simple linen shifts. Their wives and servants. Their slaves. Soon they were taking them aside in twos and threes, imported finery and homespun dropped carelessly on the parquet floors as they began their ecstasies.

Singularly and in groups, again and again, in permutation after permutation of entanglement and animal frenzy, they grew more crazed. Here two men pummeled one another with bloody fists. There, the wife of a minister knelt before a wealthy plantation owner, punching him repeatedly in the scrotum as he came, his semen spurting out as if driven forth by her blows.

*\*\*\**

Jess regained consciousness some time after midnight in the stillness of Denny's room. She was naked and alone, salty crust on her face, hair, and back. She staggered to the bathroom and rinsed her mouth. How many times had they done it? Seemed impossible. Foggily, she tried to remember what was real and what was a dream.

A dream. The thought instantly sobered her. Visions she had seen, strange alien memories from history: manic sexual abandon and increasing violence that had ended with hacked and bloody corpses lying among the discarded petticoats and torn stays. Somehow she knew in her core that it had been real.

She shuddered violently, then began looking around for her clothes. She found her underwear hanging from Denny's computer monitor. She reached for them and the screen caught her eye. It was a painting of one of the city's early luminaries. He had a visible scar on his face which she'd been taught had happened in a battle with the French. She had seen him that night, choking a maidservant in the throes of his lust until someone smashed a bottle against his head. Afterward, his teeth had flashed white and feral beneath the running blood as he beat her to death.

Denny had left dozens of windows open on his desktop. She began to flip through them. Interspersed between the porn and the pop-up ads, she could see that he'd been doing research on the statue. Every generation or two, hidden in the city's history, he had found outbreaks of mass satyrism: spontaneous incidents of bacchanalian violence and sexual abandon, as if some spirit of rapacity had bubbled to the surface, horrors that grew in scope and depravity with each event.

She felt suddenly nauseated.

Denny. There was only one place he could be.

As she made her way through the dark woods, the overwhelming pungent smell of the goat hung heavy in the air, and the sound of drums and screaming echoed through her mind. Mounds of dirt had been tossed up around the statue's base, with more being flung up from the hole as she approached. A shovel stood with its blade buried in the pile, the tags from the hardware store still dangling off the handle.

Denny crouched naked in the deep hole he had excavated, frantically clawing at the earth. She was surprised to see that the statue's pedestal extended down at least six feet underneath the ground. It was the spire of some larger structure buried in the earth at the city's heart. Denny was standing on a stone slab from which rose a fetid reeking heat. He looked up at her, mumbling and without recognition. His fingernails were torn and bloody. His manhood was engorged and impossibly large.

She grabbed the shovel from the dirt pile as he began to scramble up out of the hole. With a sickening crunch, she struck him on the head with the heavy steel blade. He tumbled back and did not move again. As she shoveled dirt over Denny and the slab she could hear the clawing and scratching of the thing entombed beneath.

# Montfort Farm

## R. Christophe Ryber

"That won't work here, Mr. Stockbridge."

Ryan turned away from the picture window looking out on the gravel driveway, where his gleaming black Audi baked in the late afternoon sun. His sharp blue eyes drilled into the lawyer sitting in the high-backed Victorian chair in the parlor, neat stacks of papers lined up before her on the coffee table.

Rebecca Kimball pointed with her silver pen at the Blackberry in Ryan's hand. "There's no cell service here."

Ryan ran his fingers through his short blond hair and frowned at the maddening lack of bars on the plastic screen. He had only driven into Greenfield a few hours ago and he couldn't wait to put its quaint covered bridges and scenic mountains in his rearview mirror. The Blackberry was his only contact with his partner, Craig Gordon. Craig was in Hartford struggling to keep their business, Fast Cat Electronics, from going under.

"Could we move this along, Mr. Stockbridge?"

Ryan shoved the Blackberry into the jacket pocket of his gray suit. He bit his lip as Rebecca Kimball let her silver pen roll out of her long fingers onto the first stack of papers. The hardwood floor underneath the thick, floral rug creaked as he paced back and forth.

"Grandma Catherine never mentioned anything about a farm," he said.

Rebecca glanced at her Rolex and sighed. "Your grandmother was a Montfort before she married Edwin Stockbridge. The only living heirs to Montfort Farm are yourself and Sophie Montfort."

Ryan stopped before one of the twin arches on either side of the great fireplace. He could smell the ashes behind the ornate stained-glass screen, with its clusters of grapes and Greek Pan prancing about with flute and golden goblet.

"If this Sophie girl is a Montfort and already lives here, then why isn't the farm passing to her?"

Rebecca brushed back her blond bangs and picked up her silver pen. She stacked the piles of papers together and opened her briefcase.

"Mr. Stockbridge, I explained the family defect when I phoned you in Hartford. I can see you're not interested—"

"And I can see you're in a hurry to get this over with."

The powder blue Wedgewood china in the curio cabinet rattled as Ryan threw himself onto the faded sofa. He pulled out his Blackberry and called up the last spreadsheet Craig had sent him.

"I have a business in desperate need of capital, Ms. Kimball. I spent six hours driving to this tourist trap because you led me to believe there were liquid assets associated with the estate. So far all I've seen is a rundown Victorian with a barn and sugarhouse."

A smile crept over Rebecca's face. "Let's cut to the chase then, Mr. Stockbridge."

She reached into her briefcase, removing a black folder. Ryan snatched it out of her hand and flipped through the documents inside. He raised a blond eyebrow, adjusting his red silk tie.

"Vale Corp? All of these shares are for Vale Corp?"

Rebecca nodded. "Olivia made some shrewd investments in the eighties. I must apologize, Mr. Stockbridge, if I seem eager to finish this, but Olivia Leighton-Montfort was a good friend of mine, and I have been managing her affairs since her unexpected death."

Ryan waved a hand in dismissal. His blue eyes widened each time he turned a page. He held in his hands the salvation of Fast Cat Electronics. If only he could call Craig.

"Get your hands off me, you piece of shit!"

Ryan jumped up from the sofa and the portfolio fell to the floor. He looked toward the back of the house, where the angry female voice continued to shout profanities, then over at Rebecca. She stood and smoothed out her pants suit. Her forced smile didn't hide the tremor in her voice.

"Perhaps it's time we met Sophie."

The wood-framed screen door slammed shut behind Ryan as he followed Rebecca out onto a thick carpet of clover and dandelions. An ancient maple stretched its great limbs overhead toward the old Victorian.

A tall man in faded jeans and a plaid shirt backed into the lengthening shadows under the tree. He stumbled as his tan work boots caught on the gnarled roots lying half buried around the tree's base. A tawny barefoot woman stalked him, her white cotton summer dress stained with purple splashes. Ryan guessed they were from the green wine bottle she waved about in one hand. Something silver flashed in her other hand, and it looked like she was threatening the tall man with it.

"Back off me, Stoddard. You ain't the boss of me."

"Sophie!"

Sophie planted her brown lips on the wine bottle and took a long swig before poking the man in the chest with the silver rod.

Ryan squinted. A flute?

"Sophie!"

Rebecca called after her again, sighing as she navigated through the overgrown clover. Sophie turned and waved the bottle in greeting.

"Hey, Becca."

"Sophie, leave poor Tom alone."

Sophie slipped past Rebecca, dismissing the incident with a toss of her tangled auburn hair. Ryan met her sullen hazel eyes as she came toward him.

"Who's Captain America?"

He shoved his hands in his pockets, maintaining his poker face. Genetic defect? Ryan had pictured some withdrawn, mentally handicapped woman, not a statuesque, outspoken alcoholic. His cheeks flushed as her body in its thin cotton sheath brushed against him. The scent of earth and wine flooded his nostrils. Her hair smelled like summer.

Ryan gave Rebecca a puzzled look. She traded glances with Tom, then nodded.

"Sophie, this is Mr. Stockbridge."

Ryan shook his head when Sophie offered him the wine bottle. She threw him a dark look over her shoulder as she sauntered back toward Rebecca.

"Yeah, the one that gets my farm."

Rebecca sighed and glanced at her Rolex again.

"It's not like that, Sophie. This is your home—always. Mr. Stockbridge is going to take care of the business end of things."

"Possibly," Ryan added, and he didn't miss the glare Rebecca shot him. Sophie dumped herself cross-legged in the grass. She set the wine bottle in a clump of dandelions and placed her brown fingers on the flute's keys.

"I don't need no boss." She raised the flute and began to play.

Ryan's eyes widened. "Bach—Sonata in E-flat major."

Rebecca nodded. "Sophie's quite talented."

Tom, clearing his throat, hooked one thumb in his belt. "I'll catch up with you later."

Rebecca nodded again and edged closer to Ryan. "She'll be like that for a while. Perhaps we could use this time to finalize the arrangements."

Ryan's blue eyes narrowed. "The Vale Corp stock—"

"Totally liquefiable. Sell it all. The farm, though, and Sophie, we have to talk about."

Ryan smiled and extended his arm. "After you."

\*\*\*

Ryan pulled on the wrought iron handle, and the red door turned on its well-oiled hinges. He squinted through the few beams of fading sunlight that cut through the sawdust clouds. The setting sun at his back cast a long shadow over the freshly swept floor. An electric motor buzzed in the darkened barn, and bright red sparks skittered around Tom's work boots.

Tom flipped a switch and the motor whirred to a stop. Another switch clicked and a bank of fluorescent lights snapped and popped to life.

"Who builds a round barn?"

The pinewood boards creaked under Ryan's leather dress shoes as he stepped inside. The grinding wheel Tom had been working at continued to free spin like the vanes on a windmill. Tom inspected the axe's sharpened edge under the flickering blue light. He nodded at Ryan.

"Pret' near everyone, at least at the end of the 1800s, when this barn was built. Better for hayin'—that is till everything got mechanized. Then they went back to rectangles."

Ryan looked over the stacks of firewood and fingered the polished wooden handles of the farm tools that hung along the walls. He hoisted a weathered pitchfork out of its slot by the door. Tom tapped the rusted tines of the fork with the butt of his axe.

"'Course we don't hay anymore. Miss Olivia got us into sugarin', which pretty much saved the place. Now the only farmin' we do is for the tourists—Indian corn, pumpkins, gourds—stuff like that."

Leaning his axe against a greasy hydraulic splitter, he added, "We use the barn mostly as a woodshed. The sugarhouse burns through a lot of wood."

Ryan set the pitchfork back into the wooden rack. "Did you know Olivia well?"

Tom's lips curled into a thin smile. "Oh, I know the Montforts. I started workin' for Miss Olivia when I got out of college."

"College?" The word was out before Ryan could stop it. He cursed himself as Tom's gaze narrowed.

"Yeah. We have them here, too. Palmary College over in Craftsbridge. Agriculture."

Ryan opened his mouth, thought of nothing to say, and nodded.

"You one of them college jocks, Mr. Stockbridge? Look like one."

"Track and field. You know—javelin, discus."

"We had cows at Palmary."

Tom grunted and shut the fluorescent lights off, his baseball cap silhouetted against the purple sky beyond the doorway. Ryan followed him out. The swollen red sun had run aground on the hills beyond Greenfield and had dyed the white spire of the Unitarian church pink. Tom pushed the heavy door shut until it clicked, then rattled it once to be sure.

"You fish, Mr. Stockbridge?"

"Please, call me Ryan."

"Fly fish, I suppose."

Ryan nodded. Tom smiled and pointed at the dark line of trees beyond the sugarhouse—old maples, white birches, gnarled oaks. Their thick trunks and towering leafy crowns stretched unbroken down the side of the mountain into the valley.

"That's Westminster Wood. You take that trail right there about a quarter mile and you'll come to Hunger Hollow Falls. There's a pool there with brookies in it."

Ryan fought down the instinctual "no." *You know squat about how this farm works, and you've already insulted the one man you really need. Who else can you leave in charge when you go back to Hartford—the drunk cousin?*

"I'd like that, Tom. Got an extra pole?"

Tom adjusted his cap and they began trudging up the grassy hill toward the gravel drive, where Tom's faded blue pickup sat parked next to Ryan's Audi.

"I'll lend you mine. Got to do another planting tomorrow while the weather holds. But I'll leave the rod in the kitchen. It's already got a fly on it. Try not to lose it. I've had it on there since last summer."

The two men paused at the edge of the drive to look at the house. Ryan could just make out the twirling form of Sophie on the wraparound porch as she spun into an *arabesque* before plopping herself down in the porch swing, her long middle finger raised in their direction. Tom grunted. His work boots crunched across the gravel to his truck.

"Have fun with that. I've got to stop at the Wright's and see Becca."

Ryan couldn't resist any longer. "You know Rebecca Kimball?"

Tom nodded. "She's my cousin. Stoddard on her mother's side."

Ryan didn't miss the gleam in Tom's eye as he leaned out of the cab window.

"Everyone's related in Greenfield. One way or another."

\*\*\*

"Piece of shit."

Ryan slurped at the steaming black coffee. He set the homemade ceramic mug, covered in purple grape clusters and creeping green vines, down next to a heart carved into the old oak desk. He traced the letters notched into the heart with his finger—ES & BM—then wiped at the grime on the computer screen with the sleeve of his bathrobe, clicking away in frustration at the coffee-stained mouse.

He pounded the blackened CTRL-ALT-DEL buttons once again, rubbing his bleary red eyes. His night in the guest room had been a frigid nightmare. Didn't they believe in heat around here? Once the sun set, a cold breeze had crept down off of the mountain and Ryan had shivered under his quilt, longing for the central air in his Cape house.

When a reluctant, frigid sleep finally accepted him, it was full of long brown limbs and defiant hazel eyes, the dulcet tones of Bach's Sonata in E-flat and . . . something less pleasant.

He had awoken to find himself sitting ramrod straight in the canopied bed, his bare skin goose fleshed in the mountain air. He had thrown the covers off and padded across the cold hardwood floor to the open window; had paused there and squinted through the predawn gloom, his hands on the window frame to lower it against the early morning chill.

Had it been his imagination or was the ground fog seeping *out of* the wood bordering the farm?

Then the thing in the dream had bubbled to the surface of his mind. At the remembrance of the shadowy, horned figure, Ryan had slammed the window shut and pulled the drapes.

The spooks of the night had vanished with the rising, yellow, midsummer sun. And Ryan had shuffled out to the dew-covered Audi in his bathrobe to grab his laptop. Now he connected a cable between the laptop and the obstinate machine on the graffiti-covered desk and powered up.

He shook his head as the lines of code scrolled up the screen. How the hell did they get so corrupted? It was like somebody had thrown a wrench in there. He let the two machines fight it out and turned to the safe at the side of the desk. He opened the folder Rebecca Kimball had given him yesterday after he had leaned over the hood of her Volvo and scribbled his signature with her silver pen. He found the combination on the back of her business card and spun the dial, left-right-left.

Nothing.

*Okay, fine.* Right-left-right.

Still, the steel lever refused to budge.

Ryan cursed under his breath and rattled the handle.

"You ain't gonna open it like that."

Ryan swiveled in the office chair. Sophie leaned against the door jamb in the same purple-stained cotton shift she'd worn the day before. Her bare toes cracked as she curled and stretched her feet like a ballerina warming up. Ryan slid back to the desk and checked the scrolling numbers on the computer.

"You know how to get it open?"

Her full brown lips bent into a smile. "Don't matter. Becca changed the combination after the funeral."

Sophie pounced out of a *pas de chat* and landed next to Ryan, her thigh sending the chair into a spin. He pulled himself back to the desk as Sophie leaned over to peer at the business card lying on the laptop keyboard.

"Yep. That's Mom's old combo."

Ryan cursed again, slamming his fist down on the desk. The laptop jumped. He needed to get his broker moving on the Vale Corp stock. Craig would bail soon, and Fast Cat Electronics would be history. How could these people not have a phone? He'd have to drive into Greenfield later, but first he needed to crack the safe.

He started as a warm brown hand covered his. Sparkling hazel eyes met his own when he looked up.

"Temper, temper, Mr. Stockbridge. You got some Montfort in you, after all."

They both jumped at the knock on the open door.

"Am I interrupting?"

Tom adjusted his baseball cap, stepping aside as Sophie stormed out of the office. Ryan shook his head, slid the office chair back. Tom lifted the bamboo fly rod he was holding and tapped Ryan's shoulder.

"Brookies bite in the mornin'."

\*\*\*

"The trail ends at the falls. No need to go farther than that. You get into the wood on the other side of the brook—things get weird."

Tom's words echoed in Ryan's head as he stared into the dark pool of swirling water. The falls rumbled deafeningly, trembling the ground underfoot.

His oxfords skidded on a wet rock, and he wrapped his desperate fingers around an overhanging branch. He hung there a moment, above the churning water, then caught hold of a flatter, drier rock.

*I'm not exactly dressed for this. If I fall in, no one will ever hear me.*

He wiped the mist off his face, pulling at his damp dress shirt. He'd left his tie and jacket at the farmhouse and had rolled his white sleeves up past the elbows. The midsummer sun blazed overhead, racing toward the zenith, but the shade in the wood on the opposite bank only seemed to grow darker.

Ryan unhooked the Royal Coachman from the cork handle. The reel spun and clicked as he stripped some line and snapped the rod back. The rod loaded nicely, and the coiled line at his feet shot through the guides on the forward cast. He shook the tip, paying out some slack, and let the fly drift.

The thunder of the falls cocooned him in silence, but he caught the changing shadows in the trees, nonetheless. His eyes shot away from the white wings of the Coachman. He peered into the darkness under the leafy branches, his hand tightening on the rod's cork grip.

There it was again.

A familiar unease crept into Ryan; its chill seeped into his limbs. There, on the far bank, was the thing from his dream. The horned shadow tilted its head, then turned and disappeared among the thick, gnarled trunks.

A cold compulsion shook Ryan out of his stupor.

*I need to get the hell out of here.*

He tossed the fly rod onto the bank and scrambled away from the seething pool. He looked up the trail, winding its way back to Montfort Farm, but his feet turned to lead.

*No, not that way.*

He spotted a thick plank thrown across the brook, its far end buried in the mossy bank.

*That way.*

He planted an oxford on the gray, weathered board and hesitated.

Into *the wood?*

Ryan shot a look over his shoulder.

*I need to go. Now.*

He bounded across the board and sprang onto the far bank, scraping against the rough trunks as his hurried steps became frantic strides. His footsteps fell silent on the soft carpet of moss and dead leaves, and the roar of the waterfall dwindled into the distance. The unyielding paper bark of an ancient white birch brought his flight to an abrupt halt.

He rubbed the swelling knot on his forehead and spun around.

*I'm lost.*

"You can see him."

Ryan tensed at the cold splash of adrenalin and backed into the trees. He looked up at the limb of a giant oak and followed the bare foot to the dangling brown leg and up to the stained cotton shift. A pair of hazel eyes burned among the leaves. Sophie sat on the branch and stretched, arching her back like a cat.

He raised an eyebrow. "See who?"

The full brown lips twisted into a knowing smile. "Herne."

Sophie raised her fingers to her temples and wiggled them. Ryan's gaze flickered among the shadows, but Sophie shook her tangled locks.

"He's gone now. He's got what he wanted."

"What's that?"

Ryan took a step back as Sophie dropped from the overhanging branch like a panther.

"You're here, of course."

They both turned as a gunshot cracked, its report echoing back off the mountain. Sophie stepped closer to Ryan and slipped a trembling arm around him, her thumb hooked into his belt loop. She nodded at the question in his eyes.

"Falls are back that way."

Ryan leaned down to hear the words fall from her lips.

"Can't shoot him no more. Herne's done all the dyin' he's gonna do."

"What is it?"

Sophie glanced up at Ryan.

"Things just got weird."

\*\*\*

"Wait."

Sophie slapped the back of her hand on Ryan's chest, and he paused. She'd led him back across Hunger Hollow Brook and through the trees, but she had shunned the trail. Ryan followed her outstretched finger to the spot where the trail entered the wood.

Tom's Red Sox cap flashed blue and red in the undergrowth as he tromped out of the trailhead. Ryan's eyes narrowed as he spotted the fly rod in Tom's left hand, then they widened at the shotgun he carried in his right.

*What the—*

Sophie grabbed his arm and tugged. He turned, his mind racing. The brown hand gripped his bicep like a vise.

"You can't go out there," she said.

"What am I supposed to do, stay in the woods all day?"

He winced as she dug her fingers into his arm.

"Who do you think that shotgun was for? Why do you think he went to the falls?"

Ryan looked into the hazel eyes and sighed. For a moment, in the wood, he had thought maybe Rebecca had exaggerated. But no. The paranoid look in her eyes, the crazy talk of Herne—

*Except you saw it, too.*

"Don't you go out there, Ryan Stockbridge. I'm tellin' you, Tom wouldn't need a gun this time of year for 'else."

Ryan pulled her hand off his arm.

"Why would Tom be after me?"

Sophie looked past Ryan and blew a deep breath. "He's gone. Out into the field. I hear the tractor startin'. Must be why Becca changed the combination, why she took Olivia's books out of her room and put 'em in the safe. They don't want you to know."

Ryan looked back toward the barn. The sputtering of the tractor had faded over the top of a knoll.

"Know what?"

"'Bout Herne, of course."

\*\*\*

Ryan chirped the lock on his Audi and popped the trunk. As he pulled out the tire iron, his ears strained to hear the puttering of the tractor. Satisfied that Tom was still busy, he grabbed Sophie's hand and dragged her into the house.

The safe was probably decent enough for Greenfield, but Ryan figured it'd been ordered out of an office supply catalog. He made quick work of the hinges and the steel door thudded on the floor. Sophie reached in and grabbed a leather bound journal.

"Your grandmother's. Before that Stockbridge fella took her away to Hartford."

As she handed Ryan the journal, a sepia-toned photo fell out of the yellowed pages, landing facedown. Ryan swiped the photo off the floor and flipped it over.

"This can't be real."

\*\*\*

He stared at the large brown eyes of the shirtless boy gazing at him out of the photograph. He was drawn to the twin prongs jutting up from the thick patch of black hair on the boy's head, just above his temples. The photograph had been taken from the waist up. Ryan was beginning to think he knew why. The back porch of the old Victorian filled the background, and there was the giant maple, only a sapling.

Sophie tapped the portrait. "Bernard. Your gramma Catherine's father and my great-great-grandfather. Herne's son."

Ryan squinted at the faded handwriting on the back of the photo.

"Bernard. Bernard Montfort."

He looked down at the old desk. His finger traced the BM inside the heart. Sophie's finger was on the ES.

"Emilia Stoddard. Catherine's mother."

Ryan looked up with understanding in his eyes. "Stoddard? Like Tom Stoddard?"

Sophie nodded, and Ryan's gaze drifted to the window looking out on the barn.

"Oh, shit."

Sophie grabbed his hand. "Wait till you see what I got upstairs."

He followed Sophie to her bedroom at the opposite end of the hall from his. He raised an eyebrow at the wooden barrels in the corner, connected to each other by plastic tubing. A crate of empty green wine bottles sat nearby. The fireplace was dominated by an oversize replica of Bouguereau's *Nymphs and a Satyr*, the unwilling beast being dragged toward a woodland stream by a tangle of naked limbs.

Sophie grabbed the half-empty wine bottle on her bureau, popped the cork, and took a long swig. She smiled knowingly at Ryan and handed him the bottle.

"Ain't no harm, not for us anyways."

He lifted the bottle to his lips.

Sophie knelt down by her bed, pulled a wooden trunk out; she opened the lid and grinned. "Wanna meet him?"

"Herne's in the trunk?"

She reached in and raised her arms reverently, like a priest raising a chalice of wine. Ryan set the bottle back on the bureau and took a step forward, mesmerized. Kneeling, he stared into the deep eyeless sockets, gazed at the row of yellowed teeth in the upper jaw, and gasped in disbelief at the curved horns protruding from the top of the skull.

"Old Samuel Montfort kept it after he shot Herne for messin' with his daughter. If it weren't for Emma meetin' Herne in Westminster Wood, you and I wouldn't be here."

Ryan reached out to touch the skull, paused, and drew his hand back. "So how many were there?"

"Well, there was Bernard—you saw him—then the male Montforts, and finally Gerard, my daddy. None of 'em lived long."

Sophie turned the skull around and gazed lovingly into the eye sockets.

"He's been watchin' over his children. He saved you from Tom today, brought you to me. He knows we're the last."

Ryan's face darkened at the mention of Tom's name. "Good God, he really was after me, in the wood?"

Sophie nodded, running a finger over the horned skull. "The Reverend Stoddard was furious when his daughter Emilia ran off with Bernard. I guess Tom must be carryin' some kinda family grudge."

Ryan stood up, went to the window, and threw it open. "I don't hear the tractor anymore." He turned away from the window and grabbed Sophie's arm.

"Rebecca hid all this from me on purpose, and I'm guessing she sabotaged your mother's computer, as well. She's working with Tom. We've got to get the hell out of here."

Herne's skull clattered to the floor as Ryan dragged Sophie toward the door. He grabbed the handle to throw it open and had time for one surprised gasp before the butt of the shotgun crashed down on his head, sending the room into blackness.

Sophie's screams pulled Ryan back from oblivion. Rough cords of rope bit into his wrists and ankles. The room sat at an odd angle. Ryan realized he was hanging off the bed, head down.

Tom threw him a wink as he dragged Sophie toward the door by her bound wrists. Blood ran down Ryan's forehead, pooling in his eyes. He blacked out.

It was there when he blinked the crusted blood out of his eyes. The horned shadow in the corner grew, looming closer. He fought the searing pain in his skull, fought to keep from slipping back into blackness. His voice croaked.

"Help me get to Sophie."

The door banged open. Ryan squirmed in the ropes. He grunted in surprise when, instead of Tom and his shotgun, Rebecca Kimball sat down next to him on the bed. Her fingers tugged at the knots around his wrists.

"He wasn't supposed to hurt Sophie. She'd be harmless with you out of the picture. No way to make any others."

The frayed rope ends finally budged, and Rebecca worked faster as she pulled out the knots. Ryan's wrists broke free. He struggled against the spinning room as he sat up, working on the knots at his ankles. Rebecca paced in front of the fireplace while he freed himself.

"I promised Olivia I would take care of Sophie. Don't let Tom hurt her."

Ryan staggered to his feet. He glared at Rebecca. "Where?"

She nodded out the window. "The barn."

***

Ryan stumbled out the front door and lurched across the clover-filled lawn toward the round barn. He wiped his forehead and grimaced at the bright red smear on the back of his hand. His bloodstained fingers wrapped around the iron handle and he threw the barn door open.

There, under the flickering blue fluorescent lights, knelt Sophie. Her brown arms were wrenched up into the small of her back and tied with frayed rope. Another section of rope held her slender neck down on the chunk of tree stump which Tom used to split wood.

Her eyes widened as Ryan stepped into the barn. Her lips moved but the screeching of the grinding wheel drowned out whatever she was trying to say. She winced as sparks landed on her cheek from the axe blade Tom held to the spinning stone. Tom looked up at Ryan. And grinned.

Ryan moved to step forward, when he noticed something out of the corner of his eye. He caught his breath as the horned shadow stepped from the darkness behind a woodpile.

He glanced back at Tom, who was rolling up the sleeves on his work shirt. The gleaming axe blade resting on the floor, the handle against Sophie's shoulder. Her lips were parted in a soundless scream, overridden by the tortured grinding of the motor.

Ryan took another step. Tom's raised finger shook as he grasped the axe with his other hand, swung it onto his shoulder. The horned shadow behind the woodpile beckoned him.

*What the hell do I do?*

The shadow drew back farther. A polished wooden handle gleamed in the cool blue light where the thing had stood. Ryan's brows knitted as he recognized the antique pitchfork. His hand shot out. He seized the long handle and lifted it out of its nook.

Tom's laughter rose above the screeching motor. Ryan turned and pointed the tines. They both knew he could never cross the barn before the axe fell on Sophie's neck.

Ryan watched helplessly as Tom's callused hands swung the axe into the air, slowing as it reached the top of its arc. He shifted his grip on the pitchfork, found his center of gravity; his arm drew back as he took two great strides forward.

Step, step, throw.

Ryan followed through just like he always had on the javelin field. The axe slipped out of Tom's fingers, fell soundlessly to the floor by the grinding wheel. Ryan started forward, but there was no need. Tom had his fingers wrapped around the tines protruding from his chest. Then he collapsed, the pitchfork handle bobbing up and down on the grinding wheel.

***

They emerged from the barn in time to see Rebecca's Volvo fling sand and gravel into the air as it sped down the driveway, veering onto the dirt road leading to Greenfield. Ryan grasped the brown arm that clutched his waist. He pulled Sophie closer—watching the shadow move among the trees at the edge of the wood.

# In Vino Veritas

## Robert Harkess

"See the blonde? The short, dumpy one?"

Marco jerked his head up and down.

"For the Master's sake take her somewhere and fuck her. We're already behind on quota for the week."

Marco nodded again. "Yes, Leo. Of course."

He started toward the girl and winced when he heard Leonides snort in disgust. Marco dragged his face into something he hoped looked sultry and tempting, and did what he could to inject confidence into his gait. It wasn't easy. Leonides was a full head taller than he was. Damn it, they all were, with broad shoulders and muscles rippling across stomachs and down hairy thighs.

Another snort, and Marco stopped again. His hands started to shake as he tried to determine what he had done wrong now. He looked at his hands—his empty hands—and resisted the temptation to slap his forehead. He changed course slightly so that his path took him to a table from which he collected a pitcher of wine and two goblets, his fingers still quivering.

He closed in on the girl and she looked up at him, her expression one of gentle confusion. The male she had entered the club with snored gently beside her. Marco flicked a glance at him and looked away. The last thing he wanted to do was draw her attention to her companion. He smiled, lopsided, and waggled the goblets.

"Can I tempt you?"

The woman giggled, looked coyly aside for a moment, then nodded. "My name is Haylee."

"Nice to meet you, Haylee," he replied, forcing his grin wider and hoping he would be able to remember the name long enough. "I'm Marco."

He handed her a goblet and poured from the pitcher. It was just wine. All of the guests had already been slipped their faerie-enhanced roofies, and the pitcher held nothing more than a cheap Californian red. Marco sloshed wine into his own goblet and put the pitcher on the floor.

He looked into the cup. It might be rubbish, but it was still wine. Just holding the goblet was making his heart beat faster. He raised it to his nose, inhaling deeply. His head swam and his tongue clove to the roof of his mouth with a sudden desperate thirst. He lifted the wine, trying for a sip. As soon as it touched his lips he upended the goblet and drained it, wine spilling from the sides and dribbling down his face like blood. His ego engorged as fast as his penis. Dropping the goblet he carried on drinking from the pitcher. Marco held his hand out to Haylee. Her whole attention was raptly focused on his groin. He had to give her a nudge to snap her out of it.

"Let's go somewhere away from this crowd," he suggested, and she took his hand.

\*\*\*

A little over an hour later Marco stumbled into a storage room next to the kitchen. He closed the door quietly, leaned against it, and slid down until he was sitting on the floor. He hung his head, only to be confronted by a view of his partially flaccid penis. He squeezed his eyes shut and concentrated on not throwing up.

He had left Haylee, wearing nothing but a contented smile, sprawled on a couch in a secluded corner. As soon as their sexual energy discharged into the collector, the effects of the wine evaporated and left him drained. He felt unclean and used. He covered his face with his hands. Before his heart rate or his breathing had returned to normal, the door shoved him mightily in the back and there was an angry hammering.

"Marco? *Marco?* I know you're in there. Get back out on the floor. Pull another pathetic stunt like this tonight and I'll pull your fucking head off and grind you for hamburger."

The door slammed into his back again, lower this time as if it had been kicked. Marco waited long enough to make sure Leonides had gone before he stood. It was different for the others. As soon as they had finished with one customer, they reached for another pitcher and moved on to the next. Some even took the famous rhomboid purple helpers. Not that they needed them. Not for stamina, anyway. But there was the rumor that the drug made them bigger than any faerie magic could, and it was cheaper. There was a lot of bravado bullshit about getting off on the look of delight and fear in the eyes of the women. Marco had tried one once. All he had got out of the experience was a bright red face and blocked sinuses. And another reason for the other satyrs to mock him. He had avoided the pills since.

He looked both ways along the corridor. Nobody was in sight, although he could hear clattering in the kitchen and ribald revelry in the "grotto." He closed the door and hurried off, hoping nobody would see him. Then he realized he was wasting his time. Leo would tell the others anyway.

He pushed through the double doors on the Mundane side and stepped down the short corridor. The disgusting creeping sensation of passing through the portal to the Unreal slithered across his body. At the other end he pushed the vine curtain aside and stepped into the grotto.

As he made his way back to the middle he passed Haylee. She was still asleep, and would be until the night ended. They had taken everything they could from her, for tonight. He turned to walk away, then leaned over and pulled a fake fur comforter across her. She was still naked, and he thought she looked cold. Or that's what he told himself.

By the time Leonides called the night to a close, Marco had screwed two more women. The others had each doubled that. Every night the club attracted almost two hundred couples, drawn by the rumors that exactly what was going on was going on. Nobody went away able to prove anything, but then nobody went away feeling anything but happy—even if they weren't sure what they were so happy about. The Faerie saw to that, as they saw to the comatose males. Even there, exceptions were not uncommon.

After the clientele—or "donors"—had left and Leo had locked up the Mundane entrances, the grotto dropped fully back into the Unreal and a shudder of relaxation rippled around the whole group. Some made sounds of disappointment, but to Marco it was a relief and a release. For a moment, at least. Leonides called them all to the heart of the grotto. It was time to see how much energy they had collected for the night. They gathered around the oak at the centre of the clearing, and Leo opened the moss-covered panel in the trunk, almost reverentially.

The hopeful anticipation popped like a bubble and was replaced with a group groan. Behind the panel, the collector crystal showed only a little over three quarters full. They had missed quota again.

Almost *en masse*, hostile eyes turned to find Marco and glare at him.

He wanted to protest, to shout out that even if he had doubled his efforts, they still would have been short. But he kept his peace. If he spoke out, offered excuses, it would only make things worse, and it might be the final straw that drove them to violence. He could feel it flowing just below the surface, looking for an excuse to flood outward.

Leo lifted the crystal out of its holder and shut the panel. That was the signal to disperse. Satyrs drifted from the grotto in small groups, muttering to each other and casting glances about, as if looking for Marco. But he was nowhere to be seen. He was not hiding—exactly—but he had found a seat on a couch that happened to be out of the way.

Leo found him. As if on a route he would have taken anyway, he casually passed Marco, just close enough to glare at him before walking off, slowly shaking his head.

"Tough night, huh?"

Marco flinched before he realized the voice belonged to Alphrein, their provider of all things faery, who was looking at him over the back of the couch. Marco wondered what the faery was standing on in order to do that.

Alphrein climbed over and sat at the opposite end of the couch. His legs pointed straight out, and the couch looked like more of a bed for him. Marco nodded, then turned his face away and covered it with his hands as he propped everything up on his knees.

"What's the problem?" Alphrein asked. "Dey giving you da goils when youse want da guys?"

He laughed at his own humor and his terrible faux-Brooklyn accent. Marco wished he would go away, but when he sneaked a look out the corner of his eye, the faery was still there. He sighed and straightened up.

"There's no problem. Honest. Just a bad night."

"One bad night is not what I hear."

"I can handle it."

"Sure. That's why you're so happy to walk out with the rest of your clan instead of hiding here until they've all gone."

Marco couldn't find anything to say, and he was starting to feel uncomfortable under the diminutive faery's gaze. "Everything's fine," he repeated.

Alphrein shrugged and jumped down from the couch. When he stood in front of Marco, they were eye to eye.

"Okay," the faery said. "But when you decide to admit there's an issue, come see me. I may be able to help." He walked off, disappearing into the undergrowth outside the grotto.

Marco also rose from the couch. He started to walk toward his own nest, and wondered if the faery might have the right of it, after all. He stopped in his tracks, shook his head sharply and barked a cynical laugh. Who was he kidding? The faerie never offered help without a price, and often offered help where there was nothing that needed fixing.

He carried on to his nest, musing over how close the faery had come to tricking him.

*** 

A week later, Marco lagged behind after everybody else had left. Only this time he sat on a stool in the middle of the grotto, hoping Alphrein would wander by.

"You look awful," the faery said, sneaking up behind him, making him flinch again. But it was less of a flinch and more of a panicked jump, really. Marco closed his eyes and took a deep breath when he realized who it was.

"I wish you wouldn't do that," he muttered.

"I know," said Alphrein, grinning widely. "But why the long face? I hear you guys made target five days out of seven, and I even overheard the lovely Leonides saying you were actually pulling your weight for a change."

Marco put his head in his hands and groaned. Somehow that made it worse. "I have been trying."

"And that's not good?"

"No." He drew the word out, whining. "It just makes me feel terrible, and the harder I try, the more I do it, the worse it gets."

"Seriously? But I thought that's what satyrs were all about; par-tay animals of the multiverse."

"Well maybe I'm just different," Marco snapped.

Alphrein raised his hands defensively. "Nothing wrong with that."

"Try convincing Leo."

"So what is it that's screwing you up so bad? I was under the impression that once you guys hit the vino, everything kind of took care of itself."

"It does. But afterward, it's horrible. Such emptiness. The others just pick up another pitcher and start again, but it makes me sick. I just wish I didn't have to drink the wine in the first place, then none of the rest would happen."

"So why don't you stop?"

"I can't. I try but eventually the wine wins. I have to go out there and take a drink, and then . . . well. And Leonides is constantly on my bad, so even if I could stay off the wine, he would kick my ass for not working."

"Good point. But can't you tell him you don't want to do it anymore?"

Marco was shaking his head before the faery had finished speaking. "Not that simple. Leo made a commitment to the Master to collect . . . It's a commitment we have to honor as a clan."

"So ask for a different job."

"Doing what? This is who we are. I either contribute, or I'm a liability. The clan can only have so many members. The only way to replace me is when I die. Then they can create a replacement."

"Unenlightened."

Marco nodded and put his face back in his hands to wallow in the gloom.

"There may be a way out of this," Alphrein said, slowly. Marco raised his head. "There's only one slight problem."

"What?"

"You need to go out into the Mundane."

There was a long silence.

"It's the only way," said Alphrein. "There's a place I know of. They have people there. People who can help with situations like this."

"Satyrs?"

"No, idiot," snapped the faery, a flash of fire flickering behind his eyes. "People who have a problem with wine."

"Really?"

The faery nodded. "Think on it first. You'd be taking a big step. Finding a way to get off the wine isn't exactly in the best interest of your clan."

"So what do I have to do? And how can I go out into the Mundane? I can't be seen. You know that's not allowed."

"I can help with that," said Alphrein.

Marco's heart sank. Here came the sting. The price. "How much?"

The faery tried to look wounded, but didn't quite succeed. "A trifle, nothing more. I can provide you with a glamour to disguise your more . . . obvious non-human features."

"How much?"

"For now, nothing. I'm just looking to do a friend a favor."

"How. Much."

"When you die, I inherit your estate."

"What?"

"The Faerie are long lived. We can take the time to speculate when we accumulate. By the time you die you could be a pauper, or you could be fabulously rich. I'm betting on the latter."

Marco said nothing, but thought furiously. Anything from the Faerie that seemed fair by definition wasn't, but he couldn't see the catch in this—and that worried him.

"You don't have to tell me now," said Alphrein. "You need to go away and think this through anyway, so . . ."

"No, I want to do it," Marco blurted, almost surprising himself. "I want to go see this person. Maybe they can help, or at least give me an option not to go on like this . . ."

"I understand," said Alphrein, a cooing sympathy in his voice. "So if you could just make your mark here . . ."

From out of nowhere a short parchment appeared, fluttering gently to land in Marco's lap, while Alphrein proffered him an ink-ready quill that had not been there a moment ago.

Marco took the quill and scanned down the document. It seemed to say exactly what they had discussed: a glamour to allow him to walk freely in the Mundane in exchange for all rights to his estate upon his death. He made his mark and both parchment and quill faded away.

"When should I go?" Marco asked.

"Tomorrow," the faery replied.

"So soon?"

"The next opportunity would be eight days hence. Can you wait that long?"

"No," Marco said, without having to think about his answer. "What do I do?"

"The glamour will invoke as soon as you leave the grotto. Leave by the normal exit to the Mundane. Take a left out the door and keep walking until you see a building with the sign *Midtown Community Centre.* Go inside, then up to the second floor. Look for the number 208, and go in. Others will be there. Say nothing except to the one who introduces himself as 'Tom.' Tell him you have come for help."

"Is that everything?"

"You must be in the room before eight. I'll tell you when to leave. Do not tarry in the Mundane."

Marco made him run over it again, just to be sure he had everything, then Alphrein wandered off into the forest.

\*\*\*

Marco trembled as he stepped out onto the street. He had never visited the Mundane before. Noise hammered uncomfortably at his ears, and he was jostled by the press of people before he had taken two steps from the door. Yet for all the mass of humanity, he had never experienced a place so dead. Nothing connected to anything else, except for brief angry flashes that made him even more nervous. Everybody on the pavement seemed to be pushing at each other, and in the opposite direction that he needed to travel. He kept close to the wall as he tried to swim upstream.

Cold, hard stone surrounded him, breaking his contact with the earth—the very thing that kept him grounded in the world. Stray emotions floated in the air around him, battered him when they drifted too close. The farther he got from the door, the greater the desire grew to turn tail and run back to the grotto, to drown himself in wine, no matter what the cost.

He stopped, breathed deeply, until he clawed back a small measure of control and stepped forward again.

Finally he stood beneath a sign reading *Midtown Community Centre.* His heart hammered in his chest and he felt profoundly alone. Even the scorn of his clan-mates was beginning to seem preferable to this.

He prevaricated in front of the double glass doors, jiggling gently from hoof to hoof and making a staccato tapping on the sidewalk. As he turned away to run back to the grotto, a hand touched his shoulder. He flinched and turned to see a human standing uncomfortably close, hands raised in a non-threatening gesture.

"Don't give up now, man. You've made it this far."

Marco cocked his head slightly to one side. "How would you know why I'm here?"

The human offered a wry smile. "You have the look." He nodded, then walked toward the glass doors, which hissed aside and allowed him through.

Marco stepped away in surprise, but not far enough to put him back in the river of humans on the sidewalk. Doors that slid sideways were a novelty to him. He almost turned away, but the human had a point: he had come this far.

Was there any harm in finding out what this Tom person had to say?

He walked hesitantly forward, flinching again when the doors slid apart before him, and on into the lobby.

It took him a few minutes to find the stairs, and he tried not to clatter too much as he trotted up them. Glamour or no, his hooves were still there and still made a sharp racket on the hard tiles.

Once he reached the second floor, finding the door with 208 on it was relatively simple, and he paused outside for only a moment before pushing it open and walking in. As he passed the threshold, a tingle of fear ran up his spine.

The room was ten paces along each side. Flat walls battered the sound of people talking from side to side. Four windows were shuttered against the night by some slatted material. Most of the furniture was pushed out to the sides, apart from a circle of twenty chairs.

A group of people huddled outside the circle, and Marco saw a face he recognized—the human who had spoken to him outside. Marco started to panic as the man walked over, smiling broadly.

"Glad you made it. I'm Tom. That was your first step, and almost the hardest. We have another new recruit today. I've already spoken to her, so we'll let her start. You just wait till I call on you, then you say the same as she says, okay?"

Marco nodded and made no protest when Tom pushed him gently toward one of the chairs. The rest of the group took that as a cue and soon all were seated. Marco looked around at them. Each pair of eyes offered him a level of acknowledgement; sometimes an encouraging smile, sometimes a sharp nod and a haunted stare.

Tom sat next to him and, next to Tom, an overweight woman who looked as though she had been weeping. Tom raised a hand and silence slowly fell, replaced by an expectant hush and rapt attention aimed toward their side of the circle. The woman stood, spoke, and Marco's throat dried up. Was he expected to do this?

There was ecstatic applause and catcalls as the woman sat down. She looked flushed, but happy. Marco realized Tom was looking expectantly at him. He swallowed hard. Tom nodded an encouragement and Marco made it to his feet. He looked around the circle of faces, all waiting on him, anticipation in every one. He drew a deep breath.

"My name is Marco, and I am an alcoholic."

Nobody moved. He had said the same as the woman, he was sure. Had he done something wrong? Then he realized that nobody had blinked since he had spoken, and his stomach began to churn.

Tom stood up and walked to the middle of the circle. He was chuckling, then he coughed and harrumphed and pulled himself together as he put his fingers between his lips and made a piercing whistle. He started to laugh again, his form slowly rippling like heat haze on a summer road, shrinking and solidifying into something very different, and Marco heard a noise from the corridor.

Alphrein started laughing again. "Don't look so surprised, Marco," he said.

"But . . . ?"

"But what?"

There was another sound, like distant thunder, coming from the corridor. Marco almost recognized it—enough to shift from upset stomach to bowels of water.

"You said these people would help."

"Did I? I said they can help with situations where people have a problem with wine. I didn't say they were going to help *you*."

Marco realized the tingle he had felt when he had entered was not fear, but his passage through a faery portal. The room was in the Unreal, or at least connected to it. He had been set up.

"Leonides loved the idea when I suggested it to him," Alphrein said, still hiccupping giggles. "He paid me even more than I'll inherit from you."

Marco suddenly recognized the sound outside the door as thundering hooves. A second later the door burst open, and the clan he had just betrayed rushed in.

# Fair Weather from that Crimson Land

## S. J. Hirons

My troubles began on paper, as they always seem to do.

The satyr I had been dealing with emerged from the back office once more. He wore that blank automaton look I have come to know and loathe every time I see it on the faces of the clerking classes as I travel. Among all the peoples and creatures of our many, mighty, miscellaneous, and mixed-up nations, that look is the one trait shared by all alike, from faun to faerie, from minotaur to man. It is the look that signifies one has passed all reasonable point of appeal. It is the look that tells you that you are about to embark upon a tour of those machines of bureaucracy any creature sane enough not to work for government agencies abhors.

He trotted back to the desk, his half-moon spectacles—hanging from his neck on a dainty chain—sitting at the very tip of his nose, pretending to put great consideration once more into the documents I had handed to him over an hour ago, pretending he wanted to find in those pages of invitation, recommendation, transit, and port-passage the detail that would enable him to enable us.

With a leathery hand he hiked his woolen kilt up a little higher to his hips and stood, cocking his horned head as though the ink on the paper before him was restless, as if it had wriggled somehow into meaningless scrawls. Behind me I felt the continuing presence of the armed guard who had ushered me forward out of the pens that filtered new arrivals through from the dock.

The clerk stopped before me and did not sit down, seemingly so absorbed in his task he had lost sense of his surroundings. He continued his perusal of our papers, as if intent on finding some clue or key upon them that would allow him to release my wife and me from this predicament. I know a man with his mind made up, however, and believe I am experienced enough in the ways of other kinds to know that look in other species, too. I knew the communication with his superiors, from which he was returning, could not possibly have brought me good news; or else why make this show of studying our documents again?

I looked back to those others, waiting in the pens; the erl-lords, and their pet dryads, with whom we had shared passage on the higher decks; the aelfes, far from the collectives their restless ancestors had confederated long ago, who had berthed in the middle decks; and the timid hobgoblin families from steerage who waited now with their heads kept low—who had learnt not to look too hopefully at anything at all in the world lest it be snatched away from them by means as varied as treaty and force; and at my wife.

Concern had begun to bloom in her eyes.

Last night I had seen for the first time how our expected child had started to change her breasts, making them bud upward into pleasantly larger handfuls than ever before. I had put dry lips to her little swell of belly and kissed it, whispered nonsense as unformed as the child inside, and she had laughed happily. The tang of her last kiss was still on my lips, despite the cup of ground neptune-seed tea this official had offered me whilst I waited for him to complete the conversation he felt he needed to have with his superiors in his office, over the wires.

I looked up at him, my chair creaking as I so realigned my perspective on the world, and this brought his attention back to me as a reality, a thing to be dealt with.

His eyes were utterly emotionless: "Master Sennufer," he said, "I'm afraid we are going to be detaining you and your wife a little longer. Please come with me."

\*\*\*

Twelve years ago I took part in my one and only protest against the practices of the Satyric Empire.

That was the year the satyrs forcibly occupied the Star-Gazer's Ziggurat on the southern border of the centaur's kingdom, Egepy.

The satyrs still claim to this day that that act was a sacred reclamation, even though their kind have never practiced Celestialism as profoundly as centaurs do; and they continue to deny that wresting the tower from the control of the centaurs was meant as any kind of symbolic gesture at all—even though all of the holy rites of centaurs revolve, in some way, around the Ziggurat and its environs.

The enmity of the satyrs and the centaurs is ages old. No scholar I've ever read has been able to pinpoint exactly how and why this conflict started, nor postulate a formula that might bring it to an end. It's a tribal thing, I suppose, as ingrained in both races as any view we observers from outside cultures might have in response to it. As with any conflict of this kind the rivalry has certain predictable characteristics: the Empire of the Satyrs and northern Egepy share a border that has always been disputed territory; the two races spring up from the same ancestral stock. In many ways the two cultures have mutual philosophies. It is, in short, the battle of one brother against another—as most longstanding disagreements always are.

A great many historians from other nations concur that the centaurs are the elder race, however, their philosophical order and their Celestialist faith pre-dating the rise of the satyrs of Swerna, a nation that so often emulates the nature of its longstanding rival. This is also what some commentators believe fuels the competitive temperament of the satyrs, and has been the principal driver of their economic and military expansions. It is, of course, virtually impossible to travel now to any land that doesn't feature some sign of Swerna's presence, be it in the trading enclaves they've established in the faerie domains, the mines and mills on the lands of the hobgoblins, or even in the human homelands my wife and I have traveled from. There the cafés and stadiums, the oil parlors and the shipping trade, are all now funded by agents of the so-called Crimson Land of the satyrs. This is one of the reasons centaurs have become more and more insular over the last decade or so and are rarely seen outside of Egepy anymore, preferring to avoid their enemy as much as possible. That retraction from the world, though, began when the Ziggurat fell to their enemy.

That same summer I'd finally finished my training as an actor and my wife Adyl, who was at the protest, too (though not with me), had had her first little pamphlet of poetry published.

Most of us students barely knew what we were about that day. As we marched down Karamir Hill and out of the campus we joined in with the throngs of more organized marchers that poured out of every street, heading toward Parliament Square and then past that, toward the Satyric Embassy on the canal side. Thinking back, it was one of the last protests of the age, a kind of bacchanal of youth and outrage coming together for one final carefree affair before the inevitable eyes of government turned our way and, by noticing us, finally found reason to outlaw such acts. But, that day, we were united in our cause, and we all lifted our voices on behalf of the centaurs even though they, wisely, were not easily found among our swelling number.

"When will there finally be," we'd sung, "fair weather from the Crimson Land?"

*Never*, came back the answer to that old centauric lay: the business of our nation with Swerna was too important for such a question to be asked again and our leaders passed laws to ensure it was not repeated.

We didn't then know that that would be the future, though. Against propriety we'd all linked arms or hands to stomp our way around the Satyric Embassy in Lymander in a kind of relentless and dizzying gyre of self-righteousness. The huge red flags of their nation listlessly draped above our heads from the turrets and towers we paraded beneath. Raisin-eyed satyrs had watched us impassively from the balconies of the buildings, their armed guards at the gatehouses seemingly unmoved by our perambulations, even when some of the more radicalized element ordered we stop and stand before the main gate to chant:

"Two Hoofs bad! Two Hoofs bad!"

I remembered my father saying that very phrase, years before, and my mother chastising him for it. He'd only been joking, but I'd been on her side of that one: it was all very well to criticize the imperialism of the satyrs, but doing it like that robbed such protest of any validity in my view and I didn't join in when my peers took it up at the protest, my enthusiasm suddenly blunted by such blundering hatred.

Seeing that this ranting wasn't pricking our enemy enough to draw blood, some of the crowd grew bolder and more boorish as the sun began to set:

"Go back to your fucking land of milk and honey, y'bastards, and leave Egepy for the centaurs!"

I may have been callow, but I was smart enough to know where this sort of taunting could lead. I gradually began to work my way to the back of the now-milling horde and up the steps of Ceramitas Bridge. From there I could see over the whole scene. In the twilight the banners below looked like the sails of a sad armada of old. Below me some of the narrow boats on the canal sped up as their pilots saw what the protestors, and myself, could not: in the rear courtyards of the Satyric Embassy the relief guards were now gearing up.

The evening was sweltering and I was regretting wearing my corduroy blazer, with all of its trendy and witty student badges, even over just the thin red T-shirt I had on beneath. I took it off and folded it over my arm, forgetting my student papers were in the inner pocket (I was fond of that jacket and wore it often).

I looked south, across the bridge, and saw four centaurs watching the protest. They stood still, with arms crossed, and seemed not to need to talk to each other to express what they were thinking or feeling: as if in abeyance of some unseen sign, they turned and cantered off toward the far parklands of the southern suburbs of the capital as I turned back to watch the protest and a cheer went up as the front gates of the embassy opened. Then that very cheer warped into a wail of more primitive outrage than any which had gone before as the billy clubs whipped up and down and phalanxes of coolly determined satyrs waded forward.

Now some of the braver pilots on the canal drew their boats closer to the wharf, letting the fleeing and terrified protestors who dashed and leapt forward toward the water board their meager decks. Some didn't make it. Those that didn't either swam to the next nearest boat, floundered in the water, or struggled back toward the cement bank and clambered back into the horrific scene above. Many broke for the alleys and side streets. I could hear car and shop alarms going off in the directions they stumbled down.

As for me, I was torn. Part of me wanted to turn on my heel and run for it like those others: I was sure the satyrs would make it to the bridge where I stood sooner or later, so keen did they seem to dispense their wisdom among my peers. On the other hand, I have to admit that some part of me wanted to run pell-mell back down the steps and join in with that diminishing band of most-determined protestors who had joined fray against the guards.

Even now I don't know why I felt that way.

I took a midway course: looking down the steps of the bridge I could see a young woman perilously close to the violence who seemed utterly frozen, in either fear or some witness's rapture, before the oncoming onslaught, and I dashed down those great steps to grab her and pull her back and out of the way. Her eyes turned on me, fierce and dark, her pupils just as dilated as any satyr's. She had ash-blond hair, loose and long in the aelfish style of the time, wore a knitted shawl of green wool over a white T-shirt. There were a multitude of silver bangles on the arm I'd grabbed.

"We have to go!" I yelled at her. "Move!"

I turned and collided almost immediately with a screaming hobgoblin lad who was wet through from the canal. With my free hand I shoved him aside and with my other I pulled. I had her hand firmly in mine and a slim and bony thing it felt as I dragged it along behind me. Through the thrum of this contact I could feel her heart and her running steps behind me as we pelted across the bridge toward the relative safety of Tambrell Park. Sirens split the city air, but we made it into the gloom of the trees before we saw any of the police vans that were now rushing toward the embassy. Their flashing lights briefly illuminated the branches around us and the iron fence some twenty feet away.

I bent down, my hands on my knees, taking great and deep breaths. Somewhere along the way I'd let go of my jacket.

That was how I met my wife.

***

The clerk and three guards led Adyl and me out of the Customs House and through a dusty yard at the back of that smaller, wooden building toward the more formidable red-stone fortress where the real business of policing their borders now obviously occurred. As we'd approached the port along the river this particular edifice had been strikingly visible for some miles, the tree line on either side cleared to serve such an end. I hadn't been daunted by it, however, as, more alarmingly, there had been a column of smoke rising from the citadel behind. I felt the uneasy sensation of realizing we had probably now ceased to exist in the minds of those we'd been on the boat with.

The clerk satyr I had been dealing with led the way with the three armed guards trailing either side of us, one of them bringing our luggage along. We were taken down some steps and into a cellar-cum-office. The customs officer handed our papers over to the guard there and left. Then we were taken yet farther down into the building, to the cells.

There's no other way to describe them, really.

It was pretty evident that this place was mostly meant for containing centaurs, what with all the straw. Our cell had what looked like two benches, set against but one wall. On closer inspection we saw that these were some form of pillory, meant for four-legged creatures. Through the iron bars on the opposite side we could see, in the gloom, a shape on the straw in there.

The door clanked behind us and Adyl and I both started, whirling around. The guard was working the lock.

"Are we under arrest?" I asked him. He didn't answer. When he looked up his mouth was tight set, and his eyes had an obdurate cast to them. I've often thought the faces of satyrs are like the masks we sometimes wear when we're acting the ancient sagas, those masks meant to show but one emotion at a time.

"My wife is pregnant," I blurted. "This isn't appropriate."

The guard gave a snort, but it was hard to tell if it was contempt or just some natural impulse. He ran a claw-like hand through the ringlets of his hair, looking over into the cell next to ours for a moment. He turned back to us and pointed to a bucket in the corner before he left.

I held Adyl tightly and whispered reassurances into her hair for a while before she reluctantly sat down on part of the pillory. I made a pillow for her out of my linen coat and she stretched out on her back as I inspected the bucket. It seemed to be drinking water with a hand-carved ladle-like dipper of smoke-wood dropped inside it. I took a tentative sip and found it was clean to the taste. I doused my handkerchief with it, squeezed it out, and gave it to Adyl. She draped it over her face and let out a desperate laugh.

"So," she said. "What do you think it is, then?"

Before I could answer, to say I didn't know, a deep voice spoke from the other cell:

"A bomb went off in their Temple of Unguents," it said. "At first light it was, during the dawn rites. Many must have died."

Adyl sat up abruptly, snatching the wet handkerchief from her face. She looked at me, alarmed. The shape in the other cell gave a kind of judder as it rose onto its legs and trotted over to our side. I was right. It was indeed a centaur. Before I'd got a good look at him, he had his hand through the bars.

"I am Rakharion," he said.

I took his offered hand and shook it. "Sennufer, of Lymander. My wife," I jerked my head in her direction, "Adyl."

"Ah . . ." The centaur leaned forward. He was bare chested, as centaurs prefer to be, and his human genitalia were covered with a short sarong of yellow silk—as is their wont when they travel abroad. He was palomino in his hind parts—the fine, golden kind—though on his right flank there looked to be a darkening cut or bruise of some sort.

"And why have you come so far along the waterways to Swerna?"

The meager light delineated his face. He looked to be middle-aged, with a waxed blond beard and moustache and tousled hair. Around his neck he wore a necklace of jade that matched his green eyes.

He lifted his arms and wrapped them around the bars—seemingly as an aid to help him stand—and shifted his injured hind out of view.

"I was invited here to teach," I answered, despite the whole context of this conversation striking me as utterly odd, "at the House of Pantomime."

Rakharion made subtle and encouraging noises, urging me to go on but, for a moment, my ability to express all that had led me here slipped away.

*\*\*\**

I've only ever personally known one centaur.

My mother is a Celestialist. My father has always called this her *unfortunate affectation*—usually when the bohemian nature of her belief reaches some climax of tiresomeness for him. Her affectation generally manifested itself in the company she kept because of her faith; an oddball mix of dreamers, rag-tag philosophers, and gypsy hobgoblins purported to be possessed of *second sight* or the ability to *true-read*. My mother particularly lapped up this latter category, always egged on by her best friend, Hebaneph—who actually taught Higher Astronomy and Telescopy at Lymander's prestigious College of Navigators.

"You'd think," my father would grumble, "that a woman in a position like hers would spear these Celestial theories on some cold spike of fact and science."

Asides like that, though, were usually muttered solely to me at some dinner party, or other social event, my mother was hosting. He'd drag me off to the corner as soon as he could so that we would have a removed view of the proceedings as my mother's friends descended into one of their convoluted and arduous treks around the theorems they felt proved their beliefs—or the blunt dissection of those that didn't—all the while nursing a tumbler of Satyric whiskey in one hand and eyeing jet-haired Hebaneph beadily as he restlessly sipped and simmered.

"As if the stars govern and foretell our fates!" he'd disparage, nudging me now and then to prompt me to refill his glass. "Let me tell you, boy, it's the single decisions that make you who you are . . . and that's all I'm saying on *that* matter."

I'd nod. I half agreed with him, but he was my father and I was just a kid of eighteen or so, about to appear in my first play, when these meetings of my mother's reached their apotheosis: a young centaur coming to Lymander to study with Hebaneph had consented to meet with them and discuss the universe. I couldn't have cared less about this. The social activities of my mother and father were becoming less and less my concern as my own calling led me closer and closer to the stage, the Academy, training, and the thought of living a life beyond Lymander.

I was still prey to the vagaries of a mother, mind you: she decreed she would bring this guest to watch me perform in *The Rider & The Wheel* as some kind of cultural exchange.

And that was how I met Yevariel.

*** 

Explaining to Rakharion how Adyl and I have lived and worked in many different nations on account of my career as an actor, it began to dawn on me that it was possible that being well-traveled was the reason we'd been held up. The thought made me relax somewhat: such journeyings as ours are easily explained. It's only reasonable to understand that an actor and a poet have a basic need to spend time in other cultures if they are to explore to the uttermost their arts.

I was even here in Swerna at the behest of one of their own! It hadn't quite occurred to me then that the satyrs could only know about where Adyl and I had been in the past via some clandestine method, as such travels certainly weren't mentioned on any of our papers for this trip.

I'd never much gone in for believing all the half-baked theories out there about some sort of Satyric Secret Service. It was in that cell that such thoughts began to be yeasted in my mind. I recognize that now. I'm not suggesting I'd go so far as to say that, now that they have the Ziggurat, they are using the power of the place to spy on the world—even though the talk I have heard about that since our trip to Swerna is couched in pretty convincing terms—but only that I think it's sensible for any reasoning person to wonder about the stolid and pre-emptive nature of Swerna's political machinations since that occupation.

I voiced my logic to Rakharion after a little while, knowing, from what he'd told me of his own journey to these cells, that he'd been taken from his lodgings that morning on the grounds that he had come out of the north to trade moon oil here in Swerna. The flimsiest of excuses—that the explosion at the temple might have required moon oil to fuel it—was all he'd been offered so far as reason for his current detention. When he'd questioned the captain of the guard about this ridiculous justification, he'd received a whack on his hind for his impertinence. He nodded now as I explained what I believed was the reason we'd been stopped.

"It's possible," he said, "for they can be quite paranoid. When my brethren spoke of this to me before I came here I scoffed. Now I have proof of it." He twisted a little, showing me the gash of suffused red on his hide.

"That looks incredibly painful," Adyl said. "You should complain. No—we should get someone down here to look at it, Sen!"

Rakharion smiled sadly at her. "Centaurs have endured worse," he said, "but I thank you for the thought. Do not trouble yourselves for me . . . although . . ." He looked at our bucket and licked his lips. "Perhaps I could ask you for some water? I have none over here, you see."

"Oh!" I felt a fool. I hadn't noticed. I dragged the bucket over to the bars and lifted the dipper to him. He took it. As he put it to his lips I saw a great resignation in his eyes. I had seen that look before. Yevariel had worn it.

*\*\*\**

I heard my mother and Hebaneph talking about Yevariel long before he arrived: they speculated he was a young prince of the realm and certainly, when he arrived, there was a particular regality of aspect in the way he held himself. But that might be true of any centaur, I guess.

*There are factions over there as bad as anything the Two Hoofs can concoct,* my father had said warningly to me once, and my mother had chastised him for using the term. *You never know,* he'd muttered to me.

The first time I saw Yevariel I was mid-performance. My mother kept her word and brought him and Hebaneph to the College Auditorium to see the play: I was halfway through the monologue in the second act (the one about heroes) when I inadvertently looked at the audience—something I'm loathe to do these days: I hadn't really mastered the art of light-housing then—and saw a dark face, gleaming eyes. He was looking up from where he had wholly reclined on the cushions and carpets my mother had brought along for him to rest on and was pressing his lips to the mouthpiece of a complimentary hookah. He parted those lips and smoke blossomed from his mouth. Still the gaze he had on me penetrated the smoke. I did not falter in performance, but there was a pause I hadn't intended.

Backstage Yevariel was full of effusive praise for the company and me. My mother was still buzzing around my playmates, and Yevariel took me aside and asked if I would meet him later that week: he wondered if I might show him around the city. So far, he murmured with a smile and a meaningful glance at Hebaneph, he had been taken only to the places middle-aged women would go to for pleasure. I was happy to agree.

We met in a small restaurant not far from Karamir Hill on a late, summer afternoon. His lodgings were to be found at the rear of the place, and the restaurant became his regular haunt during his time in Lymander.

Though the day outside was bright I found him in a dim alcove set off from the main part of the restaurant. He looked like he'd been there a while. The low table was covered with soiled plates and ewers still tacky with blackish wine, and his eyes were somewhat red rimmed from the hookah.

He greeted me with a wave of his hand through the smoke, the hobgoblin waiter bringing another carafe to the table as soon as I had nestled down comfortably on the soft cushions opposite Yevariel. A moment later skewers of chicken and lamb and little leaf-wrapped dumplings were run over from the kitchen.

As I ate we spoke of the city and of his impressions of it so far. He would be with us for a year and, over the course of that year, I would observe how he enraptured so many with his charm, his easy manners. I found him admirable, I will admit, but for me it was the sense that he was a thing displaced that I was mildly enamored of, I think: it is a familiar condition for actors to find themselves in. Yevariel seemed boundlessly rich, which is always an attractive thing when one is making new friends; willing to laugh and make mild mischief (for which his apologies would be disarmingly gracious); and he had an unerring, penetrating insight into people.

It was he who recognized I had a teacher's instincts. I think he saw that when—feeling that, at the very least, he was almost as much a guest of my family as he was of Hebaneph's—I told him about the parts of Lymander that only a native (and, especially, only a native *male*) would know: he was of a similar maturity.

Eventually, as the sun wore down the wall in a square of light, we came to the subject of the play he had seen me in. He asked me to iterate the monologue for the second act again:

"When heroes are named it takes all day," I began. "The beach is covered with flowers and reeds, flags and trees, and the gods on the mountaintop clap and weep. By moonlight the nymphs come with milk sweet as spring, and the heroes are led away, one by one. At midnight the ships come. Time winds their sails . . ."

Yevariel gestured for me to stop, tears in his eyes. "This business of heroes," he said, "it is very important in Egepy right now. These words touch me very deeply. I see from how you speak them that they touch you, too. In my beautiful Egepy we say *'mi breja, mi freyn'* when we meet one we believe has the same soul as us. It means 'my brother, my friend,' see?"

He stretched one of his strong arms across the table toward me and I took his proffered hand as though we were about to arm wrestle. "Mi breja, mi freyn," he said, soulfully, and I politely repeated it. Just then four more centaurs arrived outside the restaurant.

"Stewards of my father's house," Yevariel said. "I must speak with them briefly. They are here to arrange more suitable accommodations, but I have become fond of my little hidey-hole here."

He gave a lopsided smile which I returned. I watched through the window as he spoke to them out on the street, his arms going up and down, making cutting gestures through the air, pointing hither and thither. The other centaurs nodded and trotted away, and he returned to the table, easing himself down into the alcove and onto the cushions.

"Are you quite sure you are happy here?" I asked, eyeing the dingy restaurant: I was sure there were better places for him to lodge.

"My people are used to making sacrifices," he said.

\*\*\*

Just as Rakharion returned the dipper to me a group of satyr guards came down the steps, opened his cell, and beckoned him out. Rakharion offered no resistance. Indeed, he went without a murmur.

"He's hurt," Adyl called out to them. "I hope you're taking him to have that wound seen to."

"These are only preliminary questions," one satyr said. "And the water was for you only."

Before we could make any response to that they ushered Rakharion up the broad steps. Did it occur to me then that to have placed the water in the cell for us meant that we were headed here all along? I don't know. I do know that I have since dreamt of a satyr placing that bucket of fresh, cold water there as we stepped aboard the boat that brought us to Swerna days before.

I took a dipper of it over to Adyl when they were gone. Her eyes had hardened and she looked up the dark steps with a palpable fury: but she drank and let me wet her forehead again with a dabbing handkerchief. A sole guard returned.

"Your appellant is here," he said.

"My appellant?" I had no idea what he meant.

"Satyr. One who speaks in your defense."

"Defense? Of what?"

He didn't answer.

"Are we to come with you?" Adyl asked.

The guard shook his head. "Appellant coming now," he said and then he went to linger in the pool of blue gloom by the stairs. After a moment or two, Utag, the Director of the House of Pantomime, appeared at the top of the steps. He came down gingerly, looking fearful that either his hoofs or his toga would betray him on those slick stones. His face was tired, troubled. He and I had not met since he'd visited my workshop in Lymander.

"Master Sennufer!" he called out. As he came to the cell he stretched out his hand to shake mine, but the guard put up his billy club and halted him before we touched.

"I am sorry for all of this, my dears," he said to us, with a sour glance at the guard. "Bureaucratic nonsense is ever an obstacle when one tries to break boundaries."

I shrugged. "I suppose . . . ," I began to say, but Utag went on quite briskly:

"I will need to verify to them that your time in the hobgoblin diaspora, and your year in the aelf collectives, are merely instances of you pursuing your work?"

"Of course!" I spat. "I was *performing* in both places! And it was ten years ago! You know this, Utag!"

He nodded vigorously. "Oh, yes, yes. Indeed, *I* do. I must confirm these things for *them*. That is all."

Before either Adyl or I could voice our contempt for the ludicrous situation we were in, the Pantomime director asked, "And you never met with any political subversives in those places? Never had any conversations about Swerna or Egepy?"

Adyl made a disgusted sound.

"Utag," I said, trying to communicate to him as gently as possible, "This is not appropriate. What business is it of Swerna's whom I speak with?" I shook my head. "No. This won't do."

Utag's face fell. He looked more troubled than ever as he peered over at the guard—who just stared back impassively.

"I will see what I can do, my friends," Utag said. He leant in close and stage-whispered: "You must understand, Swerna's eyes are *everywhere!*" With a waft of his toga in the direction of the guard, he left.

***

They came and told us we were being ejected about twenty minutes later. I protested that I had a contract of work, but to no avail. Utag was nowhere to be seen when we were ushered back up the stairs and our papers were returned to us. We were told a boat was leaving soon and we would be on it. Our luggage reappeared and we were escorted back to the dock.

When we got to the wooden quay, we were led past Rakharion's head. It adorned a pole, facing east. Adyl looked away but I could not. I felt like everything that had happened had been pre-ordained, foretold somehow. I don't know why.

We were given a small cabin in steerage. Once we set off I felt the irresistible need to eject something from myself. I made my way to the shared toilets and there, standing in the stink beside the rusty, snaking pipes, hot piss tumbled out of me, making me shake like I was having some sort of seizure.

When I got back to the cabin Adyl had managed to cram herself on the small cot. She had thrown an arm over her face and would not speak to me. The boat juddered away from the dock and I went back up to the low deck, thinking that even the heavy air over the wide river would be better than the stuffy atmosphere in the cabin.

Up there, I watched Swerna slowly slip out of visibility. Smoke still lingered in the air over the red citadel. I stayed up there until the evening grew gloamy and the mosquitoes thrived in and out of the few lights along the deck.

I thought about the last time I had seen Yevariel.

I had only caught a glimpse of him as the skiff he was on slid through the water, away from Swerna. He'd been crouched between three or four horses. When he looked up, his face was black, darkened with ash, but his gleaming eyes were the same as ever. The skiff's captain had hollered some greeting at our passing boat and the faerie-lords and the aelfes and the hobgobs had waved. Yevariel had looked at me and I had looked at him. Then he had crouched lower and became obscure to me.

Would I still call him brother? Would I still call him friend?

I went back to the cabin and took off my linen coat. Adyl was asleep, her face reposed and calm, taking up the entirety of the cot. Our bags were piled up in the tight corner by our small sink and faucet. I pulled mine out and set it on the single metal chair, intending to put on a heavier coat if I was to spend the night on deck, as it now seemed I must. Instead I found, at the top of my luggage, my long-lost corduroy jacket, neatly folded and placed above all the things I had packed for our journey to Swerna. Its wine-dark color had faded and it looked dusty, as though kept long in storage. Every badge that had ever adorned it was still affixed upon its lapels. I dusted it off and looked at it for a long time before I put it on and returned to the deck and the cool night.

I looked north where the sunset's soft apricot did nothing to belie a bysening sense of mine that a storm was coming, one way or another.

# A Satyr Once...

## David W. Landrum

*A satyr once did run away . . .*
  —Sir Philip Sydney

*Whores* . . . he smiled. Lord Smart had called them "bareback riders." This one, he thought, had been worth the money to bring from London. The room where they lay was absolutely black. In the ancient days, he could see in the dark. Back then, his eyes picked up every bit of starlight, moonlight, false fire from swamp gas, the luminescence of insects. Give him a few glowworms in those old days, and he could find his way out of a dense wood on a cloudy night.

But in the absolute darkness of his bedchamber, he saw only the black. He felt the warm body beside him, softly ran his hands over the smooth melons of her breasts, down her stomach to her soft thighs and the tangle of hair about her warm little nest. She knew her trade well. She had given him a wild thrash and now he wanted wine.

He got up so he would not wake her. She must not see—though he wondered if a woman who'd been in the bedrooms of hundreds of strange men might not simply accept it if she did see. He crept from the bed to the closet that no one knew about.

In his secret room, he grasped for a bottle of brandy. When he sat at dinner parties, he sipped from crystal glasses with the delicate refinement a wealthy man was expected to exhibit. Alone, in privacy, he pulled the glass stopper from the decanter, put his lips to the spout, and let the hot, rich liquor pour down his throat. It was the best and most expensive of his stock, but what did money matter to him? His estate had been solvent for two hundred years. And he had hardly touched the treasure buried near the Roman ruins.

He rejoiced as the fiery brandy warmed him. He breathed a prayer of thankfulness to Dionysus. No one worshipped the old gods anymore, but habit lodged stubbornly in the heart.

He set the empty bottle on a table. The liquor made him want Lucy once more and immediately.

He walked over to the single window in his private room—his lair, he called it. Dawn was coming up over the forest and the hedgerows that bounded his estate.

The woods no longer teemed with fauns, satyrs, nymphs, and hamadryads. In ancient times, each grove, stream, and lake had sheltered a genius. Each river had been home to a god or goddess. The Christian religion, with its habit of consecration, had driven most of them away. Here and there, though—and especially in the rural areas where allegiance to the old gods continued to exist within the peoples' hearts—a few of the minor deities remained.

He remembered when it had all started, two hundred and forty years ago.

*** 

One day, all those years ago, when roaming free, he came across a bright, shiny object. He knew it to be a horn from his association with Roman soldiers. However, this one was curved, not straight like the Roman ones. It sparkled in the sunlight, bright, burnished, the color of gold. He lifted it in fascination.

Its weight and the beauty of the smooth shiny metal fascinated him. Almost involuntarily, he brought the horn to his lips and blew into it.

A loud, mellow note sounded. Startled, he dropped the horn. The note resonated and echoed after he had puffed into the device. As the clear, beautiful tone died away, he heard sounds that filled him with terror.

Human voices. Horse hooves. The baying of hounds.

He glanced back and saw them coming across the meadow beyond the grove of trees where he had found the horn.

As he broke free of the tree line and sped across an open space, he saw four riders and more dogs. They were on both sides of him. The human men had seen him and recognized him for what he was. They shouted, pointed, and spurred their steeds. Loud explosions of thunder (he recognized them as gunshots now—he did not know what a firearm was back then) sounded on all sides of him. Frantic, he ran. He could hear the pounding of the horses' hooves as they gained on him.

Varinius understood the local language imperfectly, but at the time he caught enough of it to know that one of them shouted, "A satyr!" Translating in retrospect, he remembered their leader had bellowed, "A thousand pound to the man who takes him!"

Varinius ran for a thick grove where their horses could not follow. An explosion sounded close to him. A bolt of pain tore through his body. He fell and rolled into the trees.

He lay on the ground, crying out. He heard the horses slow and stop. The hunters were dismounting. Smelling water, he managed to raise himself. He got unsteadily to his feet and tottered forward.

Then he remembered the lake.

He could not swim, but death was preferable to capture. Varinius stumbled to the brink of a cliff that dropped some forty feet to an expanse of deep, clear water. He felt blood in his mouth. His insides seemed to be on fire. He heard voices and the sound of feet snapping dead branches. He flung himself forward, stumbling over the edge and plunging down to the water below.

***

He reached for another bottle of brandy. Sixteen forty, he thought—the year the Civil War began and the year troopers loyal to Cromwell shot him. Lorena had saved his life. That incident, he reflected bitterly, had won him lasting fame.

He smiled as he drank down a quantity of Hennessy.

The poet Marvell had been in the hunting party. A poem he wrote, "The Nymph Complaining for the Death of her Faun," came out of the incident. It pained him. Whenever Varinius read it, he thought of Lorena.

On that day so long ago, he had fallen, hit the water, thrashed and struggled, and then gone under. As his consciousness failed, he felt hands seize and pull him. He thought his pursuers had dived in to capture him, but when he woke up he found himself in a dry cave. Beside him squatted a woman with light blue skin and long blue tresses.

Varinius tried to get up. The woman reached out and touched him.

"Don't move. You are still healing. They hit you with one of their bolts. You will heal but you are not yet well enough to stand or walk."

He groaned, feeling relief but immense weariness.

"The blessing of Almighty Zeus rest on / Your soul and on your body, goddess fair," he said, lapsing into the poetic meter he used to address female deities. "The Lord of Thunder will repay your grace."

She smiled, bent down, and kissed his lips.

"Soft," she replied. "Sleep and heal."

She gave him drugged wine. He lapsed into blackness.

***

As Varinius finished off the brandy, he reflected on human women. They did come in an assortment of shades and hues. England was a nation with many seaports, so people of many lands came here. He had slept with women who had golden skin and almond eyes, skin the color of ebony, white and freckled women, and women from India with beautiful brown bodies. Their beauties, though, were nothing compared to the blue of a Naiad's skin or the soft green of dryads when they left their existence as trees and took on flesh.

Lorena had nursed him back to health. He still sighed at the memory of her beauty. Being a water woman, she wore nothing. She had small but perfectly formed breasts, a slender muscular body, beautiful hips, a lovely cunt, and webbed toes and fingers. When he asked her if she had a lover, her eyes grew very sad.

"I consorted with Priscus for many years," she'd said. "He left when a priest consecrated the ground in his grove to build a church. For a few years, Thalia was my lover. She was the genius of a pond that joined my lake by a small stream. The local farmers dammed the stream and drained her pond to make a grain field. She died."

"I'm sorry."

"She was a sweet lover. So was Priscus. But Zeus has sent you to me."

He healed. Lorena became his lover. The main entrance to her cave lay under the water, but a long, cramped tunnel led out to a grove near the lake. There he stumbled on the treasure.

\*\*\*

The brandy had enflamed Varinius.

Lust. He crept back into his bedroom. He slipped under the covers and put his hand on the voluptuous, snoring woman. She came awake as he greedily kissed her breasts and then her lips and nose.

"You want it again already?" she groaned sleepily.

By now he could only grunt.

"Get some lotion," she said. "You've dried me out. You never stop, Morlington."

The bedroom, pitch black and shuttered, painted a dark color, concealed his goat legs, tail, and hooves (he kept his horns cut short). He found a bottle of camphor-scented cream, spread it on her mound and slit, and quenched his wine-flamed lust.

Lucy Grandville moaned, bucked, and squealed as the two of them went at it. She had fought (or, he smiled, *fucked*) her way to the status of most sought-after whore in London. He had paid a huge sum to bring her and two of her girls here for a long weekend. Of course money was no obstacle to him. He had money enough to last to the end of time.

\*\*\*

After healing from the wound, Varinius cautiously explored the grove near Lorena's lake. Hunters had torn it up, rutting through it with horses and dogs, searching for him. As he learned to speak their language (a thing Lorena insisted he do), he stealthily listened in on conversations around campfires and among farmers and herdsmen. A satyr, they said, had been spotted in the groves not far from Otter Bay Lake. Sportsmen from all over England were coming north to hunt him.

The presence of the quarry men had frightened away the

animals and birds; the droppings of the horses and dogs had fouled the soil and fertilized the weeds; and, of course, the parties of humans who wanted to kill him had ravaged the groves, dells, and meadows where he had lived for hundreds of years.

He found a new woodland in a remote location a few miles from Lorena's lake. Rumor said it was haunted. An association with ancient druidical worship made locals avoid it. An old law dating back to the time of King Henry III forbade hunting there. It seemed a safe place for him to dwell.

He noticed, as he grew more familiar with the area, an oddly shaped mound. It protruded from the ground in a circle of massive boulders covered with moss and the soil from years of leaves and grass breaking down and returning to humus. Something suggested it was not a natural formation. He dug through a gap between two of the mound's massive stones. Dirt crumbled. He felt resistance and pushed. Something gave way, and Varinius fell forward. Soil and stone rained down on him as he stumbled and rolled, shielding his head. Silence returned. The dust settled. He twisted his body around. His eyes grew wide at what he saw.

Treasure filled the chamber from top to bottom: piles of gold and silver bars, vessels set with precious stones, and containers of fine jewels. It was a fortune for a king. It would eventually enable him to live convincingly as a human being.

***

He heard Lucy groan and felt her buckle beneath him. He smiled with satisfaction. Who else, he mused, could make the top whore in Britain come? He felt a surge of passion, gripped her, and drove into her with unbridled intensity. A long, loud moan of pain and ecstasy broke from her throat as he finished. When silence came, she lightly struck his back with her fists.

"Off," she said. "You're wearing me out. No more for a while. Annabella and Cynthia are here. Ride those young colts if you want it again. I need to rest."

He kissed her and said he would let her rest. He got up, washed, and dressed. The governor of the shire would be coming by today. He planned on entertaining him royally—with pomp, a banquet, and with Annabella and Cynthia. Lucy, he had decided, would be reserved for himself.

***

What he found in the cave had facilitated his successful sojourn among the human mortals. But Lorena had not fared so well.

One day she seemed troubled. He asked her what was wrong.

"The humans are building some sort of structure on the edge of my lake," she said.

Varinius did not think this was something she should be so troubled about—two or three cottages where families could live nestled on the shore of her lake. She lived underwater or in her cave. No one would see her.

But her instinct had been right. A local entrepreneur had built a cooperage there. To bend the wood for the barrels they made, they used lye. They dumped the residue from the operation into the lake.

The fish and turtles died. Birds and deer no longer came there to nest and drink. The waters, though a beautiful deep blue, became poisonous and dead. In only a matter of months, the toxins took Lorena as well. He remembered the stages of her demise. She grew thin. Her eyes became dull. Lethargic and nauseous, she moped about her cave.

Varinius said she should find another dwelling place, but by the time he said this Lorena was too ill to travel. She collapsed one day. He carried her thin, feverish body to a grove, hoping sunshine and fresh air might purge the destroying vapors within her. She only grew more miserable and ill. He laid her under an oak. She vomited black fluid, trembled, wept, and died convulsing and screaming in pain.

Varinius buried her by the oak. As he turned, a woman, a hamadryad, materialized by the side of her grave.

She wore a white chiton dress. Her brown hair gathered on one side, she radiated beauty and dignity.

"You are the spirit who dwells in this tree?" he asked.

She nodded.

"I'm sorry I placed a corpse so near to your habitation. I will rebury her."

"You don't need to do that. The poor thing has suffered enough without having her grave disturbed." She paused and then said, "I am Ionia."

"Varinius. I would not have dug here if I'd known. I did not sense your presence."

"I don't exist as a tree enough that my presence resonates here much anymore. I've managed to find a place among the humans. You might think about doing the same yourself, Varinius."

He looked at her. The wind blew and fluttered her garment.

"Easier for you than for me," he replied.

"It will be more complicated for you than it was for me, yes. Still, I do not jest." She looked at the pile of freshly turned earth where he had buried Lorena. "They caused her death. They will eventually cause your death. I have taken steps to make sure they don't destroy me. In a short while, I will own this land. That way I can make certain this tree is never cut down. Your form is a challenge, certainly. But you have found the hoard the Roman Britons hid in the ground during the days of Boudicca. Money will enable you. You can make a place for yourself in their world as I have made a place for myself."

"You know about the treasure?"

"I know this land. Some of my roots go into the cave. I don't need any of the gold there."

He did not know what to say. She smiled.

"Come to the house four *stadia* down this road." She pointed. "I dwell there. Establish your presence. It will be your entry to the human world."

"How?"

"Disguise yourself. Use your resources. At one time satyrs had the reputation of being wily."

And with that she vanished.

***

Varinius came down to breakfast. Biggs, his valet, brought him tea and the London paper. He sat in a chair, taking in the sunlight, feeling the cool breeze blow through the open windows, satisfied to his marrow by a night of love with Lucy.

He ran his eyes over the paper. The population of the United States had reached fifty million. The Bolivian army had been routed by the Chileans in the Pacific War, and the Chileans had captured

Lima. The Empire, still reeling from the heavy losses and Maiwand, felt better now that an expeditionary force had relieved the garrison at Kandahar and were in pursuit of the Afghan rebels—who, it seemed, had suffered serious, crippling losses in the battle, making it a pyrrhic victory.

He sighed. In the past, he had had no interest in human affairs. He had lived his life in nature, in the immediate experience, not qualified by the passing of time.

Biggs brought in his breakfast of bacon, eggs, rolls, and butter. He topped the meal off with a frothing mug of ale. He felt refreshed. He also thought of Annabella and Cynthia. Since they would be the main attractions after the banquet, perhaps it would be good if he broke them in a bit. He laughed out loud. Like they needed breaking in.

As he ate, he remembered the visit to Ionia and his first time inside a human dwelling.

***

He stole clothes drying on a line. Putting them on, he shuddered. The confinement seemed unbearable—yet he knew the humans hardly ever went unclothed.

The shirt and waistcoat fit well. The trousers were a problem. His crooked goat legs did not fit easily into them. He found a pair of boots cast off in a trash heap—though they looked new and sound to him. But his hooves slid about on the soles, so he stuffed them with moss and leaves and practiced walking in them before he set out for the house Ionia said he should visit.

It loomed up before him when he turned a corner. Its towers and gables pierced the sky. A brick fence topped with iron spikes bounded it. He came to the iron gate. A servant in a powdered wig met him there.

"And whom shall I say is calling?"

He realized he had to invent a name.

"Tell her Mr. Morlington is here at the invitation of Miss Ionia."

When he heard this, he instantly became obsequious, bowing and opening the gate. Still wobbling a little in his boots, Varinius followed the man down the long lane leading to the house.

Another servant appeared at the door. The two men whispered

and the gatekeeper left. The house servant showed Varinius inside.

He found himself in a large room filled with furniture made of white and light brown wood with gold trim. Thick red cloth covered the floor. Dazzling glass ornaments hung from the ceiling. He heard footfalls. Ionia appeared on the other side of the chamber.

She had on garments that the humans wore—though in the course of his interactions with humans he had encountered mostly men, hardly any women. She was wearing a gown with a full, billowing skirt. The garment gathered at her waist, making her middle appear unnaturally thin. The top of it, cut low, revealed a wide swath of her beautiful white breasts. His blood stirred at the sight of them.

"Lady Mannering will be along shortly," she whispered. "She has left all of her property and wealth to me. In a short while you will understand why."

At that very moment, he heard a voice lilt: "O pussy! Pussy cat, are you here?"

That night Ionia met him beneath the moonlight by her oak. She slipped out of her chiton, he threw his arms around her, and they mingled in love under the sight of the chaste moon. After the rolling, grunting, and gasping was over, they sat on a mossy rock and watched the white light Phoebe shed play across the clear water of a rocky stream that ran near the oak tree where Ionia's spirit rested.

"I felt so bad for Lorena," she said. "I want to make sure the same thing does not happen to me. No one will ever cut down this oak because I will soon own it."

"How long have you been Lady Mannering's lover?"

"Four years. She is dying. I can tell, but she can't. Cancer is growing in her. She will soon sicken and perish. She thinks the weariness she feels is the infirmity of age. When she is gone, I will become sole owner of her estate."

He glanced at her beautiful, gentle body, white like ivory in the bath of moonlight. When a breeze arose and blew her hair, his blood jumped.

"You need to make provision for yourself," she said. "The men of the district talk of seeing a satyr and scour the land you once counted as your realm, hunting you. You will not be safe as long as you're living in the wild."

She paused.

"I don't want you to die, Varinius. I want you to live. I want you to be near me, to be a lover and friend. I am ripe to have a child. This only happens every two hundred years or so. I want you to father my child. But with us, it takes a lot of effort. I need you around for a long while. If you stay out in the wilderness, even in the sacred land, they will eventually find you and kill you."

He saw the truth of her words. They listened to the plashing of the stream for a long time.

"I endure that woman's embrace," she said, "only to preserve myself. You too must make your place in the human world."

"I would not even know where to begin."

"I have an idea," she said.

***

Varinius finished his breakfast. He decided he would ride over and see Ionia. Their child, Nerina, had found land of her own and married one of the local deities who had also managed to survive disguised as a human. They lived in Ely (her husband was a genius of the marshes there). He could visit Ionia, roll with her, and then return and prepare Annabella and Cynthia for the considerable business they would do tonight.

His servants got his horse ready. He still found riding awkward. Ionia insisted he learn, and he was glad he did. Still, sitting astride a fellow beast felt unnatural. His settlement in the human world, he recalled, began with riding a horse to Paige House, the manor he would eventually acquire.

***

He had learned about Lord Paige from Lady Mannering.

Two months before her abrupt death from cancer, he had sat with her and Ionia at tea. He noticed how her hand shook as she raised her teacup to her lips. It clattered when she set it down.

"Pussy tells me you are looking for property."

"I am," he said. "I own houses in London and in Hull, but my love is for the country."

"Lord Paige is selling his estate. He's flat broke, I'm told—drinking, gambling, profligacy. You could probably get it for a song." She smiled. "He even owns the satyr's grove. No one has caught the creature yet, but we are told he still lurks in the precincts."

He rode over to the Paige House. The structure, ancient, slightly medieval in its look, sat on a hill. Huge oaks surrounded it. The grounds, he noticed, had sunk to deplorable condition. Weeds choked the lawns. Grass grew through the flagstones leading to the front door. Scraggly vines crawled over the fences. He saw a pack of skinny dogs—probably hunting hounds gone feral—nosing for food in the weedy garden. No servants greeted him. He went up to the door and rang the bell.

After a long time, the door opened.

A white-haired man with bright blue eyes and a ruddy face regarded him. He wore a black frock coat and a wine-stained shirt.

"Lord Paige, I assume. My name is Morlington. Someone has informed me that you are thinking of selling your estate. I have come here to make inquiries."

"You speak English like an American," he said, his voice a gruff guffaw.

"I divide my time between Hull and London," Varinius said, improvising a story. "Thus the confusion of dialect."

"Come in," he said, turning abruptly and gesturing.

Varinius followed him inside. Paige glanced back.

"Crooked legs," he observed, a stifled laugh bursting from his lips.

"I have an infirmity—from birth."

Lord Paige only laughed again.

The house, though its interior and furnishings were magnificent, was covered with dust. A musty smell radiated from the carpets. Empty liquor bottles crowded the top of every table, the piano and piano bench, and several stairs on the staircase. Paige ambled on. Then he turned and, as if from nowhere, flourished a sword at Varinius. He tossed another sword to him.

"*En garde,*" he said, his eyes alive with mad glee.

Varinius recovered from his astonishment quickly enough to catch the blade and duck a swipe by Paige that might have taken his head off. The old man laughed wildly. Varinius did not know how to fight with a sword. He had watched the Roman legionaries train in the ancient days. Their blades were different, though, and he had never done more than observe them from afar.

The old man, drunk and half mad, wore a look of bloodlust on his face. "Let's see how well you can fence with those gamey legs," he spewed, thrusting his thin sword.

Varinius parried, turned, and thrust back, surprising the old man, who gaped at him a moment and then went after him with renewed vigor and more focus. Varinius dodged his jabs and feints. Lord Paige was skilled, no doubt, but his inebriation and the damage he had done to himself through dissolute living blunted his ability.

With the adroitness of a half animal, Varinius quickly saw patterns in his opponent's attack. He watched him (he was slowing down from fatigue), saw the right moment, rushed at him, parried, and knocked the sword from his grip, sending it high into the air.

He stepped back, caught the airborne sword and backed Lord Paige into a corner, both points sticking an inch from his throat. They faced off in silence.

"You see," Varinius said into the astonished eyes of the drunk old man, "I have worked very hard to overcome my handicap."

He paid twice as much as he should have for the estate. But he paid in gold, which Paige could not gainsay. He closed the estate to hunting so the old groves and woodlands that had once been his realm could recover their vitality through natural processes. He refitted and repaired the house, hired servants and gardeners, a cook and a valet. In a few months the place had recaptured its former glory.

Ionia had inherited Miss Mannering's estate. Neighbors grumbled that a "sapphic," as they termed her, had gotten all the old woman's land and money, but Mannering's lawyers had made the will airtight. She surprised everyone by courting (and, for effect, sleeping with) men and by being seen in London and Paris with Varinius at her side. She spent a year in Paris to have his child (a girl—dryads only bore female children).

She came back with Nerina, whom she introduced as her orphaned cousin. Everyone knew Nerina was more directly related than a cousin, but the practice of a short sojourn overseas and convenient lies afterward was common among landed female gentry who bore unexpected children, and they accepted her.

She helped Varinius adapt to the patterns of human life. She advised him (he had not thought of this) to appear to age, to announce his death, and then appear as a young son. The high-ranking gods could shape-shift easily and assume any form; lower-ranking deities possessed less spacious powers in this regard, but with practice he learned to appear older and then younger.

From his purchase of Paige House in 1710 to his current ownership now in 1880, he had portrayed four different men. Soon it would be time for number five. Ionia kept her supernatural existence hidden by a similar ruse.

They were still lovers. She seemed content with him. He ranged over a wide territory with women, but she understood and accepted as much. He was, after all, a satyr. In another thirty years, she would once again be ripe for childbearing.

\*\*\*

He made a pleasurable visit to her and then rode back home. His first guests from London would arrive in a few hours. Until that time, he would have the young bareback riders, Annabella and Cynthia, perform their famous "dance" for him (he had never seen it, but it was all the rage among the men of London). Then he would take them to his darkened chamber, where they could not see his goatish legs and tail, and decide if they were worth their price.

# Ship of Fools

## David Farland

Snow-laden pines huddled beneath their white burdens at the margin of the road, and for a moment the Ship of Fools halted as it crested a hill. Its hull was painted a merry yellow. A bitter breeze played in sails of red silk. The wooden figurehead, a fool dressed in motley, wore a comic frown, as if afraid he might run aground. From a distance, the ship would have seemed to be sailing backward through the snow.

"Whoa," Erstwhyle called to the gray draught horses that pulled the ship. The vessel had been hoisted up on axles and turned into a wagon. Every time it rolled through a town, rustics would gape and point. Inns and homes would empty as spectators gawked. Erstwhyle liked that. The bigger the crowd, the more he got paid.

Castle Crydon loomed ahead, perched upon a steep crag. Walls rose up, gray and oppressive, with merlons like rotten teeth. A dozen tall towers rose in great spires, black spears aimed at the heavens. Guards in bright red cuirasses marched along its wall like toy soldiers. No peaceful lord needed such protection.

A wretched city squatted in its shadow. Squalid houses and cheap wooden shops leaned at odd angles, as if wondering where to fall.

'Tis a sin that good trees died to create such a monstrosity, Erstwhyle thought. He liked trees, but preferred them alive and breathing. Houses were not for him. The boughs of a living pine were roof enough.

Gray clouds lowered above the castle, threatening snow. Shadow creatures moved among them, their bat-like wings flapping, slow and deliberate.

"Baron Blunder, lend me use of your eyes," Erstwhyle begged.

As a satyr, Erstwhyle had the golden eyes of a goat, with a long black horizontal slit for a pupil. He saw well to the side, but could not focus at long distances. He shaded his eyes as he peered above the castle, raising a hand to his brow where his dark horns rose, twisting as they swept back over his head. His nostrils flared, as if to catch some elusive scent in the snow. The land had the steel smell of ice.

Baron Blunder, a fat giant in his forties, raised his head up through the hatch of the ship. His face was as pale as the snow, his jowls as massive as those of a bulldog. Baron Blunder had the look of a lack-wit, but it was all for show.

"There above the castle," Erstwhyle asked, "over the topmost tower—is there something in the clouds?"

"Dream dragons," Blunder offered. "Naught but phantasms. Prince Crydon is a pompous git, if the sayings be true."

"Thought you said he was perverse," Erstwhyle corrected. "Not pompous."

"He's both. It's an unnatural union. Not unlike yourself."

Erstwhyle was the last of the satyrs. He didn't see himself as anything but human, yet every day he was reminded that he was something less.

"I want to see!" Amilee cried from inside the ship. She flung open the side door, her pretty young face so pale and free of blemish it seemed translucent. Her dark brown tresses hinted at flame.

Erstwhyle's heart skipped. "Stay hidden!" he hissed. But it was too late. She'd already popped her head out, despite the warnings.

No one was near in the woods, yet at just that instant, a dream dragon dropped below the clouds and glared at them—a monstrous creature ancient and rancid, ragged flesh stripped away from it in tatters, eyes blind and rheumy. It could have been beautiful, a work of art. It was created from nothing more than dreams, after all. But this was not something born from a summer's fancy, only a monstrosity ripped from a nightmare. A man would have to study evil for long hours to create such a specter.

Its gaze veered toward the Ship of Fools, fixed on Amilee like a rat speared to the floor, and then the dragon lifted back into the clouds.

Could such a monstrosity really see them? Erstwhyle chewed his lip. Probably not, he decided. He was a tough creature, yet right now he felt tiny and helpless.

Crydon was evil. He liked to hunt young women, girls who had been accused of crimes—petty theft, lewd behavior, gossiping. But only the pretty ones. He stripped them naked first. Those who got away lived to tell the tale; those who did not—no one ever learned of their fate.

It wasn't fair. But when were lords ever fair? And who would dare stand against Crydon?

Need had driven the three here, like a teamster with a sharp whip. Ever since the highwaymen had robbed them last summer, Erstwhyle felt drawn to this place. In a time of war, a jester's arts were needed more than ever. Yet widows and orphans had no coin to pay for entertainment, and in town markets where he once had earned good gold, he now only earned the gratitude of impoverished folks.

Crydon's gold had drawn them. Rumor on the road said that he'd pay one thousand *guldens* this night to the fools that pleased him best.

Now here Erstwhyle was, looking up at Crydon's castle. Crydon the Huntsman. Crydon Blood-Fist. The Dark Prince.

"Back in the ship, Amilee," Erstwhyle warned. "Crydon has an unsavory taste for pretty girls."

***

The Ship of Fools stopped at an inn at the base of the city. A crowd gathered to look, just as the snow began to swirl from the sky in great wet flakes.

Erstwhyle sat on the buckboard and played his lute for the crowd while Baron Blunder bought dinner at the inn. He soon came back with a gangrel of a chicken, along with buttered parsnips, stewed plums, and hard, dark bread. He brought a keg of apple cider, and they retired into the ship to eat.

As they entered the ship, a townsman peered in the doorway. "Ooh, there's a tasty tart!" he called. Erstwhyle slammed the door shut behind him, shaken.

A dream dragon might not be able to see, but now a villager *had* seen Amilee. Would he report it? Did the prince pay for news of pretty girls?

Dark was falling fast, so Amilee lit a small lantern made of bloodshot glass.

She ate little, nibbling a roll. Baron Blunder, on the other hand, shoved food down his gullet as fast as possible. All were nervously silent as they considered the evening's performance.

"You'll do well," Amilee predicted. After six weeks of teaching him to sing in the prince's native Dangolian tongue, she had no more advice to give him. She only stared down at her roll, as if gazing into eternity.

"Sure," Baron Blunder agreed with a smack of his lips. "He always does well. He'll win the prince's purse."

"Win or lose matters little," Erstwhyle said. "I'm more worried about you, Amilee." She was an outlaw, after all.

"My parents fled years ago," she objected. "He's forgotten by now."

She didn't seem frightened enough. Perhaps it was her youth. She would not say how old she was—thirteen, fourteen—but she was too young to understand the ways of princes. Crydon would never forget a traitor's family.

Baron Blunder quickly finished eating and said, "Best hurry on, don't ya think? Castle gates close at dusk."

"Aye," Erstwhyle agreed. "Drive us in."

Blunder grunted and lunged out the ship's door, then climbed into the driver's seat. With a click of the tongue he jolted the horses into motion.

As the vessel rattled and rolled, Erstwhyle peered hard at Amilee. She was a quiet girl who seldom showed emotion, and he could not read her now. Her face, lit by the lantern, seemed surreal. In only moments, Baron Blunder tapped the top of the vessel twice. They were nearing a guardhouse.

"Remember," Erstwhyle said, "there will be soldiers about. The ship can't be seen pitching or moving. And the guards might try to take a peek inside, so keep hidden. We should be done by third watch, for good or ill."

"I'll keep still," she said.

He worried though. Amilee had a fondness for taking long walks in the darkness to enjoy the light of the moon.

With that she climbed into a trunk that Baron Blunder often used as a stool. The clothes and props that were normally stored there had been shifted elsewhere in the cabin. Amilee folded herself in.

Erstwhyle went to her, held her hand, and peered into her sapphire-blue eyes. Her hand felt cold this winter's day.

"I love you," she said. "I wish . . ."

His heart stammered before it caught a beat. She'd never said that she loved him before. He was older than her, nearly twenty. He didn't quite know what she meant by "love."

As if to confirm her feelings, she leaned up and kissed him. He felt stunned. Her lips were cold and a chill rushed over him. He felt it a portent.

"I wish I was a satyr."

Erstwhyle smiled sadly. "Ah, child," he said. "Be glad that you're human. There's no place for my kind in your world."

He smiled again and pushed her down into the chest. He heard a guard outside call, "Halt!" Baron Blunder mumbled loudly as the ship drew to a stop.

Erstwhyle finished pushing Amilee into the chest and applied a heavy padlock. He climbed atop it and sat, just as guards threw open the door. Curious faces peered in.

"Boo!" Erstwhyle said. The guards' eyes widened.

Erstwhyle plucked the last flesh from the bones of his chicken, giving the guards a bored stare. They were so shocked, they fell back from the door and slammed it shut.

***

That night the Solstice Feast was already underway as Erstwhyle and Baron Blunder entered the servants' antechamber. There was no merry hearth in the huge room, only frost creeping over the threshold from outside. There were not even the faded tapestries that one would expect to hold in the heat, only cobwebs adorning the bare stone corners of the hall.

Apparently in Crydon's realm, servants were treated no better than cattle.

Three hundred bards and fools had gathered for the competition. Fear and anticipation filled the room. He saw it on the faces of black-skinned acrobats from Mansurria dressed in jaguar furs. One pretty young gypsy woman wearing silks was emptying her stomach in a corner, a victim of butterflies.

Performers had traveled hundreds of leagues for a chance at tonight's reward. Erstwhyle himself had spent weeks on the road and was now penniless and far from home.

He didn't just *want* to win; he needed it, ached for it. Erstwhyle was a fair acrobat and could dance with the best of them. As a satyr, he would arouse a sense of wonder and curiosity—if not fear. All of that worked in his favor, making his acts more memorable.

But to win a thousand *guldens*, he'd need more than spectacle. Singing and the lute were his strongest skills. He had a voice as mellow as honeyed wine, and his throaty vibrato would haunt an audience. Yet for his songs to strike hard, they needed to be sung in the tongue of his audience, as Amilee had taught him.

He hoped she was safe. She was still hidden in the Ship of Fools, parked on a great roundabout at the servants' entrance. She'd promised to be still, but there were guards strutting about—men with hawkish faces and searching eyes.

Outside, snow was tumbling through night skies. Erstwhyle brushed it from his shoulders and pulled back the hood of his great cloak, exposing his horns. People gasped. All eyes followed him as he entered the castle and doffed the cloak, hanging it on a peg.

He peered through a curtain. His rivals, the Maidens of Mansurria, sang a haunting tune to shrill pipes, while two beauties danced about the room.

Tough competition. Their beauty was ethereal, their voices sublime. And more than one of them would sleep with the prince for a chance at the reward.

Erstwhyle went to a corner and began to tune his lute when one of Crydon's lackeys, an aide to the chamberlain, told him brusquely, "You with the horns—you're next."

It was always that way. He was a curiosity, and everyone was eager to see him. But he wanted time to study the situation. Winning a competition required an understanding of the lay of the land.

"Wait," Erstwhyle said. "I need some help, friend."

The aide, a teen with a pimpled face, drew near. His breath smelled of wine. His mousey hair looked like hay. The boy kindly switched to Taldagean, a tongue common among traders. "Need help with props?"

"I need to know who in the room is out of favor with his majesty." The teen got a sly look, and Erstwhyle suspected that the boy was about to mislead him. "There's a pretty tip in it for you if this turns out well."

"The table farthest from his majesty, a red priest by the name of Typhos. You'll know him by the scar." He made a slash across his nose.

Erstwhyle grinned. The table farthest from a lord was often left for those out of favor. To have a victim for his jests—and a red priest at that—was gratifying.

Baron Blunder lumbered across the room with a bundle of juggling pins. The aide pulled back a curtain and the fools entered.

***

Prince Crydon's feasting hall was enormous. Sconces by the thousands along the walls lit the room. Each was made from a skull, cunningly chiseled so that flickering candles glowed inside. Others were set as footlights for the actors. Flames danced within them like serpents' tongues.

"Vanquished enemies?" Baron Blunder murmured. But they could not have all been enemies. Yes, there were crystal goblin skulls among them with their sharp canines and the broad skulls of giants out of the

Gwaylin Hills. But some among the human skulls were so small they had to have been taken from children.

A man who collects skulls will covet mine, Erstwhyle thought. There had been that one lord, five years back, who had tried to take it.

"Have no fears," Erstwhyle whispered lightly. "We're under protection of the guild." The Bards' Guild was a fellowship of performers—jesters, musicians, acrobats. Guild members protected one another. Any lord who harmed a guilder would earn retribution. Entertainers would quit coming to his realm or, in extreme cases, might subject him to ridicule from afar. Puppeteers might show him as a buffoon, or bards might put his failings to song.

On three sides of the room, enormous hearths were laid out. A wagon could have parked inside one. Smoke lingered in the air, a blue haze that smelled of rare sandalwood.

Erstwhyle strode forward, his small hooves clacking on the floor. Gasps arose from the crowd. Onlookers fell silent or began to whisper, "What is that?"

At the lords' tables, a feast was laid out—whole swans and platters of bread. Venison pies and sweet rolls. Mushrooms stuffed with garlic and rye crackers. Pitchers of ale and flagons of dark amethyst wine. Oranges from southern lands and the last of the year's good apples baked into tarts.

Nostrils flared. A deep hunger stirred in Erstwhyle. His kind could not resist wine.

The floor was of polished marble, deep crimson with turquoise veins. A pentagram made of silver and encircled by copper marked off the central floor, as if Crydon hoped to summon a pack of demons.

No less than two hundred lords and their ladies were in attendance. The ladies all wore pointed caps that streamed peacock feathers and taffeta. Their brightly colored dresses of rose or sapphire lifted their bosoms. The men wore leggings and tunics embroidered with gold thread.

Prince Crydon perched upon a pedestal rather than a normal table, as if he were looking down in judgment from above. His face was cowled in a royal blue robe such that Erstwhyle could not discern his features at all, only a pale, pointy nose.

Crydon clapped his hands. "Please me!" he ordered.

Erstwhyle glanced back at Baron Blunder for ideas. It would have been simpler if the prince had called for a song, or asked for a jest. Instead, he left it to the entertainers.

"A song!" Erstwhyle said. He raised his lute and began plucking the strings.

"No!" an angry voice called. It was the red priest, Typhos, eyes blazing. "Not his kind!" the priest said. "He seeks to enchant you all. Beware!"

Erstwhyle fought for control. The red priests had killed his people, murdered them in the night for their supposed sins. That was their way—to purify the earth by washing the sinners in their own lifeblood.

"I know no magic," Erstwhyle said. "I have no power, unless you find my songs enchanting."

"Kill the creature!" the priest cried, rising from his chair. But those nearby pulled him back down into place, demanding his silence.

Prince Crydon merely nodded, a sign for Erstwhyle to play.

He opened with a soft tune, "Dancing Among Moon Shadows." The song was the stuff of legend, for the proper fingering required an exceptionally rare degree of virtuosity. He sang it now in Dangolian, and the hearts of the locals melted.

The song was dark and haunting, like cloud shadows on a summer night, and began with sounds like wind sliding through trees and the serenade of crickets. As he played, Erstwhyle whistled the tune of nightingales so low, it came as if from a dream, and thus he began to skip and swirl in dance. His hooves slid across the marble floor, and the lords and ladies fell quiet, as if under a spell.

Soon, the plucking of strings evoked the sound of rain, big liquid drops falling into the song, skittering over stones, a rolling rollick that set him to frolicking. His hooves clattered upon the marble like hailstones falling. And Baron Blunder beat on a big drum: the crashing sound of thunder and lightning.

People cheered as he swirled, dancing and playing, and many stood with mouths agape, for they had never seen an artist become one with his music. There is a reason why it was said that satyrs were in league with the devil. That fear led to the deaths of Erstwhyle's parents and village, all wiped out in a single night.

People began to clap in time, and his small hooves slid over stone as if he skated upon ice. The room was in an uproar as the song reached its crescendo, but he was not ready to let the crowd go yet, not while he had them by their throats.

With a flourish he struck a transition into a new song, one of his own making. He sang:

> Hey, no, die diddily,
> Hey die-diddily, yay.

The time has come
For lute and drum
To spirit us away!

Though Erstwhyle looked as if he only had the legs of a goat, the truth was that they had the strength of a hart, and so he now did something that no human acrobat could manage. He leapt backward into the air and did a quadruple somersault, landing with a clatter onto the table—right in front of Typhos.

As he did, he reached into a small pouch that he wore around his belly, pulled out a handful of deer poop, and tossed them down. It all happened so fast, even those closest to the priest did not see it. To the observer, it appeared as if Erstwhyle had landed so hard, he'd pooped. The dry round pellets bounced on the table, falling onto a platter of cooked swan, rolling onto guests, and plopping into wine goblets.

The priest's eyes blazed and he threw himself backward with such force that his chair crashed to the floor. Women nearby shouted. One baron rose up and looked as if he'd pull his dagger.

But all around the room, others guffawed at the priest's expense. Erstwhyle glanced at Prince Crydon from the corner of his eye. The prince shook with mirth.

"Pardon me," Erstwhyle told Typhos with mock sheepishness. "Nerves."

Then he danced on the table, kicking over goblets and shoving platters aside. The priest went red.

Baron Blunder shouted, "Here now! What is that creature? Is it human? Is it a goat?"

That was the question everyone asked when they saw Erstwhyle, and as he danced nimbly over the tables, women stared at his privates and giggled, and bold men laughed out loud. He was all goat in the nether regions and wore nothing but his fur. From a distance it almost looked as if he wore animal hides for trousers. As he sashayed about, he wagged his tail in time with the music.

He was just warming the crowd up for some of Baron Blunder's comic juggling tricks, when Prince Crydon spoke.

"Where is the girl? The Ship of Fools carried three? A giant, a demon, and a sweet young girl."

The sound did not come from one place. Instead it rose like the snarl of distant thunder and began to crackle. The language was more like the hiss of a snake than anything human.

Erstwhyle was struck with an unnatural fear, for the words made his very bones rattle. He wanted to answer with his whole soul, but could not understand the question.

The crowd hushed. Prince Crydon reached out with a bony finger and made a "come hither" gesture. Erstwhyle was too frightened to move. His hips merely quivered. But he was *drawn* across the room, like iron to a lodestone, and found his hooves skating over the marble floor until he stopped in the midst of the pentagram.

The Dark Prince hissed his question again, but still Erstwhyle could not understand.

A third time the hissing came, rushing forth like waves upon a shore.

Suddenly he understood.

"She grew sick," Erstwhyle said, mustering his courage. "We had to leave her behind, days ago." He peered up at the cowled face, trying to discern whether the prince believed him.

The prince nodded as if he understood, then pointed toward the door, which groaned as it swung inward, hinges twisting with powerful force.

There stood Amilee in a pale blue dress that seemed torn from the sky of a lost summer. Her face was slack and her eyes blank, as though she were entranced. A pair of burly guards held her.

"Ah, there's the girl you were seeking!" Erstwhyle knew he had been caught in a lie. "She seems to be much recovered."

Again Crydon hissed. Amilee slid across the floor on unwilling feet until she landed next to Erstwhyle.

"Tell me everything," Crydon demanded in his serpentine voice. He pointed a finger down at the girl, and a green flame spouted from her forehead. Ghostly plumes formed, half fog and half fire, swirling in a tempest, as if all her dreams of green fields, all her hopes and longings, broke out as one.

The prince opened his mouth—a vast black cavernous mouth—and the green fog swirled up into it. Suddenly his eyes blazed within the hood, a cold piercing light.

"I shall *have* her," he whispered, his voice coming from everywhere and nowhere. It circled, hissing in dark corners, then lashed back from the opposite direction.

"Wait," Erstwhyle begged. "Please!"

"She is an outlaw," Crydon said, "child to my enemies." He reached for her, and Amilee began to surge into the air, rising toward him like a dying ember rising into the night.

Erstwhyle had never seen such powers.

"No!" Baron Blunder shouted, distracting the prince. Amilee fell, a puppet whose strings had been cut.

"No?" the prince simpered.

Guards lunged and grabbed Baron Blunder. He was huge, but not strong. Three guards pulled him down, dragging him back in a chokehold.

"No!" Erstwhyle urged. Amilee had done nothing. There had to be some justice in the world.

Erstwhyle knelt above Amilee. "Please, oh Great Prince, do her no harm. She was but a child when her parents were outlawed. Take me instead."

Prince Crydon glared down. Erstwhyle could not see his face, but the prince's eyes seemed to bore through him. "What would I do with you?" he asked, the words hissing and snapping in far corners.

"My head," Erstwhyle said lightly. "It has served me well all of my life, and it would serve you well."

"I need no counsel," the prince replied. "The fools in my court give counsel enough."

"Then use it for a sconce," Erstwhyle said. "Imagine—with my horns, it would be the jewel of your collection." He raised his hands in an expansive gesture, and the glowing eyes of the dead seemed to peer down.

Erstwhyle reached up, stroked his own horn, as if polishing it.

Prince Crydon laughed, and suddenly a spell was broken. It was not the portentous laugh of a demon, the distant snarl of a dragon. It was the laugh of a commoner, of a peasant at an inn enjoying a mug of ale with friends after he has heard a good jest.

"A fine offer," Crydon said. "As noble as I have ever heard. Such nobleness should be honored. You win, satyr. The thousand gold *guldens* shall be yours. I have never met a man who could match your skill with the lute, and that leap was stupendous. Though I find your sense of humor to be rather coarse . . ."

Erstwhyle cocked his head and wondered. Had this all been an act? Had the prince simply sought to unman the troupes that played before him? No, it couldn't be. Erstwhyle had heard too many dark tales. Yet he wanted to trust his luck.

The prince reached down and took a golden goblet from the pedestal. A servant raced forward to fill it with deep-red wine.

"This goblet has been in my family for six hundred years," the prince said. "The weight of the gold alone is worth more than a thousand *guldens*." He stood and stepped down from the pedestal, then leaned forward to hand the golden goblet to Erstwhyle. Before he did, he raised it in the air. "A toast, to the greatest fool in all the land!"

"Huzzah!" the lords and ladies shouted, raising and draining their own mugs. "Huzzah! Huzzah!"

Erstwhyle saw the prince's face then—black eyes filled with madness, too full of light, a small black beard over a manly chin, a leering grin. There was an expression on that face that Erstwhyle had never seen before.

Hunger?

Rage?

The prince lowered the mug to the satyr's lips. Erstwhyle dared not refuse. The wine was swirling in the cup, raging in a torrent, a tornado funneling down into an invisible drain. It was as dark as blood.

He gingerly took a sip. It was the sweetest wine that had ever touched his lips, made from summer-ripe cherries.

Wine does not affect satyrs the way it does humans. It does not absorb so slowly into the body. Instead, the liquor slammed into Erstwhyle's brain, pounding like a hammer. Not only was the wine sweet, it was stronger than anything he'd ever tasted.

In an instant he was swirling and struggling to remain upright. People laughed and pointed. "Look at the goat man!" a woman scorned.

Erstwhyle grinned drunkenly at her.

"A song!" someone else shouted, and Erstwhyle took up his lute and began to play.

He capered about the room, spinning as the wine had spun, weaving and playing, lost in song. As the crowd started to clap, he sang:

> Me mother was a milkmaid
> Me da a Billy goat.
> And on the night I was born
> they took me for a mooncalf
> And threw me in the moat!
> Hey, no, die diddily,
> Hey die-diddily, yay.
> The time has come
> For wine and drum
> To bear us all away!

Erstwhyle danced as the people applauded. He searched the room for Baron Blunder, but saw only grinning skulls along the wall. He peered about for Amilee, but smoke stung his eyes and he stumbled, and in a moment he forgot where he was, lost in song . . .

\*\*\*

He woke in the dead of night. He did not wake all at once. He first became aware of a scraping and wondered what it was. But his mind was groggy, and he went back to sleep.

Moments later, he felt a jolt and heard scraping again. Then he felt a tug.

Someone was pulling him by his left hoof. Outside. Through the snow.

The wine had so dulled Erstywhyle's senses that he could not react and merely fell back into a stupor.

"Get the door," someone said in a gruff voice, and he was pulled along through a doorway. He managed to open his eyes a slit. A burly soldier in chainmail had him by the foot. The chamberlain's aide carried a torch, leading the way. They entered a strange room that smelled of copper.

"Leave him," the soldier said, dropping Erstwhyle. The fat soldier wiped sweat from his brow with the back of his sleeve.

The aide had carried the torch to the far door and stood staring at it. "Shall I fetch the butcher?" the lad asked. His voice sounded buoyant and jolly.

Erstwhyle suddenly realized that something was very amiss. *Wake up!* his senses warned. *Wake up!* But his muscles wouldn't move. So he continued breathing steadily, as if he were fast asleep, and closed his eyes.

"Don't rouse him," the soldier said.

"Perhaps we should tie the creature," the aide suggested.

Erstwhyle recognized the voice as that of the aide who had helped him earlier. He felt so betrayed.

Both men squatted over Erstwhyle, and he wished that he had a knife, but he had not been able to carry any weapons into Crydon's hall. He nearly moaned when he realized that he no longer had his goblet either.

Where is Amilee? he wondered. And Baron Blunder?

The soldier finished tying his wrists, then went to Erstwhyle's legs. Afterward, he grunted and rose. The door scraped the floor as they opened it, and chill air blasted into the room. Then they were gone.

Outside, the chamberlain's aide asked cheerfully, "What do you suppose satyr tastes like?"

The soldier laughed. "Sort of like goat," he said, "with maybe a bit of fool thrown in."

Erstwhyle lay still as their footsteps receded, crunching over ice-covered snow.

He knew this place now. The coppery scent he'd detected was blood, blood so thick that it had seeped into the dirt floor. He was at the shambles, the kill shed where the king's butcher slaughtered animals.

He couldn't imagine that someone would want to eat him. It seemed so . . . unnatural.

But then he remembered that look in Crydon's eyes—the rage and hunger—and realized what it meant.

Erstwhyle stilled his heart and found his throat feeling tight and dry. Satyrs get drunk more quickly than do humans, but the effects wear off more quickly, too.

He pulled hard upon the leather cords that bound him. They were stiff and icy.

Human feet are easy to tie, because they are so large. Not so with Erstwhyle's sharp little hooves. He kicked at the bonds and struggled free, stumbling to his feet. Then he pulled at his hands.

As a satyr he was stronger than a human; his training as an acrobat had made him stronger still. Now he strained. The friction warmed the cords. With every twist and pull, the leather stretched. In moments he broke free.

He opened the door and stood looking out. The chill air had teeth as sharp as a wolf cub's. A thick fog covered everything, as dense as gruel, yet the full moon provided a gloomy light. A dog was barking at the castle gates, and in the distance he could hear horns blowing—not the deep throaty call of war horns, but the high song of hunting horns.

*Amilee!*

He imagined her running through the cold night, barefoot and naked, while Crydon chased her upon his charger with a boar's spear in hand, dogs yapping wildly on her trail.

It would not be a fair hunt in the snow. She would not be able to escape, not with her footprints providing a clear trail. She would not be able to outrun him for long before the cold took her.

Yet what could Erstwhyle do?

The castle gates would be closed, the drawbridge up. With his horns and hooves, he could not just sneak out, even in this fog.

Urgency swept through him. He wanted to help Amilee. He needed to be sure that Baron Blunder was alive. He wanted vengeance. He could not do everything at once.

Amilee and the prince were far away, and he didn't know where Baron Blunder might be. He decided to check the Great Hall.

A satyr's eyes are better than a human's in the dark. Though the night was fast coming to a close, the shadows were deep. He made his way through town, stepping more quietly than a human could in the snow, for his sharp hooves made very little sound.

He followed the aide's track back to a servants' entrance at the palace. He pulled open a small door, which moaned softly as swollen wood scraped paving stones, and nearly fainted when he spotted a guard in the dark, with a dying lamp above him. The guard, a fat sot, sat in a chair by the door, snoring lightly. A huge mug of ale rested at his side, empty.

Erstwhyle crept in, closed the door behind him, and stole the guard's weapon—a strange long kris made of black metal. The kind of thing one might use when making sacrifices.

Erstwhyle crept along a corridor to the Great Hall and peered through a curtain. The fires in the hearths had burned down to smoldering embers, and most of the candles in the skulls had been blown out. There was no sign of Baron Blunder or any of the guests.

A lone waif hummed an old folk tune as she bent over a table, scrubbing it clean:

> I love you, and I always will.
> Till the mountains fall forever,
> And the moon stands still . . .

Upon the podium sat the prince's dinnerware. The golden goblet gleamed in the ruddy light.

He gave it to me, Erstwhyle thought, and then he stole it back and tried to kill me. A murderous rage built.

He'd have to check the roundabout for Baron Blunder. But first there was a small matter of vengeance.

He crept through the room as silently as possible. His hooves made tiny clattering sounds on the marble floor. The waif didn't seem to notice.

He reached the podium, climbed the steps, and grabbed the heavy flagon. There was a platter and dinnerware all of gold, too. He took the forks and knives, tucked everything into the belt pouch, and used the platter as a breastplate.

As he slunk down from the podium, he heard the serving girl emit a soft yelp. She gaped at him in surprise.

With a single leap he crossed forty feet and drew his black kris, then swung it and stopped the blade an inch from her heart. "Quiet!" he hissed.

She gasped, chest heaving, and looked as if she might faint. She was young, only sixteen perhaps. She had wheat-colored hair and eyes that were robin's-egg blue. Her skin was pale as cream, and like all serving girls in castles, she had that "hand-picked" beauty to her, with a doe's legs and lashes.

"Oh, sir," she begged too loudly. "Spare me!"

"Quiet!" he demanded again.

"But I know thou art a lowly creature, given to animal pleasures," she said, trembling. Tears leaked from the corners of her eyes as she came to a hard choice. "Do with me as you will! Satisfy your lusts upon me, but please, please let me live!"

Erstwhyle groaned. The red priests had done their job well on this one—telling tales about the unnatural lusts of satyrs in order to justify their crimes.

"Look, you seem like a sweet girl," Erstwhyle assured her, "and under better circumstances, I might even hope to court you. But right now, I'm looking for a friend of mine. Big fellow? He came in the Ship of Fools."

"He left—hours ago," she said. "All of the bards and fools departed. Soon after you won the goblet . . ."

"My friend would never have gone without me!"

"But it was said that you took your cup and left," the girl continued, still scared out of her wits. "The guards said they let you out the city gates. You were afraid that someone might steal your prize."

Of course. The prince had sought to cover his crime. Half the bards and fools in the country would be hunting Erstwhyle now, hoping to purloin his golden cup.

Even Baron Blunder . . .

"Last I saw Baron Blunder," Erstwhyle said, "he was being held by the guards."

"They let him go," she said. "He stormed off in a rage. He was quite wroth with you!"

Was it true? Had Baron Blunder been persuaded that he was so faithless?

*It's the horns. And maybe the tail and hooves. People never trust you if you've got horns and hooves.*

Erstwhyle must have scowled, for suddenly the wench nearly swooned, and he had to grab her with his free hand to catch her.

She moaned, eyes half closed, and begged, "Please, sir, take me if you must."

"Perhaps I'll rip your bodice another time, milady," Erstwhyle quipped. "But if you could manage to remain quiet for a few minutes, I'd be forever in your debt!"

Conveniently, she let out a sigh and fell limp, so he laid her gently on the floor.

He went to the guests' cloak room and found his great cloak still hanging on its peg. He donned it, pulled the deep hood up to cover his horns, then crept out the way he had come, past the sleeping guard, and into a chilling fog.

He slunk through the pre-dawn. Ice crystals entered his open mouth with every breath. The air smelled of fresh bread and firewood, for the bakers were up cooking for the troops. He passed a hovel and heard a baby cry and a mother trying to quiet it. Otherwise, the fog and cold smothered all sound. He wondered how to escape the castle and realized that he'd have to go over the wall.

He reached the base of some stairs leading up to the top of the wall. A young guard stood there, peering through the mist and darkness.

"Is someone there?" the guard asked.

Erstwhyle crept closer, then raced forward. He threw back his hood, showing his horns and golden eyes.

The guard shouted, fumbling for his blade.

Erstwhyle rammed him with his horns and sent the lad flying. By the time he pulled his sword, Erstwhyle was darting up the steps, three at a time. He reached the top, just as the guard began shouting.

Erstwhyle peered down through the fog. Castle Crydon was perched upon a huge crag. No human could have hoped to jump from it safely.

The first drop over the wall was only twenty feet, and he found a nice little outcrop there, with perhaps four inches of ledge. Beyond that, all was fog.

He leapt, landed soundly on the ledge, and slipped on icy stone. He went sliding down a slope, grabbed at a small tree, which slowed his fall until it yanked free. He spotted another perch twelve feet down below and leapt for it.

A boulder came bouncing past his head, pushed from the wall above.

He gave a startled cry, dropped to a tiny ledge, and held his place. Rocks and ice went rolling past.

He waited for a few seconds, then began taking a circuitous route, bouncing from one tiny outcrop to the next—a feat only a mountain goat could have managed.

Another set of boulders came tumbling through the fog. Shouts of "Get him!" rose from the walls. Arrows whizzed past, fired blindly.

He raced west a few paces, and in twelve leaps reached the bottom of the hill. The river that might have swirled around it was covered in ice and snow. The only sign that water lay beneath came from dry cattail rushes that clustered along the banks.

Erstwhyle feared that it might be too thin to hold his weight. Hooves were great for leaping around on rocks, but tended to split ice like a dagger. He sometimes wished he had the monstrous feet of humans, as unnatural as they looked in the animal kingdom.

There was only one way to test the ice. He leapt out as far as he could and landed with a belly flop, sliding.

He was only a dozen feet from the shore when he heard a soft crack and waited to fall. He was painfully aware of the weight of his gold. He swore not to part with it, even if it meant drowning.

On hands and knees he crawled three paces before the ice broke and he slipped under . . .

*** 

Two hours later, Erstwhyle slogged along a forest road in his wet cloak. A thin film of ice had formed outside it, which created a surprisingly nice layer to hold in the warmth. The interior was lined with rabbit fur, and though he felt sopping wet and miserable, he was warm enough.

*At this rate, with my body heat, it should only take a few weeks to dry out!*

What made him more miserable was thoughts of Amilee. The hunting horns had gone silent long ago, which meant the huntsmen had found their quarry.

It was not hard to follow Prince Crydon's trail. A dozen hunting horses and thirty dogs will make a mess out of fresh snow. Among their tracks, Erstwhyle found those of Amilee—the bare footprints of a young girl.

With the coming of dawn, shadows were fleeing, and the fog began to lift. Stark pines, almost black beneath their mantle of snow, rose up on each side of the trail.

Erstwhyle had passed through town in the darkness and had spotted the Ship of Fools outside an inn, but Baron Blunder was nowhere to be seen. Erstwhyle hadn't been able to wait for his old friend. So he'd forged ahead.

Now, as he topped a hill, he heard the jangle of mail and harness, the tired panting of dogs, the clop of hooves. Crydon's hunting party was returning.

Erstwhyle leapt off the trail, raced a hundred yards, and dove beneath a small pine. The cold needles beneath it carried a musty scent, and he bellied down, tried to see his own tracks. His prints stood out in the snow.

His heart pounded in terror as the hunting party came riding into view. Hounds sniffed at his trail. One let out a keening cry.

The red priest rode up and peered at Erstwhyle's tracks. "Milord," he shouted, "a stag passed this way! A large one. Shall we give chase?"

Erstwhyle suddenly wished he had dropped more deer pellets into the man's food.

Prince Crydon rode up, resplendent in black: his cape, fish-mail armor, and the long hunting lance he bore tipped with blood.

The hounds sniffed at the ground, peered up at their master, tails wagging, eager to continue the hunt.

Crydon's dark eyes flashed. "Looks like a trophy," he said, keenly interested. Then his shoulders sagged. "But that damned girl wore me out . . ."

He turned and rode away, his retainers at his back.

\*\*\*

Erstwhyle found Amilee in the snow—naked, pale from blood loss, and freezing cold. She had a single wound to the belly. A lance had run her through. She was lying with blood dribbling from her mouth. She had put a bit of snow over the wound, as if to stanch it.

The rising sun lay hidden beneath a lid of gray clouds, and Amilee looked as if on a bed of swan's down. He blushed to see her pale breasts revealed.

To Erstwhyle's surprise, she still breathed.

"Amilee!" he cried as he neared, taking off his cloak and laying it over her.

"My love?" she panted. "Is that you?" She peered about blindly, moaning in pain.

"Stay still," he begged. "Can you move?"

For a moment she struggled to take a breath; then she said, "He caught me . . . after sunrise. Should have . . . let him have me . . . sooner."

Amilee lifted her head, propped herself up, but a gushing sound alarmed Erstwhyle. He peeked beneath the robe and saw blood ooze from her wound. He wouldn't be able to move her for fear that she'd bleed out. And he couldn't let her stay, lest she die of cold.

He took her hand, found it as chill as ice. He searched for words to comfort her, but none would come.

She looked at him, smiled faintly, her blue eyes seeming to bore into him. "Get me to the ship," she said. "Dress me . . . dress me in my old brown dress."

He knew the one—a peasant's dress, the one he'd first seen her in. A dirty and worn thing lying crumpled in a trunk. She hadn't worn it in weeks.

"I will," he promised.

She seemed to pass out. He feared she might never speak again. Then she roused enough to say, "Carry me back to Littleford, to me mum. I don't, don't . . . want to be buried here."

"Did he . . . did he ravish you?" Erstwhyle begged. He hated the Dark Prince. Yet somehow he imagined that if he had confirmation of the deed, he could hate the man more.

She began panting and suddenly gripped his hand with ferocious strength. Her back arched. She let out a cry, and then a moan, as if she'd just had some grand notion.

Amilee stopped breathing. Her hand fell. Tears threatened to blind Erstwhyle. Oh, how he fought them.

***

The satyr was still holding Amilee's hand when the Ship of Fools came rumbling near an hour later. In the frosty air, Erstwhyle was shivering, teeth chattering. But he hadn't dared remove his robe from the girl.

Instead, he dreamt of vengeance.

*We are bards, protected by a brotherhood. This girl was my charge.*

But that wasn't quite right. *He* was a bard, not Amilee. She'd only come to teach him. The fact that he loved her would change nothing in others' eyes.

But the prince had stolen Erstwhyle's reward and tried to have him butchered. For that, the Dark Prince would be ridiculed and scorned, humiliated in every land. Bards would sing of his base desires.

It might not sting much, but who knew? Merchants who might have traveled to the land would now shun it. Lords who might have offered support would turn away. Songs and crude jests had unseated more than one king.

Erstwhyle recognized the pounding hooves of draught horses, the creak of an axletree, and the squeak of oversized wheels as Baron Blunder drove up.

"Whoaaa . . . ," Baron cried to the horses. He sat for a long moment. When he spoke, his voice was rough with emotion. "Poor lass! Think we can bury her in this hard ground?"

Erstwhyle shook his head. "I promised to take her home, to her mother."

Baron Blunder grunted approvingly.

Erstwhyle picked up the girl, so small and pliant, and staggered to the wagon. Baron Blunder opened the door, and they laid her upon her bed. Erstwhyle found the waif's dress, still dirty and stained, and pulled it onto her, then laid a blanket over her. He wouldn't be able to sleep in the ship tonight, maybe not for many nights.

He climbed out and stood in the daylight.

"They said at the castle that you took your gold, then slipped off into the night. I thought I'd never see your tail again," Baron Blunder said.

Erstwhyle shook his head. "It was a lie. The prince stole my prize and tried to have me killed."

Baron Blunder said, "There's a good song in that," and then fell silent.

Erstwhyle's thoughts were clouded. "His men will be hunting me. I had to leap down from the castle wall." He knew that tracking him would not be hard.

*** 

For long hours Baron Blunder used the lash and sent the horses plodding up little-used roads, into remote mountain villages that wouldn't see three strangers in a winter. The snow grew deep as they climbed.

Erstwhyle knew that if they could get high into the mountains, the snow might cover their tracks. The skies were heavily laden, gray as slate, and by midday snow did indeed begin to fall. Two hours later a strong gale kicked up, and big flakes began to swirl around them.

The baron chose strange roads, going ever higher into the mountains. There were no signs to guide him, but he seemed to know the way. He had been at this a lifetime.

At last they reached a fork in the road. One trail climbed while the other dropped into a serene valley. There were no cottages or fortresses as far as the eye could see—only dark empty forests and falling snow. Down in the valley, wolves began to howl.

"Which way?" Erstwhyle asked.

Baron Blunder shrugged. "I've been lost for hours."

Erstwhyle studied the trail helplessly. Baron Blunder urged the horses uphill.

"Why this way?" Erstwhyle asked.

"I'd rather die of frostbite than by wolves."

\*\*\*

Exhaustion took its toll. As night began to fall, Erstwhyle nodded off and woke to find Baron Blunder carrying him, struggling to open the door to the ship.

"What's happened?" Erstwhyle asked.

"Get some rest," Baron Blunder said. "I'll drive through the night." He bore Erstwhyle into the ship, which seemed warm and quiet. Outside the wind wailed.

Erstwhyle felt dazed. He listened to the shrieking wind and felt desolate. "Aren't you going to sleep?" he asked.

"Not tonight," Baron Blunder said. "I think that we've made it safe. No one is chasing us."

*No, we did not make it safe. Amilee did not make it.* Erstwhyle's heart ached.

\*\*\*

In the dark, a dream came: Erstwhyle was perched upon a snowy crag with the wind swirling around. Below, the valley was filled with the howling of wolves.

As he trembled, he looked up into the storm and saw something flying toward him. Vast were the wings, perhaps a hundred spans, and the creature was dark, like the clouds at the heart of a hurricane.

In seconds it was upon him—a reptilian head with teeth as sharp as shards of ice. As it wheeled past him, he smelled the terrifying odor of putrefaction. It was dead, old, and odious.

A menacingly low voice echoed from everywhere and nowhere. "Let the hunt begin . . ."

Erstwhyle woke and knew it was no normal dream. It had been a sending. The Dark Prince was coming!

\*\*\*

Midnight found the Ship of Fools climbing into the forest, struggling through the snow.

Baron Blunder had taken a lantern, and now he forged ahead of the horses through the storm, lighting the track. Erstwhyle drove. To both the right and left were dangerous ledges, dropping into the forest.

Erstwhyle had no idea where they were going. He only hoped that somewhere higher in the mountains, the trees might be thick enough to provide shelter and Crydon would give up the chase. Snow was falling, enough to cover their trail. With luck the strong winds would blow away any traces.

Suddenly there was a cracking sound, and the whole wagon tilted. Erstwhyle had driven off the road. He imagined the Ship of Fools plunging down the cliff, and his heart pounded. Everything went into slow motion.

He leaned left, tried shifting his weight so that the wagon would stop tilting. If it went over, he'd have to jump for safety.

For long seconds the wagon canted, and Baron Blunder rushed back, pulled the horses by the reins, and urged them back onto the road. The horses forged, straining and stamping their hooves until the ship righted.

Moments later they rounded a curve and found a mountain crevasse. Tall pines rose up on either side of the road, and Baron Blunder pulled the horses into their shadow. A few feet ahead, trees had been chopped down, but only a few. The road simply ended.

Erstwhyle realized they were on a woodsman's trail.

"We'll stop here until this storm blows over," Baron Blunder said.

The baron freed the horses from their harnesses, led them into the shelter of the woods, and then started a campfire. He was good with fires, amazing in fact, and soon the two of them were sitting beside a blaze. They had little to eat, only a bit of dark bread, some raw onions, and parsnips.

Still, the blaze pushed the shadows of the forest back, and they sat in the warmth of its glow, while flames licked the air and embers went wafting upward, like stars rising into the night. A haze of blue smoke soon filled the little glen.

They had a glum meal, and long into the night, Erstwhyle caught Baron Blunder staring at the wagon. They had known each other so long, they hardly needed to speak. The baron longed for bed, but would not sleep in the same room with a dead girl.

"You think he's hunting us?" Baron Blunder asked.

"I know he is," Erstwhyle said. "I had a dream."

"What kind?"

"I dreamt that I was on a cliff. A dream dragon flew overhead and said—"

"Let the hunt begin," Baron Blunder finished. The fat man looked up sheepishly and shrugged. "I had the same dream, like a daydream, only . . . I felt it in me bones."

"Do you think he'll find us?"

The baron shrugged. They'd done all they could do. Baron Blunder wasn't the kind to resent fate.

A voice boomed through the woods, circling like a hawk, hissing and snarling, "I've found you!"

Erstwhyle and Baron Blunder leapt to their feet, eyes searching. Erstwhyle peered down the road, the way they had come, but saw nothing.

"Run!" Baron Blunder shouted, turning for the woods. However, before he had a chance to run, a black arrow sprouted from his back. Then two more. He cried out and staggered forward, dropping to the ground.

"Hold!" Erstwhyle shouted. "We're bards! We're under protection of the guild!"

In that instant, shadows seemed to stretch from the woods and coalesce into shapes. On the road a dozen mounted men appeared—huntsmen with the Dark Prince. Hounds in spiked collars and leather masks the color of blood lunged forward, barking.

The prince laughed. "Fool! You think the guild can help you? Why, you left my castle a day ago, crept out with your reward. And who is to say what happened here, so far in the woods, with only the wolves as your witnesses? Most likely, it was some robbers that found you."

The silence had been an illusion, Erstwhyle realized. Crydon had ridden him down, with huntsmen and horses and dogs. Erstwhyle had never heard a sound.

He peered to his right and left, overwhelmed and confused. What was real, what was not? Were these men mere phantasms, like the dream dragon?

"So, please me," the Dark Prince said, his voice whispering among the pines. "You will take off your clothes and run. This time it will be a proper hunt."

Erstwhyle hesitated. To race through the woods in the dark was a sure way to break a leg, or attract wolves.

"How do I know you're even real?" he said.

"Strip off your clothes," Crydon said. He urged his mount forward and with his black lance pierced the satyr's chest.

A powerful illusionist might show images, even create sounds. But he could not make a spear prick a man.

Erstwhyle gulped, let his cloak slide off. He stripped off his tunic, revealing the curly hair on his chest, the belly ring made of Sardakian gold.

"Now, run," the prince hissed. "Run for your life!"

Erstwhyle found his nerve. "No," he said. "Fight me. You're not half the man I am." He rabbed the lance and jerked it.

The Dark Prince struggled momentarily, then let go. Erstwhyle fell backward into the snow, and the lance went flying.

The Dark Prince laughed and drew his great sword. "Ha, so there is some fight in you, Goat Man!"

Erstwhyle was on his back, weaponless and weary to the bone. His friends were dead. If I'm to join them, he thought, I'll give a good accounting.

He leapt to his feet, then grabbed a burning log from the fire and waved it like a torch, startling the Dark Prince's horse. It reared, and the prince raised his sword, prepared to swing a killing blow.

The Ship of Fools exploded.

The side door blew out, slamming into the prince and knocking his horse sideways. The prince rolled and jumped to his feet. Dogs snarled and yapped, and the prince's retainers fought to control their own mounts, which neighed and bucked.

In the door to the ship, Amilee stood in her dirty dress, which billowed in the stiff wind. She was as pale as ever, and for the first time Erstwhyle realized that she had been no paler in death than she had been in life.

Her face was a feral mask of rage. She leapt toward the Dark Prince, arms spread wide—and *flew* across the clearing. In one swift motion, she twisted his head and ripped it off. As blood gushed up from his carotid artery, spurting into the air, she brought down her mouth.

"Vampire!" a huntsman shouted, and taking control of his mount, spurred away. The other horses were whinnying in confusion, and in the meager firelight Erstwhyle spotted the priest trying to control his horse.

Erstwhyle lunged past Amilee, slamming his log into the back of the priest's head, while hounds yelped in terror and raced off into the night, into the storm.

\*\*\*

~ 113 ~

"A vampire?" Erstwhyle asked later, as he sat beside the fire with Amilee. It made sense now. He remembered how cold her touch had been. And he recalled how, at first, he had been amazed that she would want to join a troop of fools as they traveled the world.

*Of course she needs to travel. She needs to feed.* It explained her penchant for long walks in the moonlight. Yet it still amazed him.

"For four years now," Amilee admitted. "I didn't want to tell you. I was afraid that you'd be afraid."

The fire crackled and a log shifted. Sparks began floating toward the heavens, and she took his hand. Her own was very cold.

"I was afraid," he admitted, "that you were afraid. I mean, I'm only half human."

She nodded. She looked content, as one does after a full meal.

"You're man enough for me," she said. But her voice was timid. "Am I . . . woman enough for you?"

He looked into her eyes, and fire gleamed in them, sparkling, like a pond on a summer's day. "You're so alive. I thought you were gone."

"I needed . . . soil from my homeland," she said. "Without it, I was weak. He knew that. It's why he always took off our clothes."

*Of course, there had been dirt on that old dress!*

"You gave me my life back," she whispered and leaned forward for a kiss. But just as his lips were about to meet hers, she twisted away, aimed lower, and he felt her cool tongue moisten his neck. A numbness seemed to spread out from her touch.

"May I?" she asked. "It won't hurt."

Eternal life? he wondered. With the woman I love?

How could it hurt?

***

Hours later, the Ship of Fools rode down out of the mountains, leaving the heights and the snow behind. For a while it stopped at a crossroads on the highway, and there Erstwhyle dragged the body of the Dark Prince to a tree and tied it so he hung from his hands.

*There should be justice in the world. This man tried to rob me. He killed my friend and tried to eat me. He made young maidens run naked in the woods, hunting them for sport.*

So Erstwhyle hung him beside the road. Before he turned away, he cut a couple of steaks from the prince's backstrap to eat on the road. He left the Dark Prince as a warning to would-be tyrants.

# Blood & Beauty

## Jeff Chapman

He scented the father and the six daughters before he heard them. Every new moon they danced, skipping through the heather, leaping and spinning. Their hair waved in the breeze, golden at the scalp before darkening to green along its length.

The monstrosity crouched lower into the blackberry brambles. Gray hair grew in wavy strands around his loins and legs, which ended in cloven hooves. His torso and arms suggested a man but wiry, yellow hair veiled his white skin in a jaundiced halo. A black mane ringed his face. Deep-seated yellow eyes peered over a broad, flat nose, and from the tip of his nostrils through his upper lip sliced a cleft from which his tongue shot to taste the air. Retractable claws adorned his fingers.

Ignoring the tantalizing berries, the half lion, half satyr risked inching forward to admire Feena, his lust and love. If they saw him, the dryads would vanish into the forest, driven off by his ugliness.

He watched for hours, yearning to hold her, to touch her tender skin. Twice she danced within reach. A single bound and she would have known the strength of his grasp, suffered his lips and tongue, but Salton checked his desire: he wanted her love.

When the dryads left the clearing, Salton rolled onto his back, waiting for limberness to return to his aching knees. He must have her. The old father dryad would suffer, but surely he wouldn't sacrifice them all to keep one.

Their magical hearts beat deep in the forest in a grove all but inaccessible to the woodsman's ax. Salton journeyed daily from his cave to caress Feena's tree, to lick and sniff her sap, and to offer his devotion. Each hemlock grew perfectly straight with delicate branches fanning out from its bole. The new growth emerged dark yellow as if the branches were tipped with gold.

The father's tree stood in the center beside a blackened, limbless trunk, which marked the mother's grave where lightning had done its worst. She must have screamed as she burned alive. Salton thanked the gods he had not heard it.

The father recoiled as Salton approached, creaking and bending as if the satyr-lion brought forth a mighty wind. Salton touched the father's bole and pressed his fingers into the furrowed bark. "Is my ugliness a threat, Lerhem? I had no part in how nature made me. Let me love your daughter."

Lerhem did not speak. The dryads, the squirrels, and even the birds fell dumb with anticipation.

"Your silence insults me." His cleft parted as he snarled through jagged teeth and red gums. "You condemn me for nature's abuse, but I *am* master of what I do."

Claws shot from his fingers and he dragged the points through the furrows, cutting to the tree's flesh. Lerhem screeched and his branches shook.

Salton withdrew his hand. His claws folded into his fingertips. "I can hurt you in ways unimaginable."

Delicate whisperings flitted among the trees like butterflies. Then the chatter ceased and a deep voice resounded in his head.

"Such a union would be unnatural. It is forbidden."

Salton roared at the sky, baring his cat fangs from point to root. The hemlocks quivered, as with the first gusts from a storm.

He raised his claws and looked about the circle at so much beauty and perfection. How could an honest plea for love be forbidden? His hand snapped downward, leaving a five-fingered gash across Lerhem's trunk.

***

"Did you hear that?" asked the elder of the two woodsmen. The handle of his ax rested on his shoulder and graying hair poked below the edge of his red, wool cap.

"It's too far. We shouldn't be going this way." Like his father, the son carried an ax and wore a red cap, but his black hair curled up below the neck, and a thick coil of rope hung from his shoulder.

The older man stopped. They were following a deer trail and something else through a stretch of unexplored forest. The noonday sun stabbed at the broad-leaf canopy overhead, pressing the forest to yield from the black of night to the cloudy gray of twilight. Squirrels scurried among the oaks. A woodpecker's knock reverberated. A grunt told them of feral pigs feasting on nuts. All these sounds were familiar and unnoticed except when they chose to listen.

"These woods are strange, Father. I can feel something here."

"Aye. Perhaps we should go back. But look at these oaks. No one has ever cut here."

They craned their necks to see the treetops well over a hundred feet above them.

"Too big for us," said the son. He pointed at the base of a massive bole. "Would take five men, maybe even six or seven, just to circle that."

Three delicate notes from a flute fluttered past.

"That," said the father.

The son shook his head. "What is it?"

The father broke through the undergrowth toward the source, drawn like a wolf to blood. The son followed, his senses clouded and dim. He felt drunk, not the way of the mead he drank to excess with his friends, but on enchantment. A witch might live out here or faeries, coaxing them to a cauldron or an Eden of no return.

For hours they traveled in fits and starts, leaving the oak and walnut forest for hemlock and pine, resolving to turn back only to plunge ahead again when the flute whispered. They emerged from the forest into a grove of golden hemlocks, which grew in a ring around another hemlock and a denuded bole, gray and cracked from the weather.

They gaped at the perfectly proportioned trees, at the green boughs tipped with gold, a species living only in myth.

"It can't be," said the son. "It's an illusion. We're bewitched."

"A gift," answered the father. "We were meant to find these." He stepped toward the fairest tree, grasped the lowest branch and broke off the tip with its mixture of green and golden needles. "Is this an illusion?"

The satyr-lion hiding in the shadows winced as his beloved shrieked. Already the unanticipated had soiled Salton's scheme. Though these woodsmen could not hear it, the trees screeched and screamed like horses in a burning stable.

With one hand Salton pressed the halves of his cleft lip together and with the other brought the hollow reeds bound with grass to his mouth. The notes diverted the woodsmen.

"And this is the grandest of them all," said the father, approaching

Lerhem. "Go on, see if you can reach around it."

The son embraced the trunk but his fingers did not touch.

"At least six more hands," said the father. "We must keep this place secret."

"Who would believe? It will take us a week to drag these home through the woods." Startled, he pointed to five parallel gouges in the bark.

"A lion, possibly. Marking his territory," said the father.

"It's too dangerous here."

"The woods are always dangerous and so is a prize worthy of song and story. We should cut one now."

The son pointed at Feena. "The fairest and the lightest."

Salton sucked in a breath. His lips quivered and his fingers shook as the two men approached Feena. The dryads squealed like dying rabbits, piercing his eardrums and shattering his concentration, which he needed most for the spell.

He squeezed his eyes shut, focusing on the words, on the two men who must forget. He repeated the words, catching their rhythm, for if that rhythm was imperfect, the spell would fail. Notes shot from the flute toward the men, who stopped before landing their blow.

They looked at one another, searching for a glimmer of comprehension, a landmark in a fog bank, but found nothing. Where? Why? What? The questions rolled about in their minds, sloshing to and fro, and in unison they shouldered their axes and strode from the grove, following the obscure path that had led them there.

\*\*\*

The boy crouched lower behind a fallen log and fountain of ferns as his father and older brother marched past, staring ahead, not speaking or singing, not smiling or frowning. Their sharp eyes did not scan the forest at all: most unusual and dangerous.

He looked back to the golden hemlocks, then slunk along the trail until he was out of sight and hearing. A giant boar crossed their path, grunted, and shook his tusks. But the men marched toward it, and if the boar had not charged away, they would have fallen over the beast's bristled back. They suffered an enchantment. About this, the boy harbored no doubts.

As the father's grip loosened, the branch that he had broken from one of the hemlocks fell out of his hand. The boy picked it up, not fully believing what he had seen until he felt the prick of the green and golden needles in his palm. He dropped the branch in a satchel, where it joined the berries he had been gathering.

The spell wore off as the pair reached familiar woods and the men began wondering at the passage of the day without cutting any trees.

The boy caught up to them. "No luck today, Father?"

The men exchanged a troubled glance. "We didn't find a tree worthy to cut today, Doran." He slapped his youngest son's shoulder. "I hope your berry picking was more profitable."

"Not so much," said Doran. "But I did find a worthy tree. I found a golden hemlock."

His older brother laughed. "And I saw a centaur mounting a river nymph."

"You saw a dying pine," said the father. "You're as likely to see a golden hemlock as a satyr."

The two men laughed as they turned toward the cottage.

Doran pulled the branch from his satchel. "Is this a dying pine?"

\*\*\*

Salton brushed the rounded nubs of his claws across Feena's trunk. The wiry hair growing on his hands and fingers caught in the bark, but he took no notice. He hummed a ballad, stroking Feena in time with the music, as if Feena was a violin and Salton the bow. The dryad giggled from the tickling.

"I would never let them hurt you," he whispered.

"No, you would not. But could you stop them?"

Salton growled deep in his throat. "You underestimate me. I would have torn their limbs and sliced their throats and drenched your roots in their blood had they struck you."

"And if they had chopped at my father or sisters?"

"They didn't. They chose the most perfect."

"If you are to have me then you must speak plainly."

"Then tell *me* plainly," said Salton. "Will you have me?"

"Do my father and I have a choice between life and death?"

"It was your father who refused me. To be ugly is to be cursed in his eyes. But do you blame me for seeking a lover's bliss?"

"I've reproached you for what you did. Not why you did it. My father is calling you."

Salton pressed his cheek against Feena and shot his tongue through his cleft to catch a drop of sap. "It won't be long, my love."

"I cannot leave without my father's permission," said Feena.

But Salton did not answer. He well knew this and growled as he approached Lerhem.

"You play reckless games," said Lerhem. "For centuries we stood here undisturbed until an abomination showed death the way."

Salton shrieked, his cry echoing through the woods and valleys as he slashed Lerhem. Amber rivulets sprang from the gouges. "Give me Feena and I'll protect you. I'll stand between all of you and any threat."

"A harbinger of danger as our savior? Your promises offer no comfort."

The grove shivered with whisperings, urgent and plaintive. Salton struggled to pick out the individual voices, to determine their tone, whether for or against him.

Lerhem groaned. "You have imperiled us, who are rooted to the earth, the victims and beneficiaries of happenstance. I do not trust your spells, but since you value your desires above our eternal destruction, we must accept your protection. I expect nothing fruitful from this union. Let us never speak of it again."

\*\*\*

Salton gathered reeds growing in the shallows of a lake and wove them into a pallet which he laid over dried moss. Across the pallet he sprinkled flower petals from every orchid he could find. His wedding bed complete, he hunted a stag, creeping up on the foraging animal at the edge of a meadow. He sprang onto the beast's back, sinking his claws into its flank and chest before crushing its windpipe between his jaws. He savored the blood dripping from his mane and hands, blood lust driving him to eat his fill, consume it raw, but for his bride he resisted.

He roasted the deer on a spit at the mouth of his cave until the meat glistened and bubbled with melting fat.

His preparations consumed a day and a night and though Lerhem and his daughters feared the time when the sun crossed the sky, Salton went to collect his bride just as the sun rose behind the eastern peaks.

"Will you hide among the hawthorn to set an ambush or wait in the open to frighten any comers without a fight?" said Lerhem.

"Today, I take my bride home." Salton stroked Feena's cheek. "Strategy is tomorrow. You've made me wait long enough."

"You brought them here," said Lerhem. "You've given away our secrets."

Salton took Feena's hand and led her from the grove, from

Lerhem's blustering, from the whispering trees.

"Father and my sisters are very frightened by what you did when you brought the woodsmen. We should not leave them during the day."

"The woodsmen have forgotten everything, and I've prepared a feast and a bed of flowers for you."

Salton talked as they trod the forest, recounting his hunt for orchids and the slaying of the stag. He bade her to sit on a log in the cool shadow of his cave's entrance. He tore meat from the roasting deer and poured wine in wooden cups. Feena nibbled at the meat, respecting Salton's kindness. The wine she gulped and after the third cup Salton moved the flask within her reach.

He ate his fill, swallowing chunks of meat whole and snapping bones to suck the marrow. Grease and wine clotted his mane. He recounted the many nights he'd watched her dance. Feena listened and smiled and when his confidence overflowed, he risked a question.

"Do you find me repulsive?"

"You're a creature with talents, like any other. Your music is certainly not repulsive."

"Ah, my flute. Many days my only companion." He wiped his greasy fingers on the goat hair covering his thighs, then raised the hollowed reeds to his lips before turning his back so she would not see him holding his cleft together.

He played a lively tune, tapping a hoof with the rhythm, and Feena danced around the ashen coals that smoked beneath the stag's carcass. His flute bore magic and any song had the power to bewitch a mortal, but Salton had no magic to bewitch a dryad.

"Why do you turn your back?" she asked.

"I am shy."

"You needn't be." Feena leapt and pranced about the coals to a song in her head. "Why would I laugh at such sweet sounds. You must play for my father and sisters when we dance in the clearing."

"I want nothing more."

"I'll speak to Father. He'll think differently when he hears you play."

Salton laid down his flute. "Could you love a face like mine?"

"I could love the man behind it, if he no longer threatened my family."

"There was no other way."

"You didn't try. You could have befriended us, entertained us with your music. Other satyrs have done so."

"Perhaps I acted rashly, but your father is stubborn."

"Cautious. As he must be. He cares only for my welfare."

"As do I. Come see the bed I've prepared before the flower petals lose their fragrance."

He took her hand and led her into his cave. His hooves clicked against the stone floor. He lit two torches, whose light revealed the pallet covered with flowers. Feena crouched to admire his work. Her beauty glowed in the wavering, yellow light. Salton stood in silhouette, his ugliness for a moment blotted out.

Feena stretched out atop the flower petals, which curled around her shoulders and hips like water. She rolled her head, taking in the myriad scents and then beckoned Salton to join her. He caressed her and bathed her with his lips, repeating "I love you" after each kiss. He could hold back no longer and mounted her, fulfilling his longings of many years. He thrust gently, taking her virginity, and as they moved together, she writhed beneath him and moaned with what Salton assumed to be passion.

Her cries multiplied. Her movements became erratic. Her fingers dug into Salton's shoulder blades. Equating her response to his prowess, he redoubled the fury of his lovemaking, his hooves clacking against the floor in time with his thrusts. Feena cried a long, diminishing scream, and then her arms went lax, sliding off Salton's shoulders. Her eyes rolled back as white as snow, and she vanished, leaving Salton to thrash about in the pool of flower petals, unfulfilled and alone.

He leapt to his hooves, cursing whatever magic Lerhem had used to summon his daughter and defile their agreement. He grabbed his flute and ran toward the hemlock grove, shouting curses. "I'll strip all the bark from his bole," he swore, "and set a fire at its base."

Dusk fell as he ascended the knoll to the grove, hoarse from running and shouting. The sun burned red to the west above the treetops. Salton stopped. The fading light flooded the grove unfiltered. Seven stumps, their tops hewn roughly with axes, sweeping to points and ridges like snow-covered mountains, marked what had once been. Sticky rivers of sap oozed from the wounds and trailed to the ground where woodchips lay scattered around each stump. Gold and green needles littered the ground, the hallowed ground of Salton's love.

The great trees lay where they had fallen, all pointing east as was the woodsmen's custom, some paean to the gods that Salton did not understand. He stumbled among the remains and counted six logs. The woodsmen had shorn the branches from two of them.

He knelt beside Feena's stump. They had taken her. He roared, wrapping his arms and legs around her decapitated trunk, and mixed his tears with her sap until the sap liquefied and Salton's tears and Feena's blood ran together.

He rose when the moon shone overhead, its gray light touching upon the hallowed ground for the first time in centuries. The grove was silent and empty. Feena's words echoed in his head. *You brought the woodsmen. We shouldn't leave them alone.* But he had seen the woodsmen work before. Tomorrow, they would bring horses and more men.

He followed the trail left by Feena's log, where the woodsmen had dragged it through the forest. The trail reeked of Feena. When he stepped from the woods into the garden behind the woodsmen's cottage, a pair of dogs barked, but Salton silenced them with a few notes from his flute.

Stepping over the sleeping dogs, he searched the yard but Feena's bole was gone, too valuable perhaps to leave unsecured. Following her scent brought him to the woodpile where her smaller branches had been stacked to cure with the other firewood, pieces of his beloved reduced to kindling, fuel for the family's cook fires.

He knelt before Feena's remains, took up his flute and played a tune in a minor key that leapt and fell with a building frenzy. At first his body tingled, then it ached, then his blood burned through every vein, a poison to him and any creature.

With the last of his failing strength, he gashed his neck with his claws before collapsing across the stack of Feena's branches. His blood boiled out of his neck and soaked the wood with toxins. The satyr's body diminished and evaporated. Salton's flute lay where he had dropped it, beside the woodpile and free of blood.

***

"Doran. Doran," called his father from outside.

His mother nodded, so Doran left his porridge to attend his father.

"Old Mrs. Cowper wants two bundles of wood. Take a satchel. She'll have seven onions for you."

He nodded and hurried inside to fetch a bag. An errand meant a trip through the village, a chance for something out of the ordinary to happen. His mother bade him to count the onions, and as he passed through the doorway, he met his older brother carrying firewood.

"The new hemlock," said the eldest brother to his mother. "Father says it's ready. That it'll burn sweet and hot."

"What?" said Doran. "I should be here when it burns."

"There's plenty of it to burn, little brother. We have all winter."

"Your brother's right," said his mother. "Now you have a reason not to tarry."

Doran frowned. Arguing would get him nowhere. He stomped outside where he'd tied the bundles of firewood and slung them over his back. He took off for the village, resentment driving his legs to a trot. He had led them to the hemlock grove. He should be the first to smell the wood burn.

Inside his tunic, the flute he had found beside the woodpile months before thumped against his chest with each stride. At least he had held the gold coins that the man at the mill had given his father for the logs. His father said they were now a rich family.

His trot slowed to a walk. He greeted the neighbors he passed but to their surprise did not stop to talk. The old woman Cowper put seven onions in his satchel, one at a time with a trembling hand. He set off for home, intending to follow the road and brook no distractions, but a sweet, young voice at a turn in the lane stopped him.

Amilee, the blacksmith's daughter, beckoned to him from a stand of birches. Doran left the path for the trees. What was some smoking wood to Amilee's bosom and lips? He had kissed her once, a hurried peck, but the memory had lingered for days. Her family guarded her virtue like a king his crown jewels. The father had ambitions for her marriage and a woodsman's son did not figure into them.

But maybe, Doran thought, with the wealth of the hemlocks, his prospects had risen.

"Why haven't you come to see me," Amilee said, "to tell me all about the hemlocks?"

"You know why I don't come to see you." They threaded their way deeper among the birches. As always, she teased him without mercy.

"You should ask my father to be an apprentice."

"And sweat over a hot fire all day?"

"And see me every day."

"Apprentices aren't rich, Amilee, but a finder of golden hemlocks is."

"Will you find more? I would love to see one."

"I don't know. I might have a knack for it, so maybe."

Doran sat beneath two birches whose boles joined at the ground. Purple and yellow wildflowers stared at the sun amid the grass cropped short by flocks of sheep on the common pasture. Amilee tucked her skirt under her legs as she joined him. Her black hair was braided into plaits tied behind her head. As an unmarried woman, she did not cover her hair.

"How did you find them?" she asked.

"It's a secret."

"Even from me?"

Doran touched the flute as he scratched his chest. "Listen to this. I've been practicing." Notes tumbled from the flute as Doran blew into the reeds and some coalesced into a melody.

Amilee giggled. "You plan to be a bard now?"

Doran ignored her. Amilee swayed, weaving to the current of the song; her eyes narrowed and her lips pursed. Doran played more as the music inspired him and Amilee seemed to enjoy it. She scooted closer, pressed her bosom against his arm and crossed her legs over his. The heat of her breath inflamed his cheeks like the bellows in her father's forge.

He stared at the tops of her breasts exposed above her bodice and followed their curves to the crease in between. So close he could touch them with the slightest move of his hand from the flute. Her softness stirred his heart to beat in rhythm with his playing.

Amilee knocked the flute from his mouth as she smashed her lips against his, pushing with her legs as if to climb into his body. Doran had spied on his brother with a girl once, so he knew something of what to do, but Amilee took him for a ride. He held on to her, simultaneously aroused and put off by her aggression. He'd thought her a virgin; coy as a spring flower, maybe; but still a virgin.

Amilee turned her back as she tightened the lacings to secure her bodice. A red bruise marred her shoulder where he had bitten her. She fiddled with her sleeve to cover it but the fabric slid down after each attempt and the bruise peeked over the edge of the linen, like a red fox at the entrance of its den. Her bosom trembled as she sniffled.

"What's wrong?" he said.

She turned to him and her eyes filled with tears. One spilled over her lashes and streaked down her plump cheek. Never had she looked so beautiful and vulnerable, no longer the teasing flirt perpetually out of reach. He wanted to feel her again. He sat up and reached for her shoulder. Amilee slapped his hand away, striking his wrist so hard that he yelped. She jumped to her feet, pulled up her skirt, and dashed through the birch trees toward the road.

Doran rubbed the red mark on his wrist, wondering what he had done wrong. When he saw the bag of onions, he cursed himself and the girl. How long? The sun had passed noontime. His mother would be furious if she wanted those onions for supper, and she would tell his father to use a switch on him.

He took three long strides through the birches, stopped, cursed, and came rushing back to find his flute among the crushed wildflowers.

No smoke rose from the chimney as he approached the cottage. Very odd for midday. A sick sense of dread ushered away his fears of punishment when he stopped before the partially open door, hanging idly from its hinges. No talking, no clatter, no noise at all spilled from the house.

He pushed the door and it creaked. He had never heard it creak before, had never opened the door to silence. He stepped inside and let loose the bag of onions, which thudded on the floor. One rolled out and stopped against his brother's arm. His family lay across the floor boards, their faces swollen and purple, their eyes bulging. An acrid smell fouled the room and wisps of yellow smoke wavered in the sunlight streaming through the windows. His eyes burned and he doubled over coughing.

He backed out the door and tripped, falling over and tumbling away from the cottage. As he lay on his stomach retching, he felt the flute against his breastbone . . . the flute that he'd found beside the woodpile, beside the hemlock wood.

# When the Faun Fell

## Rhys Hughes

After I graduated and successfully applied for a position with the Institute of Practical Cosmology I was sent to a remote part of Wales to operate an experimental telescope with the intention of confirming or refuting one of the oddest hypotheses of the origin of life.

Accordingly, I set off one cold day into the mountains on a rattling old locomotive that crawled along the rusting warped rails of a narrow-gauge railway. I was the only passenger in the gloomy carriage and I soon began to entertain doubts as to the ultimate wisdom of the abstruse career I had chosen. But it was far too late to turn back.

It might seem rather perverse to locate an important observatory in any of the so-called Celtic lands, for they are notorious nurseries of rain, mist, fogs, and other brumal inconveniences. The clouds rarely part and there is a joke that the inhabitants have no idea what the sun and moon look like. Once I laughed at the absurdity of that. Not now.

But the telescope that was my destination was a radical new type, fully cloud proof, or so Professor Regardus insisted. He had designed it himself over a period of nine years and considered it his greatest accomplishment. Perched on the peak of Mochyn Budr Mountain and immensely long, the longest telescope ever conceived, it actually poked *through* the blanket of water vapors into much clearer, purer skies.

I huddled more snugly into my coat, pulled my hat down over my ears, and rubbed my gloved hands together. The bleakness of my surroundings was so complete that I stopped looking out the window. It was unbearable for more than a few moments at a time. I shut my outer eyes and replayed in my mind the scene prior to my departure.

\*\*\*

A walnut-panelled office in one of the older wings of the Institute was the lair of my personal tutor, Professor Bo Regardus, highly respected among his colleagues both for his imagination and precision. I stood before him on a rug of curious design, an ultraviolet spiral with frayed edges. Was it supposed to represent a distant galaxy?

But the man perched on the oddly shaped chair behind the impractical rhomboid desk seemed oblivious to the peculiar furnishings around him, doubtless because of familiarity. He stared at me with eyes full of a subtle humor that I found slightly disturbing.

Then he spoke in his unique baritone, and I had the impression he was far away, at the end of a long corridor. Only Professor Regardus is able to speak loudly and quietly at the same time. I have never met anyone else who can do this unsettling, useless trick.

"Well now, Mr. Livers! You have worked hard all term and passed the final exams with flying colors—and allow me to suggest that a study of how colors stay aloft might one day be a fruitful area for research—and so I have selected you as the prime candidate for a special project of great importance to our academic reputation . . ."

I waited for him to continue. He licked his wrinkled lips with a tongue that glowed purple in the rhythmic gloom.

"Panspermia. That's the word for it!"

"I dare say it is," I agreed.

"An attempt to confirm or refute the hypothesis; that's the task. Do you appreciate the significance of this mission I'm entrusting to you? Proof of the extraterrestrial origins of life! It will change all our assumptions about biology, chemistry, and cosmology."

I nodded but I felt awkward and so I gazed around the room, desperate to find an alternative focus for my eyes, to wrench them away from those wrinkled lips and bobbing chin. On the far wall of the office slanted a portrait of Harry the New, the little king or *regulus* of our newly independent land. I stared at that.

Panspermia. The hypothesis had been around for a long time. The idea that microbes originate in the vacuum of outer space, in gas clouds or in the hearts of comets, that they fall onto planets and seed them with life, a beautiful contagion spreading complexity and perhaps eventual sentience throughout the universe. Scientific heresy but plausible enough; and fame waited for any man who demonstrated its truth. The professor noticed the direction of my gaze and turned his head.

Then he jerked a bloated thumb at Harry the New.

"It'll be a major scientific achievement for Wales, for this overlooked country of ours, this drenched clump of black hills and narrow valleys. It should put us back on the map again."

In reverence, Regardus regarded the regulus.

"What do you say?" he prompted.

I accepted the assignment, of course. And off I went.

\*\*\*

My name is Frampton Livers and I consider myself to be a champion of diligence and precision. Others share this opinion of me. I'm not given to delusions or fancies; and even when I sustained a blow on my head after a bookcase toppled onto me, my subsequent dazed ravings were muted and realistic. But how muted is the real world? The wound healed slowly and for months I wore a purple bruise that covered my forehead. I grew attached to this color, exactly the shade of certain plums and the style of prose we are urged in essays to eschew.

The rattling old locomotive finally reached the end of the line. With a groan that made my own grumbles redundant, it shuddered to a halt, and I stood and opened the creaking door of the carriage. It was as if I stared at a painting done by a depressed surrealist.

Framed by the rusty door, the landscape was rustier.

Brownish clouds foamed against the sides of Mochyn Budr Mountain, and the peak itself twisted like a mad goat's horn into the ceaseless black rain, large oily droplets of which were caught by the wind after falling to the unseen valley floor and swept back up, so that every wet globe had a second chance to spatter a poor forehead.

On the very tip of the gnarled peak was perched the

observatory, but it showed only its filthy white base. The rest was lost in the thick vapors and I had a sudden suspicion that perhaps the top had been chewed away by the acidity of the drizzle, leaving only a smelly stump like a dinosaur's foot. Should I turn back at once and forget my mission? Before I had the opportunity to seriously consider my options, the locomotive departed in a mockery of stealth, freewheeling on its ugly iron wheels with squeals of self-hating laughter. I was trapped up here.

***

So I puffed the remaining distance to the door of the observatory, and with the key Bo Regardus had given me I went inside. I found myself in a tiny antechamber that contained only a hat stand. I divested myself of my coat and hung the dripping thing up. Then I passed through into the next room, the work area, the place of starlit truth.

The eyepiece of the telescope was located here and it was connected to the smooth length of the tube and the length of this tube was remarkable. Up it went, and up, to the roof of the dome, through the roof and through clouds, and still up, and somehow I knew that it kept going up until it was out of the atmosphere and in cold space.

I marvelled at the ingenuity of the man who had constructed the device and all my doubts vanished and I became dedicated to my mission again, a research student worthy of the name. And it seemed to me that I should begin work as soon as feasible.

There was a modest kitchenette in the farther corner and I prepared tea in a teapot and dipped my hands into the biscuit tin, for when in Wales do the same as the Welsh; it's the safest way.

After this repast, which was all the more comforting for the sounds of the rain lashing the outer walls but unable to get me, I rubbed together my palms and said to myself, "Frampton! It's time to make the wise professor so proud of you that he literally explodes with admiration, smirching that rug of curious design in his office with his monumental brains." Naturally I meant that only as a primitive metaphor.

And so I fixed my best eye to the eyepiece, but there was no peace for my eye; not for my mind or my poor soul.

At once I was transported beyond this mundane world.

I floated free in the unhappy vacuum.

Stars and planets forced themselves into my brain, jumping down the tube and through my dilated pupil, and tightrope walking along my optic nerve to the security of my pulsing lobes.

"That's odd!" I said as I tore myself away. And it was.

\*\*\*

I had realized that there were no lenses in the instrument. It was simply a hollow tube of immense length that connected space with the ground. The audacity or stupidity of this design so bewildered me that I was forced to boil the kettle for a second session of tea.

As I dipped my umpteenth biscuit into the muddy brew in my delicate china cup, patterned with pictures of coal miners and other typical Welsh conceits, there occurred to me the suspicion that somebody had stolen the lenses, perhaps a disgruntled farmer in a valley below the mountain. After all, this was a region of crass superstition.

But that didn't make too much sense. How could a simple farmer reach outer space to snatch the big lens from the far end of the telescope? It isn't possible to escape Earth's gravitational pull in a tractor. Much more likely that the lenses were never included in the first place, a probability that led me to conclude the observatory was a trick.

Or if not a trick, then a deliberate scam, a way of claiming government research funds and diverting them into private pockets. Bo Regardus as a master conman, an academic thief; the notion wasn't wholly risible, but if this truly was the case, why send me here?

I drained my teacup and returned my face to the eyepiece; and my eye once again flew among the constellations.

"Ingenious!" I breathed softly, as understanding came.

There was no fraud involved at all. This telescope didn't require lenses because it operated on a new principle.

The layers of air inside its length were at different densities, packed on top of each other like sheets of ultra-pure glass, so light from the universe was refracted through lenses made of *air*.

The arrangement worked superbly. It was wonderful.

"Frampton Livers," I said to myself, "you have been given a

chance to make cosmological history with this magnificent invention, so don't spoil your prospects with a distrustful mind."

I don't enjoy berating myself but often it's necessary.

As I continued to observe the multitude of stars and nebulae, an object as tiny and dim as a spider's chin swam into my field of view; and though it should have been insignificant when compared with the glittering gems of the firmament, it compelled my attention. I frowned darkly, squinted at it, unglued myself from the eyepiece, wiped my sodden forehead with my sleeve, switched eyes and focused again.

The speck was still there and now it was bigger . . .

\*\*\*

Over the following hour I watched it closely and it grew steadily and then I realized that it was inside the telescope and was spiralling down the tube toward me. Something alien and weird had entered that immense hollow cylinder, the *starpipe* of dreams, and was plummeting to the ground with a silent shriek. Taking a series of deep breaths, I calmed myself and made the necessary calculations in my head.

It's common knowledge that an object that enters our atmosphere from the void will burn up unless it is sufficiently large and robust. And yet the conditions inside the telescope were milder than those outside: the layers of rarefied air were softer, less prone to generating friction, and lightning strikes were also extremely implausible. I deduced that the object would survive the fall and impact the ground.

The ground in this particular case was the floor of the observatory, or if I didn't remove myself, my own face.

It seemed wise to leave before the critical moment.

From the rate at which the object grew in size, I estimated the time of its arrival as ten minutes into the future. Basing my actions on this figure, I transferred myself with reasonable haste into the antechamber, where I retrieved my raincoat. I then opened the outer door and braved again the elements of our more prosaic world, the lashings of remorseless rain that slapped the exposed skin of my hands and forehead like the bitter tears of one hundred thousand betrayed wives.

Hiding behind a rock, I waited for the collision.

***

But it never came. The clouds frothed and glooped over the summit of the mountain, lapping the base of the lopsided observatory until it resembled the largest toddler in existence paddling in milky coffee, but there wasn't any hint of an explosion, no sparks or rubble. Nothing but the howling of the sour wind. I continued to wait anyway.

Thirty minutes later, it became clear that the expected catastrophe was a dud, some sort of illusion, and I returned inside to inspect the results of the strange object's fall. But everything was the same as I'd left it, so with a sigh of frustration I stepped to the eyepiece of the telescope and placed my eye against the metal. Then I screamed.

The visage of a laughing goat peered back at me!

I toppled over in astonishment and clutched the eyepiece for support, but it wrenched itself off the instrument, opening the hollow tube, and the impossible goat plopped out, hooves kicking.

A musty smell assailed my nostrils, I felt warm wet breath on my neck, and slitted yellow eyes swam before me.

Then I tumbled and rolled; and the goat came with me, in my arms, an awful and absurd companion to share an accident with, and we ended up next to the kitchenette. Its wispy beard tickled the inside of my left elbow and I shrugged myself free and stood erect.

But the goat was up before me; and then I saw that it had only two legs. It was a man.

But not a real man; a combination of man and goat.

Some sort of satyr or faun . . .

"How did you get inside the telescope?" I cried.

He leaped onto the kitchenette worktop, stood with hairy hands on hips, and smirked down at me. "I really don't know what you are alluding to. I know nothing about any telescope. This is an artificial womb, a birth canal that connects the up with the down."

My legs became wobbly. "You speak human language?"

"If you prefer, I can talk my own."

"No, no, I like it this way."

"We drift free in the vacuum of interstellar space in the form of seeds, at the mercy of the solar winds and the gravitational currents. Many of us land on inappropriate worlds; we have no choice. So when we see such a miracle as this tube protruding from your world, we have no hesitation in making use of it. So would you if you—"

"Were a goat too," I finished his sentence for him.

He corrected me. "A star goat."

I accepted the rebuke without protest. Clearly he was more than just an ordinary goat. There was something unassailable about him; he gave off a sequence of sparkles that weren't dewdrops in his hair but something else, the sharp glints of an adamantine compound. He was half goat, half man, but also half mineral; and if those fractions add up to more than one, I can only respond that *he* was more than one too, in fundamental essence and bearing. I felt overawed in his presence.

Now I comprehended why I had timed his descent to Earth incorrectly. I had assumed his shape was getting bigger simply because it was nearing my eye; whereas in fact he was turning from a seed into an adult goat man and growing bigger as he fell. So he had seemed closer than he was. The professor would laugh at me for making such an elementary error; I knew this. But I couldn't wait to take him back to the Institute and demonstrate him in front of my peers. He was divine.

\*\*\*

We waited in the rain for the rattling locomotive and the goat wore my raincoat and hat, his astral strangeness hidden from the gaze of normal folk, who would misunderstand him.

Without any protection, I sagged under the onslaught of oily droplets that lashed me like quicksilver ball bearings, stinging my eyes, blanching my skin, turning my hair into tendrils.

"Now I understand why it's called Panspermia."

"I beg your pardon?" he said.

"The theory that life originated in deep space. Pan is the god of your kind, isn't he—the head star goat?"

He ignored my question. "Here's the train."

The black monstrosity groaned up the rails toward us, flaking rust as it went, coming to a squealing halt, but juddering horribly like a man who has swallowed hundreds of springs and is dying in bed as a result. The driver beckoned to us with a gesture that might have been a challenge to a duel and we painfully climbed aboard.

During the long journey back to the semi-civilization of the city where the Institute is based, I studied my travelling companion from the corner of my eye, for it is not yet illegal to steal glances. He seemed satisfied by his situation and the topaz orbs of his eyes blinked merrily at the sombre scenery outside. I imagine that bleak valleys and withered farms compare favorably with the nullity of outer space.

There still remained the mystery of how he could speak my language, but I settled this question in my own mind by telling myself that it was an example of magic, pure and simple. It's a truism that star goats shouldn't be expected to conform to the conventions of surface animals. And yet at no point did I dare ask him for his name.

***

We stood before Professor Regardus, the space satyr and myself, on that rug that resembled a map of a galaxy; and the smooth walnut-panelled walls glowed warmly in the light of the lamp that pulsed on the rhomboid desk; and I waited to be praised fulsomely.

But the professor took it all in his stride, a stride much longer than any I had beheld before, mental or physical, and he merely waved a hand and said lightly, "Yet another one. Excellent!"

I frowned and spluttered, "He is conclusive proof of the correctness of the Panspermia hypothesis, isn't he?"

"Oh, I don't think we require even more proof . . ."

I was shocked and retreated a step.

Regardus gazed at me critically, but there was no unkindness or even disapproval in his expression. He said: "Mr. Livers, do you mean to say that you believed what I told you the last time you stood here in front of me?"

"Why yes, of course. A research project of the utmost importance. An innovative telescope on Mochyn Budr Mountain. Are you about to inform me that those were merely illusions?"

"In a sense, yes, dear Frampton. There is no telescope on that peak nor has there ever been. It's an incubator, a device for accelerating the growth of the star goats from loose seeds to adults in just a few hours. The way I see it—and I must stress I'm not the only one—is that the humans have made a mess of this world. They have lost a sense of magic and the hope and wonder that accompanies it; so it seems a good idea to encourage as many star goats to settle here as possible."

"You talk about humanity as if you don't belong."

He shrugged. "If I had told you the truth at the beginning, you would have refused the assignment, deeming me mad. You had to experience it for yourself; you had to deliver a star goat in person. There was no other way of winning you over to our side."

"Are you going to publish my results or not?"

"No. It's best to keep everything a secret until enough of the star goats are in place to make a real difference."

I was seized with a strange impulse. I overturned his desk, crouched forward, and lifted him off his chair. "You're a goat too, aren't you? You are a satyr from space just like him . . ."

And to my eternal shame, I yanked his trousers down.

"Now I'll learn the facts!" I cried.

But his legs were human legs, hairy but not hairy enough, and it was clear that his slippers sheathed feet rather than hooves. I fell back and I saw my future career crumble like one of those rotting farmhouses up in the blasted valleys; but the professor calmly rearranged his clothing and righted his desk and then said softly: "That was *my* reaction when I was first told."

His voice was rich, a unique baritone, and once again I had a feeling he was far away, at the end of a long corridor or inside a tube connecting Earth with the Beyond. And I knew at once that I would dedicate all my talents to the cause, to the secret integration of the star goats, to the next renaissance of my own weak species.

I fell to my knees and rolled my eyes in an improvised gesture of utter submission; but then my vision happened to alight on the portrait of King Harry the New, and I saw clearly and with an expanding inner mirth what I had never noticed before. His horns.

# Satyrday

## Howard Phillips

Being a mythical creature in the modern world is a pain in the ass. And when your ass is a goat's ass, it's a monster pain.

My name is Darren, and I'm a satyr, bleeding from the stomach and chest on the top-floor balcony of a high-rise apartment complex.

I flatter myself to think you'd like to know how this all came to be. Well, I have to put it in context, so I hope you're ready to walk a mile in my hooves.

First let's talk about satyrs.

MYTH: We're jovial little pipe-playing goat men that dance around drunk, banging forest nymphs.

I ain't jovial. I play the saxophone. I dance like a three-legged centaur. And I don't have a nymph fetish.

FACT: We have an epic penchant for alcohol, sex, and music. Call them our Achilles heel.

I binge drink for breakfast. My libido's as active as Artemis's bow. And I know a jukebox better than Apollo.

I didn't cast the fucking mold, all right? There's some kind of pantheon irony in the fact that "satyr" is a near homonym with "sate," because our addictions are insatiable. I'd file a complaint, but Dionysus is busy running breweries in Ireland, and Ares is vacationing in the Middle East.

That said, I wake up this morning at the crack of noon, hungover, with a hooker named Sally, naked but for a pair of plastic antlers.

Yeah, she's a human. We work because she has dissociative

disorder, making it hard for her to distinguish fantasy from reality.

But her ass is Zeus's magnum opus.

I smack her on her finest feature and tell her to get dressed; I'm flying to Hollywood. I'm not, but it's the only thing that gets her moving.

She dresses into her magistrate uniform and tries to leave my apartment through the refrigerator door. I show her the right exit, kiss her on the cheek, and tell her I'll see her tonight.

I turn on Tchaikovsky and sip a bottle of Bailey's on the balcony. The city below is a mosaic of stone, glass, metal, and flesh, dimly lit by smog-filtered beams of Helios's cosmic orb. Car engines, pigeon wings, and a murmured choir of voices assimilate into a discordant urban symphony called "Friday Afternoon."

Inside, I polish off a jar of kalamata olives and wash it down with the rest of the Irish cream; the breakfast of chumps.

Then I jerk off to Yo-Yo Ma in the shower, pretending my dick's a cello bow.

I throw on some baggy jeans, a hoodie, and boots with gel inserts fitted to my hooves. And then I don a fleece cap over my horns and pop my hood up. My human disguise: satyr incognito.

I lock up, leave out, and wait in the hallway for the elevator. Inside, Señora Esperanza is coddling Gordita, one of those glorified hamsters humans call "Chihuahuas." When I get in, the dog starts huffing and yelping like Darth Vader squeezing a whoopee cushion.

It can smell me, and it knows something's up. I try to make light of it. "She can smell her own kind," I say. No one suspects a half goat of a professed canine. I force a laugh.

"*Eres un perro?*"

Señora Esperanza asks if I'm a dog.

"*Si,*" I answer. "I must be. My mother always told me my father was a dog. And my father always told me my mother was a bitch. So biologically . . ."

"*Ay caramba!*" she exclaims. "*Vaya con Dios.*"

She crosses the air in front of me and gets off on her floor.

"Woof," I say, as the elevator door closes.

Downstairs in the lobby, Lenny the security guard is watching porn on a computer monitor. He pulls up solitaire when I walk by and crosses his ankle over his knee to hide his tented Dickies crotch. "I looked up that word on dictionary-dot-com," he tells me.

"Yeah?" The sound is still going on the minimized sex screen. The panting and moaning don't mesh well with the stacks of cards displayed on the monitor.

"Yeah." Lenny coughs and hits mute. "Satyriasis: uncontrollable or excessive sexual desire in a man. Like nymphomania in a woman."

"You got it," I say with double meaning.

He looks offended. "That's what you think I have?"

I hit the volume button on his keypad.

The speakers resume, sounding a screaming orgasm.

Lenny blushes and hits mute. "Well maybe you just think that's what I've got because that's what you've got." He smiles, proud to be on the offensive.

He's right, in a manner of sorts, only his condition is my identity. "Don't make me your scapegoat, Lenny."

"Scapegoat?" I hear him pulling up dictionary.com as I walk out the door.

I head to the station and squeeze into a tight-packed subway car. Two stops in, my mother calls, long distance, from Greece, only she blocks her number so I can't tell it's her.

"Hello?"

"Darren, it's your mother. I'm going to talk for thirty seconds and you're going to listen. I'm worried sick about you, up in that big city all alone, never calling to tell me you're all right."

It's been thirty seconds and she's still going. Meanwhile, my ass is brushing against nine different people in the overcrowded compartment. I'm trying not to draw any attention to myself, but I've got this shrill voice squawking through the speaker. People are starting to look at me.

"Mom, now's not a good time," I cut in.

But she's already built up momentum. "Your father's having a kidney taken out in August. I keep telling him to cut back on his drinking, but he's all like, 'I'm a satyr,' and this, that, and the other."

More people are paying attention, eavesdropping on my conversation. I tighten my hood and lean in toward the window. "Mom, I have to go."

"It's dangerous in the city, you know? People get stabbed and shot all the time. Can you imagine a satyr going into a public hospital for treatment?"

"I have to go, Mom." I hang up the phone and try to look as

normal and uninteresting as possible, but my heart is beating like a horny old man in an erotic movie theater.

I slow my breathing, get off two stops early, and walk. My head aches like I've been cleaning my ears with an oil drill. I stop at a local dive for a drink.

Aphrodite's fairer twin is gracing a silver barstool.

I hear the distant twang of Cupid's bowstring and take a seat beside her. My vision dallies on her ample bosom, double D's cresting in the mouth of a V-cut halter top.

Velvety amber tresses flow sumptuously as caramel liqueur over her silken carnality. I want to pour Shiraz down her smooth, sculpted calves and sip the runoff from her toes.

"Macallan twenty-five," I tell the bartender, still fixed on the belle at the bar.

The aged scotch trails a smooth familiar burn down my throat, pooling in my stomach.

I strut beside the goddess and hit her with my best line. "Hello." I gaze into her honey-brown eyes as only a satyr can, wild as an animal yet soft as a poet. A waft of sweet, floral perfume sends my hormones on the fritz, an intoxicating blend of lavender and vermouth. "I'm Darren."

"Marcy," she sings. I let my touch linger after our handshake and she returns my smile.

"*Merci,* Marcy." I mean it when I say it.

She laughs. "Thank you for what?"

I pause, staring. "Your captivating allure."

Demur, she smiles and blushes. "I'm meeting someone here." She seems sad to confess it.

"I forgive you," I say without thinking.

She giggles, but stops abruptly and stares uncomfortably high over my head. Behind me there's a hate-filled, two-eyed descendent of a Cyclops, spewing anger like furnace heat.

To the chest at eye level, I say the first thing that comes to mind: "Fee-fi-fo-fum." It doesn't help matters.

The titan lifts me off the ground by my hoodie collar like I'm just another dumbbell. Face-to-face, I can smell the cheeseburger on his breath and envision myself as pulverized goat souvlaki.

Where's Heracles when you need him?

In a swift and sudden rush of movement, he pulls me in and

throws his bodyweight behind a head-butt, smacking his skull against mine.

The room turns into a ringing white flash. When I come to, a second later, I'm standing there, dazed but fine, and he's sleeping on the floor like a drunken corpse.

The big dummy didn't know that beneath a couple layers of thin cloth I've got horns to shame the Billy Goats Gruff.

Marcy's got her hands on her cheeks in some kind of shocked arousal. In my bottom periphery I see the rhythm of her breasts in heavy breathing. I step so close that our lips are an inch apart and she can feel my erection on her thigh. "So, where were we?"

She kisses me, lightly on the cheek, unzips my pants, and sticks a napkin in my fly with her number written on it in lipstick. My eyes follow her ass out the door.

I scram when the bartender calls the cops.

Running like a human is difficult with the inverted knees of a goat. It resembles the hobble of a constipated cripple. I slow to a saunter when I'm out of eyeshot.

I duck into a Holiday Inn and slide into the conference room, ten minutes late for the Mythical Creature Support Group meeting that had already begun.

I mouth "sorry" to the mermaid in the wheelchair with the blanket over her "legs," pointing to her watch.

"I feel like Atlas, burdened by this world of secrets I have to carry every day." The speaker is a gorgon with sunglasses on, snake-hairs sedated and tied into a bun. "Why do we resist the urge to step out and say *I am?*"

The mermaid moderator nods. "I think it's because we expect rejection. A minotaur goes for a walk in the woods in Orleans, California, gets filmed, and people are screaming *Sasquatch* for years. A hydra goes for a dip in Loch Ness, and all the Scotts are yelping *Monster.*"

"And so we never try, for fear of failure?" the gorgon asks.

"Failure costs," the mermaid answers. "But someday, someone will try, and it will be better for us all . . . or not."

As usual, I don't say anything during the meeting. Words are a sorry substitute for action. And, for now, inaction seems the proper action. I sound like Socrates' grandfather.

I walk home after the meeting, drink a bottle of Kentucky

bourbon, and rub one off before I head to work.

The Labyrinth jazz lounge is a dusky seclusion tucked into a maze of back alleys. Subdued black lights bathe the darkness in a dull purple glow, allowing patrons to haunt the shadows and indulge their vices in private misery.

I mingle around until stage call, and then take up my sax and sit, spotlit on the stage. I drown thought in the bass and snare of the lead-in, tapping a hoof to the underbeat, and then give music the reins.

My "voice" joins in, crisp and as squeaky clean as Cerberus's balls, what with three heads and all. My sad tormented wail is worthy of the Underworld.

My cheeks swell like a puffer fish trying to blow out birthday candles, as I bare my soul. I'm surprised to find it sadder than I thought.

I think of Marcy and how I can never see her again, lest I be unmasked. I think of the mermaid in the wheelchair struggling, depressed, through her secret coexistence. And I think of myself, enslaved to programmed instincts, routinely suffering insatiable desires.

A fiery dirge rails against the silence, screaming where I cannot, each note a short-lived fairy dancing the air unseen.

And then I think about tomorrow, its bland repetition and bleak prospects, and the tempo falls like Icarus. The band stops now, and it's only the sax, singing like a well-tuned goose's lullaby.

I am Orpheus. I am Prometheus. I am a dissatisfied wooden doll pretending I'm a real boy.

Silence comes, accented now by earlier melancholy.

Applause follows. It's an ovation. I realize I'm shaking and tears have wet my face. Across the bar men and women are raising their glasses. I've never played so well before.

In that momentary triumph, spotlighted in the crowd's eye, I want to rip my fleece cap off and bleat, to reveal myself in the wake of grand approval. Isn't it better to be hated for who you are than loved for who you're not?

My resolution falters and then fails as the clapping ceases. I need a drink.

The bartender says it's on the house. And patrons send a slew of drinks my way.

Drunk, I exit through the blurred gateway, which should be the back door.

The alley outside is as dark and foul as Hades' short hair. I stumble out with an overflowing tip jar tucked under one arm and a handful of salted barroom peanuts.

"I'm a satyr," I tell a rat, a bottle, and a trash can.

I start up Mount Olympus's little nephew. Streetlights are swaying overhead like bulb-sized fireflies. I try to use the line in the concrete between the sidewalk and the curb to walk straight, but it's not working. I've got enough booze in me to intoxicate a Girl Scout troop.

I stop on top to gain my bearings, maybe navigate by the stars. But I'm no Argonaut.

I don't know where I am, but some guy in an alley does. And so does his knife. The blade slides into my belly like I walked into a hip-high unicorn. I go down like Troy.

Now I'm lying in a puddle of my own blood. The fall shatters my tip jar, sending dollar bills everywhere. The masked man starts stuffing his pockets with red-green currency before reaching into my pocket.

"Not the napkin," I whisper, grabbing the bandit's pant leg. He kicks me in the face. My hat goes flying off, unveiling my twisted curling horns.

"Holy shit!" my attacker shouts. "What the fuck?" He throws my money down and takes off running, Marcy's napkin still in hand.

I struggle to stand, tears running down my face. "Wait!" I scream. "Take the money." I just wanted to be mugged the same as anybody else. I throw salty peanuts in his direction.

It's just as well, I tell myself. Marcy would curse and run if she knew.

I'm bleeding. I'm drunk, lost, lonely, and bleeding.

Eventually, I stagger home, gore running warm and sticky through my fingers as I hold my cap over the wound.

I open the door to the apartment lobby, dripping blood onto the glossy tile floor. Lenny puts his porn on pause and looks up. "Darren?"

"Scapegoat," I confess.

I see his eyes run the gauntlet of emotion: surprise, betrayal, fear, anger . . .

He draws his side arm and fires all ten rounds. One catches me in the chest, and breathing gets hard. Empty, he throws his gun down and runs.

The elevator door opens. Inside, Señora Esperanza stands frozen in horror, holding whimpering Gordita up as a body shield.

"Baa," I say, spewing blood and spittle. She runs. *"Vaya con Dios,"* I call after her.

I get off on my floor, and Sally's waiting in the hallway. Her normalcy is surreal. "Hey, Darren."

"Not tonight, Sally," I manage between wheezes. "I'm flying to Hollywood." She nods and leaves without a question.

I unlock the door and enter my apartment, alone as I'd been all day. Somehow, I'm horny and thirsty . . . again.

"Know thyself," the Oracle says. Dying, my purpose becomes as clear as a ghost wrapped in cellophane.

I strip down to my mythical birthday suit, my hairy goat haunches wet with blood, and walk out on the balcony where my day started at noon.

And here we are, together now. It's midnight.

Standing on the edge of the rail, I greet the world. "Hello."

And then I take one small step for a satyr, one giant leap for myth-kind. Pedestrian gasps, camera flashes, and a choir of reporters will assimilate into a breaking-news symphony called "Satyrday."

# Opiate of the Lonely One

## Fel Kian

Late afternoon melded like liquid metals into early evening. The waft of metropolitan excess, waste, disinfection, and rot—each vying for supremacy—was inescapable. In the courtyard behind the Hotel Syrinx the miasma was even more prominent, as someone had tried to mask the lingering stench of a recent garbage pickup by sprinkling cheap perfume against the bins.

Martin tried not to gag. He coughed into his fist and took deep breaths of his own clean palm. The scent of the liquid soap from the office restroom was anything but comforting, but it was better than the alternative. A scraggly rhododendron mocked him with a shake of its leafy frame.

It was a wonder that plant life existed at all in this human-made cesspit of bricks and glass and mortar. Martin's hatred of the city had not diminished in the few lackluster years he had lived there. Indeed it had intensified beyond all reasonable proportion. Yet this was where he needed to be, a bustling metropolis of opportunity, the heart of modern progress. It was an affliction he had brought upon himself, one he privately bemoaned but nevertheless endured.

"Is there something you want?"

Martin had been milling about the courtyard for an hour, lost in speculation and growing apprehension, trying to recall who had tipped him off about this relatively unknown rendezvous point. Perhaps an online chat room or an overheard conversation between two licentious execs. It scarcely mattered now.

He smiled at the dark-haired youth eyeing him with reservation . . . or envy, perhaps. Envy at the sight of his fancy shoes, creaseless suit, and necktie. No, not envy—but disdain. Martin had come directly from the office. He had not taken the time to go home and change into something less formal. That path led to hesitation, a chance to back out and delay another day, another week. Another lifetime. No. Sometimes the only way to live life to the fullest was to bypass the safe, the rational, and leap into the fray.

Besides, he didn't need a second fix; he feared overdose.

"Yes," said Martin. "I suppose I do."

"I'm guessing that's not a badge in your pocket?"

Martin shook his head. The youth was lovely. He had sharp cheekbones and a taste for glamour. Eyeliner accentuated his long lashes and a touch of rouge drew attention to his soft lips set against a hard mouth. He cast cautious glances around the courtyard, although they were alone and a short dash to a major street.

Martin withdrew his hands from his pockets and held them up. "No, I'm not a cop or a social worker or some nut job. Though maybe I am a bit nuts to hang around here while the sun goes down."

"You got cash?"

"How much are you asking?"

The smile he flashed Martin sent his heart aflutter. The blood rushed south, and Martin turned his head in as casual a manner as possible, trying to shield his mounting excitement and the overt joy he felt for his resurrected libido.

"Depends," said the youth, "on what we're talking about."

Martin told him. Negotiations ensued and ended abruptly. The youth had all the chips. Martin was new to this sort of exchange of services, and the youth had pegged him right off as a newbie and milked him for more than he might usually have gotten away with. Ultimately, Martin was compliant. The final sum wasn't unreasonable. Not for him anyway, who would have gladly paid double for a boy so lovely.

"Okay," he said once Martin had dished out half the payment on good faith. "I'm going to make a call on my cell. In ten minutes I'm going to make another one. Then another when we get to your place, and then one more before I leave."

Martin frowned. "I assumed this was all going to be anonymous."

"You can listen to what I say. It's just a precaution."

"A precaution?"

"It's my thing. Call me paranoid."

"No, sorry, I understand."

"Safety first."

"Right." The perpetual nagging doubt Martin had fought hard to repress was beginning to surface. Maybe this was not such a good idea. Maybe he should have gone to the video store instead, or spent the night downloading from some preferred websites—although these were pale alternatives to flesh and blood. He'd made it this far; farther than he would have imagined. The boy had a right to be cautious. In his line of work it was probably as necessary as using a condom.

And he was attractive, tantalizing, sensual . . . downright *hot*. Really fucking hot! He was wearing leather pants that beautifully described his trim and round buttocks. The black-collared shirt was buttoned down to reveal just a glimpse of that smooth, tawny chest. A veering bulge even hinted at his endowment. The kind of smolderingly beautiful hunk Martin would surreptitiously ogle from a distance and quickly memorize for later recall, once he was alone and horny.

He made the call then, saying only, "It's me, yeah, we're leaving," and hanging up.

"Right," Martin repeated. "Let's go then."

"Lead the way."

He took side streets and alleyways, moved swiftly across quiet residential neighborhoods, and cut through two small parks, one of which had a rowdy gaggle of teens around the swing set, who were too busy mucking about to pay them the slightest attention.

Martin never once glanced back. He reached a district of militant townhouses, zero traffic, and one stray black cat. Not a curtain stirred; no bored or nosey neighbors here. It was the sort of dead pseudo-suburban street that made you believe you had entered The Midwich Cuckoos novel.

Once Martin had climbed the steps to his door and put the key in the lock, the boy was there, standing next to him, smelling of cloves and cinnamon. Martin went in first, then stood aside in the narrow hallway, letting the boy pass in order to shut and lock the door behind him.

The youth edged sideways, lightly brushing his lovely rear end against Martin's crotch. Professional technique? Martin wondered, but not unhappily. By now he had a raging hard-on from a battle of suppression he had (somewhat gladly) fought and lost en route.

Don't be premature, he chided himself.

The youth turned left into the living room and without permission or prompting made himself at home on the leather sofa. Martin hated the trendy "modern look" of most homes, with their leather furniture and surgical steel coffee tables and minimalist decor—but the fetishist in him loved the smell and feel of leather and vinyl. The youth's attire certainly complemented the furniture.

"Nice pad," said the youth. "Smells kinda funky though. Earthy." He glanced around, perhaps looking for potted plants, but didn't spot any. "What's your name anyway?"

Martin moved into the adjoining kitchen, visible through a partition in the wall. His reply was delayed as he grabbed two glasses from the cupboard and a bottle of red cabernet sauvignon from below the counter.

How was he to reply? Should he use his real name? Was there any harm in that? Or would it be more thrilling to role play?

"Brian," Martin replied, hoping to sound genuine. "Brian Kinney."

The youth nodded, unimpressed. He withdrew his cell phone again. "Okay, Mr. Kinney."

"Brian."

"Brian. Gotta make another call."

"Be my guest," said Martin, but the youth was already talking, a rapid succession of *yups* and *yeahs* and *all rights*, and it was over.

Was that inane chatter or some sort of code? Martin mused.

"Wine okay?" Martin came into the living room.

"I don't need a drink. Got any beer?"

"I'm afraid not . . ."

The youth smirked, but accepted the glass.

"What should I call you?" said Martin.

"Whatever you want."

"Justin?"

Justin shrugged, took a tentative sip of the wine, and pulled a face. Noticing that Martin was watching him, he smiled, dipped his little finger into the glass, and drew a crimson streak over his lips as if applying gloss, then slowly licked it off.

Martin reached for his wallet, took out the remainder of the bartered cash. The boy's gaze instantly flickered to the money as Martin set it on the table, an instant of weakness revealing itself: he was like a starved animal catching his first glimpse of nourishment in too long an interval.

Justin stood up and went over to Martin, who was now sitting on his black leather recliner. His pants swished and creaked when he moved. He knelt and unzipped Martin's fly.

"You're a big boy, Brian."

Martin sighed.

"I'm gonna gag on this beast."

But Justin was a pro: he didn't gag once. He brought Martin close to the edge a couple of times, but backed off at Martin's gentle command.

Martin was in his own world. A private mantra circled inside his head. He had to keep a firm hold on the reins, or else he'd blow his load in one go, which was no good. He might not have the opportunity to recover and then come a second time. He wanted the whole experience to last. A gradual build up in lieu of a transient eruption. So he filled his mind with thoughts of death; death to prevent premature ejaculation. Death to prolong the pleasure. The boy was good, too good. He needed a rest.

Martin disengaged himself, and carefully tugged his sensitized manhood back into his briefs. He gave Justin's crotch a tentative stroke, feeling a tumescence there. The boy emitted a sexy little moan to show that he was not altogether impassive or displeased.

"Let's go up to the bedroom," said Martin, rather breathlessly.

Justin drained his glass. "A top off first?"

Martin turned and bent as he grabbed his drink from the coffee table, losing sight of Justin for an instant, which was long enough. He was slammed in the face before he had fully righted himself.

The force of the blow wrenched his head and broke his lower jaw, shattering two or three teeth in the process. He fell to his knees, blinded and confounded by the pain. The wineglass, however, did not suffer even a hairline crack. Martin had always been proud of his glassware; it was sturdy stuff.

***

Justin didn't wait for the old fart to recover. He retracted his arm and delivered a second, more powerful blow. Martin's elbow connected with the rim of the coffee table on his way down, and Justin didn't know if the resultant crack was the wood splintering or the poor bastard's skull caving in. Nor did he care. Martin slumped, unconscious, over the staining red wine that was seeping into the rug.

Justin bent down and placed the glass under his nose to make sure he was still breathing. Satisfied, he shoved the money into his pocket and, not without some difficulty, heaved Martin over his shoulder and carried him upstairs.

He laid the dirty old bastard on his bed and took a moment to admire the room, decorated with framed, erotic photography and bondage gear aplenty. Kinky, but too much so. This was one hardcore fetishist, but it seemed as if he was overcompensating. The photographs were difficult to discern, even at close range.

He leaned forward to examine one and then jerked back. He

realized that what he was looking at was the bole of a tree carved into the likeness of a young girl, who was frozen in a state of agony—or ecstasy—and transformation.

It was incredibly real; in fact, parts of her looked rather . . . fleshy. This wasn't erotic at all. He didn't want to look at any of the others.

Worry seized him. He was wasting time. He raced back downstairs and scrambled to find some duct tape. He disembowelled the front closet, swore, and then shoved everything back. He checked the small bathroom, to no avail, then moved into the kitchen, but found nothing beneath the sink either.

He began randomly pulling out drawers and stopped.

"Okay," he muttered to himself, panting slightly. "Take it easy. Stop acting like an amateur."

There was an order to things. As long as he stuck to the plan he had nothing to fear. First, he told himself, make the call. He made the call. He related the address and the condition of the victim. "Fine," he finished. "I'll see you."

Second, he found a rag and wiped the fingerprint trail he had left behind. Next came the duct tape, which he eventually discovered in a toolbox in the guestroom closet. By the time he had the still unconscious Martin securely bound, there came a sequenced knock at the door.

A slimmer, taller youth in a tan leather jacket slipped through as soon as Justin opened it. He began to greet him but was cut off.

"Call me Justin. In case the fucker wakes up."

"Fine," replied the other boy. He was about the same height and build as Justin, but he had longer hair and a feral grin that accented his canines. "Who am I then?"

"Ted."

"Sure. Whatever. You think he'll wake up?"

"Not any time soon. And if he does there's a likely probability that he'll need a CAT scan."

"You brained this one too?" Ted slipped into the living room. "What's with you and knocking people on the head? Is it symbolic or something, like revenge for having to *give* them head?"

Justin grinned. "No, I like that part."

Ted lifted one of the glasses, and as he examined it he remarked, "You fuck him first?"

Justin smirked and shuffled off into the kitchen. "Christ, Ted. Don't start acting all jealous. We've got a job to do. Let's just clean the place out and go, all right? It was as much your idea as mine—"

"Yeah, yeah—all right! What's this guy got? Can't be much if he lives in a townhouse."

Justin rifled through the kitchen drawers and cabinets. "He's a suit. He's gotta be loaded. Just go check out his wristwatch. Posh stuff. And earlier I saw . . . here, look at this." He held up his find. "How's this for posh? Pure fucking silver."

"Are the walls thick enough, you think? Anyone see you come in?"

"Look, we're safe. Sooner we get this stuff in the van, the better."

Ted moved into the kitchen and grabbed Justin by the waist. "Didn't bring the van," he said, yanking him forward so that their pelvises joined. "You give me a fucking boner in those pants, you know that?"

"Come on, not now. What do you mean you didn't bring the van?"

"Traded up for a convertible."

"Great. So we've got a hot car sitting outside?"

"We've got a hot rod in here."

"Would you quit—what the fuck was that?"

Ted swerved around and reached behind his belt. They stood side by side, staring at the cellar door. They had both heard it: a muffled groan.

"You put him in the cellar?" Ted asked.

"No. Upstairs. You packing?"

"Just this." He pulled out a bowie knife.

"No gun?"

"You kidding? Do you have any idea how expensive guns are?"

Another groan, this one sharper and more precise, as if it knew it had an audience. There was a jarring quality to it as well which resonated in the walls.

Ted grinned and reached toward the door to the cellar. "Creepy shit. Think this guy's some kind of serial killer?"

"Wait."

"Why?"

"I don't know."

"Come on. It's a cliché, but when you hear shit coming from a stranger's cellar, you gotta check it out. You ready?"

"I can't believe we're doing this."

"Man up," said Ted.

"I'm manning up," Justin snapped back.

Ted swung the door open, and a humid waft surprised their senses.

"Smells like an arboretum down there," whispered Justin.

A faint illumination crept up from below, lighting the descending steps but little else. Ted carried on ahead, plunging forward in a foolhardy attempt to seem braver than he felt. There was no railing. Justin warily followed, the tension mounting with every booming creak of his leather pants. He wished he'd had the foresight to take them off. Then again, rushing barelegged into a john's cellar wasn't a very dignified thing to do.

But neither was getting caught by the cops. What were they doing? A stolen car parked right outside, a concussed victim duct taped to his bed upstairs—it was time to leave, not go rooting around some asshole's cellar. Justin no longer wanted to find out what the source of the noise was. He wanted to get the fuck out.

"Ted . . ."

Phosphorescent lamps lit the spacious cellar. The walls were lined with potted ferns and ivy. There weren't any windows but the air flow was somehow regulated, and the humidity was quite high, giving the illusion of a sticky July despite the fact that it was a week into November outside.

Justin navigated around the bizarre cellar in a daze. The ground crunched beneath his tread, as his wandering feet carried him next to Ted and in sight of a creature shackled upright to the wall. Justin gripped Ted's elbow but Ted shook himself free, moved forward, and blocked his view.

"Ted, don't!"

"Like hell I won't. Do you know what this is? Come here, take a look. It can't bite you."

"For fuck's sake," protested Justin, albeit feebly; curiosity gnawed at him from the inside. He peeked over Ted's shoulder.

It had horns, goat ears, and a hairy chest that blended naturally into unwashed wool from the waist down. It was pallid, underfed, and pathetic looking. It observed them observing it, and groaned—which was not the most accurate description of that unearthly, nerve-jangling sound, but Justin could think of no other way to put it.

As well as being captive it was injured, maimed: both of its nipples had been sliced off, and a stream of glittery, jade-tinted blood leaked down either side, forming puddles under its hooves and spreading. Its all-too-sentient, bloodshot eyes pleaded with them.

*Set us loose let us free.*

"What did you say?"

"I didn't say anything," Ted said absently, hypnotized by the rise and fall of its emaciated chest.

Justin shook his head. "You . . ."

*Gawk at us like some caged animal human beasts and hear our agony.*

He'd been looking right at Ted when it happened—when the words steamrolled out of his mouth—but they weren't his. They belonged to something else.

Ted frowned. "Why are you looking at me like that?"

"Nothing, sorry."

The creature was communicating through Ted—without Ted's explicit awareness—using him like some sort of voice box. Justin didn't know quite how to tell him. Ted probably wouldn't believe him anyway.

The faun groaned again, this time louder. It was a symphony of sounds, layered with grief and longing; a mingled cacophony of suffering beasts, wounded, dying. It assaulted them with its unmitigated intensity. An atavistic response caused them both to cringe, and they had to cover their ears and wipe their faces.

Then suddenly it was over, and the air vibrated in the aftermath.

*Little beasts avert yourselves but it drills deeper.*

"Tell me you heard that," said Justin.

"I think the whole fucking block heard that," Ted replied.

"No, I mean . . ."

*He is awake the anger gives strength he is coming let us go be our savior.*

"It's talking to me," Justin said.

"What?"

"The . . . this thing." Justin pointed a shaky finger. "It's saying shit, but it's using your mouth."

"It's using my mouth?"

"You don't know you're doing it. Honestly, can't you hear yourself?"

"I think the trouble is, you're not hearing *yourself* talk."

"I'm not crazy. I know I heard it."

"Yeah, well, it's all fucked then." Ted sighed and was silent a moment, considering.

*He feeds takes with complacency he drinks from us.*

"It's doing it again, isn't it?" said Ted. "Judging by your expression."

Justin nodded.

"Fine." Ted slapped his trouser pockets in resignation. "What's it saying?"

"It's saying," Justin began, then stopped and listened, staring at the ground all the while. There was no noticeable change to Ted when he became the conduit, only a slight parting of his lips, but the effect of seeing him used like that was very unsettling.

Presently, the faun became more verbose. Gaining momentum from

Ted's temporary passivity, it described its predicament in one flowing, uninterrupted sentence.

"The guy upstairs," Justin explained, "is feeding off him."

"Feeding? What do you—"

Justin silenced him with a wave. He pointed upward. "The fucker's a junky. He's impotent. He's drinking this thing's essence, slowly killing it."

"Jesus. You mean he's using this thing like Viagra?"

"This isn't funny."

"Trust me, I'm not laughing."

The floorboards announced a presence moving above them. Ted and Justin screwed their eyes to the ceiling. The vegetation had burgeoned, spreading in disharmonious geometry over the ceiling, seemingly trying to burrow through the wood and concrete. The closer they were to the creature, the more it smelled of rain-damp soil and elms and inchoate memories of the wild.

They heard Martin distinctly, walking above them, pacing like a leisurely predator.

"You said you tied him up!" said Ted.

"Like a goddamn cocoon."

"Obviously not that fucking well."

"Fuck! He couldn't—"

"Just . . . shut up, for Christ's sake."

*Living mortal tasting god blood gaining god power stronger stronger.*

"What?" said Ted.

Justin repeated what he understood of the phrase. Ted hefted the bowie knife, his expression solemn and contemplative.

"Ted, you're not thinking you'll . . ."

"Strike while the iron's hot," replied Ted, flashing his trademark grin. He shrugged off his jacket, relieving himself of the weight.

"Ted!" Justin caught his elbow.

Ted swung around, the humor evaporating suddenly from his grin. He raised his arm, and before Justin could deflect or parry, the blade nicked his cheek. A shallow cut, but it packed a vicious sting.

"Who the *fuck* is Ted?" screamed his assailant. "I'm myself—I'm fucking *me*, you goddamn prick. What's my fucking name?"

It was no use telling him to lower his voice. Justin sighed. "Hector."

Hector raged behind furious eyes, through choking panic. "That's fucking right! Hector! Not fucking Ted or Tom or Dick. And who the fuck are you?"

Justin shook his head, mouth sealed.

"Don't think of holding me back," said Hector.

He turned. Neither of them had heard the approach. The light of the cellar had dimmed. The air was thicker, more pungently earthy than before.

Martin's countenance far outweighed Hector's in malice. He struck like an adder, grabbing the boy by the throat with one hand and clamping his wrist with the other.

Hector exhaled a curt gurgle of surprise and dropped the knife. Martin's grip tightened. Hector began to kick and thrash, emitting amputated sounds of pain from his diminished larynx.

Justin clearly heard the bones crunch in Hector's wrist. Then Martin grunted as the heel of Hector's boot connected with his breast. His hold slackened, and they collapsed, continuing to fight.

Justin didn't need to see or hear anything more. He ran in the other direction, the illumination ebbing by the minute. The shadows elongated. The vegetation thrived, expanding and exuding the scent of the woodland sheath. Justin's heart palpitated in his throat. He hated the woods. Being lost among the trees at night was a very specific nightmare to him. To be segregated from civilization like that, bombarded by vines and bats and God knew what else, without a soul in earshot to hear you scream for help . . .

His chest burned. The ground had become uneven. Sweat blurred his vision, and eventually his coordination rebelled and he tripped, landing face first in the slop. He sat up, sputtering.

How long had he been running? Where the hell was he? He looked up. He couldn't see clearly; he thought he saw a speckling of stars beyond the canopy.

The faun rattled his chains, a feeble noise, but enough to catch Justin's attention. He stood, trudged forward. The dimensions of the cellar had completely altered. The distance from the foot of the steps to the faun had increased exponentially. Where he was . . . was an uncertainty; an eclectic environment that appeared to exist in two places simultaneously, the intangible coupling with the tangible. The "how" was beyond his understanding—or so he assumed before he gazed down at himself. His hands and legs were covered in the creature's shimmering blood. The blood was responsible, creating a splintered reality wherein one world bled into another.

This was all vague extrapolation on Justin's part. Metaphysics wasn't his strong suit. He gleaned one simple fact of the matter: the blood was copious, which meant the creature didn't have long to live.

The faun lifted its head, the simple exertion causing a ripple of pain to cross its hairy visage. It gazed at Justin with those forlorn orbs and parted its mouth, but no sound came out. Perhaps it now spoke without words, but Justin's mind was unreceptive to that mode of communication.

"You want me to release you?" he asked.

The faun nodded, an almost imperceptible response.

Justin tested the shackles, but the knots held like glue. "I can't do it even if I tried," he said. "What do you want from me?"

Slowly, painstakingly, the faun turned its head to the left. From that direction, in the distant depths of a veld darkness that Justin didn't even want to fathom, the soft lament of reeds could be heard. A song of mourning, and a beacon besides.

"I can't," said the boy. "I just can't," said the youth who'd been called Justin.

But the faun no longer stirred, and the pipes played on, beguiling and irresistible.

# Unmixed Wine

## John "JAM" Arthur Miller

Gladys drove her yellow Humvee through the countryside, marveling at the orange rock that dominated the Ozarks. Although she'd been to her grandfather's farm many times in the past, the orange rock always made her feel as if she were entering a new world, standing on the threshold of luminescence. Stones the color of pale carrots surrounded the gravel road, triggering memories of childhood journeys along the same route.

Decades ago, vacationing with her parents had turned into ginger chasms of imagination. She remembered arriving at her grandfather's farm and playing tag with the calves in the fields, a little eight-year-old girl running with four-legged friends through fertile pastures. Cows were dull and unremarkable when fully grown, but as calves they were playful. They'd sneak up on Gladys while her back was turned, running away when she gave a surprised yelp.

*Don't go off by yourself, Sissy,* Grandpa always told her. *There's a lot of critters on this property, things that would drive city folks crazy if they saw 'em.*

Now a successful marketer for Hasbro Clemons Inc., one of the largest toy companies in America, Gladys wondered why she'd come back. Was she driving *to* something or *away* from something?

She felt her past reaching for her with promises of adventure; at the same time she felt the pressures of corporate America and the need for escape.

Thinking of the deadlines and commitments awaiting her return depressed her. Her smile faded. She glimpsed her reflection in the rearview mirror while backing up after missing the turn, her frown deepening. Sometimes she hated herself, loathed who she had become.

After her divorce, she'd put herself through school, holding two jobs, telling her friends it was all so her daughter could go to college. But the truth was, Gladys had been chasing the American Dream, trying to become someone, trying to be *somebody*. Anybody other than a poor, divorced single mother.

She paused to gaze at her reflection, wondering where the years had gone. What separated her from that little girl who had run with the calves thirty years earlier? Where had that sense of exhilarating freedom gone? She was still pretty, despite the crow's-feet. She brushed the wisp of hair from her brow and checked her lipstick, as if she were about to enter into a meeting with her account manager.

"Relax," she told her reflection. "This vacation is for you, Gladys."

She always talked herself up like this—positive thinking—but it wasn't helping. The only thing that seemed to matter was the freedom she'd felt as a little girl in this wide open space, that playful sense of liberation while exploring the three ponds hidden among the farmland's crooks and crannies.

*This is your land, Sissy.* That's what Grandpa used to tell her. *Eventually, the land claims its own.*

Thick clumps of trees grew alongside the entire stretch of gravel; beyond sprawled a great green cornfield. The road she'd missed cut through these trees and bisected the cornfield.

As she put the Humvee in gear, something moved through the brush to her right. She saw a flitting shadow in the trees. Breaking branches indicated massive weight. The scent of greenery and moss crept through the open window, along with the musky scent of a large animal.

*Don't get too close to the bull,* Grandpa had perennially warned. *And stay out of the corn.*

Then the shadow was gone, just as quickly as it had come.

A shiver raced down her spine, and she let out a nervous laugh.

"God, I need this vacation."

The animal had been in her imagination, the thoughts of a little girl coming back to haunt her. Perhaps *something* had been there . . . But her inner child had exaggerated the moment, pulling her into the past.

Stress melted off her in waves.

As she drove through the clumps of trees into the cornfield, she failed to notice the movement beside the road. She didn't see the large silhouette within the shadows of cornstalks. She was so intent on the farmland spread out before her that she didn't see the figure step out behind her ride.

Before Gladys lay the cornfields, pastures, and the old farmhouse set atop the hill. Behind her wafted a cloud of corporate-world dust and a set of purple eyes glowing in cornstalk shadows beside the road.

The Humvee's tracking system turned into four-wheel drive and clung to the hill, her eyes remaining fixed on the farmhouse.

*Welcome home, Sissy.* Even though she lived three hundred miles away, Grandpa always told her, *This is your home. We have a bond with the land, don't we?*

"Grandpa," she whispered.

\*\*\*

She passed through the gate and into the farmyard, saddened to see how useless it had become; with no cattle there was nothing to keep in or out. The wooden barn leaned precariously to the right, as if it might drop from exhaustion.

At the farmhouse Gladys backed up her Humvee near the side door leading to the breezeway. She lowered the tailgate and removed a suitcase, a cell phone pressed between shoulder and ear.

"I'm supposed to be on vacation, Bob."

"Of course you are," Bob said. "But this won't take a minute of your time, sweetie."

She cringed at the word. *Sweetie.* Bob had been buttering her up for months, trying to charm his way into her pants. He'd already bedded down two other marketers, young coeds fresh out of college. His reputation as a shark was growing, and not just in business. Gladys didn't want to be counted among his burgeoning list of conquests.

"Bob, I'm forty years old."

"Yeah, turns me on."

"Very funny." She laughed despite herself. "Listen, why did you call? Is this so important that it can't wait?"

"Well, when you put it that way . . ." Bob spoke slowly, measuring his words. "There is a nice restaurant down the block from where we work."

"Bob, you're not asking me out on a date, are you?" She entered the farmhouse, letting the screen door slam loudly behind her, emphasizing her words. "Because if you're calling me during my vacation for something so frivolous . . ."

"No, no," Bob said. "It's just that the restaurant would be a nice setting to meet with clients, to schmooze them."

Bob always used the word *schmooze* when discussing clients. To Bob it was a "salesperson approach" to run clients over and fast-talk them into a corner. This was the exact opposite of Gladys's approach and the reason Hasbro Clemons had hired her. Gladys formed symbiotic long-term relationships with clients, while Bob's sales approach usually just irritated them.

"I'll check the restaurant out." Gladys glanced at the clock and groaned. "Listen, Bob, can't this wait until I return?"

"I guess so," he admitted with a sigh. "It's just that . . ."

"Bob, I'm not going out with you, if that's what you're getting at." She looked around the kitchen, wondering where to set her suitcase. "You're the accounts manager on my team, and you know the rules about dating fellow team members."

He cleared his throat.

*Some men are like roosters, Sissy,* Grandpa had warned her when she became a teenager. *They act like the entire world's a chicken coop full of hens.*

"Bob, you there?"

"Of course, Gladys. And I agree wholeheartedly." Before she could respond, Bob quickly added, "I'll see you when you get back."

He hung up.

She sighed and shut her flip phone, wondering where the towers were, wondering how she was receiving a signal this far in the sticks. Even out here the stress of the corporate world was trying to get her.

"I'm here, Grandpa," she whispered. "I'm here."

*I know, Sissy.*

Tears sprang to her eyes. The wind picked up outside, strong enough to blow the living room's gossamer-thin curtains. They seemed to be reaching for her. She watched them until the wind died down.

"Very funny, Grandpa."

She could almost hear him chuckling.

She wasn't sure whether she believed Grandpa had actually made the wind blow or not, wasn't sure of anything anymore. All she knew was that she belonged.

It felt like destiny.

***

In the morning, she awoke to the sensation of fresh country air blowing through the open bedroom window. A rooster crowed in the distance, not near enough to be annoying. She smiled, remembering

Champ—Grandpa's old rooster that used to fly straight at her father whenever they visited, landing on his head.

*It's because of your red hair, junior,* Grandpa said. *He sees you as just another cock in the coop.*

Dad hated that damned rooster, but Champ followed Gladys wherever she went, sometimes running her father off to protect her when she got in trouble for missing dinner. Always because of too much time spent with the calves.

After Champ died he became a favorite story handed down through the years like a family heirloom. Until her parents passed away in that two-car accident two months ago. Now there was no one left to enjoy the tale.

That's why she was here: to examine her inheritance, to make painful decisions. Should she let Grandpa's farm go or hang on to the past? She desperately wanted to recapture the land's magic.

Gladys got out of bed and started toward the kitchen where the coffee maker was pumping liquid caffeine into a pot. She felt groggy even though she hadn't slept this good in years.

A cool breeze wafted through the kitchen window. With the breeze came a strange odor.

"What the hell?"

She went to the window and opened the screen, leaning out while sniffing. Beneath the sill were several large hoof prints. Same animal's scent she'd gotten a whiff of in the cornfield yesterday. She wondered if the neighbors had lost a cow.

*Stay away from the bull!*

"Thanks, Grandpa!"

She slammed the window shut and went to the kitchen table. Her cell phone lay on the counter, light blinking. She had set it on silent after talking to Bob. Upon seeing it, she groaned and checked the Caller I.D.

"Shit." Sure enough: Bob. "Can't you just leave me alone?"

She'd return his call later, after her morning coffee, and after sprucing up the place. One of the treasures of staying on her grandfather's farm was the fresh country air that flowed in through the windows. Gladys just wanted a warm mug in hand and to relish the sweet country breeze.

But it wasn't just the fresh air; it was waking to the sounds and feel of the country. She tried explaining it to her city friends, but it was impossible. Even the *feel* of this place was peaceful, able to lull Gladys into daydreams, like fishing at one of Grandpa's three ponds. *You can't buy that kind of feeling,* she'd tell her friends.

Though she was certain others enjoyed peace of mind from living in the country, there was something *different* about Grandpa's land, something mystical and pure, as if the land called to her, as if it seeped into her bones with cozy warmth.

The land had always had a hold on her, even while she was three hundred miles away. She sometimes dreamed of being a little girl again, eight or ten, running with the skipping calves, playing tag while dull-eyed cows looked on. Occasionally, a dangerous bull with long horns appeared in her dreams, stamping its hooves as it approached, as if to say, "This is *my* pasture, damn it!"

In a few of her stranger dreams, people with purple eyes pranced over the land.

She poured herself a mug of coffee and sat at the kitchen table, turning her cell phone over so that she wouldn't have to watch it blink. Gladys let out a hesitant sigh. She used to be able to sigh without restraint, one smooth exhalation, but not for many years now. Lately it was as though her lungs held on to the breath, as if her body was trying to prevent any oxygen from escaping. And so her sighs flowed out in broken spurts.

"If only I could relax, Grandpa."

*Have a seat, stay a while.*

She giggled.

\*\*\*

Grandpa's land undulated with hills that ended before three valleys, where the ponds were hidden by tree groves. Gladys headed for the pond by the willow tree. She drove Grandpa's four-wheeler through a mile stretch of corn, then bobbed through bumpy pasture that had once served as grazing ground for over five hundred head of Holstein cattle. The pasture gave way to woods and groves.

At first she couldn't remember where the pond was situated, having been away from Grandpa's land for five years. She detested the fact that her corporate world had stolen so much from her.

But after a half hour, she found the weeping willow reaching above the trees. The willow was the most recognizable landmark in the area, surrounded by elms and maples and cherry trees.

As she drew closer, the smaller trees filled the sky, blocking sight of the larger weeping sentinel, and she ended up losing her way a couple of times.

*The land can become your friend if you let it lead you, Sissy.*

She kept recalling Grandpa's words, until those words became louder, as if he were sitting behind her, whispering into her ear. She grew accustomed to it.

She also began listening to the land, *feeling* her way to the weeping willow.

Her city friends just wouldn't get it. But Grandpa would.

Finally, the ground turned into a slight decline, then a gully. She heard the sound of bubbling water, and was delighted when the gully turned into a brook. This brook hadn't been here last time she visited, back when her parents were still alive. Mother Nature was always reshaping Grandpa's land, creating a kind of natural earth art.

She stepped off the four-wheeler and followed the brook as it wound through clumps of miniature knolls and moss-covered trees. Finally, she stood beneath the cool shade of the willow. Nothing grew within thirty feet of it, as if the other trees could sense its eminence.

She brushed the long tendrils forming a green curtain aside, approaching the trunk. She touched the tree's bark, an intimate gesture.

"Hello, my friend."

She swore the tree shuddered.

Bob would tease her about being a tree hugger.

*Oh well*, she thought. *He will never see you anyway, my friend.*

She walked to the edge of the branches, sitting beneath tendrils swinging in the wind, the green curtain opening to form a small window. The algae-coated pond was reflective glass, surrounded by yellow reeds. She saw the large rock she'd used as a child to jump from into the deep part of the pond.

Here there was peace, a place of contemplative relaxation. She sighed, amazed that the oxygen rushing from her lungs flowed out in one smooth exhalation—no hesitancy, no halting spurts.

*There's a sense of freedom in these hills. The stress of living in that mouse maze of a city just falls away whenever you visit. Tell me it don't.*

"You're right, Grandpa."

She attributed it to the land, the healing balm that touched her soul. But maybe Grandpa really was with her, tending to her himself. Maybe he wasn't just in her imagination. Maybe the little child within was giving Gladys's worn soul the person she loved most.

She sprawled out, leaning back and staring up into golden splotches of sunlight fighting through the weeping green. Two dragonflies buzzed past, hovering near her face before flying over the pond.

The softness of the downy earth conformed to her body. She sank, content. The air, rich with lush fragrance, seeped into her pores like sunshine, and she might as well have been lying on feather pillows.

A peaceful feeling enveloped her, and she fell asleep, mesmerized by the land.

\*\*\*

Gladys woke staring into golden shafts of sunlight. Then she saw a man's shoulders. From her vantage point, she guessed him to be about eight or nine feet tall. The wind whipped the willow's green tendrils, giving her a view of his muscled torso.

Nobody could be that tall, she thought, as a heavy grogginess filled her mind with fog. She saw butterflies fluttering over the pond, heard the brook behind her gurgling. The buzz of dragonflies combined with the warmth of sunshine oozing into the pores of her skin, hypnotic.

"Just a dream . . . ," she muttered, smiling at her sudden arousal. She reached between her legs, pushing her fingers down the front of her pants.

How long since she'd last done this?

But there was no self-consciousness, no right or wrong now, as she brought her hand out of her pants and licked her fingers. No child could sneak into her bedroom. No relative could interrupt her. No chance of being caught. Alone and in the moment, she hesitated only briefly, wondering whether she was half asleep and actually touching herself, or completely asleep, dreaming.

As the weeping willow's green tendrils swept over her body, the man appeared, at first facing her, then with his back to her. Her imagination took control as she fantasized, taking the man into her body, spreading her thighs to allow for a smoother transition, arching her back to ease the melding of two beings into one.

It felt so real. She suspected this was what people called a lucid dream.

He was inside her. She could smell his musty odor—which turned her on—and feel him sliding through her wetness, both bodies gyrating. A pheromonal rush of seduction captivated her senses. Her skin tingled, and a great heat burned between her thighs. Need was all she felt, a rich hunger so pure that she cried out.

Soon she was moaning, her back against the damp grass, the

sounds of nature amidst a familiar rhythm she'd thought she'd never experience again. She knew this was a dream because the man was hairy from the waist down—well, not his penis, that portion of his body was perfect—but the rest of his lower extremities were that of a goat. The dream felt real, as did the orgasms exploding through her body. So powerful that she couldn't help blurring fantasy with reality. But goat-men didn't exist in the real world, where corporate lawyers ruled politicians for the sake of the almighty dollar.

She didn't want to think about reality. She only wanted this man, this stranger, desired him deeper inside. A fantasy come to life, a lucid dream of pent-up sexual aggression; she wanted him to ravage her, to make love to her harder than anyone had ever done before.

Her whimpers became moans, then moans became screams of ecstasy. One orgasm tumbled into another, until it all blurred into one unified sensation, one whirling orgasmic universe containing only the sound of passionate screaming. Hips pushing out and up, thighs spread and giving as much as she was receiving—pure energy—she seeped into this universe, pouring herself into the fantasy.

Exhausted, she fell back asleep, her clothing torn. Already her eyes were closing, her gaze flowing down her lover's body, from his nipple rings and chiseled chest to his rock hard abdominal muscles, until finally she was drifting further along, to shores where her imagination had never ventured before.

\*\*\*

When she awoke, she was reaching for herself, wanting to feel herself again, when she heard a loud noise. It was the familiar pounding of a hoof against the earth, like a bull stamping. The ground vibrated beneath her, and Gladys quickly rose and began pulling her clothes back on. But her shirt was torn, ripped down the front.

"What the hell happened?"

She had no time to consider this. The beast was back. The same musky scent she'd smelled the day before filled the air. The thing was hidden in shadows and moving intently toward her. The tramping of hooves came nearer. Judging from the sound of its passage through the woods, the thing was huge, whatever it was.

She looked around, disoriented, trying to find the four-wheeler. She must have slept most of the day, because already the sun was low, hanging just above the trees beyond the pond.

On the ground around her were the impressions of hooves pushed deep into the soft earth, and deeper impressions closer to the pond, as if the creature had been thirsty after a rowdy romp of sex and—

*Stop it!*

But the thought wouldn't leave her mind. Weren't her clothes torn? Wasn't she sore and wet?

She saw a strange cup where she had been sleeping. It was gold with two large handles on either side, the kind of thing she'd seen in movies depicting ancient Greeks. Gladys remembered drinking something syrupy sweet, like honey mixed with wine, but her mind was still foggy. She couldn't be sure.

Had she dreamed it, or had someone put something in her drink? Had she even drunk anything?

She couldn't be sure of this either.

She picked up the cup to smell it and determine if anything else had been added to the wine, but whatever was in the woods suddenly began moving toward her fast. She flung the cup aside and ran from the weeping willow.

She raced past elms and the stumps of cherry trees, out past the edge of the woods where the pasture began. When she got to the four-wheeler, she found it destroyed, the engine torn out. Surrounding it: the deep impression of hooves.

"Damn it!"

The beast was still coming for her, through thick briars and brambles. So loud, getting more so as it neared. She thought of the pasture she'd have to run through. And then there was the road going through a mile of corn.

But she had no choice.

She took off sprinting, remembering something Grandpa used to say: *You need to put your feet on the ground, feel the pulse of the earth beneath you, otherwise you lose your connection.*

She ran, her ankles bending each time her foot landed in a pothole.

After a short distance, something burst from the woods behind her. A heavy branch flew past, nearly clubbing her head. She heard the snort of a large animal. The sound vibrated in the air, almost a baritone of raw power. It sounded like a two-ton bull.

The earth shook as the creature got closer. It seemed to be almost upon her, about to bear down on her. She risked a glance over her shoulder, but saw only the strange man at the perimeter of the woods, the one with the cloven hooves and hairy legs, stroking his erect penis.

*You're not real! Can't be real!*

She heard the sound of clomping hooves, as if a horse ran alongside her, but there was nothing there. She slowed and as she did so, the sound diminished, and she realized the goat man wasn't chasing her.

She looked down and screamed; she saw cloven hooves instead of human feet. Tendrils of her shredded jeans blew in the wind, and she saw white hairs sprouting up all along her legs.

"No!" She looked back at the thing that had drugged and ravaged her. "You bastard."

The goat man flinched, shoulders bunching. Then he lowered his head and charged. Ram horns grew from his skull with each step, thick and looping over his pointed ears. He roared, and Gladys ran as fast as her hindquarters would carry.

*This land will save you if you save it first, Sissy. This land will be your salvation, as will the moon and stars. All you have to do is remove the city stink. When you do that, the woods will move through you.*

The moon was rising, and she felt a cold strength shining down from above, giving her energy, empowering her to run faster than she'd ever run before. Perhaps it was her new mutation, the goat legs that propelled her so quickly. Yet she couldn't deny the exhilarating power the moon possessed, beaming down, passing *through* and energizing her.

Was this what Grandpa had meant about the woods moving through her?

Despite the fear she felt in the pit of her stomach, new sensations beyond anything she'd ever sensed swept through her: the earth, moon, soil, and trees—all of them speaking to her, all of them rejoicing in her newfound strength.

How had she ignored these sensations her entire life?

She heard the ground vibrate beneath her trampling hooves; felt earthworms and insects tremble under her tread. She smelled rotted bodies of fallen trees and remains of dead animals, buried and absorbed, making the soil nutrient rich. And the grass communicated a scent, bringing to mind all things of the earth, both predator and prey.

*There's music in these hills, Sissy. Music that most people never hear.*

The wrath of the goat man swept through the pasture. It was a presence, an angry power that dominated and subjugated everything in its path. She felt his sexual need, but his anger was stronger, a meteor cutting through the air, making it difficult for her to breathe.

He was just behind her, his hooves pounding out an angry rhythm.

Somehow she had made it to the cornfield, but the road was still a good hundred yards away. She lowered her head and blasted through stalks of corn. Tingling sensations pricked her scalp, and when she reached up she discovered horn nubs.

The goat man roared again.

At that moment she wouldn't have been surprised to see him step out before her, wouldn't have been surprised to see anything preternatural. Wasn't that what she was now? Wasn't she becoming one with the night? A goat lady similar to her enraged lover?

She began laughing hysterically, unable to run while thinking about rutting with the goat man, because reality had become so ridiculous.

*It's in your blood, Sissy. The land, my genes—it's all tied together through our bloodline.*

She stopped and turned around. The goat man stopped as well, breathing hard, his breaths slapping against the cornstalks, moving them like wind.

Gladys breathed deep and hard and sighed, the sound of a great beast. She was taller than the stalks of corn, towering over the tassels—she must have grown a good two feet.

What was this great power that had transformed her?

*The land changes you, lets the beast out.*

The satyr following her—for that's what he was—gestured at the top of the hill. She followed his finger and her gaze settled on Grandpa's house. Every light was on. The sun had set, and rectangles of yellow light spilled from the windows onto the grass.

Who had turned on the lights?

She felt a vibration in her pocket. When she removed the object, she found her cell phone. It seemed alien, vulgar. She dropped it and smashed it with her cloven hoof.

Her companion growled and gestured again toward the farmhouse, urging.

She loped up the hill, hooves crunching ginger gravel along the road. She didn't take the time to open the two gates. Instead, she cleared each by a good foot. Her clothing felt restrictive, and she began to undress.

When she let her shirt and bra trail behind her, she suddenly forgot about Hasbro Clemons. When she ripped what remained of her pants away, thoughts of Bob, work, and the city dissipated. Each piece of clothing shed as though it were her world, her life, her civilization.

She remembered from her childhood, learning in Bible school about Eve's purity before she ate of the fruit. Gladys realized evil no longer existed for her; a sense of liberating freedom became available. She had lost the knowledge of good or evil. There was only need, hunger, lust, and laughter. In the innocent mind of a child locked in her mythical body, there was no tomorrow or yesterday, only right now.

She approached the house, stepping onto the front porch. The door opened and a familiar face appeared, the body hunched over because of his large size.

She gasped.

"Grandpa?"

He gave her an ornery grin.

Did people have to become angels when they died? Did they have to become ghosts? Maybe people could become damn well whatever they pleased. Maybe some people chose to become satyrs, like Grandpa.

It didn't matter. All she knew was that her grandpa had come back, and that was enough.

"Welcome home, Sissy."

She wiped tears from her eyes and hugged him, both naked yet unselfconscious.

He led them to the kitchen, both of them stooping. On the kitchen table was the same type of cup she'd seen beneath the weeping willow.

"It's a *kylix*," Grandpa said. "It holds unmixed wine."

"For what purpose?"

He smiled and stomped his hoof. "To let the beast out."

He held the kylix out to her, and she took it greedily. No corporations or players trying to get into her pants, no right or wrong, no shame or guilt.

She became as a little girl before Grandpa, drinking the unmixed wine. Right and wrong fled before the intoxication that infiltrated her mind. She heard the music of the forest, the tune of the land. Felt the joy of Luna and the dance of Nature. She began moving her hooves in tempo, a rhythm that had to be felt, not heard.

"What is this, Grandpa?"

He grinned. "It's the Sicinnus, Sissy."

"Sicinnus?"

"The ecstasy dance given to all satyrs."

She stamped her hooves and raised a cloud of dust from the kitchen floor. Then, remembering her parents, she became sad.

"Won't Mom and Dad be joining us?"

Grandpa hung his head. "I'm afraid they didn't hear the call of the land."

He held her hand and she wept for them. Then they left the unnatural farmhouse and went out into the night. There were other satyrs waiting, first ten then twenty. Grandpa said that female satyrs were called satyresses.

"Like me," Gladys said.

"Like you, Sissy," he agreed.

Beneath the full moon they experienced the rhythm of an unheard tempo, heard the music of the wind whipping through the trees. Mother Nature sent clouds, and thunder clashed like cymbals. They shed civilization like clothing, until they danced naked before the heavens, no knowledge of right or wrong, their slates wiped clean.

In the Sicinnus they found freedom; in the dance they became one herd, one mind.

Vibration from the earth—the planet's ecstasy—flowed up her hooves and into her hindquarters.

The satyrs let it flow like liquid night.

Soon she was dancing with her male lover beneath the weeping willow. She made him want her, and he did the same for her.

They both sang Luna's song, beneath rain falling like unmixed wine, falling from the kylix in cleansing waves.

# Gameplay

## Dy Loveday

A shadowy face appeared on the car windscreen. Rain lashed the glass, blurring the contours, but I recognized it all the same. Litter slammed into the image, flattening the three-dimensional lines, before a chilly wind picked up the scrap and tossed it under the car idling next to me. My fingers slipped on the steering wheel, knuckles white beneath freckled skin.

"I can't help you." I grabbed the familiar cross resting on my chest. It dug into my palm, and by now it should have scorched the flesh. But of course God didn't even bother doing that nowadays. The form on the windshield faded, and I released a breath.

The streets teemed with life: people with umbrellas intermingled at a pedestrian crossing, while commuters and buses competed for a path through the maze of peak-hour city traffic. Gathering dusk and a downpour had mustered the crowd to a chilly intersection. The traffic light diffused through the rain, showering the dashboard with blood red, and the engine throbbed beneath my feet. My eyes watched the road—the black soulless ice glaring straight back at me.

Shoppers and workers hurried home. To eat and rest beneath the covers, toes tucked in, warm and comfortable. Doors latched and children safe, their books and games locked away.

The rain pounded on the pavement, trammeling like the echo of drums.

My mind drifted back to the past, memories rising to the surface. Back to the entry of my parents' house where my older sister's jeans hung on the circular stairs, inviting me to cross the threshold and discover why seventeen-year-old Jocelyn had discarded them on the banister. Our mother had crumbled beneath my sister's requests for videos and chocolate and had left her alone in the house. Jocelyn was probably up there with her boyfriend, messing around with the slack-mouthed drummer who watched her like she was his favorite eye candy. The greenish tinge to her face that morning had tricked our parents into letting her skip school. The conniving bitch got away with murder while I always ended up disappointing everyone. Not quite as elegant, not quite as smart, nowhere near as believable in my efforts to show interest in other people.

I spat a curse that would have earned a look of fury from my mother and skipped upstairs, running my fingers over the jeans before poking them over the side of the banister so that Jocelyn would have a hard time finding them. Those extra seconds of searching might get her caught.

In the hallway, Jocelyn's door filled my vision. I pushed it open, just enough to peer through a gap in the paneled wood. The dried, powdery scent of orange jessamine floated on dust motes. A slice of light shone from the bay window across the carpet. A bed, unmade, lay like an invitation, as white as Jocelyn's lies. Pillows were gathered up on the padded headboard, cool rectangles resting against a navy leather surface.

The drums beat louder.

The bathroom was halfway concealed by the adjoining door. Inside, the sound of Jocelyn and her boyfriend lingering, touching. The truth was I was jealous of what she symbolized—her smooth red hair and perfect features—and the way she moved through life unapologetically, her attention focused on acting and heading east. Whereas I would probably end up a bored civil servant in local government, buried beneath mounds of forms and paper clips.

*Drip.*

Water trickled from the spout of the gold dolphin tap, the last drop quivering like silver drool. The hair rose on the back of my neck, but I stood still, transfixed.

I heard a murmur, a muffled scream. My sister's artist fingers with their long nails lifted from the water and gripped the thick lip of the tub, staining the smooth expanse. At first I thought she'd painted her hand in nail polish. Thick trails of blood-red water dripped to the floor, running in rivulets across the tiles and down the drain. My hand lifted in response, pressing the door wide and the scene froze in a terrible tableau.

*Plop.*

A huge shape shifted in the mirror and a silver saw blade flashed in the light. Dark hands clasped the disk, the arms long and curved and raised as if in prayer. My mouth opened wide, ready to cry out. The razor-edged blade twirled and lowered in a movement so fast it was a blur.

Jocelyn's fingers twitched and her back arched, flowing hair trailing like waterweed over the edge of the tub. Crimson sprays of blood hit the white tiles. A tiny noise escaped my throat. I stepped back, eyes darting everywhere, my head filled with a buzzing noise.

"Glory be to Thee, O Lord Abaddon," a man chanted.

*Run. Run. Run.*

My sister's voice screamed in my head and for once I obeyed. I turned, dashing into my room, floorboards silent against the blood thumping in my ears.

"Where are you, Victoria?" The voice was rough and gravelly. Wind whistled in the background, a thousand drums reverberated in the echo, along with my sister's whisper.

*Hide.*

I slid beneath the draped covers of my bed, trembling. A sob rose and escaped. How did he know my name? My arm pressed against a sharp edge. I panicked, thinking the intruder waited there, taunting me, only realizing at the last moment that it was the book I'd purchased from the antiquarian store last week.

*Please play with me, Jocelyn.* The torn binding admonished me, reminding me of several nights before. I'd taped a triangle on the floor and begged my sister to join me, leading her by the hand into the inner circle, our shoulders hunched close enough for the scent of rosemary to waft from her hair. For once Jocelyn agreed to go along with the game, her eyes filled with something like pity, angering me more than her usual contempt.

I'd droned meaningless Latin from the book, the stench of cremated nail clippings, urine, and crushed snail shells burning my nostrils. "Powers that be, show my future love to me," I'd chanted. Nothing happened. I folded a small piece of red silk and placed it in the silver cup along with petals that I'd stitched together in nine jagged lines. "By the power of fire, I command thee." I picked up a black candle and poured wax into the cup.

Jocelyn was smiling but I could tell she'd lost interest. Her gaze drifted to the bedroom door.

"Stupid bastards," I'd said, reluctant to let her go. "Useless pathetic entities, rotting in hell. What do you know about life—or power, for that matter?"

The silk caught fire, a burning conflagration that sparked onto the rug. Black eyes materialized on the wall, pupils narrowed to tiny pinpricks. They glanced over Jocelyn's face and body, then flicked to mine. Smoke swirled and a triangular face appeared like ink seeping into litmus paper. Tiny writing marched down the wall, the undecipherable wedges and squiggles chipping the plaster. Jocelyn careened out of the room, screaming. And later our parents grounded me for playing a stupid trick and causing trouble. The stains reappeared no matter how many times I scrubbed and scrubbed.

"I hope you enjoy living with the results for a few days," my mother said. "Serves you right for being so destructive. You know how sensitive Jocelyn is."

She wouldn't listen to the truth, and I wasn't surprised. The woman had never liked me, and she took Jocelyn's side in every argument.

"Come out. Come out. Wherever you are," he said in a singsong voice. "You know I'll find you." Deeper, huskier: a guttural growl.

My hand rested over my mouth, hiding a broken whisper. "Jocelyn. I'm sorry. Help me."

Wisps of black vapor curled around my bedroom door and I trembled, hiding in the darkest corner. The cloud took the shape of a goat and peeked beneath the dangling quilt, finding me under the bed. My sneakers dug into the wooden boards, and I let loose a full-throttled scream, throwing my weight back—but the smoke followed, sticking to my body like boiling tar.

The substance divided, some cascading into my mouth and nose, bringing the taste of rot and decay, while more coiled around my neck, forming a solid chain. The smoke thickened in my throat to an oily consistency, drowning my sobs. An arm dropped from the bed, reaching for the end of the fetter. My shoes squealed as he dragged me out kicking and gasping.

A creature with dark skin covered in flashing glyphs lay on my bed, completely naked. His grin exaggerated the distorted, irregular-shaped skull, a macabre parody of a human face, with horns flowing back from a widow's peak.

"My summoner. Well met." He opened my mouth with a sharp claw attached to a cloven hoof, splitting my lip. A long gold chain rasped out of my throat. He kissed the chain and placed it around my neck.

The constriction in my chest eased and I wheezed, choking and inhaling a convulsive breath filled with the scent of wild animal.

He licked his hoof and pointed to the wall. "An entrance to the Underworld. But you'll need to earn it first."

Flames danced in his black eyes as he invaded my thoughts, giving cold comfort with a tender stroke of claw against cheek. The sinking sun sent needle rays through the glass, tingeing his skin with an umber glow.

"Let me go."

"You called me." He smiled, both coy and modest at the same time. "Thus entering into negotiations. Your sister's soul awaits a decision. What shall the arrangement be?" He placed a black claw on his lip, as if thinking.

I lay bare before his gaze, his fetid stench diving down into my lungs. My hoarse cries overshadowed the grind of car tires spitting gravel on the driveway. The front door slammed as someone walked into the house and the creature shifted his focus to the greasy saw blade held in his left hand, the edges smeared with Jocelyn's blood.

"Pretty child." He cupped my cheek. "Come now. Make a choice. You? Or shall I take your sister?"

Mother suddenly called out for Jocelyn. She'd found the jeans. Her footsteps pattered up the stairs, on the landing now.

"Shall I remove your mother as well?" He bent down and whispered in my ear. "Imagine life with just your father. Sweet pecks from his mustached lip. You'll get anything you want with both women gone. I'll even give you an ability to make things more interesting. Eternal life? Telepathy? What about the ability to foresee the future or manipulate your mundane world? All for two silly women who can't understand what it's like to be you. Such a clever girl, my Victoria."

*No. No. No.*

My sister's face darkened the windscreen. Her lips mouthed the words, *Save me.*

My mother's discordant screams tortured my ears.

*Drip.*

I licked wet lips, tasting salt. The car engine revved.

*Stop this. There's nothing you can do to change things. Eternal life was the deal.*

The satyr's voice joined the others in my head, the faint sound of drums and piped music prickling my skin.

My hands with their scarred wrists came off the steering wheel, hiding my adult tears. The tires of my car peeled rubber as I accelerated across the intersection.

And for just a moment the blaring horns, tearing metal, and iron-rich blood filling my mouth tasted like freedom.

# Layin' A Brodie

## J.S. Reinhardt

Keith received the e-mail simultaneously at every one of his addresses at 1:13 in the afternoon on a Friday. The message was brief and worded in such a way that he couldn't help being interested. His job was to find news after all, to stay plugged in to the goings on of society. It was more than his job; it was his calling.

Nothing like this had ever come through his inbox, though.

The e-mails were all the same: four simple lines and a name. When he had his tech guys trace the address they came up short. The sender was good. Even the Nigerian scammers couldn't hide their trail as well as this guy had, which made the allure of his story even stronger.

The name alone wormed its way into his every waking moment. The sender referred to himself as Penelope of Mantineia's son. Keith did some research and discovered that Odysseus's so-called faithful wife had spent a lot of time on her back, legs spread, while her hubby was out and about. Her son could be anyone.

The body of the e-mails though . . . those words sat in Keith's head like a smoldering coal. They crawled up and down his spine and sparked in his brain. Those words would not leave him alone until he met their author and found out whether or not his suspicions were accurate—which is what he eventually decided to do.

On the other side of the worn wooden door—a door he traveled twenty-four hundred miles to stand in front of, the last thirty of which were on the back of a mule with a hand-drawn map to guide him because the locals didn't venture into these hills (they said so before calling a blessing of Allah over him)—dwelled the sender of that cryptic e-mail.

He knocked three times, and when the door slowly creaked open the smell that wafted out was one of an animal's den. His head swam, and before he could right himself, the ground rushed up. Maybe it was the altitude, or maybe last night's *aushe sarka* had been slightly off. Or maybe it was the fact that this was really happening—he was meeting the sender of the message, and what he had feared looked to be true . . .

\*\*\*

"Mr. Lantain."

The voice was distant, drawn out, and cloudy like he was hearing it from the other side of a wet towel.

"Mr. Lantain, wake up."

Keith's head felt like a wet towel, actually. Cold and heavy. He could smell exotic spices and something cooking. The world drifted back to him. He was in Afghanistan, here to interview the man who'd sent him the e-mail. Keith opened his eyes and the back of his head grew its own freight train pulse.

"You mustn't move right now, Mr. Lantain. You struck your head when you passed out."

"What?" Keith scooted back on the bed. The pounding tempo sped up inside his skull. He was in a small shack, darkness barely held back by the glow of a fire. A kettle steamed in the hearth. The coals fluttered, undulating as he stared into them. The voice came from the shadows beyond a small table.

"Sometimes the altitude gets to people. Sometimes, my appearance." The man stepped forward into the flickering light, and Keith's breath stopped short in his chest. He was not fully a man.

Closing his eyes, Keith focused on his breath. Under the smell of the stew and its strong spices sat that stale animal stench, like a city zoo on a hot summer day.

When he opened his eyes again, the man-thing was lighting a large candle in the center of the rough-hewn table. Keith recognized what the creature was.

"You're a satyr?" The words came out like someone else's.

"Not just any satyr or faun, Mr. Lantain. I am All, the one you surely know of as Pan."

"The son of Penelope of Mantineia."

"That is correct."

"I don't believe you."

"I don't ask that you believe in me, Mr. Lantain. I only wish that you hear the story I have to tell. That is why I wrote you."

"Are you telling me that you, Pan, an ancient Greek god of the forest, now lives in the mountains of Afghanistan and uses the Internet?"

"I am *the* god of the forest, Mr. Lantain, get that straight. As for the e-mails, I simply hired a young boy from the village at the base of this valley to send them. He brings me the supplies I need, as well as runs errands for me."

"If you're *the* god of the forest, why are you living in these bleak mountains?"

"Something powerful is hunting me and no forest on earth is safe because of it. Simple as that. I've been hidden here for some time and I cannot return to the fields and forests of Greece, and thus I'm afraid this place will be the end of me. That is why I summoned you here. I am dying, Mr. Lantain."

"What, are you going to sacrifice me, make stew from my meat? How is it that I, a mere mortal, can help you, a god?"

The beast laughed so loud the small windows rattled. "I'm beyond the benefit of sacrifice now. You can help me, Mr. Lantain, by listening to the story I have to tell and sharing it. The story is the tale of your kind. Perhaps knowing the truth will allow you to gain control of your own fate once again. I'm afraid it may be too late for you, though. Far too late."

Keith thought about what the e-mail had said as he pulled the printed text from the chest pocket of his jacket, unfolding it in the dim light. He didn't need to see it to recite the message:

*I know what has gone wrong with civilization. I was there when it happened. Come to the village of Keshem where the tribe of Persians called Afghans live. I have a story to tell you.*
*Mr. Roman Faunus*

"Yes, and here you are." Pan stood up and walked to the kettle, his hooves thumping in the dry dirt of the shack's floor. Pulling a small bowl from above the mantle, he ladled some of the aromatic stew into it. "You must eat this and finish the bowl. It will heal your injury. Then, you will sleep."

"I shouldn't sleep. I shouldn't even be lying down." He tried to get up and the pressure in his head pushed against the back of his eyes. Keith settled into a sitting position. "So tell me this story."

"Only after you finish the stew." The goat man handed Keith the bowl. "By morning you'll be fine. Eat, please, Mr. Lantain. Then rest."

Keith was hungry after all, his stomach reminded him. He dipped a large wooden spoon into the bowl and began to eat. It was spicy, the vegetables perfectly done, and the aroma made the throbbing in his head slow. He wished there was meat in it, goat meat, but considering the chef that didn't seem appropriate. Keith laughed. "This is really good, what is it? I've spent time here and I've never had this kind of stew before."

"It is an old recipe, Mr. Lantain." The goat man smiled, his teeth peeking out from behind his wiry Billy Goat's Gruff goatee.

Keith shook his head. "Shouldn't you have horns?"

The beast lowered his head and parted the shaggy hair. "Just like these, I imagine?"

Two small horns, curled like those of a ram, were there just above the pointed ears. Pan shook out his black hair and all was hidden again.

It seemed this creature was, at least, a satyr. Whether or not it was Pan still remained to be seen.

Keith shrugged. "I thought they'd be larger."

The two laughed and Keith scooped out the last of the vegetables, then finished the dregs. "That was really good, um, Roman?"

"Roman was just a clue for you, Mr. Lantain, one you seemed to have overlooked. I've told you my name." The goat man walked over and took the bowl and spoon from him.

"So you want me to call you Pan, then? Really?"

"That is the name I was given, so yes."

"Well then, Pan, you can call me Keith."

Keith felt warm and calm; the bed felt soft underneath; the blanket, heavy on top of him. The fire whisked at the chill in the air with dark orange flames, comforting in their mild heat.

Pan smiled at him from across the shack, then turned and pulled out a small velvet bag from a cabinet next to the fireplace. When he turned around Keith could not hold back a small laugh. From the bag, Pan produced a set of old wooden pipes.

"Well you certainly look the part now, I can't argue with that."

Bringing the pipes to his lips Pan began to softly play a song that penetrated every molecule of Keith's body. The small shack swooned around him, the world slowly turning on an axis centered over his heart. Everything focused on his chest, every bit of every thing tied to his core. A giddy laugh slipped from his lips, flesh tingled, hair stood on end, and Keith drifted down into a deep sleep, knowing it was indeed Pan playing this music of the ages for him.

Putting his pipes away, Pan looked down into the fire. It was perhaps the last time he would play his beloved music. The chatter of birds across the roof was joined by the clatter of small hooves on his porch. Wildlife, sparse as it was this high in the cold mountains, had come to his song—as they had come for millennia.

Tossing one last log on the fire to hold over until morning, now just a few hours away, Pan settled down into his straw bed in the corner of his final home.

Tomorrow he would tell his story. Then he would be free.

***

Keith woke to the smell of baking bread. Pan was nowhere to be seen, and he wondered if last night had in fact been some twisted dream. That smell just under the sweet baking bread, the faint animalistic scent, told him it might've been real. But when the ancient god clomped into the shack with a load of firewood, there could be no more question about the reality of the situation.

"Good morning, Keith. I trust you slept well? How's your head?"

Keith felt his scalp bit by bit under his shaggy black hair, exaggerating the movements. "I feel great." He stood and stretched, then dug in his bag for his notebook and mini-recorder. "When shall we start the interview?"

"Relax. Although time is of the essence, we do have enough to enjoy some bread and coffee first." Pan dropped the firewood, brushed his hands on the coarse hair of his legs, and pulled a dark loaf of leavened bread from a cubby above the hearth. "Fine by you?"

"That looks wonderful, and coffee sounds great, yes. I'm just going to set everything up."

"As you wish."

They shared the warm bread—a fine loaf with dates and thick crust—and the dark, aromatic coffee. Pan stoked the fire and Keith tested his recorder as snow-laced wind kicked against the windows.

"I'll be recording everything and taking notes as needed." He depressed the record button on his mini-recorder and leaned toward it. "Somewhere in the mountains east of Keshem, Afghanistan, I'm speaking to Pan, the Greek god. He is approximately six feet tall, with dark wiry hair. Two horns, smaller than those depicted throughout the ages. And his lower half is that of a goat. Pan has called me here to tell a story, one he insists humanity must hear." Keith looked up. "Does that about cover it?"

"Yes, it does, thank you." Pan smiled, and Keith returned the gesture.

"Okay, I'm ready when you are."

"Then we begin. You're familiar with the three-day festival that occurred in New York State in 1969, Woodstock, correct?"

"Yes, of course."

"I was there. It was supposed to be about peace and love, two things that are important to me, as you may know." Pan sat down across from Keith. "It turned out the brown acid was not as bad as they had said. It was Andrew Allison that was the bad trip.

"The sixties saw the creation of a more independent woman, and from that independence a whole cultural movement was born. By the time August of nineteen sixty-nine had arrived gender, race, religion, income, power, or sexual preference didn't matter anymore. From the Port Huron Statement to Tim Leary preaching 'Turn on, tune in, drop out,' the arc of change in consciousness and connectedness was astounding. The rampant bourgeois hyper-consumerism, repressive thinking, traditional outlooks, and growing rifts between the haves and have-nots were becoming a thing of the past. Revolution was happening, and individual empowerment bringing forth a truly humane, human culture was underway."

Pan got up from the table and poked the fire with a long iron rod. Sparks flushed up the chimney. "But listen to me. I sound like some sentimental fool waxing about the good old days."

"I brought plenty of tapes."

Pan nodded and took his seat again.

"So anyway, there I was on Saturday, somewhere between Sly and the Family Stone and The Who—incidentally, I still don't understand why either band was at Woodstock. But let's not digress.

"Taking a break from people-watching, I ran into our friend Andrew Allison. Old Andy was considered a square in the parlance of the times, someone who couldn't get his mind outside the box society had put him in. What mattered most to him, in order, were his car, the career waiting for him at his father's law firm once he passed the New York bar exam the following spring, and the 3.8 million dollars he knew he would inherit after his grandmother passed away. She was on the way out too; it would be a matter of weeks, maybe days, before she succumbed to the brain tumor that had turned her into a blathering idiot."

"Did you know Mr. Allison before Woodstock?"

"I knew his type. The sixties in America was my time in the New World, you might say. Men like Andrew were projects of mine, they needed to be of the time, not just pass through it unchanged." That Pan felt some kind of emotional tie to this Andrew Allison was not lost on Keith.

"You might be wondering what a guy like Andy was doing at Woodstock. So was I that fine summer evening. It wasn't the music or the revolution. It was one thing and one thing only that brought him to that field in upstate New York. Same thing that makes men do damn near everything from wage wars to earn wages. God's gift to Man. I love some of the names you've come up with over the years: furburger, cooter, muff, the old pink taco. Whatever men want to call it, pussy is the great manipulator. When you look up the definition of manipulate, your dictionaries say 'to change by artful or unfair means so as to serve one's purpose.' Do you know of any women out there who can say they've never used their pussy in an artful or unfair way to get something they wanted?"

"Not personally, no." Keith shared a laugh with his host, like two regular guys talking in a bar.

"Where was I?"

"You were talking about Andrew."

"Yes. Andy at Woodstock was as out of place as tits on a turtle, as they say. Now isn't the English language a beautiful thing? I mean, it can be so descriptive. For communicating what is going on in a person's heart or mind, I don't think there has ever been a better language. There I go again. I'm a bit preoccupied these days . . ."

Keith leaned into the recorder. "I should add that, earlier, Pan mentioned being hunted and that his time is growing short."

"Yes, but back to the story you came to hear. With his close-cropped hair, well-defined muscles, and bright white teeth, Andy was better suited for the polo field than Yasgur's back forty. But Misoula Robinson was a hard thing to talk out of an idea. See, Misoula was a tall, dark, and very sexy waitress at a jazz club Andy frequented. Most of the regulars and employees at Parlay's Lounge thought Andy was a narc, but Misoula hadn't judged him. At first he didn't give her a second look. She was a negro after all and for some reason Americans thought very poorly of blacks. If only you humans had known back then that you all came from the same stock, if you traced it back far enough.

"Misoula was drawn to Andy, went out of her way to get his

attention, and eventually she started to worm her way into his head. She was as forbidden as that apple Eve plucked down in the garden, maybe even more so if Andy wanted to keep his name and birthright of wealth and power. Eve ended up in a pretty bad place after all, right?

"A few heavy-petting rounds in the alley behind Parlay's, followed by late-night rendezvous in her fifth-floor apartment in the Village. Andy tried pot for the first time, drank gallons of Mateus, and watched Misoula's hips sway as Miles ran the voodoo down. I love Miles's music, it is similar to mine. Very similar.

"The exotic smell of her sweat . . . and her dark foreign skin. She was enchanting. When Misoula said Andy should drive her and two of her friends upstate for that hippie music festival, there was no way he could say no.

"So flash forward to Saturday. Our good friend Andrew was three hits into his first acid experience, loving every psychedelic minute. Released from the pressures of his family, Andy was cutting loose. Misoula was happy to see her white buck following her down the path of enlightenment. Despite her airs of free thinking, sex, and society, she had a drive deep inside her to make something of herself."

Pan stood up and paced across the small shack several times before continuing.

"As our players assembled in a small grassy field beyond the stages and crowds, an idea started to form in my head. What if these were the new children of Eden? What if, with a little help from their friends, as old Joe sang, a real change could start right there?"

Keith interjected, "The sexual revolution was long underway. What else were you interested in?"

"Love, man! It isn't just about sex with me. Humans always think it is, but really I'm all about love. Love for yourselves, for those around you, for the world you inhabit." Pan's ears twitched and a big smile crossed his face. "So there I am watching Misoula and her two friends, Karen and Selma, and the man of the hour, Andrew Allison. For once in a long while I have a little faith in what a few kids like them could achieve. So I start playing my song and sure enough those kids start stripping off what few clothes they were wearing to dance among the cattails and high grass. The night animals circled the field, as they often do when I play my song, and joined in the festivities. It had been a long time since I found enough motivation to play my music. I was on fire that night.

"Fornication wasn't my idea, but it sure was what my music was meant for. Man, woman, beast, they all engaged in the procreation of their kind, with my tune as the rhythm behind their hips. I was caught up in it as much as anyone else, tail twitching in time to their undulating hips, breath blowing hot over sweet Syrinx."

Pan glanced over to where his pipes were stored. "I never noticed him in that field, that badass motherfucker who had something else in mind. When that old slanderer got an idea in his head there wasn't a damn thing I could do about it." He looked around his small shack seeming to wish for someplace to go. "I thought I was kin, but in my heart I knew I was no kin of his; he had used me before. Sure, you stupid humans confused me for him all the time . . ."

"It's the horns," Keith said, rubbing his own scalp.

"The horns." Pan leaned over and grabbed the two curled horns perched above his ears. "So I have horns and that subterranean cocksucker has horns too. That doesn't mean we're related, you dig?" His nostrils flared with a huff, and he stopped to collect himself before continuing.

"There I was getting down when Satariel started laying down his own unrighteous groove. Let me tell you, when Mr. Cifer gets rolling, stand back. He's one bad mamma jamma. My dream dissolved and his took over from there. Karen and Selma didn't pick up his intentions right away, but Misoula and Andy did. I saw it in their eyes, glowing like some irresistible fire." Pan leaned onto the table, close to the recorder, and Keith leaned away from him.

Pan was seething, but there was something else too.

Keith wrote down one word: guilt.

Pan leaned back and closed his eyes. "That was how it all started. My intentions weren't for the whole damn planet to go off the fucking reservation, man. I wanted that love, that groove, that last chance boulevard to become their chosen path. I felt like the Bard's Hamlet in that field, watching those four kids pick up what that deceiver was laying down. Alas, poor Humans! I knew them, Horatio."

Pan sprang out of his chair. "I may have let the boogey man in, but those four invited him to sit down and stay a while. And so he did. But you already know that, don't you? That's why you're here, isn't it? You ask all the time, how did it happen? Where was the wrong turn that ended in the fucked-up world you're living in now? Killing yourselves with your proud looks and lying tongues, hearts devising wicked plots as fast as your feet run into mischief. Hell, you know the rest of those seven deadlies, and you know how they weigh on every one of you forsaken sheep.

"I've been watching the whole damn world go right down the

drain. That world I love so much, all the creatures great and small, all the lovely plants, and all those fantastical creations you dismissed as fable, those were the first to go, as blind greed and lust stole your imagination."

"So, are you blaming yourself for letting . . . well, I assume you're talking about Satan, right? For letting Satan take control of humanity?"

Pan was silent a long time.

Keith couldn't believe what he was hearing. The half goat, half man Greek god of antiquity was taking the blame for turning humanity into a bunch of self-righteous, greedy murderers.

"Those four kids sucked up every last drop of the Angry Man's song, hook, line, and sinker, as they say. The rest is your history, the reason you're all in the predicament you're in."

"But how can four people have caused all the problems which have been visited upon humanity since the summer of 1969?"

"They weren't just four regular people after that night, don't you get it? They were sycophants, toadies, minions of the devil, fucking kiss-asses to the universe's biggest asshole. When Satan is driving the tour bus, you're a fucking rock star. Anything can happen.

"So those kids, led by Andrew Allison, fueled by the devil himself, and initially funded by Andy's 3.8 million dollars bequeathed to him by his dead grandmother, changed the course of America. And we all know: as America goes, so goes the world."

Pan had a wild look in his eyes, and for the first time Keith was sure about the creature's identity.

"Those kids left Woodstock before the moon set that night and the screws began to turn. The girls worked on pushing babies out, little incarnated spawns of the devil, and sired some of the most successful land developers, bankers, lawyers, ad men, and corporate executives the world has ever seen. Thirteen total, when all was said and done, and no I'm not going to tell you their names."

"What do you mean you're not going to tell me the names?" Keith leaned forward and clicked off the recorder. "Without names how can you expect me to check up on anything?"

"Without the names, Keith, you'll be protected. Just tell the story, that will be enough. You can guess who those rotten spawn are anyway, and so will those who read this story."

"And then what, Pan? What do you think will happen?" Keith stood up.

"We'll get to that later. Turn that thing back on please."

Keith set the tape in motion again.

Pan nodded and continued.

"While all this was going down, Andrew was investing and making millions, funding weapon manufacturing, despots and madmen, medical and pharmaceutical research—you know those pills baby boomers are popping like candy to make it through the day for whatever ailment du jour? You can thank Andy for them.

"He had all those big-time icons of the age off'd too: Hendrix, Joplin, Lennon, Elvis, Morrison, the list goes on and on. It was all part of the plan that started when the Deceiver laid hands on that loon who orchestrated the Tate and LaBianca murders. See, that rat bastard had thought old Charlie was going to be his son to walk the earth. But crazy is as crazy does. Charlie got the ball rolling against the whole revolutionary movement with those killings in California, and as Andy worked his possessed wonders on the icons of that era the dream faded faster than a sheet in the sun."

Keith had to hold back a laugh: it sounded ludicrous.

Pan settled down into his straw bed and let out a sigh. He looked like a tired old animal, laying down for the last time. When he glanced up at Keith, his eyes were distant. "Here is the thing though, man, are you ready? Are you really sure you can handle this?"

"That's why I came, to hear this story."

"I may have started the party, but Satan's plan never would have worked if dang near every last one of you hadn't *wanted* it to work. If you hadn't had that seed of greed and lust growing in your guts, the world would be a different place. If you had managed to really, truly give a shit about your environment, about the resources given to you, about your fellow fucking man, that rat bastard's plan never would have worked. Andy and his long line of progeny and partners would've just been another group of assholes in the history of mankind."

Pan leaned forward, his face twisted into a mask of distress.

"That's the thing with the devil. He knows just what to serve up, just the right ingredients to make you belly up to the chow line and eat his shit. You're here though. Maybe you're the one who can bring this whole ship back around a hundred and eighty degrees."

"I'm just a reporter, Pan, a journalist. Not a revolutionary. And to be honest, I don't think people want to change. Is there anything happening right now that is all that bad or all that new?"

"Oh it's happening, Keith, and it is getting worse. I have to have faith in Man, now more than ever. My time is almost up and we're getting close to the end of the story. Don't leave me wishing I had done more. I can't have that be my last thought."

"They don't have faith in you anymore. You're just a myth, an old dusty story."

Keith stood up and turned to look out the small window at the darkening valley. A tiny flare arose in the fire, the sizzle of sap filling the air. He turned back to his recorder and stopped the tape. "So tell me, Pan. What is it you want humanity to do? Hardly anyone believes in a god anymore, let alone a god like you. And if they don't believe in God how can you expect them to believe in the devil?"

"I don't expect you to convince anyone. But some will believe, some will hear the truth in this story and maybe trace the changes back and see those that have turned the tide. What culture has whipped around in a brodie like this—ever?"

"Humanity has turned on itself over and over. You've been around to see that, haven't you?" Keith walked around the table and sat down on the bench across from Pan's straw bed. The fire crackled, and Pan lowered his head to let out a breath.

"I have been around a long time, but I tell you now that the devil is to blame. Bring my story to light, put the wheels of change into motion once again—but for good this time. Let nature lead the way. That's all I wish."

Keith stood up as a blast of air rushed through the small shack, causing the fire to gutter. Pan settled back against the wall, looking up at Keith's eyes.

"Wish in one hand, shit in the other, though, right? You know which one will fill up first, Pan. You know all too well, don't you?"

But those eyes were not Keith's anymore. They weren't even human. They were the black eyes Pan had been dreaming of—the ones chasing him down.

Keith's face melted like a ball of wax.

The fire grew larger and the air in the shack grew so hot that the straw under Pan began to smolder. The king of all satyrs tried to get up as the transformation was almost complete. Satan, deep-red flesh stretched thin over sharp bones, face contorted in laughter, sharp teeth glistening, black horns rising from his bald head, stood looking down at him. His voice boomed toward Pan.

"Hey there, old friend. So nice to see you again." His wings unfurled and his cloven hooves stomped the ground, pushing Pan back onto his straw bed. "No need to get up. We're almost done here."

Satan's tail whipped through the air with a crack. Black hair sprouted as his hooves scratched into the dirt floor.

"So, you thought you could run and hide from me? You thought you could fuck with my plan?"

Satan's long fingers reached out, jagged nails dug into Pan's chest, and he laughed as the claw marks turned black and cauterized with his fiery touch. The satyr yelped in pain.

"And by the way, I never did thank you for that night. While I could have done it without you, you certainly did make it easier."

Pan shrank back, curling into a whimpering heap.

"That's right cry, you silly little animal. You were never a god." The devil leaned away, his roar reverberating in the small shack and echoing down the valley. Villagers later recounted that the sound was like the very earth opening up to bellow.

Bright blue flames engulfed the shack, Hell itself right out in the open, and in a matter of seconds Pan's flesh seared, blistered, and began to char. His agony was nothing but a brief flutter in the fire as his remains were rendered to ash. The wind howled and flurried around the tempest pyre.

Satan danced in the ashes and sang out in a challenge to the god that had cast him down. For he had succeeded in eliminating yet another of his long-time nemeses. With one wide flap of his diaphanous red wings, he took to the air, and Satan flew off into the night.

\*\*\*

It was a full month before the young boy who had dared to run errands for the man-beast in the mountains traveled back to the small shack; all he found there was charred earth. Kicking through the black stones he wondered if what had happened to the man-beast had anything to do with the horrible cry which had scared the elders of his village.

Picking up a charred piece of wood, he saw a small black and silver rectangle, softened at the edges.

It was a small tape recorder, like the ones in the American police shows he watched online. He pressed the small play button and was surprised by the hiss of blank tape crackling out of the speaker. He rewound the tape and jabbed the play button again. The distorted voice of the man-beast stuttered from the recorder.

". . . that seed of greed and lust growing in your guts, the world would be a different place . . ."

He pressed stop again and went down the mountain. His best

source of income was now gone. Maybe he could make some money selling the story about the half goat, half man that he'd run errands for over the last eight months.

The recorder was too melted to be worth anything so he chucked it over the ledge and watched it shatter on the red stones below. Thin magnetic tape spooled out into the frigid wind.

He pulled the zipper of his worn jacket up higher and watched his feet trundle back to his village, wishing he had some way to make enough money to get out of that backward collection of mud huts.

Machine gun fire echoed over from the next hill.

Maybe he'd join in the fight against the Americans.

He spun around when he heard someone whistling behind him, a song he didn't recognize.

A little boy was following him down the trail. He didn't remember passing him. He didn't recognize him from his village either. As the boy got closer he saw he had black eyes and a smile full of sharp glistening teeth.

# Witchcraft & Devilry

## Bennie L. Newsome

Terrance held the digital camera to his face, ensured that the subject was centered within the device's LCD screen, and took the picture. The camera beeped, made a clicking noise, then saved the image to a memory card. He lowered the camera but continued to stare at the fountain.

Thirty-two-year-old Terrance Harris was a freelance graphic designer. When he was not working on projects for his clients, the man busied himself with a personal website, *Witchcraft & Devilry*. It was for this website that he came to Birmingham, Alabama; the fountain before him, located at the hub of the historic Five Points South District, was the focal point of his journey.

"*The Storyteller*," he muttered.

Terrance moved around the landmark to capture it at different angles. Within the broad circle of the fountain, bronze animals in green patina, all larger than life, sat on pedestals just above the water's surface. Five frogs, their faces turned up, spat arcs of water that crossed at the center. Between them were larger sculptures: a lion cub, a hare riding a tortoise, and a tiny deer resting on a dog's back. But it was what captured these animals' attention that gave people pause. Though the fountain's plaque called it a ram-man, anyone who knew their Greek mythology could see it was a satyr.

Sitting on a tree stump, he held an open book in one hand and a staff in the other, an owl perched at the top. The creature had the head of a ram, its large horns curving to the back of his head, and wore a Br'er Rabbit suit.

The scene was whimsical, the sound of the water soothing.

*But that is, indeed, a satyr,* Terrance mused, taking another photo.

He first saw a picture of *The Storyteller* fountain back in his New York City loft while surfing the Internet. The satyr snagged his attention right away, but it was the article beneath the picture that made him want to see it for himself. According to the writer, a lot of the natives believed the artwork to be evil. After seeing the satyr on the glowing monitor and reading this claim, Terrance knew right away he had to document the fountain and post it on his website.

In his quest to secure firsthand information for *Witchcraft & Devilry,* Terrance had traveled to the site of the Salem Witch Trials in Massachusetts and journeyed to Adams, Tennessee, where the famous Bell Witch Haunting was supposed to have occurred.

He never actually witnessed anything supernatural and really had no desire to. The articles he posted online were mostly speculative, given strength with local rumors. Personal encounters with the supernatural were not his goal. He cherished his life too much to tempt the powers that may or may not be. He was just a sucker for a good old-fashioned ghost story.

Terrance circumvented a couple of homeless people who were sitting on the rim of the fountain and took a picture of the subject while making sure to include the Methodist church in the background. That image alone was a contradiction. The Methodist Church was known for their strict adherence to the rules and regulations of the gospel, yet a fountain housing a satyr sat mere yards from the humongous building with its Italian-style architecture. The fountain was situated on one of the intersection's five corners—city property, true—but it was basically in the church's front yard.

*And let's say there's nothing remotely evil about it,* he thought to himself. *The artist who created it has made many more sculptures which are showcased throughout Birmingham and the animalistic carvings are as innocent as they come. This fountain just happens to be the first with a ram-man.*

*But perhaps this is simply an illustration of Aesop's fables. I mean, you have the tortoise and the hare, you have a dog, and you have the storyteller. However that doesn't dismiss the fact that sitting in this fountain is a satyr, a being that represents wine and sexual pleasures, which is a complete affront to the church behind it.*

*Furthermore, in the satyr's right hand is a rod, which denotes power. Perched on the top of that rod is an owl, personifying knowledge. Therefore it claims to be a powerful and knowledgeable being. In the satyr's left hand is a book, symbolizing teachings. As the king of speculation, I can rightfully say that this satyr is supposed to be a powerful and all-knowing being promoting teachings that are in contradiction to the church. Devilry!*

Terrance smiled at his conclusion. Even if his findings were totally off base, *The Storyteller* fountain was going to make a great addition to his website—especially when he obtained some testimonies from the superstitious locals.

He began taking pictures of the surrounding landscape. Even during the middle of a work day, there was a lot of pedestrian and automobile traffic. With dozens of apartments nearby, a gigantic university just down the street, and several hospitals in the area, Five Points South remained a bustling place; the district had a little something for everyone.

Across the street was a barbecue joint. The curb in front of the establishment was lined with cars and there happened to be a steady stream of people going in and out.

*Southerners sure love their barbecue,* Terrance thought with a crooked smile.

Next door was a nightclub that wouldn't be open until later that evening. On the same block was a tattoo parlor, music shop, pool hall, tax preparation center, National Guard recruitment station, and several restaurants. Terrance captured it all on camera.

"This is going to be the easiest story I ever had to cover," he said to himself, taking a picture of a sign jutting out from a nearby lamppost that read *Five Points South,* beneath it a yellow star.

*It could be an ordinary star, but it will sound better if I say it's an undercover pentagram.*

He took a picture of the five corners that made up the intersection. Cleverly designed to represent a star, perhaps? The five frogs in the fountain were probably chosen to represent the Five Points South area, but when Terrance was done the animals and the stars and the intersection were all going to suggest a pentagram—the symbol used in witchcraft and satanic rituals. He might even suggest that some of the locals secretly worshiped the devil.

"Excuse me, mista."

Terrance turned around. A homeless man stood next to him, his head full of dirty stringy hair, his beard unkempt, and his face covered in dirt. He wore a filthy dress shirt and a pair of grungy denim jeans. He smelled like shit, too.

"What can I do for you?" Terrance said, stifling a gag.

"Listen here, man. I ain't had nuthin to eat in two days. I'm just lookin for a little change so I can get me sumthin to eat. I ain't tryin ta get high, I don't drink, I just need ta get sumthin to eat. You can buy tha food, if ya want."

"Not necessary," Terrance said, turning to face the fountain again. "How about this? You give me a little information, and I'll pay you for your time."

The man's eyes lit up. "Well, what cha need to know?"

"Rumor has it that this fountain is evil. What can you tell me about it?"

The homeless man glanced at the artwork and quickly shook his shaggy head. "Shit, ain't nuthin evil bout dat dere founten. Dat's Bob."

"Who?"

"Bob. Da ram-man. Dat's what us homeless folks call im, anyway. Ain't nuthin evil 'bout Bob. He just homeless like us. Through da cold weatha, and tha hot weatha, Bob has ta bear it just the same. People call im evil cause he misunderstood—just like us homeless folk. People call us all sorts of thangs, but tha day ends and tomorrow comes and it's tha same ol' thang. What can ya do?"

"You got a point."

Terrance no longer felt able to endure the man's fetid odor, so he reached into his pocket and struggled to remove a bill from his folded wallet without exposing it. He glanced at the bill he was holding and fought back a groan of disappointment. At least it wasn't a twenty or higher. "There's a ten for the information," he said.

"Thank ya!" the homeless man cried. "And God bless ya, brutha!"

"You have a good day," Terrance said as he turned to walk away. He wanted to be gone from that heavily homeless-populated area as quickly as possible, before word got out that some fool tourist was near Bob's fountain handing out free money.

\*\*\*

Several minutes later Terrance slid the keycard into his room's lock and waited until the indicator light on the door went green before pushing down on the handle and strolling into his room. Once inside, Terrance kicked off his shoes, then retrieved his black satchel from under the mahogany desk.

He wasn't normally a paranoid man, but he trusted the shifty-looking hotel staff about as far as he could throw them. The idea that Southerners were the most friendly people in America was a lie propagated by the media. All that separated them from New Yorkers or Californians was their southern drawl.

With the TV on—dispelling the room's eerie quiet—Terrance lay back on the bed and took out his laptop. He connected his camera to the computer and began transferring the Five Points South images onto his hard drive.

When that was done, he'd start typing up the article for his website. But he needed to interview some more people. The homeless man's talk about a misunderstood satyr named Bob wasn't going to cut it for an interesting horror story.

*I'd love to talk to some of the Methodists. Wonder how they feel about the fountain sitting on their front lawn? Maybe I can find some locals who don't consider the satyr a homeless comrade.*

He decided to go to the club he saw and do some research there. *Possibly even bring a young lady back to my room . . . to interview.*

He grinned as he decided to give the people of Birmingham—the women in particular—another chance to redeem themselves as hospitable Southern folk.

\*\*\*

Eventually the sun went down and an orange moon took its place in the darkening sky. Instead of going to sleep like a nice, respectable neighborhood, Five Points South came alive, even more so than during the day.

The streets were lined with cars, and more vehicles crept through the avenues looking for places to park. The sidewalks were crowded with women wearing their finest or skimpiest clothing and men showing off their most happening gear. The restaurants were still serving food, and the goth chick stood outside her tattoo parlor talking to the guy who sold guitars. Across the street billiard balls smacked together amidst loud talking and raucous laughter.

Terrance sat on the rim of the fountain, watching the activity, getting a feel for the place. The water splashed in the pool behind him, providing a steady stream of background music to the scene before him.

As the festivities continued without any sign of stopping, the church bells rang behind him. After the final toll, there seemed to be a split-second suspension of time in which everything froze in silence. Then the murmur of the streets rose again, but it was different; the water in the fountain no longer sounded in the background.

He turned to look at the figures in the pool. The steady stream of water that shot from the frogs' mouths trickled to a slow drip, then ceased altogether.

*Ribbit!*

It was slow at first, but then the croaking increased in both volume and tempo. The five frogs began moving. They shifted around on their pedestals, changed positions, then came to a dead halt, their faces no longer turned upward. After a couple of final croaks, the fountain was silent and water emitted from the frogs' mouths again. But the streams no longer flowed in arcs. Instead, they shot straight across, intersecting at just the right points, forming a pentagram, which encompassed the other denizens of the fountain.

A red glow emanated from the pool of water, and the other animals began to stir. The hare shook out its fur and fell from the tortoise's back as it crawled to the edge of the platform and dove into the glowing water. The lion cub stood and began pacing atop its small pedestal, and the dog nipped at the deer on its back.

Then the satyr rose. He stood tall on his hooves and stretched his metal body as if stepping out of a vehicle after a long ride. With sinister eyes, he looked around at the crowded street, and a small smile touched his ram lips. The satyr banged his staff on the platform, causing the owl to take flight and then return to its perch. The satyr held the book out before him, cleared his throat, and proclaimed in a loud, clear voice, "Let the fornication and inebriation commence!"

***

It was around three o'clock in the morning when Terrance came stumbling out of the boisterous and flashy club Twenty-Seven with his arms around the thin waist of a young lady. The woman did not have the sexy accent of a southern belle, but Terrance discovered something else he liked even more about her—she had less morals than she did clothing.

"Are you coming back to my room or not?" he said.

She smiled coyly. "Where're you staying?"

"The hotel at Twentieth and University."

"Well . . . I guess I can make sure you get to your room safely."

He gave a slight nod of his head. "Whatever you need to tell yourself, sweetheart."

The pair proceeded down the crowded sidewalk and started to turn the corner, but something in Terrance's periphery made him stop in his tracks.

He'd caught a glimpse of the satyr wading in the fountain back across the street.

*Impossible!*

He turned and stared, squinting.

The woman followed his line of sight, but failed to see anything unusual. "What is it?"

Terrance waved her off as if shooing away a fly. "Go to the hotel and . . . go on and wait on me . . . I'll be along shortly." He was drunk as he staggered to the curb.

"How can I go to the room and wait for you? I don't know what room you're staying in. I don't even have a key."

Terrance didn't hear her, nor did he notice as she returned to the club. He stepped into the street, stumbling into traffic. Cars came to screeching halts. A horn blared and the driver stuck his head out the window, shouting at Terrance.

"Oh, you shouldn't go through all that trouble to make me feel at home," Terrance mumbled, unfazed. His sights were trained on the fountain, where the satyr was waving his staff and open book, like a television preacher delivering a sermon.

Terrance received a few more honks and a heap of curses, oblivious to the commotion, before coming to a standstill in front of the fountain. And this time he really saw it, the frogs spraying streams of water in the formation of a pentagram.

*I'll be damned.*

The notion that his trumped up story was real did little to comfort him. Had he been sober he would have gotten on the first plane out of there. Instead he did something he would regret for the rest of his life.

He called out to the satyr.

"Bob?"

The dog jumped to its feet, barking at him ferociously, as the deer hopped from its back and stepped aside.

Terrance flinched and was about to run away when he realized the dog was confined to the fountain. He shifted his gaze and noticed all the other animals staring at him.

The satyr, as if interrupted, turned to Terrance, seeing him for the first time. An appalled look appeared on the ram-man's carved face and as he raised his brow, the sound of bending metal cut the air.

"Who the hell is Bob?" the creature demanded.

"Oh, shit!" Terrance wheeled around and grabbed the first person who passed by.

"Hey!" the woman cried.

"Aye, man! What's your problem?" the woman's boyfriend asked as he moved to break Terrance's hold.

"The satyr . . . it spoke to me!" Terrance said, his breath reeking of alcohol.

The boyfriend scowled, put an arm around his lady's waist, and the couple hurried away.

Terrance turned to face the angry satyr once more. Then he spun again and yelled after the fleeing man and woman, "The satyr is not sitting on his stump! The thing is walking and . . . he talked to me! I swear!"

Another group of people walked by.

"There's something wrong with this fountain!" Terrance screamed, alarming them. They hurried away just as quickly as the couple had.

"They cannot see what you see," the satyr said. "And I do not rightly know how it is that you see the truth. Perhaps you have chosen to see what others prefer to ignore. The question is why?"

Terrance watched in awe as the satyr came wading toward him

through the shallow water. He opened his mouth to speak, but the words refused to come out.

The satyr stopped at the inner edge of the jet-stream pentagram and stared quizzically at Terrance. "You're that man who was out here taking photos earlier. I'm sure you've heard the saying, 'Seek and ye shall find.' " The creature held open his arms as if inviting Terrance for a hug. "Well, apparently you have been searching for a devil, and now you have found one!"

"I wasn't looking for a devil...not exactly," Terrance stammered.

"Now that you have found me, is there anything you wish?"

He thought about the question, then slowly shook his head.

"No? You don't wish for power? You have no desire to be granted that which the Heavens have denied you? Don't you want to know the secrets of the universe?"

He shook his head again. However unreal all this seemed, he knew better than to ask anything from the Devil.

"I think I understand," the satyr said. "Your search is derived from pure curiosity."

"Like I said, I wasn't exactly looking for you. I just . . . I think I should be—"

"Wait! Before you go, may I ask you one question?"

"Okay." Terrance's heart beat rapidly.

"Much obliged," the creature said, his eerie smile sending chills down Terrance's spine. "How is it that you enjoy the pleasures I provide while not bearing my mark?"

Terrance quickly shook his head. "I didn't . . . I . . ."

"Oh yes, you have. You are clearly intoxicated by the beverages I supply to this area. And I assume you have been enjoying the pleasurable company of my beautiful women?"

"Well . . ."

"You see, Five Points South is like an exclusive club, and in order to enjoy the benefits, you must have the stamp of admission. That way everyone knows you have paid the price and you can come and go as you please. Free to partake of anything your heart desires."

Terrance was no Bible scholar, but he knew that to accept the mark of the beast (any beast) was to sentence one's soul to eternal damnation. Living his life in ignorance was one thing, but to know he'd be going to Hell when he died was quite another.

"Well," he began hesitantly. "I guess I'll be going."

"Leaving so soon?"

With his clawed hand holding the book, the satyr indicated the scene behind Terrance. "Why, the party is just getting started."

Terrance took a step back and then turned around. It had already been dark when he exited the club, but the street seemed even darker now. And though the stygian blackness was enough to unnerve any man, it was not the catalyst for the large urine stain developing in the crotch of his pants. What had really sent him spiraling was all the people. Walking along the sidewalks, going in and out of the club, or eating outdoors at the bistros, they talked and laughed and went about their business as if there was nothing out of the ordinary. They did all this with a red cloven hoof print glowing on their foreheads.

"You see? They have all been marked and they don't have a care in the world. They are content because I take care of my children. You can be like them, if you would only accept my mark."

Terrance trembled as he slowly turned to face the looming satyr. "The mark of the beast," he muttered in disbelief. "I thought I was coming to get a good story, but this is more than I bargained for."

"THE MARK OF THE BEAST?" the satyr bellowed.

The animals cringed. All except for the dog who bared its teeth and growled.

"EVIL? You know what? I had you pegged all wrong. I thought, surely he can't be a pious man. He's drunk off his ass, there's no way he could belong to that group of imbeciles."

The satyr looked over his shoulder and glared at the Methodist church. The demonic creature spat. "The mark of the beast," he reiterated with a bit more calm. "Evil. That sounds like Christian talk."

Terrance didn't know what to say. He was afraid that any amount of talking would only worsen his predicament.

"Are you one of those Methodists, boy? No, wait, let me guess. Baptist, Catholic, Pentecostal? Maybe one of those 'refuse to take a side' Non-Denominationalists? No? How about Jewish, Jehovah's Witness, Muslim, Buddhist? I don't give a rat's ass what you cling to! None of them are kosher with me! Not a one!"

The satyr's mood shifted gears as he looked to the other animals sharing his fountain. "We have us a God-fearing man here, boys.

What do you think we ought to do with him?"

Terrance's frightened eyes went from the shrinking deer to the barking dog. His gaze darted to the lion cub, which stalked around on its pedestal, rumbling, then leapt over to the hare. The only animal not paying him any attention was the turtle that swam around in the pool.

*Doesn't he get a vote?* Terrance found himself wondering.

Above him, the owl hooted, and when Terrance's head snapped upward, it stared down at him with huge eyes.

"It seems the majority has spoken," the satyr said. "You either give me your soul, or you give me your life. The choice is yours."

"That's not much of a choice," Terrance said. Tears had started down his face. "Now I see . . . I see why they call you *The Storyteller*. That's just another way of saying *The Liar* or *The Deceiver*. No matter what choice I make, I'm dead."

The satyr fixed Terrance with a horrifying scowl. "Is that your final answer?"

Terrance wiped away his tears and began to back away slowly.

*It can't harm me,* he assured himself. *It wants me to believe it has that, but it can't even pass beyond the pentagram. None of them can.*

"I guess that is your final answer."

As soon as he heard these words, Terrance turned to run but stopped short. The crowd of people stood before him, stretching as far as he could see.

With pitch-black soulless eyes, the horde glared at Terrance, the hoof print on their foreheads pulsing red.

Terrance screamed. The sound had the same effect as a starting pistol, signaling the possessed mob to rush him. His bloodcurdling shriek rent the sky.

\*\*\*

A few hours later, when the sun took its rightful place above the world, the lifeless body was found by a couple of sanitation workers going about their morning routine. The man was face down in *The Storyteller* fountain, floating among empty alcohol containers and a few used condoms.

The artwork itself appeared undamaged. Five bronze frogs sat on their pedestals, with their faces turned up, each sending streams of water that met in the middle of the pool. The hare rode its nemesis, and the lion cub sat on its hind legs, and the dog lay with the deer atop its back.

Overseeing them all was the satyr. The metal creature had reclaimed his seat on the bronze stump. One hand still clutched the nine-foot staff with the owl perched at the top, and in his other hand was the open book.

The only thing out of place was the drowned tourist.

According to both the police and coroner's reports, Terrance had consumed too much alcohol and passed out in the fountain. With his face submerged in water, it had only been a matter of time before he drowned. The anchorperson on every local news station would announce that it was a tragic accident, ignorant of the fact that Terrance had died on his quest for witchcraft and devilry.

# To Dance Among Your Puppets

## W. H. Pugmire

The masked hermaphrodite reclined on the chaise longue in his bedchamber and admired the fauns and satyrs that he had painted on the ceiling. His papier-mâché mask, which his own hands had fashioned, aped *Le Stryge*, except that the artist had given the daemon but a single horn. He had, since youth, been attracted to grotesque, fantastic things. Indeed, it had seemed like a kind of birthright: for his mother had read to him from Greek mythology since his infancy, and by the time he turned seven he was a genuine pagan, intoxicated with the beauty of Grecian things, one who built altars to Pan and Persephone. He had watched the dancing dryads and satyrs in the woods at dusk, and had mimicked that dancing when alone in starlit fields.

His mother, slightly mad, had hinted strange things about his own relationship with the creatures of myth, at times bending to kiss him just above his double sex. Before she had lost her leg, she used to climb with him in times of twilight to the attic, her special realm. Her artistic gifts, which she had bequeathed to her delicate offspring, had been put to particular use in the attic, the ceiling of which had been studded with tiny points of phosphorescence that caught and held light once the source of radiance had been extinguished, and thus after the attic lights had been switched off it appeared that the ceiling was covered with a multitude of tiny stars. Between the slanting walls of the peaked roof, his mother had fastened crude wooden rails, from which she hanged a series of the puppets that were her source of livelihood, except that these puppets in the attic were quite different from the beautiful and harmless creations sold to the public; for these puppets represented the creatures that had captivated her lunatic mind, her replications of Cerberus and Charybdis, of Medusa and Lamia. When she opened the three attic windows and allowed the night wind to rush into the attic room, she would dance with the wind-tossed figures, sometimes tilting so as to kiss the wings of Sphinx or hoof of goatish Pan.

The masked hermaphrodite remembered that distant time when his *mère* had first insisted he follow her up the ladder to the trapdoor that opened into the attic space. Dusk had fallen, and she had carried a candle with her. He watched as she pushed open the trapdoor with the back of her shoulders, and as he crept into the dusky place the woman scampered so as to light other candles. He studied the incredible creatures that hanged on their strings and began to move as his mother pulled open the room's small windows. And then the woman reached toward a ball of twine that rested on an antique table, and he marveled at how whitely his mother's teeth gleamed as they tore into the twine so as to produce four strips of lengthy cord which she dangled in the air as she tiptoed toward him. He wanted to please her (she was his only love), and so he joined in her madcap laughter as she tied the ends of cord to his ankles and his wrists. She tugged in time to her tapping feet, and he moved as her living marionette. How heavily she breathed as she helped him to pirouette. He laughed and looked up at her as his cords began to tangle, and the luminosity of her eyes astounded him, they looked so like the eyes of a Grecian goddess.

Languidly, the masked one pushed himself out of the bed and found the footwear that he had fashioned from bits of wood and leather, the outlandish espadrilles that resembled cloven hooves. He had used some of the cord from the attic to construct the soles and found the shoes easy to walk in despite their width. He stood for a moment to listen to the heavy evening wind that had awakened him from dreaming, the wind that reminded him of how long it had been since he had visited the shadowed attic. Stepping into the darkened hallway, he drifted to the ladder and clutched its frame. A mere silhouette in deeper darkness, he lifted his feet off the floor and began to ascend the ladder, until his masked head touched the trap door. One frail hand pushed above him and felt the movement of wood, and a smell of neglected things rushed to him. He pulled himself up into the familiar space and reached for the pull cord that activated electric light. Long fluorescent tubes hummed and blinked on, but their glare was far too brilliant and he quickly pulled the cord again. One thousand white points shone on the peaked ceiling, one thousand new-born stars; and beneath them hanged diminutive creatures of Grecian myth, the creations of his mother, his stillborn silent siblings.

The wind sounded outside the windows of the room, those windows that seemed alive with swaying nebulous shapes. His eyesight had adjusted to the darkness, and so he crept to the windows and opened them. Ah, the fragrant wind! It hastened past him, into the room of puppets, those creatures that began to sway and jostle. Laughing, he hopped into the madness of movement, spinning around, around, while the figures knocked against his head. He whirled in the wind until vertigo oppressed him, sending him to the floor in a heavy fall that split the surface of his mask. His monstrous countenance fell from him, and the myriad points of light fell on his beauteous face. Wearily, he shut his eyes and called a woman's name. How strange, to hear his own name echoed so manifestly on the wind.

The hermaphrodite opened his pale eyes and saw how the sky above him was like a funnel in which a multitude of stars revolved. Swimming among the stars he beheld an artificial fraternal horde. Puppets no longer, they moved their sentient arms and beckoned him. And then she appeared, out of darkness, into starlight. Her beauteous eyes were those of a goddess, as he had always suspected them to be. Her enchanting hands moved with significant motion, and he felt his wrists and ankles lift. He paid no attention as his hooves and clothing fell from him, revealing the glory of his double gender. He rose, into the funnel of shifting starlight, toward the hungry mouth that ached to kiss him once again.

# The Briggs' Hill Path

## Josh Reynolds

It was 1921. The image in Harley Warren's hands was carved from a strange dark wood and polished to a soft gleam. His fingers traced the contours of wooden hips and thighs, exploring crevices and curved protuberances, grasping the shape of the thing. The wood felt alternately rough and smooth beneath his fingertips. A thrill passed through him.

"What is that?"

Warren looked up from the image, blinking in momentary confusion. He smiled a moment later, placing the image down on his desk. "Back so soon, Carter?"

"Regrettably so; I wasn't able to find any of the items you asked for. I say again, what is that?" Randolph Carter said, gesturing.

The two men were a study in contrasts. Carter was tall and lantern-jawed, with a goggle-eyed New England face. He dressed primly, in an almost archaic fashion.

Warren, on the other hand, was dressed in an open opium-smoker's robe and silk Ottoman trousers. He had handsome wide features that nonetheless could be disturbing in the wrong light, and a mane of too-long honey-colored hair.

"What is what?" he said, sitting back in his chair.

"That. That!" Carter's gesture became sharper. Warren looked down at the image in his hands as if surprised to see it there.

"This?"

"That," Carter said. "It's hideous."

"It's a woman," Warren said, quirking an eyebrow.

Carter shuddered. "Not any woman who ever existed, thank God," he said.

"Your worldliness is exceeded only by your open-mindedness, my friend." Warren put the image onto his desk and idly rubbed the steel rings that occupied four of his fingers.

Carter frowned, but didn't rise to the bait. He had shared Warren's Charleston home for close to three years now and had become used to his friend's acerbic commentary. "I take it that it only recently arrived?" he said instead.

Warren pulled a cigarette case out of his dressing gown's pocket and flipped it open, taking one for himself and offering the case to Carter, who demurred.

Lighting the cigarette, Warren said, "Special delivery from a friend in Massachusetts. It was found in an estate sale. It's a curious thing, eh?"

"Yes," Carter said, looking at the image more closely. It had been carved from a single piece of wood, and with great skill and patience, that much was obvious. But the shape it had been carved into . . . curls of carven hair and ivy sprouted from the sloped skull, showering back in a shaggy mane, from which a quartet of curving horns projected. Instead of legs, the jointed hairy limbs of a goat, with heavy hooves that provided sharp contrast to the almost delicate hands, which were clasped between the ankles.

Despite Warren's earlier assertion, it was no woman. It was feminine, true, but to such a degree as to be too much of a good thing, with too many soft curves. The face was almost featureless in its perfection, with eyes that seemed to pull at him for all their sightlessness. They were just wood but they seemed darker, somehow, than the rest. The image smelled of—what was it?—something familiar, and his extremities tingled.

"Briggs' Hill," Warren said.

Carter looked away from the image, blinking. "What?" he said.

"Briggs' Hill. Near—ah—Zoar, I believe the town is called." Warren sucked on his cigarette thoughtfully. He ran a finger across the length of the image. "The owner died, and her belongings passed into the hands of her creditors."

"Where it should have stayed," Carter said. "It's horrible." He shuddered again, rubbing his arms.

"Matter of opinion, I expect," Warren said.

Carter looked at him, frowning. "Why did you want that thing?"

Warren shrugged. "Why do I want anything?" He indicated the rest of the closed-in porch that served as his office. Freestanding shelves, overstuffed with books and folios of all types. The floor was covered in yet more books, piled haphazardly. Statuary and iconography from one end of the globe to the other occupied what free space remained—African hate-fetishes and Auckland grindlywags competed for space with Catholic saints painted in the colors of the Loa and Inuit whalebone statues.

Warren hunted the unknown through yellowed pages and across rolls of papyrus and cowhide, looking for any gleanings of old knowledge left behind. He looted tombs—or paid others to do so—and collected the detritus of centuries with compulsive glee.

As far as Carter knew, the knowledge was its own reward. Warren had an obsession with *knowing*, which sometimes drove him to altogether unpleasant lengths.

Still, Warren's obsessions, though ugly, had their uses. They'd saved Carter's sanity, if not his life, when he'd come to Charleston, soul sick and half mad, and a half-dozen more times since.

Warren collected the hideous and the beautiful in equal measure, and Carter occasionally suspected that he, too, was a part of his friend's collection. This latest acquisition was nothing out of the ordinary. And yet the questions arose unbidden to his lips.

"Yes, but why this thing, specifically?" Carter said. "It's—"

"Intriguing," Warren said.

"Not the word I would have used."

"No, I suppose not. A number of unusual rumors abound about Briggs' Hill and Zoar; the usual strange noises and the like . . . black-winged things flitting across the moon and such." He waved a hand, adding, "Witch gossip, mostly."

"But," Carter probed, knowing Warren *wanted* to be prodded. "There's something else, isn't there?"

"Well, that depends, don't it?" Warren smiled. "What do you know of night visitors, Carter?"

Carter blinked. "By which you mean . . ."

"Incubi. Or succubi, in this case," Warren said. "Night hags, spirits of the quiet moments, bringers of the little death," he went on, seeming to relish each word.

"I—oh—no, nothing," Carter said hurriedly, his face flushing.

Warren's smile grew. "A puritanical upbringing isn't conducive to certain kinds of knowledge, eh?"

"No." Carter frowned. "What does this have to do with anything?"

"The men of Zoar fear music and goats," Warren said. His attentions were back on the grotesque statue. He stroked it affectionately, and Carter's hackles rose as the light coming in through the window made the icon look as if it were thrusting itself up to meet

Warren's fingers. "Even today they make the lords of old Salem look hedonistic by comparison. But some say this is only a mask—that by night they consorted with—well—" He broke off abruptly and looked at Carter. "You wouldn't be interested."

"If you knew that, then why even bother?" Carter snapped.

"Aren't you snippy this evening."

Carter opened his mouth to reply, but then closed it. He turned and left the porch, shaking his head.

They ate in silence and retired in the same manner. Carter to his room and Warren to a hammock on the porch. But Carter lay awake, waiting for dreams that never seemed to come anymore.

Sometimes, he was thankful for it. At other times, he wondered whether the bargain he'd made to save his soul had damned him to stultification. His dreams had once threatened to kill him, but Warren's teachings had helped him to dull his dreaming mind and to lock it away from the greater seas of sleep. Unfortunately, it often made rest hard to come by.

He rolled over, eyes closed, trying to ignore the sound of the night waves slapping against the Battery. Warren's Charleston home overlooked the sea, and its sound was omnipresent. Carter had a pronounced distaste for the sea, but he was beginning to enjoy its fruits, despite his reservations. Another of Warren's contributions to what he called his "Carter project."

Carter opened his eyes, looking up at the ceiling. The cracks there seemed to look down at him, as if they formed the features of a larger face. He blinked. The room was stifling. He sat up and went to the window, wrestling it into submission.

A sea breeze slipped in, curling around him, and he leaned against the frame. A soft rain began to fall, growing harder by the minute. Falling drops beat a stinging tattoo upon his exposed hands and face.

There was a strange smell on the breeze, not the salty taste of the sea, but something else. Carter coughed as the smell grew stronger. He felt flushed and his nightshirt was uncomfortable against his skin.

His bedroom door creaked. He turned as it swung open. "Harley?" he said.

There was the clop of a hoof on wood. The smell enveloped him, pressing on him from every direction. It was a musty smell, like a goat pen on a hot day. And then, it was something else again, something more pleasant and less brutish.

Carter stumbled forward, as if pulled by the scent. He felt intangible fingers drift across his cheeks and jaw, grasping at him, forcing him on. The sound of hooves rattled before him, and he broke into an awkward run, following them.

When he got downstairs, the door to the porch was wide open, as was the door from the porch to the backyard. The latter was a jungle of untended, hardy foliage—kudzu, elephant ears, and ferns, as well as sharp-trunked palmettos. Books lay scattered and open, their pages flipping in the quiet wind.

There was a pressure against his back, rough and smooth at the same time. It was warm—no, hot . . . terribly hot. Something wet and agile dabbed the length of his neck and he jerked forward, his shoulder connecting painfully with the doorframe. As he turned, he caught a glimpse of something lithe and feminine dashing past him on ghostly hooves, out into the backyard.

Curiosity warred with other, baser desires; but Carter followed, stepping out into the wet night, trampling ancient wisdom beneath his bare feet. Warren was, of course, already there.

Carter's friend stood among the sword-bladed palmettos, chest bared to the rain and the dark, arms spread as if in benediction.

"H—Harley?" Carter said.

Warren turned. His eyes were dark slits. "Can you feel it, Carter? The path is opening just for us."

"Path?" Carter said. "What path?"

A trill of laughter slithered through the rain and rustle of leaves. A shape moved through the shadows between the trees. Carter spun, but for some reason his eyes could not focus on the house only a few feet away. Fingers played in his hair and down his spine, eliciting a shiver from him.

Warren was still speaking. "Horned god, Ms. Murray? No, no I think not," he said, his words tripping over one another. "Not a god of fertility but a goddess of fecundity, eh Carter?"

"What?"

Warren whirled, grabbing Carter's face almost tenderly, his fingers caressing the edges of Carter's eyes. He hauled the other man around and stood close behind him. "Look! Look at her!"

Carter looked. She swayed beneath the trees, balancing on cloven hooves, her fingers trailing across the bark of the palmettos. Lush vines of kudzu slid across her skin as she stepped forward. Rainwater rolled across the smooth curves of her heavy breasts and down the flat pane of her stomach before disappearing into the hairy recesses between her oddly jointed legs. Arms stretched above her horned head, she thrust her hips forward, one leg placed in front of the other.

A sound like music trickled from her full lips, teasing Carter's ears and sending a pleasant sensation along his spine. Her head nodded in time to some distant harmony and her pearly horns sliced through the rain, the tips catching and flicking drops in a shimmering halo.

"What is she?" Carter whispered.

"I'm not sure," Warren replied, his voice hoarse. "I hadn't quite expected to encounter her so soon, but, then, it has been several weeks since . . ."

"Since what, Warren?" Carter asked.

"Since she was last sated," Warren said, shoving him forward. Carter stumbled to his knees, eyes wide.

"Warren, what—" he began, his fear pulsing through him in quivering spurts.

"Sorry, old boy. I'm not the one she wants. I tried my best, but, well, you know women."

"No!" Carter said. He tried to get to his feet as the dancing hooves brought the she-thing closer to him.

But Warren's iron grip held him down on all fours. "No? Then it's time you learned," he murmured.

Carter struggled ineffectually as the goat smell washed over him, hot and perfumed. He twisted his head, but slim fingers tangled in his hair and wrenched his face up. Music splashed across the surface of his mind as she spoke and Warren released him, stepping back.

"She's as old as time, Carter. All sin and fire. She demands nothing that no man is unwilling to give. Life unbridled, unbound. The old woman of Briggs' Hill was her priestess, her prophetess, and the men of Zoar her secret shameful worshippers, delivering her nightly offerings."

Warren's voice faded into silence, and Carter could hear him stepping back and away. Another voice took his place.

It whispered, "*IA* . . . ," as the she-thing pulled Carter to his feet; her features were blurred, all save for those eyes, eyes that burned into his and filled him with a painful heat. He staggered forward, clutching at the smooth flesh. His fingertips sizzled as he touched her, and she flowed into him, teeth nipping at his earlobe. A twisting, turning tongue squirmed across his bare chest, trailing glistening strands of saliva in strange burning patterns.

"*IA—IA* . . ."

She was known by many names . . . Ishtar and Hathor, Astarte and Cybele, the black she-goat who yearned only for man's love in the form of seed and blood. Her names skidded across his stumbling mind, insinuating themselves into his consciousness even as her fingers and tongue probed his flesh.

"*IA SHUB-NIGGURATH . . .*"

His breath came in stifled gasps as he reached up and took her horns, yanking her closer. Her pelvis ground into his, and he could feel the coarse brown hair of her lower extremities through his pajamas. The hairs seemed to curl and convulse as they tore his pants like thorns.

Clawed fingers descended, cloth ripped, and he was naked. Head thrown back, he writhed stiffly as she slid down him, her voice drowning out his thoughts, her touch plucking his nerves.

He wanted to pull away, to flee, but neither his mind nor his body was his own. A skirl of distant pipes sounded beneath the rumble of thunder. Her teeth flashed as she dragged them gently across his belly.

Carter gasped as she seized him, and a moan escaped his throat. He felt as if he were burning from within, and his body moved on instinct. She turned, her claws leaving bloody trails across his arms and chest, and sank forward, her horns dipping in readiness.

As the rain pelted down, Carter took her, and her voice changed in pitch, scratching joyfully at his soul. Somewhere, buried beneath the lust and inflamed hormones, his mind shrieked at the obscene nature of the congress.

"Carter . . ." Warren's voice tugged at him.

What had Warren said before? Was this what had afflicted the men of Zoar in the night?

Hooves dug into the ground as they strained together. Her claws flashed, tearing at him.

"Carter!" Warren said again.

Pain swept over him and his eyes sprang open.

"Carter! Damn it! Carter, WAKE UP!"

Carter tried to focus, but something blocked his vision and bound his limbs. He realized he was still in bed, still fully clothed. Something indescribably foul crouched on his chest. He tried to scream and caught sight of Warren standing over him, face twisted in an expression of horror and disgust.

Strange syllables were fired like bullets from Warren's lips, and the undulating, goatish mass uttered a shrill, inhuman shriek in response. It expanded and contracted like a plume of smoke, twisting in on itself as if weightless, yet somehow managing to keep Carter pinned in place.

He thrashed, trying to free himself. Warren grabbed his arm and thrust his free hand forward, stiffened fingers carving sigils on the humid air. As Warren yanked Carter off of the bed, the shapeless thing cycled up and around and spilled past them, still shrieking.

"What—what—what—" Carter babbled.

"A few choice phrases of mimetic verse I learned from a friend in Tibet, enough to shatter the thing's link to your subconscious." Warren pulled Carter to his feet. "Are you hurt?"

"No. No. What was that?"

"Something unpleasant, come on," Warren said, heading downstairs. Carter followed him on shaky legs.

"I saw it, but it wasn't like that, it was . . ." Carter shook his head, trying to put his dream into words. "What was it?"

"A remnant of an older time, something—ah," Warren said. The wooden icon of Shub-Niggurath sat where he'd left it on his desk. "A memory of a ghost of a thing," he said as he picked up the statuette gingerly and carried it toward the fireplace. "I had hoped to add this to my collection, but obviously it's still dangerous, even with its owner's passing."

"You—you knew?" Carter hissed. His skin crawled as Warren started a fire.

"I suspected. But I hoped it would come for me, as opposed to you. Unfortunately, you're a much stronger dreamer than either of us gave you credit for."

The fire blazed to life and Warren tossed the image into it. "There. That should do it."

The woman shape seemed to twist and turn in an attempt to escape the flames, and Carter felt a stab of something inside him.

The dream hung heavy on his mind, and he could taste the salt of her kisses and feel the rough press of her limbs. Part of him yearned to dive headlong into that fireplace and rescue the thing. Then, the wood cracked and blackened, emitting a shrill whine that might have contained a trace of music in it—but, then again, perhaps not.

Regardless, Randolph Carter shuddered and looked away.

# Goat Songs

## Mark Valentine

The wooden door had swollen in the rain and the paint, once bright yellow, had peeled away, leaving large patches of streaked bare wood. He pushed hard and it grudgingly opened. A thick odor descended upon him, the same one that seemed to linger in every secondhand record shop he had been in: an acrid mixture of patchouli, sandalwood, and sweat. Except that this one had another sharp tang to it, really rich and rank: French cigarettes, he guessed, like those fat cylinders of black tobacco he'd once smoked himself.

He nodded at the counter. He hardly needed to look to know who would be there. They were nearly always the same: men with gray flesh that seldom saw daylight, a large never-quite-white T-shirt from concerts ten years ago, and an unbarbered beard, often full of crumbs. There was also something grave and slow about them, as if they lived in a world where time went on differently, a dimension that only existed in these sorts of shops.

He'd lost count of how many he must've been in. There were a lot less than there used to be. Most weekends, he'd take a train or bus to some obscure provincial town, work through the market stalls, junk shops, and charity shops (hard work in its way, and usually for nothing much), and keep a look out for any surviving record shops. They were usually in back streets and had names like Rock of Ages, Second Spin, Wax Works, or simply, for the less imaginative, Bob's Records.

He'd started young, when he was seventeen, and all his friends were buying disco records or painting themselves up for the New Romance. They didn't call to him: what did were the heady days of the sixties (which also happened a lot in the early seventies, but time was never neat like that). He loved the hazy psychedelic albums, with their cover designs of flowers, pixies, and mushrooms; the spaced-out drones from primitive synthesizers or mishandled sitars, with their images of deep, star-strewn space; the triple gatefold concept albums about Nirvana, Arcadia, Atlantis, and other way-out places. They were well out of fashion when he began collecting them, and he bought boxfuls for a few shillings each. But now their rarity, even more than their weird qualities, was much better understood, and it was desperately hard to find anything out of the way or unheard of. He still followed his rite of visiting distant little towns, but it was as if the search itself was now as important to him as the finding. It had become just what he did.

He began to thumb through the racks of musty, dog-eared albums in the Rock section, starting properly at *A* and working his way through the letters one by one. Flip, flip, flip, the tired old titles he always saw, making his spirits sink. By the time he got to *D*, that creeping sense of despair had begun to steal over him. What was he doing in this draughty, smelly shop, what was he doing in this dingy, sodden town, what was he doing with his life even, on his own in a rundown rusty caravan without wheels, hidden in the corner of a nestle-infested field, hooked up to an uncertain power supply? The collection was better housed than he was. It had a shed to itself, from which he would fetch records to play, alone at night. Or he would play Record Roulette: roll a dice, count the albums from the number thrown, and you must play that. All the way through. Then roll again and start where you left off . . .

He realized his fingers were flipping automatically, and he wasn't looking at the sleeves. He stopped, sighed, and let his arms drop to his sides. And then he did something that he never did, or hardly ever, only if the bus or train was due and he had to hurry. He skipped over the letters and went straight to the place where he really wanted to look, under *S*. He stood in front of it, the section that was always the biggest, and he stared, as if willing it to hold what he wanted, the rarest album ever, the mythical work he had never seen.

He stretched his pale hand out slowly, as if he were taking part in some ritual, because he practically was. Then, very carefully, he drew the stacked records toward him, one by one.

It wasn't a bad selection. Sublunar was here, those cosmic travellers; Stray Horse, the country band; Swiftwillow, the dreamy folkies; Saturn Temple, the overlords of occult gloom; and . . . and . . .

He froze.

His fingers stopped, and he swallowed. He hardly dared to look properly. But it was there, all right: *Goat Songs* by Satyr. He had seen enough pictures of the album to know it at a glance. The title and the band's name were done in curled lettering, all adorned with thorns, and there was a painting showing an English lawn, with croquet hoops, flower beds, a fold-up chair and table, and a jug of lemonade. A Tudorish sort of house could dimly be seen in the background. A girl's straw hat lay negligently on the grass, as if it had been thrown aside. There were shrubs of laurel in a virulent green, and topiary cut into curious swirling shapes, not quite rooted to the ground.

Despite the title of the album, he knew that there would be no goat or mythical creature to be seen, just the placid, genteel garden vista. Except if you looked carefully, and he was looking very carefully now, there they were, right by the edges of the shrubs, a pattering of marks in the grass: the marks of cloven hoofs. And, trailing through the bushes, fading off into the edge of the picture, was a pink ribbon such as a girl might wear about her, like a sash.

He stared at the album cover as if he could will himself into the scene. None of the blurry reproductions he had viewed in collectors' magazines or guides did it justice. They were no more than a gray ghost of the full eerie splendor he now saw before him. He stole a glance at the guy behind the counter, who was ruminating over a crossword and taking no notice of him. He stood in front of the album a few seconds longer, as if to preserve the precious moment. Then, with gentle delicacy, he reached slightly forward and enticed it into his fingers, as casually as he could.

He stared once more at the cover design, then turned it over. The other side was much plainer, simply a wash of a faded, fawn colour, and the essential facts delineated in a deep brown ink. He checked the track listing and they were all there, the five titles whose general shape he knew by heart, four on side one and one long track, nineteen minutes, on side two. Shape only because all five were entitled in Greek lettering, which apparently even when translated (yes, some aficionado had taken the trouble) didn't mean anything in that old tongue, other than a sort of set of exclamations. So they were known instead, uninspiringly, as "Goat Songs I to V."

He would have to have it, even if the record itself was badly scratched and smeared, but he still thought he ought to check. That was part of the ritual also: always ease the sleeve out, span your hand from the label to the black rim, and tilt the disc to the light, so that the sheen would show you where the blemishes were.

With painstaking care, he reached inside, teased out the white envelope, with its crackling cellophane centre. He put the album cover down carefully and took out the holy thing itself, the record that he, and hundreds of others, had so long sought. He was fearful that he would stupidly drop it, so he let his moist thumb and forefinger touch the edges, something he always tried to avoid. In the dim light of this shack of a shop, lit by a single bare bulb, it was hard to see for sure, but there didn't seem to be much wrong. Perhaps the slightest hint of scuffing here and there, and something had been incised in the run-off groove, some sort of crude symbol, probably not a pressing mark. A couple of curves, like parentheses. But from his long years of experience, he thought the record would play well enough. He replaced it in its sleeve, and slotted that back in the cover, pausing once more to admire the cover painting.

He realized he had not dared to look at the price. There wasn't one. He turned the record over several times, looking for it. The excitement of the find was still keen upon him, but he also now began to feel a heavy dread. If you had to ask for the price, did that mean it was going to be vast, well beyond his range? And yet it hadn't been kept behind glass, in a special case, as was usually the case with records known to be rare. Did they really know what they had here?

He set the record right again in its niche in the *S* shelves, and quickly scanned back to the other albums. They each had a small oblong sticky label on the front top left—he wished they wouldn't do that, it always left a residue of gray skin—and the price was written in smeared blue ballpoint. They were at the lower end of usual: not a giveaway, not a collector price.

Well, there was nothing for it. He flicked back to pick up Satyr's album and take it to the counter. For a few moments his heart pounded when it wasn't there, wasn't where he thought he'd put it back: he flipped frantically, making the albums thud against each other and raising a haze of gray dust, until his trembling fingers found it again and took hold of it firmly by the corner. It was as if the damned thing had deliberately tried to elude him, had gone off to hide in the dimmer recesses of the racks.

There was no point in looking for anything else now. He didn't even go to see if White Lantern's *Mothlight* LP was there, his second (but now, he hoped, promoted to his first) greatest want. He took his find as calmly as he could to the drowsy gentleman at the counter, who was perched uncomfortably on a three-legged stool.

The deep, rank smell he'd caught when he entered the shop emanated out in greater waves now, that mingling of joss sticks and continental cigarettes, and some sort of riper, rawer stench he could not really place. The shopkeeper, or the guy looking after the place, whichever he was, had thick gold rings on most of his fingers, bearing the signs of modern witchery—a horned figure, a pentacle, an ankh, and, less commonly, what looked like a black moonstone.

The album was turned over in the adorned fingers a few times, and there came a noise from the throat, halfway between a grunt and a bleat. He waited in what seemed like a long brittle silence, broken only by the curious ululation.

"It's priceless this, mate."

Here we go, he thought, talking it up.

"Yes?"

"Ha ha, just kidding. I mean it hasn't got a price, you see?"

Oh very funny.

"Yes, I couldn't see one."

"Nice cover."

"Mmm."

"Well—say a tenner?"

Oh yes. That tenner was tendered with the utmost celerity.

"Need a bag?"

"No, thanks."

No. Just need to get out very, very steadily, but very quickly, before anything changes. Before the shop folded in on itself and he was lying on the bunk in the caravan and the rain was leaking through the hinges of the skylight.

***

All the way home on the rattling, creaking green bus, he held the album carefully and thought of everything he knew about it. Made in 1970 in the far west of Cornwall, it was said, sometime after the Glastonbury Fayre, by a group of four musicians nobody had heard of much then, nor very much since. Singer with acoustic guitar, then one each on flute, fiddle, and a girl on tambourine. But not what you could call folk music, supposedly, at least not English folk music. No fol-de-rols and no gallant highwaymen nor sailors neither. Somebody had once done a feature on them in a fanzine, a huddle of pages stapled together, and they had photocopied a few interviews from the freak scene of the time. What Satyr was about, it seems, was going deeper back, to the very origins of music, to the sounds the ancient Greeks knew. Of course, in those times they had a lyre and a syrinx and a cithara, it said, not modern instruments, but Satyr claimed they could still get close to the spirit of what the Greeks heard.

The other odd thing about them, he remembered now, was a bit of a gimmick: they didn't give themselves names. They said they were all Satyr. So the interviewer then had had to refer to them as singing Satyr, flute Satyr, fiddle Satyr, and girl Satyr. Nice idea, but a bit too outlandish really, and much good it had done them. The album, and the band, had vanished without a trace. The seventies wore on to a weary and disillusioned end, and they fell well out of fashion. Only a decade or two later did the old word of mouth begin to tell of them. Whispers passed among the red-eyed collectors at fairs and at the meetings of the Society of the Seventies.

He got off at the village green, resisted the urge to go and have a celebratory drink at the Black Lion because something might get spilt, and took the rutted cart track through the woods to the concealed plot, no more than a paddock, where he was allowed to keep the caravan, and to live (if the council never found out), for a few quid in hand or a bit of jobbing work every now and again, when the farmer remembered.

The rain had stopped and the leaves of the oak and ash were translucent with jewelled green. The birds sang in delight at the bounty the rain had brought, and a pale sun gilded the gray clouds. Away on the horizon were the low blue hills, little mounds and cones that always seemed to call to his soul, in their misty indigo haze. There must have been temples there once, he sometimes thought, shrines hidden in the hollows. Perhaps he would go to find out one day when his collecting days were done. His foot slipped in a rut, and he clutched the precious album more closely to him.

Round the corner, and his decrepit old caravan came into view. Many days he loathed it, this tin box where he lived, and wondered why he had never made the effort to get on, find a job, find real friends (not just collecting friends), maybe even get a girl. One gray day succeeded another. He grew sick even of his albums, and very lonely. He'd walk into the village for no particular reason, just to talk to someone, in the pub or the post office. But there were also days when he seemed to have all he really wanted, even the list of albums he didn't have, since that gave him dreams and a purpose.

He tugged on the corroded chrome handle, and the door sagged open toward him. The place was a bit of a mess, he had to confess. He put the album down carefully on a shelf where he could not possibly sit on it, and began tidying up. He knew it was daft, but he wanted to enjoy the great find in the nicest surroundings. And he also knew he was putting off the moment when he had to find out whether the album was as legendary as its reputation.

After fifteen minutes or so, it was as neat as it was ever going to get. He fumbled in a drawer and found a packet of Pan incense sticks. He lit a few so they stuck upward like a smoldering crown. The spirals unwound and he snuffed appreciatively: there was something in the perfume, just some elusive hint, that reminded him of the shop. He thought he might as well make a real ceremony of it too, so he uncorked the bottle of Macedonian red wine someone had given him when he'd helped get their car out of a ditch. By god, it smelt like vinegar, almost as acrid as, as . . . yes, as that blessed shop again. But it tasted all right, good enough anyway.

All he had was a portable record player in lurid orange leatherette, found in a junk shop. He liked it because it reminded him of the early seventies, when it would have been quite an in thing. He took great care to get the right needles for it, that was important to save your records. Sometimes he paid more for a stylus than his food bill for a week. It didn't matter. That old music was what mattered.

He took *Goat Songs* out of its cover and out of its inner sleeve and carefully lowered it onto the spindle. He moved the playing arm and the turntable started up at that slow, hypnotic 33 rpm speed he knew so well, which almost seemed a part of his own inner rhythm. He lowered the needle onto the outer groove. There was the satisfying sound of the sharp point drifting over the spirals. He knew he was holding his breath.

A fanfare-like acoustic guitar burst out in great chords, and the tambourine shivered across them. After a few moments, this gave way to the most extraordinary sounds he'd heard from a human throat, a snarled, goatish singing, soon joined by sinister flute and violin flourishes. Then a young woman's ethereal voice echoed as though from some deep cavern, in a beautiful, imploring chant.

He found himself entranced. The pace was fierce, frantic even, and yet it did not sound like rock. There was no deep bass pulse or thudding drum, no wailing guitar: the sounds from the instruments were pure, untreated, and yet no less urgent. Oh yes, certainly: *Goat Songs* was all he had hoped, as weird, as wild as its repute. He felt a surge of delight well up in him, and wondered if he had ever been happier. The thrilling, and so rare, so precious music, the wine that blazed in his veins, the fine surges of incense, all swept over him so that he did not want these moments to end.

In his imagination, he dwelt upon the lovely, but also rather sinister scene on the album cover. It was as if he *felt* the colors: the vivid green of the lawn, the lurid yellow of the lemonade, the pale straw of the fallen hat, and the fluttering pink of the torn ribbon. And then he laughed to himself, and he remembered the marks of the cloven hooves, and he saw himself barefoot, placing his own soles upon the marks, and how the hollows they made seemed to seep around his feet, drawing them in.

But the mud of the hoofmarks was not clammy or cold. It was fiery. He danced upward and found that he was cavorting on the lawn, singing, prancing, uttering at intervals incantations, he and the others, his four companions. As the last song on the first side shimmered into silence, he found his eyes were closed, and this vision began to fade. He was swaying a little in a blissful reverie. All around him the overpowering, musky stench rose in waves and he snuffed at it with deep, animal pleasure.

Out of the silence, gently, as one who conducts a solemn ritual, he felt toward the disc, turned it over, and set the next side going. Then he sank back again. The needle clicked over the opening grooves with that well-loved scuffling sound. And the scuffling continued: the fifth song did not start. Ah, so there was a little fault then. Not a serious matter. He bent forward and placed the stylus closer to the first track and waited. Still only that sound of slow, spiraling, circular pacing. Some little trick, perhaps, to fool the listener? But nothing else began. He found himself being drawn in to the monotonous, regular rustling, like something ... like something making its way through tall grasses, through bushes and twisted trees. Like hooves, like cloven hooves, pacing steadily, stealthily . . .

# Uncle Kantzaros

## Iain Grant

People might find it hard to imagine how Nell could possibly fail to see such radical change come over her, but those people, just like the rest of us, perfectly aware of the invisible progress of the hour hand, are still capable of looking up at the clock and declaring, "Is that the time?"

Nell's life seemed to be composed of nothing but monumental yet incremental transitions that inevitably took her by surprise. By the age of twenty-three, she discovered that without effort or choice, she had acquired a job in a gray and windowless call center which she neither liked nor was suited to, a flat in a converted Victorian townhouse furnished with items that she could not recall buying, and, most baffling, she had acquired a man called Robert who might be regarded as her boyfriend or possibly just a work colleague who she had sex with from time to time and who had once told her that he thought he sort of loved her and if he didn't then he certainly jolly well liked her a lot.

It was in this manner that, over the course of months, Nell acquired a pair of goat legs, complete with hooves.

It started as four large calluses, two on the ball of each foot. Actually, it started on the day when she realized her sensible flat shoes were too small. Actually, it started one Sunday morning when Robert rolled over in his bed, ran his hand up her leg, cleared his throat and said, "My, how continental." She protested that she had shaved just the day before. Robert said he didn't mind. Of course he didn't mind. He, like her, was a great accepter of change.

The following month, she shaved, applied depilatory creams and hot waxes, and eventually made an appointment with her doctor. During the same period, she found her feet beginning to ache, her shoes suddenly too small, and saw the skin underneath her toes and the balls of her feet harden and thicken.

The doctor inspected Nell's legs and suggested that it might be hormonal. Nell pointed out that at the age of twenty-three she was hardly likely to be menopausal. She asked the doctor about her aching and inexplicably larger feet. The doctor suggested bigger shoes.

Nell tried larger shoes and took to walking around her flat barefoot. She didn't realize that she had also taken to walking on tiptoes until Robert pointed it out one evening when he'd come round for a spag bol dinner and a bit of a cuddle on the sofa. She tried putting her heels down on the ground but it felt sickeningly wrong, as though it would unbalance her and tip her backward.

As her feet narrowed and her toes became encased in skin and nail, she abandoned shoes altogether. She surrendered her legs to the hair not long after that. She invested in a number of floor-sweeping skirts to wear outdoors. These did not go down well with her supervisor, Josephine, who thought they looked suspiciously "folksy."

Embarrassment at her physical state led her to break up with Robert. Nell found this hard to do, not because of any emotional attachment, but because she remained unsure as to whether he was actually her boyfriend. At work she spoke to him, about people and time and moving on and sort of said that she probably wouldn't be inviting him over again anytime soon, and he nodded and said it was ok and went back to his cubicle, leaving her wondering if she had actually managed to break up with him or not or whether they had ever been together.

And then, on the first of December, she pulled back her duvet and looked at her crooked legs in the condensation-streaked light of day, at the tufty brown hair that covered each of them from hip to cloven toes and, like an optical illusion being revealed, saw with soft surprise that she possessed, had possessed for several weeks, a fine pair of goat legs complete with hooves. The only thing she did in the light of this knowledge was to make an experimental purchase of dog shampoo to wash her goaty fur. She was unconvinced by the results.

\*\*\*

Nell prepared for a quiet Christmas. On the last Friday before the holiday, the office underlings at the Blame 'n' Claim call center decamped to the nearby Harvester pub and Nell found it easier to be dragged along than resist. She sipped a rum and coke and smiled whenever anyone looked at her. Robert approached her with a badly wrapped present, told her that it was just a little something for both Christmas and birthday and then almost kissed her once, bobbing his head like a chicken, and then succeeded on the second attempt, but sort of missed and kissed her on her cheekbone. Nell found herself ridiculously touched by the gesture, thanked him, downed her drink, and went home to have a cry.

By the time she got there, she couldn't be bothered to cry and instead put her one present under the Christmas tree by the television and did the previous night's washing up.

There was a knock at the door. She dried her hands and opened it to find on her landing a short man with thick wavy hair and a scruffy beard. He held an umbrella in one hand and a tall bottle in an off-license carrier bag in the other.

"Hey, hey, hey!" he exclaimed, spreading his arms wide.

"Yes?" said Nell. "What can I do for you?"

The little man shrank back immediately and gave her a hurt look. "Is that any way to greet your favorite uncle?"

Nell frowned. "You're not my favorite uncle. I don't have an uncle."

"That you know of," he said with a waggle of his brolly. "I am your Uncle Kantzaros. Your only uncle, ergo, your favorite uncle."

"What do you want?"

"I come to bring an end to care and worry!" he declared, his voice raised once more, his arms open to embrace her.

"No thanks," she said and shut the door.

As she turned, there was a loud thump, a yelp, and a whimper. She opened the door again to find the bearded man clutching his hairy knee. His lip was trembling.

"I banged it," he said. "Very hard door."

Nell looked at his little goat legs and hooves and at the roguish glint in his otherwise pathetic eyes.

"My uncle?" she said.

He sucked through his teeth and rubbed his knee. "Kantzaros. Kalli Kantzaros. You should have a sign. It's a very hard door."

"Were you trying to kick it in?"

He shrugged. "Worth a try."

She sighed, stepped back, and ushered him inside.

"For you," said Kantzaros, passing her the off-license bottle as he hobbled in.

"Oh, what's this?" she said without enthusiasm as she opened the bag.

Kantzaros trotted into her kitchen, his wounded knee forgotten, and reappeared with glasses.

"Wine," he said. "The end to care and worry."

As she poured, he whipped off his scarf and threw it onto the table. He took a glass from her and drank deeply. She gestured to his legs.

"Are you . . . ?"

"Staying long?" he said, jiggling his empty glass at her. "No. Till the last day of Christmas, no longer."

"No, I was asking . . . saying . . ." She refilled his glass. "You appear to have goat legs."

"Ah. Or is it the goat that has mine? Drink up."

The wine looked cheap and nasty, the label indicating neither grape nor country of origin, and she sipped it cautiously. However, its taste was not the poky vinegariness she expected but a warm, rounded fruitiness that spoke of golden summer days, of sunlight on leaves, of wide cloud-speckled skies.

"That's nice," she said.

"Nice?" he replied indignantly. "Is that what passes for acclaim these days? That Bacchus should hear such damning praise! Where are your poetic metaphors of joy? Where are your superlatives?"

"I mean it is *very* nice," she said.

He humphed. "You're obviously not drinking it right."

He pressed the tip of his brolly under the base of her glass, tilting it up so that she was forced to drink it or spill it. She swallowed in desperate gulps and gasped when it was done.

"Better," said Kantzaros. He snatched the bottle from her and charged their glasses once more (although she hadn't seen him drink his second). "And do you?"

"Do I what?" said Nell.

"Appear to have goat legs."

He poked at her skirts with his brolly.

"Never you mind what's under there," she said with a laugh. The wine seemed to have gone straight to her head. "Have you eaten?"

"More than once," he said.

"I think I could rustle up an omelette or something."

"You have the omelette. I'll have the something," said Kantzaros.

She cooked while he drank and then they ate and drank together, and although she had no wine in her flat, and he had definitely brought only one bottle, there were at least six empty wine bottles on the table when he put his knife and fork down and pushed his plate away.

Kantzaros passed wind.

"Charming," she said.

"You're welcome," he replied drunkenly. "Such a meal deserves thanks. It is the season of gifts, after all." He focused slowly on the one present beneath Nell's tree and went silent.

"You've got a gift for me," Nell prompted.

"Have I?" he said in loud confusion. "Not yet. Let's see. When I was king, I . . ."

"You were king?"

"Shush. When I was king, I offered another the gift that everything he touched would turn to gold."

"No thanks. I know that story," said Nell.

"It would make everything look jolly—" he paused to hold down a belch "—Christmassy."

"No thanks."

"Oh. Course, there's nothing more Christmassy than an old goat. The old Yule goat. You ever been to Scandinavia?"

"No."

"Lovely, lovely part of the world. All those . . ." He made a wobbly hand motion. "You know?"

"Fjords?"

"Maybe," he said. "Think I need to throw up now."

"Bathroom's that way. Through the bedroom."

As her uncle vomited noisily into the toilet, Nell made a

half-hearted attempt to clear away the plates and tried to work out how she came to have a drunken satyr in her bathroom. *Was* he a satyr? Or a faun? Or just a goat man? Was he even her uncle? And, seeing as he wasn't in any fit state to go anywhere else, where was she going to put him up in her one-bedroom flat?

It took her a good while to realize that everything had gone quiet in the bathroom, and she went to investigate, only to find her uncle in the gloom of her bedroom, sprawled face up across her bed. He was very still.

"Uncle?" she said softly. His eyes were closed. She leaned over him. "Kantzaros."

He chuckled faintly and licked his lips but that was all.

"So I'll sleep on the sofa then," she said and then saw something on the brow of his head. His wavy hair had fallen back and beneath it she saw two stubby protrusions.

"You have horns."

"Course I do," he slurred. "Two on me 'ead and a horn o' plenty just for you." He grabbed at the fur-matted mound of his naked groin to make his bawdy point and giggled.

"Disgusting," she said.

She was at the door when he said her name.

"Nell. Nell."

"What?"

"You want to know the truth?" he said.

"What?"

He beckoned her over. She hesitated.

"C'mere," he growled.

She went to the bedside.

"The best thing for a man is not to be born at all," he said. "And, if already born, to die as soon as possible."

She looked at him. "Get some sleep," she said.

He was snoring before she had left the room.

*\*\*\**

Nell woke to the sound of banging. She sat up, cautiously tested the crick in her neck that had come from a night on the sofa, and looked round. It was afternoon. And it was Christmas Eve. There was no sign of last night's meal on the table. Kantzaros's scarf had gone from the back of the sofa. There was, in fact, no indication that a boozy satyr had been in her flat at all. She was quite prepared to accept that she had dreamt the whole scene, except there was the banging coming from the bathroom.

She got up, noting blithely that she had no hangover, and went into her bedroom to find Kantzaros, in his scarf, hanging from the top of the bathroom door, swinging it from side to side and seeming to do his best to pull it from the wall.

"What are you doing?"

"Waiting for you, my dear."

"I meant what are you doing to my door?"

"Just testing it. Some of those screws are very loose, you know. Shoddy workmanship."

"Could you stop?"

"I could do a great deal many things."

She coughed.

He looked at her and then dropped to the floor.

"But you're up now," he said. "Let's go."

"Where are we going?"

"I need to pick up a couple of presents. And a priest."

"You need to pick up a priest?" she said.

"And a couple of presents. Chop chop. Let's go."

"In a minute," she said. She went into the bathroom and closed the door firmly.

"Are you seriously going to wear that?" said Kantzaros as she came into the lounge fifteen minutes later.

"What?"

"That," he said, pointing to her skirts with his umbrella.

"What would you rather I wore?" she said.

Kantzaros gestured to his own unclothed lower half.

"You can't go out without anything on . . . downstairs," she said.

"Why? Donald Duck does it all the time."

She looked at him for a long time.

"The skirt stays," she said, the conversation over.

\*\*\*

~ 229 ~

They walked arm in arm along the snowy high street. The passersby appeared not to notice Kantzaros's goaty legs at all, and Nell wondered if they would notice if she whipped her skirt off and exposed her own to the world.

"Here," said Kantzaros, stopping outside a shop Nell had never seen before, a dingy-looking thing with a low doorway and leaded windows.

"Won't be a minute," he said. He ducked inside and shut the door when she made to follow.

She tried peering through the windows to see what he was up to, but the glass was dirty and all she could make out was two figures shifting and gesturing by what appeared to be candlelight.

When Kantzaros emerged much later he carried two parcels, one red with green ribbon and one green with red ribbon.

"That wasn't a minute," she said, stamping her hooves against the cold.

"That's what I said," he replied, grinning. "And now a priest."

"Where are we going to find a priest today?"

"At midnight mass."

"It's not midnight yet."

"Time for a drink then."

In the pub, Kantzaros drank and talked, and at midnight they stumbled giddily out to a nearby church from which came the sound of singing.

"We're late," said Nell.

"Best time to arrive."

Kantzaros rattled the door latch noisily as they entered. The carollers turned as one to look at them.

"Excuse us!" he said in a loud voice and trotted across the flagstones to an empty pew near the front.

He picked up a service sheet and gustily joined in the song. Nell had half expected him to sing the wrong words out of tune, but he sang with the others in a rich baritone that dwarfed the rest of the congregation in tone and passion. By the end of the verse, it was as though the carol had not existed, had not been worth singing until Kantzaros lent his voice to it.

When the last note faded, Kantzaros nodded to the parishioners to soak up the praise he imagined they were silently heaping on him.

They then sat down for the sermon. Kantzaros grunted approvingly at everything the vicar said, throwing out a "hear hear" every now and then. The young vicar gave them a stern gaze and tried unsuccessfully to ignore them.

They passed the vicar on the way out. Nell shook his hand politely.

"I hope you enjoyed the service," he said stiffly.

"Bloody loved it," said Kantzaros, pumping his hand. "Can I just say something, vicar?"

"Yes?"

Kantzaros stretched himself up to put his mouth to the vicar's ear. Nell didn't quite make out what was said but the tone of it was clear as was the sudden reddening of the vicar's face. The young man backed away as though slapped, swinging his vestments and looking around wildly in embarrassment to see if any of his congregation had heard.

"See you next year," said Kantzaros, patting him on the shoulder and running off laughing.

Left with the poor vicar, mortified and apoplectic, his mouth working silently like a fish's, Nell decided the best thing to do was leave, so she ran too and, somehow, running made it funny and then she began to laugh.

Eventually she caught up with Kantzaros on the corner. The satyr was bent over, catching his breath.

"Hoo!"

"Was that it?" said Nell.

"Hmmm?"

"You wanted to find a priest so you could whisper vulgar comments in his ear?"

Kantzaros nodded happily. "It's expected. We spend eleven months of the year underground, sawing away at the roots of the world tree . . ."

"There's a world tree?"

"Of course. Do you doubt your brother's word?"

She stopped. "Brother?"

He pulled a face. "Uncle. King. Brother. What does it matter? It's all good."

She made a skeptical noise and started walking. "So you saw through the roots of the world tree. Why?"

"To bring about the end of the world, of course," said Kantzaros, falling in beside her. "An end to care and worry."

"Why would you want to do that?"

He shrugged. "It's expected. Anyway, that's for eleven months of the year, but at Christmas, just when the tree's cut all the way through, we're allowed up into the world above."

"So I've got you all Christmas?"

"I know! Wonderful, isn't it? All the way through to Epiphany. Twelve days, like the song. Of course, I know a better version of that. Who wants two turtledoves, when you can have two plums, two melons?"

"Ah, crudity," she said.

"All the best things come in pairs. Well, apart from one thing," he said lewdly and would clearly have made another crotch-waggling gesture if his hands hadn't been full of presents. "Can't count any higher than two, anyway. There are some numbers I can't bear to speak."

"What? Like three?"

He recoiled and spat. "Horrible holy number."

She nodded. "Wondered why you didn't go up for a sip of communion wine in the church."

"Waste of good grapes," he said sourly and then suddenly brightened. "Which reminds me . . ."

"What?"

He raised one of the presents.

"It's Christmas day."

\*\*\*

At her flat, in the dim light thrown off by the Christmas tree's fairy lights, she sat and opened the green parcel with red ribbon. Inside, nestling on a thick cushion of tissue paper, was a long-necked bottle of dark green glass with a waxy cork stopper. Nell lifted it out. It looked very old.

"Wine?" she said.

"An offensive suggestion. It's nectar."

"What? Like the stuff bees drink?"

"Hardly."

He suddenly had glasses in his hand and equally suddenly the bottle was open. As the rosy-red liquid was poured, Nell caught the honeyed scent of the drink.

"This," said Kantzaros with quiet seriousness, "that Thetis used to anoint Achilles, that Calypso offered to Odysseus. Nectar."

He offered her a glass, clinked his gently against hers and they drank. It was a powerful and heady drink, as strong as any spirit but dressed up in the warm, rich flavors of every sweet thing she had ever loved.

"Wow," she said.

"Hmmm," said Kantzaros. "Better than 'that's nice' I suppose."

The glass was empty and she put it down clumsily, noting that the brew had already reached her limbs.

"And this one?" she said, indicating the other parcel.

"That one's for January the fourth."

"You're staying until my birthday?"

"Of course. But what's this?" He leant across the sofa, plucked Robert's badly wrapped present from under the tree.

"Oh, no," she said. "It's going to be embarrassingly rubbish."

"Fantastic! I can't wait."

As she reluctantly opened the parcel, Kantzaros nibbled on a strip of wrapping paper.

Nell pulled back the leaves of the box to reveal a selection of steel kitchenware: spatula, whisk, potato peeler, and cheese grater all sat in the bowl of a colander.

"I always moaned about not having enough utensils," she said.

Kantzaros nodded. "That's . . . um . . . hmmm. Who is this gift from?"

"Robert."

"And who's Robert?"

"I don't know. I really don't," she said, smiling. She jiggled her glass at him and he obligingly topped it off with nectar. As she drank, she luxuriated in the physical warmth it transferred to her.

"Drink of the gods, eh?"

"You betcha," said Kantzaros. "Tantalus was condemned to eternal torment for daring to steal it."

"And you?"

"Huh?" He looked at her and his roguish grin wrinkled oddly. "Damned and blessed in equal measure. I am the night on the town and the morning after."

She reached forward and ruffled his hair. Her fingers lingered on his stubby horns. "You are the very devil, Kantzaros."

"There is a certain superficial similarity."

He put his hand to the crown of her head, felt the smooth, hornless curve of her skull, and then brought his hand down to cup her cheek.

"So where's my Christmas present?" he said.

She stood up and bent to put a kiss on his forehead. He smelt of darkness.

"That," she said. "And a sofa to sleep on and a blanket to keep you warm."

"A fine exchange," he replied.

***

On Christmas morning, while Nell prepared dinner, Kantzaros crouched by the fire and stared at the colander that Robert had bought her.

He was so intent on the thing that he failed to notice her set the table or even bring the dinner in.

"Kantzaros," she said.

He looked up. "Oh. Sorry. They used to leave them out for us in the old country."

"Colanders?"

"Sieves, I suppose. In hope that we would be fascinated by them and be distracted from our mischief-making until dawn."

"It's just a colander."

"But all the little holes!" he exclaimed. "Don't you feel the need to count them all? Huh?"

"Right," she said. "And given that you can't count above two means . . ."

"Well, quite," he added.

"Fauns are OCD," she mused.

There was wine with the food and when there was no more food there was still more wine.

Kantzaros made extravagant toasts, many of which Nell did not understand. He told tales of the "old country" and of the schemes and ploys of the beautiful centaurs, of his battles of wits with the hare and the wolf. He spoke of kings and heroes and, in his growing drunkenness, it was uncertain whether he was speaking of them or to them. And Nell, in her own drunkenness, imagined that she caught glimpses of those he spoke of, shades that hovered in the corners of the darkening room.

She drifted into sleep with stories wrapped around her, her head lay on a cushion of soft green leaves and moss, and in her dreams, she was lifted up by the cavalcade of characters in her uncle's stories and taken with them on their endless journey.

*** 

On Boxing Day, Kantzaros lay on the sofa with his scarf over his eyes and groaned in pain and repentance for his night of drinking.

"You drank more the other night," said Nell. "Why the hangover today?"

"Because," he said through gritted teeth, "today is a day for hangovers. The world has gorged itself and now is the day to sweep away the leavings and put the boxes out for the tradesmen, to pay the piper and acknowledge the fragility of everything."

"If you say so. Can I get you anything?"

"The crushed bark of the willow tree."

"You mean aspirin."

"It sounds better the way I say it," he muttered.

*** 

On Saturday, along with the food and alcohol, Kantzaros produced from nowhere a set of bagpipes, a peculiar furry octopus with dusty clay legs. The music he played was simple at first, a mere nursery rhyme, but then, as his fingers leapt from pipe to pipe to pipe with spidery dexterity, the tune branched out into numerous distinct melodies that wove around one another, sometimes fighting for dominance, sometimes spiralling up to some heartrending height as one.

When—and Nell couldn't say whether Kantzaros had played for a minute or a day—when he stopped playing, he gave her an expectant look.

"A better piper than a caroller?" he asked.

"That was astounding."

"Ha!" he barked. "You would call the finest wines of Arcadia merely nice but are astounded by a man with an inflated goatskin."

"A relative of yours?" said Nell wryly.

"Yes," said Kantzaros. "But I didn't like him very much." And then he grinned with a mouth full of peg-like teeth and she didn't know what to believe.

\*\*\*

Snow blew in from the east and the world became a colder and grayer place. And by contrast the fairy-lit glow of her little flat was made warmer and more colorful until she was spending her days in a whirlwind haze of Arcadian wine and the songs and stories of her uncle.

And then it was suddenly New Year's Eve and she surprised herself by dancing along to Kantzaros's pipes, and at midnight he raised his glass, yelled, "Janus, you'll never see me coming, you two-faced bastard!" and bounded across the furniture, leaping from chair to table to chair before pulling down a shelf and falling to the earth with a bump, surrounded by books Nell could not remember owning.

\*\*\*

On New Year's Day, they walked in the park and threw bread to the ducks on the ice-covered pond. Every crumb of bread Kantzaros threw seemed to transform midflight into a stone, and he hooted with glee each time one of his stones struck an unwary and sometimes terminally surprised duck.

Nell put her arm through his and gently steered him away from the pond and toward the Victorian glasshouse at the centre of the park.

She tugged at the edge of his scarf. "Is it deliberate?"

"What?" said Kantzaros.

"The scarf. The brolly. You look like wotsisname out of those children's books by thingy."

"Ever loquacious, dear niece."

"You know, *The Lion, the Witch and the Wardrobe*."

He spat on the ground. "That foul piece of Christianization. Yes. You refer to Mr Tumescent the Faun. Cast into the role of petty Judas, you'd note."

"I don't think that was his name."

"Who's the expert here?"

She frowned at him.

"So what's it like underground?" she said.

"Dark," he replied.

"I mean, do you really live underground, sawing through the world tree and that?"

"It is what I said."

"I mean . . . I didn't know if it was a metaphor or something."

"Have you ever tried living in a metaphor?"

"Where will you go when you leave me? Where will you actually go?"

"Mmmm. Do you think I am a dream? A fantasy? A mental delusion?"

She nodded and then said, "I mean, if this is a mental breakdown I'm having then I would heartily recommend it to others."

"Thank you." He squeezed her arm affectionately. "There *are* dark places in this world. Gray, windowless caverns. And the world tree has many roots to be sawn through. What separates me and mine from the great galumphing human race is we know what we're doing and we're wise enough to give it a rest from time to time."

*** 

The following day, she left for work before he woke.

After the last few days, the Blame 'n' Claim call center seemed ethereal and otherworldly. Despite the holiday season there were plenty of calls to field, but she couldn't keep her mind on the job. She stumbled over her script and lost the thread of things more than once.

She went to the coffee machine for a caffeine boost and a chance to collect herself. Nell found a group of office underlings around the coffee machine, sharing a joke. Robert was among them.

"Hey," she said.

~ 237 ~

"Hi there," said Robert. "How was your Christmas?"

"Oh. I had a mad uncle drop by for a couple of days."

"I thought you said you didn't have an uncle."

"I didn't know you paid attention to things I said."

He paused lengthily and Nell realized that she knew less about Robert than she thought.

"Thank you for the present," she said. "Very . . ."

"Practical."

She smiled. "Nice," she said. "It was very nice."

"I think 'nice' is even worse than 'practical.' "

"My uncle liked the colander."

"Good for him. Frankly, I might as well have sent you a big sign saying 'cook for me.' Next time, I'll cook."

"You don't cook."

"I will, next time," he said.

"Next time?"

He coughed awkwardly. "And New Year?"

She shrugged. "Took the mad uncle to the park so he could throw stones at the ducks. You?"

"The best," he said and that caused a wave of laughter from the underlings around them.

"What?" said Nell.

"Oh, nothing." He grinned. "We had a very good New Year."

There was further laughter from the others. It was dirty and secretive and hurt her, not because it was directed at her, but because it suggested that Robert, who she had never thought as special enough to belong anywhere, did not belong exclusively to her. She was surprised to find herself feeling and thinking such things.

Something must have shown on her face because he touched her arm tentatively.

"You could have been there," he said.

"Yeah," she replied hollowly.

"But you could have," he said. "All you had to do was turn up."

She nodded silently as she backed away.

\*\*\*

Before her front door had even closed behind her, she angrily ripped the skirt from her waist and flung it across the room where it swept the tacky little Christmas tree from its stand and fell down behind the television.

Kantzaros, who had been sleeping on the sofa with the colander over his face, sat up, put down the colander and the wine glass he'd been holding, and looked at her violent handiwork.

"Taking down the decorations already?" he said blearily.

Nell wiped away the snot and tears with the back of her hand. "Why me, eh?" she said.

"Hmmm?"

She gestured at her bare legs and gave an involuntary stamp of one of her hooves.

"I didn't ask for these."

"You have there some mighty fine goat legs, Nell. Stirs something in a man, I tell you."

She gave a suppressed yell of rage. "Who the fuck would want mighty fine goat legs?"

"Goats?" suggested Kantzaros.

She picked up the nearest thing to hand, which turned out to be Kantzaros's bagpipes, and lobbed them inexpertly at his head. They bounced off his face with a sharp, discordant squeak.

"I want you out of here," she growled and then stormed into her bedroom, threw herself on her bed, and buried her face in her pillows.

A short time later, she heard the bedroom door open.

"You were conceived and born in the Chinese year of the goat."

She rolled over. Kantzaros stood in the doorway, very still.

"And you're a Capricorn," he added.

"So was Jesus," she said. "He didn't have to put up with hooves and fur, did He?"

"Any child born during the twelve days of Christmas can become one of us."

"Really?"

He nodded. "And with me for a father, the odds were against you."

She sat up suddenly. "Father?"

He spluttered. "Father. Uncle. Brother. It's all good."

She shook her head.

"There are antidotes," he said.

"Really?"

"I could bind you in ropes woven from straw or garlic stalks."

"Not sure if I've got any in the flat."

"There's the singeing of the toenails thing, too." He looked at her hooves. "Mmmm, maybe a bit late for that."

"I just want to be normal," said Nell.

"No you don't," said Kantzaros vehemently. "You want something and you just need to be strong enough to recognize it."

"What do I want?"

From nowhere he produced two glasses of wine.

"I don't think alcohol is the answer," said Nell.

"No. Alcohol is the axle grease of thought and conversation and decision and deed. Wine is part of the journey, not the destination. Drink up and we'll be on our way."

She shook her head but took the glass nonetheless. He sat down on the bed beside her and stroked her leg. Nell watched his fingers burying themselves in her fur.

"Why goat legs?" she said.

"Why not?"

"But why goat? Why not sheep or cow or horse or dog?"

"Or chicken."

"Or chicken."

"Goats are intelligent creatures. Inquisitive. And even when you think you have them tamed, there's still that bit of wild left in them. We're not docile like sheep or cows. You can never trust a goat."

"Can't I trust you?" said Nell.

He squeezed her thigh, tenderly but powerfully. "Absolutely not," he said. "The desert tribes knew our power. The Arabs called us *azabb al-akaba*, the 'shaggy demons.' The Israelites called us *se'irim* or 'hairy men' and tried to placate us with gifts and sacrificial offerings."

"Get away."

"S'true, till that bloody Moses character anyway, with his 'you shall no more offer your sacrifices to the *se'irim* after whom you have gone a-whoring.' Makes it sound like they were a-whoring after me all the bloody time. Fat chance. Anyway, it was a short step from there to blaming the sins of the tribe on a goat and sending it out into the desert to die."

"A scapegoat?"

"Right. But it takes a lot more than a desert to kill a goat. And, the way I see it, if you keep heaping sins on a goat for long enough, that goat'll get to thinking . . ." He drained his glass and looked through it. "Belief's a powerful thing."

He stood up and took her by the hand into the lounge, where he sat her down on the sofa and refilled their glasses. "And speaking of gifts and offerings," he said and pulled down the red parcel with green ribbon from the mantelpiece and placed it in her lap.

"It's not my birthday until tomorrow," said Nell.

Kantzaros looked at the clock on top of the television. "It's true. We could wait for five hours."

They sat in silence for nearly a full minute before Nell growled and opened the parcel.

The V-shaped object was dark and had the greasy shine of something that had been held by a thousand different hands. She couldn't tell if it was made of stone or wood or some strange metal, as she lifted it out.

"Pipes," she said.

There was one mouthpiece leading to two pipes, set at an angle to one another. Carved trails of ivy—or maybe it was actual ivy—twined around the pipes and bound them together.

"More pipes," she said.

"Ah, but these are different from the bagpipes," said Kantzaros.

"Well, I can see that. The absence of a bag for one thing."

"Not what I meant," said Kantzaros. "The bagpipes are mine. These *auloi* are yours."

She smiled. "I can't play."

"Belief," said Kantzaros and got up in search of a fresh bottle of wine.

While her uncle made investigative noises in the kitchen, Nell put the pipe reed to her lips and blew. The pipes produced a harmonious two-tone note.

"And you said you couldn't play," called Kantzaros.

She experimentally covered a hole with her fingertip. The notes changed although perhaps not for the better. She tried other fingerings until she managed to produce a harmony equal to the first.

"Here," said Kantzaros, thrusting a glass at her. "Piping is thirsty work."

"I've only just started," she said, but drank regardless.

"Wine improves music," said Kantzaros. "And more."

"It only makes it appear to sound better."

"We live in a world of appearances, don't we?" He picked up his bagpipes. "With me now."

He began a simple tune. She watched him and his hands on the pipes. She found a configuration of notes that, to her ear, harmonized with his pipes, and when his fingers galloped on into other variations and counter-harmonies, she kept the simple tune going. Cheeks puffing, he nodded in approval and played on.

His pipes were louder but the sound she produced was clearer, purer, more akin to a brass instrument than the woodwind she held in her hands. While his music skittered and bounded, melodies running like animals through the shady and twisted woods, her music was the sunlight, sometimes concealed by his music, frequently revealed in unusual ways, but always there, a constant.

And she realized, in a way that she could not articulate properly, that there were other constants at her disposal. There was the air, high, cold, and capricious. There was the water, filling the emptiness with its gentle relentlessness. And the earth too, a limitless realm of rich chord-filled depths. The possibilities of the instrument opened up in front of her like a yawning pit, and she balked with a momentary vertigo but, with her uncle's wordless encouragement, she launched herself into it, taking control of the music from him and guiding the melody into new territory.

"The auloi were invented by Marsyus, the wisest of the satyrs," said Kantzaros.

He had stopped playing but Nell carried on. She wasn't sure she would have been able to stop if she had wanted to. She had given the music free rein and it rode her with a certain inevitability.

"Some say that the auloi were invented by Athena who tossed them aside when the puffing of her cheeks ruined her pretty little face," said Kantzaros. "Whatever, Marsyus was the master of the pipes and there was no greater musician in all the world. He knew this too and challenged Apollo to a contest: Marsyus versus Apollo, the auloi versus the lyre, freedom versus reason. Apollo was the god of light and truth. Marsyus was the emissary of the great Dionysus; Dionysus the giver of unmixed wine; Dionysus the hidden ruler, the false man; Dionysus the wild, the liberator, he of the loud shout; Dionysus the big-balled, the black goat, the goat killer, the winnower; Dionysus who brings release from care and worry."

As Kantzaros recited the litany of names, Nell felt, as she had in previous evenings, the shadows gather in the corner of the rooms and the corners of her eyes, and through Kantzaros's invocation, something more beautiful and more terrible than she could bear to look at took form in the room with them.

"In such a contest, only Dionysus could win," said Kantzaros, "but Apollo can never admit defeat and Marsyus was forced to pay for his hubris for daring to challenge a god. Apollo took him to a dark and windowless cavern and flayed the skin from his back and left him there for dead. I still carry the scars," he said, wincing.

She played on but her eyes twitched questioningly.

"But Marsyus and the auloi survived, down among the roots of the world tree. And he rises still to lead the Bacchanalia, the cult of drunken frenzy."

And she saw without seeing, could not see but knew, that there was not one figure in the room with them but several, a host of them emerging from the moonlit copse behind her, moving in time to her music.

"And the dance will go wherever it will," said Kantzaros, smiling at the forms in the shadows. "The ladies of the dance offer their gifts, their wine, their bodies to whomever they meet, and kill those who refuse them."

There were other instruments accompanying hers now, cymbals and drums and things she could not imagine, and Nell felt the power she held ripple through her, a caress and a shiver. Kantzaros raised his hands high in welcome, a wine bottle held in one of them.

"We shall share our Bacchanalian mysteries with those willing to learn, the mysteries of fig and ivy and pine, mysteries of bull and goat. The bull whose horns we drink from. The goat whose hide makes our wine sacks."

He grinned at those assembled. "For what is an old goat for, if not for storing wine?"

He drank deeply and his smile broadened and his voice grew larger and more resonant than humanly possible.

"We lead the dance," he said, "and everyone must follow us or perish."

She stopped blowing. The shades who accompanied her did not vanish instantly but faded back into the gloom, their music disappearing like a balloon slipping from a child's hand.

Kantzaros looked at her, waiting for a response.

"I like that," she said.

"Of course you do," he replied and pointed at the clock on top of the television. "It's midnight."

"My birthday."

"My last day in the world above."

"Let's make it one to remember."

\*\*\*

People might find it hard to imagine how the minions at the Blame 'n' Claim call center could possibly fail to see the radical change that was worked upon them that day, but those people, just like the rest of us, perfectly aware of the invisible progress of the hour hand, are still capable of looking up at the clock and declaring, "Is that the time?"

Each person in that office found a way into that other world. Some entered the building humming tunes they imagined they heard on the radio. Some had heard the echoes of birdsong in the trees in the sculpted lawns by the car park. Some, driving in, had been fortunate enough to glimpse the cavorting figures emerge from the Harvester pub, their faces raised in exultation to the sky. Those witnesses carried their experiences with them into work, like seeds in their pockets.

During the morning, several callers made mention of the unusual voices they heard whilst on hold, strange and sibilant, enticing them with offers, though of what they couldn't be certain. Then there was the old woman who sat in one of the toilet cubicles (a toilet cubicle that was now a dark and mossy bower and yet quite clearly still a toilet cubicle). The crone uttered prophecies to every woman who would stop and listen and read the fortunes of those few who dared ask. Then there was the music that began to bleed in through the office PA system, a constant rolling tune that was sometimes pipes and sometimes drums and sometimes voices. The music was utterly natural. They all knew the tune. They had always known the tune.

And when the call handlers and paper shufflers heard and saw that the music wasn't coming from the overhead speakers but from the instruments and mouths of the party makers who were now among them, this too seemed obvious. New Year's may have been nearly a week gone, but it was still the season for parties.

The parade of drunkards wound its way through the aisles of tiny cubicles, encouraging folk from their chairs with offers of wine and food (a banquet of food was set out by one wall, trestle tables laden with platters brought in by a catering company that no one had booked). Few of the minions questioned any of what was going on about them. Even fewer questioned it once they had a cup of wine in their hand or, better still, in their belly. Kantzaros's wine was heady stuff, and many of Nell's coworkers were soon stumbling about drunkenly.

Nell watched Kantzaros hopping from hoof to hoof in the midst of a circle of women, making loud, lewd, and ecstatically received boasts about his "horn of plenty." Turning with a smile, she saw Robert refilling his cup at the drink machine (which had spontaneously decided to produce golden frothy wine), and as she saw him, he lifted his head and saw her too. He gave her a little wave. Another Nell would have returned the wave but it was a tiny gesture that indicated too little to signify anything. Now, for today at least, she was not a woman of tiny gestures. She glared at him, not unkindly, and blew on her pipes, raising the volume and tempo of the music that she controlled.

A ragged cheer and drunken laughter rippled around the room, spinning the party onward into dance. Drummers and singers, bare-breasted call handlers and wine-addled desk jockeys, locked arms and seized waists and kicked their legs to the music.

"You want to dance?"

She stopped playing, leaving the music to its own whims.

Kantzaros stood beside her, leaning on the banquet table and nibbling on something red and papery.

"I don't dance," she said.

"Everyone dances."

"I don't. I do many things but I don't dance."

He humphed at her but said nothing.

"You do know you're eating a napkin," she said.

He spat gently and inspected the chewed thing he held. "I was wondering what it was. Well, you know, as a great man once said, try everything once except . . . um . . ."

"Folk dancing and incest," she prompted.

He frowned deeply at her. "No. Tin cans and cardboard." He shook his head. "Folk dancing and incest? Where did you hear such rot? I bet you've never tried it."

"Which?" said Nell.

"Watch," said Kantzaros. "And play."

He turned on one hoof and sharply raised one knee, a sharp motion, like a whip-crack, cutting through conversations and demanding that every eye be on him. He turned and switched feet, cocked an elbow in one direction and thrust his face in another. It should have looked ridiculous, Kantzaros stepping out with jerky sudden movements like a spastic chicken, but it transcended absurdity and became something profound and compelling.

"Play!" he commanded, snapping into a fresh pose.

Nell put her pipes to her lips, picked up the tune and moulded it to Kantzaros's movements, transforming the people's dance into theirs—hers and Kantzaros's. She stepped in behind him, and not to her own surprise—because surprise would indicate that she was something other than in perfect control of the situation—but to her glowing pleasure, she lifted her naked legs in time with his, shifted, pivoted, and kicked. The men and women of Blame 'n' Claim, ecstatically drunk, unkempt and at peace, fell in behind. In addition to the bells and drums, some took up improvised instruments and joined the music with stapler castanets, filing-tray tambours, and paperclip shakers.

Nell spun and flung her head back and, seeing Robert pulled toward the dance but clearly hovering at its edges, cast a trilling countermelody over him, dragging him to her side, his cheeks flushed and his eyes glistening.

"Eu-oi!" sang Kantzaros, and the crowd sang it back to him.

"Eu-oi! Eu-oi! Eu-oi!"

They progressed through the room until everyone had joined the procession, willing subjects of the Bacchanalia. With heads thrown back and eyes glazed, feeling the drumbeats guide their limbs and the melody tug at something more elusive, they abandoned themselves to dancing and capering and felt themselves filled with a spirit that was not their own.

They danced out into the reception area. Josephine came running up from the ranks and threw herself in front of the double doors, her arms spread wide to bar their exit. The dancing did not stop but Kantzaros drew to a halt in front of her.

"You're not going anywhere!" said Josephine hotly, glaring at Nell.

There was laughter and booing.

"Come on!" yelled someone.

"Have a drink!" yelled another.

"This is wrong!" shouted Josephine.

For a moment, just for a moment, Nell was struck with an unpleasant thought, a peculiar connection made. She remembered the story of the Pied Piper of Hamelin, piping away the children of the town, luring them into a cave, never to be seen again. But the fear vanished as quickly as it had arrived. Kantzaros was not leading these people into the darkness. He was leading them out, into the air and freedom.

"The dance will go wherever it will," he said to Josephine.

Julie from Accounts tried to press a cup of wine into Josephine's hand.

"The ladies of the dance offer their gifts, their wine, to whomever they meet," said Kantzaros.

"Just look at yourselves!" shrieked Josephine, gesticulating at their dishevelled, half-naked bodies.

This did not have the desired effect. The merry folk of Blame 'n' Claim looked at themselves and one another, decided they liked what they saw, and cheered.

Kantzaros dipped his head forward and danced onward, sweeping Josephine aside like a garden gate, and out into the winter's afternoon. As their breath misted in the air and the cold pricked their eyes, they fought back with loud voices and enthusiastic leaps and turns on the icy path leading down to the road.

"You can't do this!" yelled Josephine, chasing after them. "There are calls going unanswered in there, claims waiting to be made."

"We lead the dance," said Kantzaros, "and everyone must follow us or perish."

Nell did not see, yet perfectly comprehended, what happened next: Josephine, running, stepping on a patch of ice, slipping. Nell heard the dull thump and the scream and incorporated that high pure note into the tune.

They led the tipsy, pissed, and near-catatonic across the ring road, past the retail park, and on toward the town center.

The wild procession collected all in its path, and the throng, both real and imaginary, grew and grew. And though Kantzaros and Nell led it, it eventually reached such enormous proportions that it became impossible to distinguish what was the Bacchanalia and what wasn't, and as the alcohol flowed and the music spread and the short day ended, it wrapped itself around the world, and with the kind of logic that only the truly drunk are capable of, the dance of Dionysus simultaneously became the world and vanished from it.

***

Nell and Kantzaros, alone once more, danced up the stairs to her flat and spun in each other's arms on the landing until nausea and laughter made them stop. As Nell fumbled for her keys, Kantzaros stumbled and slammed against the door.

"Ow," he declared slowly. "S'very hard door."

"I should put up a sign," said Nell with difficultyand let them in.

Kantzaros rebounded off the sofa and then the wall before slipping, by chance more than design, straight through the kitchen door. There was the sound of many pieces of crockery almost breaking.

"Time for one last drink," he said.

"No!" shouted Nell.

His head poked round the doorframe, the bottle of nectar in his hand.

"No?"

Nell placed her auloi on the table and patted them as one would a sleeping child. "Never say it's the last drink," she said.

Kantzaros jiggled the dark bottle in the general direction of the clock.

"Less than an hour to midnight," he said with a rueful smile. "The world tree's healed. I have work to do. Those tree roots won't saw through themselves."

Nell wilted. "You mean this is it?"

"Yup."

He popped back into the kitchen and returned with two glasses. He pressed one into her hand.

"A toast!" he said.

She looked into her drink's yellow-green depths. "Why?"

"What?"

"What have we achieved?"

"What were you expecting?"

She swept her arm down to indicate her hideous goat legs and then up and round to the unlovely flat she had somehow acquired and then, lacking the sufficient appendages, grimaced to indicate the formless unchosen life she had similarly acquired. He looked at her blankly.

"Oh, what's the use?" she said and turned away and went into the bedroom.

She stood at the foot of the bed and knew that he stood behind her.

"I expected things to change," she said. "But all we did was drink far more alcohol than was good for us. We've spent more time drunk than sober. We've pressured everyone else into joining in just because we wanted them to and only did what we've done because it seemed a good idea at the time."

"Dear girl!" said Kantzaros softly. He took her by the elbow and turned her to face him. "You have it entirely wrong."

"Really?"

"What we did was drink far more alcohol than is good for us. We spent more time drunk than sober. We pressured everyone else into joining in just because we wanted them to and only did what we did because it seemed a good idea at the time!"

He grinned widely and there was definitely a twinkle in his eye. "If that's not an achievement, I don't know what is." He raised his glass. "A toast, my love. An end to care and worry."

She raised her glass and clinked it against his. "An end to care and worry," she said and drank and then leaned down to plant a kiss on the corner of the small satyr's beard-wisped mouth.

"You are, without a doubt, my favorite uncle."

"Or brother."

"Or father or king. It doesn't matter. It's all good."

She drained the glass and felt the intoxication flood her cheeks, her body, and head.

"Definitely my last drink," she giggled and then, the back of her knee connecting with the bed, toppled backward. She grabbed at Kantzaros for support, dug her fingers into his shoulder, and pulled him down with her. Something bounced off the mattress and smashed against the wall but they were laughing and barely heard it.

\*\*\*

Nell woke to the sound of her phone ringing. Something felt different, felt odd. She stretched. She was alone in her bed. Kantzaros had gone although his not unpleasantly earthy smell still clung to the bed sheets. That wasn't the odd thing. It was something else.

The phone continued to ring.

She reached out for it blindly, not ready to open her eyes to a new day.

"Hello?" she croaked.

"Oh no, you don't sound well."

"Robert?"

Something in the freshness of his voice, or perhaps the faint noises in the background, made her suddenly wonder what time it was and she came awake more fully.

"I was just checking that you were all right," he said.

"I'm fine." She rubbed her sleepy eye with her knuckle.

"There's obviously a virus going round," he said. "Either that or a lot of people throwing sickies today."

"Hangovers will make people do that," she said.

"Hangovers?"

"Yeah. You know because of . . ."

She didn't continue. She just knew the conversation that would ensue if she tried to talk to him about what had happened the day before. She didn't know if it was Kantzaros's magic or not.

"Virus," she agreed. "Yeah, that'll be it."

"Do you need anything?"

"No," she said, scrunching her toes. "No, wait."

"What?"

"I want you to come out with me on Friday night."

"Special occasion?"

"Our first date."

"What about our first date?"

"We'll have it on Friday night."

"But . . ." He stopped. "Okay."

She flung back the bed sheets and covered her grinning mouth to stop herself laughing into the phone.

"Some food and drink," she said and looked at her ten pink toes, wiggling in the condensation-streaked light of Epiphany. "And maybe even some dancing."

# Contributors

GENE O'NEILL is best known as a multi-award nominated writer of science fiction, fantasy, and horror fiction. O'Neill's professional writing career began after completing the Clarion West Writers Workshop in 1979. Since that time, over 100 of his works have been published. His short story work has appeared in *Cemetery Dance Magazine*, *Twilight Zone Magazine*, *The Magazine of Fantasy and Science Fiction*, and many more.

JOHN LANGAN received his M.A. from SUNY New Paltz and his M.Phil. from the CUNY Graduate Center. His stories have appeared in *The Magazine of Fantasy & Science Fiction* and anthologies including *The Living Dead* (Night Shade 2008), *Poe* (Solaris 2009), *By Blood We Live* (Night Shade 2009), *Supernatural Noir* (Dark Horse 2011), *Blood and Other Cravings* (Tor 2011), and *Ghosts by Gaslight* (Harper Collins 2011). His first collection *Mr. Gaunt and Other Uneasy Encounters* was published in 2008; his first novel *House of Windows* appeared the following year. With Paul Tremblay, he has co-edited *Creatures: Thirty Years of Monster Stories* (Prime 2011). His essays on horror writers have appeared in *Fantasy Commentator*, *The Internet Review of Science Fiction*, *The Lovecraft Annual*, *Lovecraft Studies*, *The New York Review of Science Fiction*, and *The Weird Fiction Review*. He has served as a juror for the Shirley Jackson Awards. He is an adjunct instructor at SUNY New Paltz, where he teaches creative writing and gothic fiction.

JODI RENÉE LESTER is a writer and editor. Her short story "The Guixi Sisters" appeared in *Midnight Walk: 14 Original Tales of Terror and Suspense*, which won the Black Quill Award for Best Dark Genre Anthology and a nomination for the Bram Stoker Award. She is currently working on a novel as well as several editing projects, while continuing to write short fiction. Jodi had the honor of studying with Dennis Etchison and is a member of the Horror Writers Association. She grew up in Southern California and now lives in South Carolina with her husband Mike and their three cats Bruno, Mathias, and Klaus. She can be followed on Goodreads at www.goodreads.com/author/show/2970826.Jodi_Renee_Lester.

K. H. VAUGHAN is a refugee from academia with a Ph.D. in clinical psychology. In his other life he taught, published, and practiced in various settings, with particular interest in decision theory, forensic psychology, psychopathology, and methodology. He lives with his wife and three children in New England. Information on upcoming releases can be found at www.khvaughan.com.

R. CHRISTOPHE RYBER lives in Hardwick, Vermont, where in addition to penning short fiction and poetry, he tutors English and studies writing and literature at a local college.

ROBERT HARKESS shares his writing time with his real-world job in a major ISP in the U.K. He lives just north of London with a wonderful wife and two attention-seeking furdragons and blogs at www.rbharkess.co.uk.

S. J. HIRONS has been previously been published in *Clockwork Phoenix 3* (Norilana Books), *Subtle Edens: An Anthology of Slipstream Fiction* (Elastic Press), *Daily Science Fiction*, SFX magazine's *Pulp Idol 2006* anthology, *52 Stitches* (Strange Publications), *Title Goes Here* magazine (Issue #1, Fall 2009), *A Fly In Amber, Farrago's Wainscot, Pantechnicon Online* and *The Absent Willow Review*. He has upcoming stories in *The Red Penny Papers* and at *faepublishing.com* and some critical writing appearing in *Interfictions Zero* from the Interstitial Arts Foundation.

DAVID W. LANDRUM lives and writes in western Michigan. His speculative fiction has appeared in scores of journals and anthologies, including *Dark Distortions, At First Bite, Midnight Thirsts, Roar and Thunder, The Horror Zine,* and *Danse Macabre.* His novelette *The Gallery* is available from Amazon.com.

DAVID FARLAND is an award-winning *New York Times* bestselling author in science fiction and fantasy, with nearly 50 books in print, published in over 20 languages. As a novelist he has worked with such major franchises as *Star Wars* and *The Mummy.* As a video game designer he worked on games such as the #1 international best-seller *Starcraft: Brood War and Xena.* Currently, Dave is finishing up the last book in his Runelords series while he prepares to take the series to Hollywood. His latest novel *Nightingale* begins a new young adult fantasy series, has been garnering rave reviews, and has won five awards so far this year.

JEFF CHAPMAN writes software by day and speculative fiction when he should be sleeping. *Tales of Woe and Wonder,* available in the Amazon Kindle store, collects nine of his fantasy stories. He lives with his wife, children, and cat in a house with more books than bookshelf space. You can find him musing about words and fiction at www.jeffchapmanwriter.blogspot.com.

RHYS HUGHES was born in 1966 and began writing fiction from a young age. None of his early efforts saw print, mainly because he never submitted them anywhere or even showed them to anyone else. Those stories have all been lost. Eventually he began sending his work to editors. His first published story was called "An Ideal Vocation" and it appeared in an obscure anthology in 1992. Encouraged by this "success", he then proceeded to bombard the British small press with hundreds of tales for almost two decades. His first book, the now legendary *Worming the Harpy,* was published by Tartarus Press in 1995. He has published many volumes since then, chiefly collections of short stories but also a few novels, in several languages.

HOWARD PHILLIPS is a veteran with multiple combat deployments afflicted with terminal wanderlust, a perpetual student raised by books, and a professional liar, that is, a fiction writer.

FEL KIAN'S first novel *Indigo Eyes*, a gothic fantasy, was published by Immanion Press. He has been indulging in imaginative fiction since he learned to read, and only stops writing these days to help raise his baby girl. A sample of his work and other information can be found on his website, www.fel-kian.com.

JOHN "JAM" ARTHUR MILLER once owned an online publication. He once had some notoriety within a few writing circles. Then he died. In fact, he's writing this bio now as one of the living dead. While lying to rest his 70+ publishing credits and much hubris, he currently rejoices in his new life of freedom, caring little about a world that looks upon him as a zombie born anew from arcane faith. Currently he is training to be a minister.

DY LOVEDAY has a M.A. in creative writing from Adelaide University and she is a graduate of the Odyssey Science Fiction Fantasy Workshop 2012.

J. S. REINHARDT writes across the horror genre, with work appealing to everyone from young adults to those with an affinity for the more extreme and explicit situations. Stay abreast of his latest works by visiting his website www.jsreinhardt.com.

BENNIE L. NEWSOME is a writer and graphic designer from Birmingham, Alabama. He is the author and cover illustrator of *The BoogeyMann* (YA horror/humor), and the author of *Life is no Fairytale* (YA romance/humor). In addition to his two novels, Bennie has been published in several anthologies; including Hallmark's *Thanks, Mom* which is scheduled for publication in May of 2013. For more information, check out Bennie's website at www.bnewsome.yolasite.com.

**W. H. PUGMIRE** has been writing Lovecraftian weird fiction since 1972, making his first sale to *Space & Time* magazine. He devoted himself to writing for the small horror magazines until Jeffrey Thomas published his first collection in 1997. His newest books include *The Strange Dark One, Uncommon Places, Some Unknown Gulf of Night,* and *Gathered Dust and Others. Bohemians of Sesqua Valley* and *Encounters with Enoch Coffin* will appear in limited hardcover editions in 2013. He is presently attempting to write his first novel, a work inspired by August Derleth's *The Lurker at the Threshold.* Pugmire dreams in Seattle.

**JOSH REYNOLDS** is a freelance writer of moderate skill and exceptional confidence. He has written a bit, and some of it was even published. For money. By real people. His work has appeared in anthologies such as Miskatonic River Press' *Horror for the Holidays,* and in periodicals such as *Innsmouth Magazine* and *Lovecraft eZine.*

**Mark Valentine's** stories have appeared most recently in *Seventeen Stories* (2013) and *Selected Stories* (2012), both from the Swan River Press, and his tales of occult detectives can be found in *Herald of the Hidden* (2013) and *The Collected Connoisseur* (2010, with John Howard), both from Tartarus Press. He has written biographies of the Welsh mystic and supernatural fiction author Arthur Machen and the diplomat and fantasist Sarban. He edits *Wormwood,* a journal of the literature of the fantastic, supernatural and decadent. 'Goat Songs' reflects his love of old vinyl records, particularly the obscurer albums of the Seventies by such artists as Titus Groan and Comus. He was briefly in a progressive rock group, Ruins, before getting involved in the Eighties indie tape scene, with The Mystic Umbrellas, Radio Dromedary and a recording of a lighthouse foghorn.

IAIN GRANT is an author of short stories and novels, ranging from contemporary literature to fantasy and horror. His short stories have appeared in numerous magazines and anthologies. His contribution to the critically acclaimed *Roads Ahead* anthology from Tindall Street Press was singly praised by the *Guardian* newspaper (September 2009). He is perhaps best known for the comic novel *Clovenhoof*, co-written with Heide Goody. The follow-up novel (which follows the continuing adventures of the earthbound Satan and Archangel Michael) will be published by Pigeon Park Press in late 2013. Iain's first solo novel *A Gateway Made Of Bone*, a sprawling SF adventure, was published in 2012. This has been followed by the Birmingham-based thriller *In Other Hands*, and the mind-bending murder mystery *IAMNOWHERE*.

# About the Editor

AARON J. FRENCH (a.k.a. A. J. French) is currently a book editor for JournalStone Publishing and the Editor-in-Chief for *Dark Discoveries* magazine—a professional, internationally distributed print magazine specializing in dark fiction, currently on its tenth year of continuous publication and distribution. He has worked with and

edited such authors as David Liss, Norman Partridge, Gary A. Braunbeck, Thomas Ligotti, Steve Rasnic Tem, Jonathan Maberry, F. Paul Wilson, Glen Hirshberg, John Shirley, and many others. In 2011 he edited *Monk Punk*, an anthology of monk-themed speculative fiction and *The Shadow of the Unknown*, an anthology of nü-Lovecraftian fiction. Aaron also served as co-editor for *The Lovecraft eZine* for several months in 2012.

Aaron's fiction has appeared in many publications including *Dark Discoveries, Black Ink Horror, Something Wicked, After Death...,*

*Beware the Dark, Chiral Mad, The Lovecraft eZine,* and others. His zombie collection *Up From Soil Fresh* was published by Hazardous Press in 2013. Also in 2013 "The Order," Aaron's occult thriller novella about a Lovecraftian secret society, was published in the *Dreaming in Darkness* collection. He is currently an active member of the Horror Writers Association. His collection of mystical fiction, *Aberrations of Reality*, was published in 2014 by Crowded Quarantine Productions.

Aaron is pursuing a Religious Studies degree from the University of Arizona. His nonfiction articles on Thomas Ligotti, Alejandro Jodorowsky, and Karl Edward Wagner have appeared in *Dark Discoveries* magazine, while his online column "Letters from the Edge," focusing on the occult, spirituality, rogue scholarship, esotericism, and speculative fiction, is featured regularly on the *Nameless Digest* website. His academic papers "Toward Christian Renewal" and "Journeys of the Soul in the Afterlife: Egyptian Books of the Afterlife and Greek Orphic Mysteries" were published in the peer-reviewed journal *The Esoteric Quarterly*. He is currently a member of the ESSWE, the European Society for the Study of Western Esotericism.

# OUT OF TUNE

CHRISTOPHER GOLDEN

DAVID LISS

DEL HOWISON

GARY BRAUNBECK

GREGORY FROST

JACK KETCHUM

JEFF STRAND

NANCY KEIM-COMLEY

KEITH R. A. DECANDIDO

KELLEY ARMSTRONG

NANCY HOLDER

SEANAN McGUIRE

SIMON R. GREEN

LISA MORTON

JEFFREY MARIOTTE

MARSHEILA ROCKWELL

EDITED BY

JONATHAN MABERRY

NEW YORK TIMES BESTSELLER

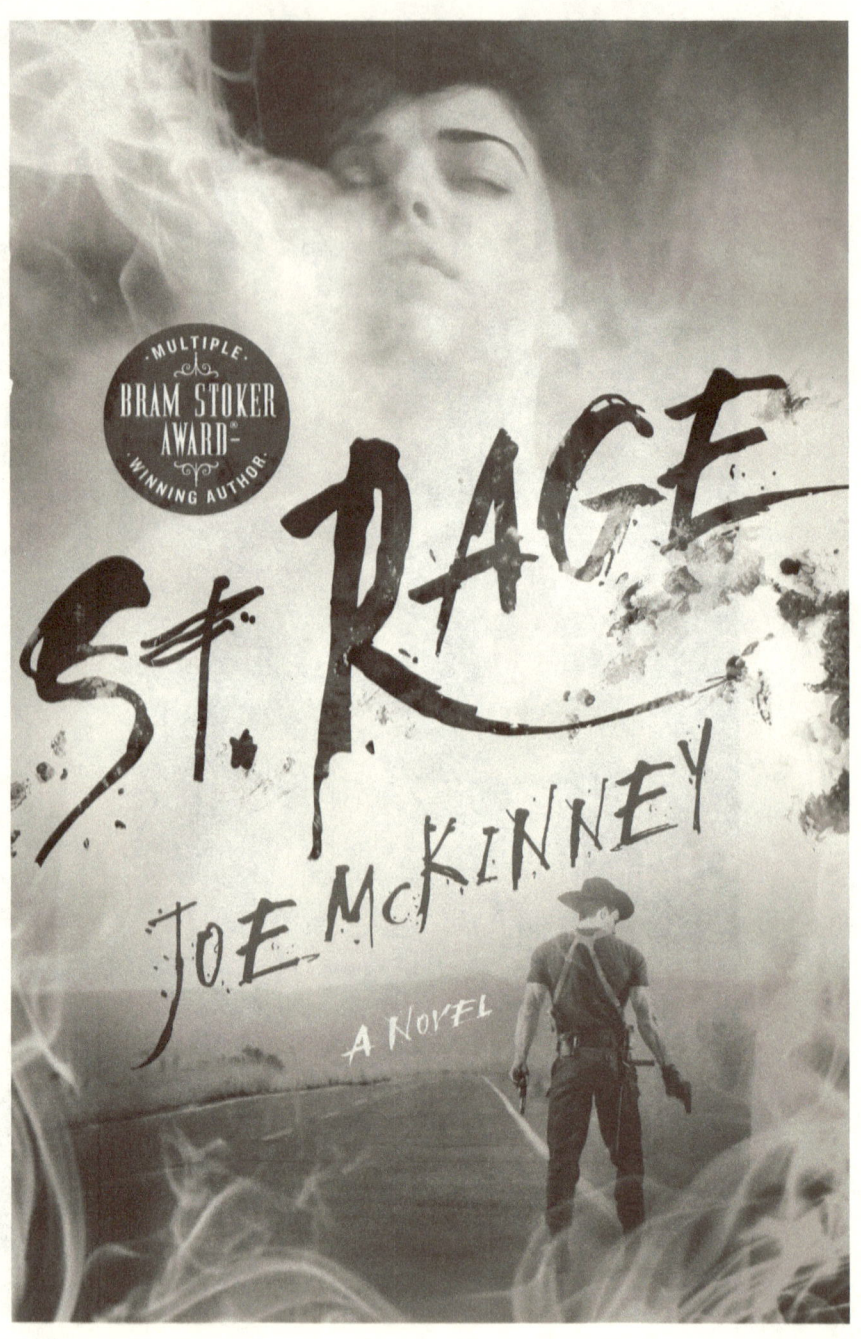

MULTIPLE BRAM STOKER AWARD® WINNING AUTHOR

ST. RAGE

JOE McKINNEY

A NOVEL